AURORA'S EYES WIDENED IN SURPRISE.
THE ROOM WAS EMPTY.

A movement behind the door snapped her head around. The Apache leaned nonchalantly against the wall, his brawny, bronze arms crossed over his bandaged chest. His gaze was dark and sensual and intense.

He kicked the door shut.

Frissons of awareness fired along Aurora's nerve endings. Her unbound hair swirled around her shoulders in a fiery cape as she turned to face him.

Stalking Wolf studied a red-gold strand that had landed on her lips. *"Boca bonita,"* he murmured, lifting it off with a feather-soft touch. Beautiful mouth.

Aurora took a deep breath. She was a doctor. He was her patient. But no other patient had invaded her dreams as the rugged Apache did night after night. And no patient had ever made her so aware of being a woman.

DESTINY'S WARRIOR

KIT DEE

AVON BOOKS ◆ NEW YORK

AVON BOOKS
A division of
The Hearst Corporation
1350 Avenue of the Americas
New York, New York 10019

Copyright © 1997 by Melitta Dee
Inside cover author photo by Jon Wolf Photography
Published by arrangement with the author
Visit our website at **http://AvonBooks.com**
Library of Congress Catalog Card Number: 96-95496
ISBN: 0-380-79205-2

First Avon Books Printing: July 1997

AVON TRADEMARK REG. U.S. PAT. OFF. AND IN OTHER COUNTRIES, MARCA REGISTRADA, HECHO EN U.S.A.

Printed in the U.S.A.

WCD 10 9 8 7 6 5 4 3 2 1

To the Chiricahua Apaches
May you come home again.

Acknowledgments

I would like to thank Charlotte and Phillip Titla of the San Carlos Apache Nation for their friendship and for sharing the Old Ways. With them I attended ceremonies of The People where I could feel the beat of the Drummers' Drums and hear the Songs sung by the Singers.

I have invented some ceremonies for this story.

Chapter 1

Tuesday, June 27, 1876

"**A**urora Elizabeth, are you done yet?" Major Artemus Spencer's voice boomed down the hall of the hospital at Fort Bowie, Arizona Territory.

"Ssh, Papa, you'll wake the baby." Aurora emerged from the women's ward and hurried toward him. "I'll be right out."

"I'll wait outside." Her father retreated to the shady veranda, letting the screen door slam behind him.

Aurora slipped off her bloody apron and stuffed it in the hamper beside the front door. Stepping outside, she gasped, stunned by the searing heat. "Good Lord, I didn't realize how hot it really was." Unbuttoning the top two mother-of-pearl buttons on her lilac-colored dress, she plucked at the bodice, seeking a bit of breeze.

"The adobe walls keep the hospital cool." After twenty-five years in the Army, Artemus stood the only way he knew, ramrod-straight. "Is it a girl or a little trooper?"

"A boy. He and his mother are sleeping now." She fished in her skirt pocket for a handkerchief and wiped the perspiration off her brow.

"You look as if you could use some rest yourself."

"It was a difficult birth, Pa. I knew it would be as soon as I examined Mrs. Baker." She shuddered at thought of the black laundress giving birth in her canvas-walled shack. "That's why I had her admitted to the hospital. Do I really look that bad?"

"You look like you're out on your feet, child. Go back to the house and rest."

"Not yet." She raked her fingers through her hair. She'd swirled it up into a knot earlier, but the flaming copper strands had worked loose and curled around her face. "I want to be here when Bonnie Mae awakens. So far she's doing fine, but I don't want anything to go wrong. She's my first patient here, and she deserves the very best care I can give her."

"There will be more."

"I know. People need doctors out here. That's why I came. But I've been here three weeks already."

"Rome wasn't built in a day, and neither is a medical practice. You've got to give people a chance to know you. Soon you'll be so busy you won't have time for me, so I'm going to enjoy every minute we have together. We've got sixteen years of catching up to do." He crossed his arms over his dark-blue shirt and surveyed her. "Your mother would be so proud of you. You're carrying on her family's tradition of helping people. I can almost feel her looking down on us and . . ."

His Adam's apple moved up and down as he

swallowed. Abruptly he turned and marched to the railing. Resting his hands on the white wood, he gazed at the distant mountains.

But Aurora had a feeling her father was seeing another place and another time. Wanting to give him a chance to collect himself, she sat down on the long wooden bench beside the door. Rob Roy, her collie, who'd waited on the veranda all day, trotted over and nudged her hand. She petted the dog she'd brought west with her.

A distant bugle call floated over the fort, its tones shimmering in the still air.

"What's that?" Artemus straightened, instantly on full alert. No wooden stockade guarded the fort, and he scanned the surrounding hills, looking for the source of the call. Slowly a column of men and horses appeared on the crest of a hill. "Something's wrong. Kreutz and his men are supposed to be guarding Apache Pass, not back here."

"What could be wrong?" Joining her father at the railing, Aurora studied the riders. Their dark-blue uniforms contrasted with the bright yellow bandannas most had pulled up over the lower half of their faces, to protect them from the thick clouds of dust stirred up by the horses.

Captain Kreutz led his men down the long slope into the fort at a trot. That was when she saw him.

The Apache.

He ran in the choking dust beside Kreutz's big black charger. She knew none of the Apache scouts—the tame Apaches, as the troopers called them—would be running among the horses. It was too dangerous.

"I'll be damned. He's captured a hostile." Artemus pulled his battered black campaign hat forward a bit to shade his eyes as he peered at the riders.

"A h-hostile?" Suddenly Aurora was seven again and huddling against her mother's skirts as Kiowas circled their wagon train and killed people to the right and left of them. Then had come the arrow that wounded her mother. Fear parched her mouth as the heart-stopping war cries of Kiowas echoed in her mind.

Then she shoved the fear away. She was grown up and a doctor now. And by God, she would not let fear rule her!

As the soldiers neared, Aurora noticed the Apache's hands were tied in front of him. Her eyes widened with shock when she realized that Kreutz grasped the end of a rope knotted around the Indian's neck. Kreutz spurred his horse into a canter, forcing the prisoner to race alongside or strangle.

When the Apache stumbled, Aurora gasped and leaned forward, as if to help him. He caught himself, though, grabbing the rope to relieve the pressure on his throat.

Kreutz didn't look back to see if the Apache was still on his feet as he led his patrol past the women clustered in front of the officers' quarters. He halted at Headquarters with a dramatic flourish, but before he could dismount, a soldier spoke to him and pointed at the hospital. Reining his horse around with a vicious motion, Kreutz spurred the animal. It leaped forward at a gallop.

The Apache was jerked off his feet and dragged along behind, clutching the noose.

"Oh God, no!" Aurora screamed softly, her hands pressed to her mouth. The rest of the soldiers galloped after Kreutz, their horses' hooves striking the ground so close to the Apache that she couldn't tell if they were trampling him or not.

By the time Kreutz halted in front of the hospital, she was shaking with fury at his senseless cruelty. How dare he treat anyone, even a hostile Apache, like that? Did the man have no common decency?

The mingled scents of hot leather and sweaty men swept over her. Kreutz and her father were speaking, but their words faded as Aurora's attention focused on the Apache.

Bracing himself with his bound hands, he got to his feet and stood beside Kreutz's horse. He was coated with white dust, which gave him a ghostly appearance in the bright sunlight. But there was nothing ghostly about the way his broad, smooth chest rose and fell as he drew great gulps of air into his lungs.

He was bruised and bloody. His tan pants were still tucked into knee-high moccasins, but his white shirt was so badly torn that it hung in tatters from his wide shoulders. Blood mingled with the rivers of perspiration pouring down his glistening copper-colored body.

Lifting his bound hands, he brushed his long ebony hair back from his face. The movement loosened the noose around his neck slightly, just enough for her to see the angry red welt where the rope had bitten deep into his flesh.

He needed a doctor. He needed her. Aurora drew a deep breath, then stepped forward.

Her father put out his arm, barring her way. "Where are you going?" he asked in a low voice that didn't carry.

She frowned. "To see how badly hurt that Apache is. He's bleeding and—"

"You'll do nothing of the sort." His voice was

stone-hard. Aurora glanced at him, shocked. "Look at his eyes. Look and see what's in them. That's a Chiricahua Apache. A killing machine. He doesn't want your help."

Only when the Apache's gaze swung to her did Aurora understand what her father was trying to tell her. Hatred blazed in the Indian's eyes. She took an involuntary step back. Instinctively her hand came up to her throat in a protective gesture. *My God, he may be captured, but he's not conquered. He may be a prisoner, but he's still a wild, free warrior in his own mind. An Apache.*

"Good afternoon, Miss Spencer, a pleasure it is to see you." Kreutz's thick Prussian accent rasped across her nerve endings like a rough file. With a theatrical flourish, he removed his black Stetson and bowed from the saddle. "Worry not. The Apache can't hurt you. I have him well secured," he said, jerking the noose around the Indian's neck.

"I'm not worried about him hurting me, Captain." She didn't trust herself to say more, not when she was appalled by his treatment of the prisoner.

"Doesn't Mrs. Baker need you, Aurora?" her father prodded.

"He needs me," she said stubbornly, nodding at the Apache.

"You'd really help an Indian?" Her father gave the Apache a hate-filled look. "After they killed your mother?"

Aurora frowned at her father. This hatred of Indians was a side of him she hadn't seen before. "But Papa, I told you it wasn't like that at all." She rested her hand on his arm. "Believe me, it wasn't the Kiowas that killed her. It was the Army doctor."

He shook his head. "Someone has filled your head with nonsense, child—which is understandable, considering that you were only seven. I've read all the reports of the Kiowa attack that day. Your mother wasn't the only one killed."

"Papa, I was there. You weren't. And I may have been a child, but I know what I saw." She had vowed that day that never again would she stand by helplessly when someone she loved was injured.

Her father's lips thinned. "Damn it all! I know what happened that day. And I know the Apaches, which you do not. Save your medicine for people who need it." He gestured at the Apache. "That savage doesn't."

"But—"

They turned at the sound of a commotion near the end of the column of men.

"Hold it, Captain. Stay right where you are," shouted a tall, gaunt man, whose black frock coat flapped around his legs. Horses snorted and shied as he hurried up the line with a large camera and tripod bouncing on his shoulder.

Aurora shook her head. Only Pincus Jones would wear a coat in this heat. With his thinning gray hair, sallow complexion, and sunken eyes, Pincus looked as though he was ready for an undertaker, but Aurora knew the well-known photographer was stronger than he appeared.

"Captain, I'd like to get a picture of you and the prisoner for the *Sentinel*," Pincus said as he set up his camera. "I want to get some stories and photographs that show the folks back home what our boys in blue are doing to meet the Indian menace."

"Happy I will be to oblige, Mr. Jones." Emmett Kreutz doffed his hat, revealing his broad face. "We will get Apache closer so you see the noose around his neck. Hold him, Corporal. And his hair pull back so Mr. Jones can show what a vile heathen he is.''

''Yes, sir.'' The barrel-shaped corporal swung off his horse, grabbed the Apache, and yanked his hair back.

At that moment Rob Roy leaped off the porch. Barking madly, the collie lunged at the Apache.

''No, Rob Roy! No!'' Lifting her lilac skirts, Aurora raced down the stairs and collared the dog before he could bite the prisoner. Kneeling in the dust, she held onto the yapping collie, shushing him.

The men backed their horses away, clearing a large space around Aurora and the Apache. She was so focused on holding the dog that it took her a moment to notice the silence that pooled around her.

Slowly she raised her head. She was kneeling almost at the feet of the prisoner. Her gaze locked with the Apache's. Beneath his hatred she saw intelligence and something else, something she couldn't begin to identify.

Two troopers held the prisoner's arms tightly. A third cocked his revolver with a metallic click and pointed it at the prisoner.

The Apache took no notice as he stared down at her. He was taller than the troopers and the friendly Apaches she'd seen around the fort. He shifted his stance slightly, and the sinews beneath his copper flesh rippled with power. His primitive maleness sent a shimmer of awareness cascading through her. Surprised, she looked away.

''Fear not, Miss Spencer.'' Emmett Kreutz's voice

ripped the moment. "My men have him. Hurt you he can't."

"I'm not afraid of him, Captain. I just didn't want the dog to bite him and add to his injuries. He already has enough."

Kreutz's eyes narrowed, but his voice was smooth as a politician's. "Your sympathy for these murdering heathens is commendable, but you can't show them kindness. They see kindness as weakness. They understand only war and killing."

"I'm afraid I find that hard to believe, Captain." Aurora's lips thinned as she glared at Kreutz, then she pointedly turned her back and dragged Rob Roy onto the porch.

Only when she stood deep in the shadows did she look back. The Apache was still watching her. And in that stolen moment, there was a connection between them. The breath froze in her throat.

Then he looked away.

He'd made it! He was in the enemy camp!

Stalking Wolf surveyed the corral where the Bluecoats had imprisoned him. It filled the space between Headquarters and the hospital, and would be easy to escape from as soon as he'd learned enough about the White-eyes' plans.

Two soldiers emerged from Headquarters. As they walked toward the corral, the chains they carried clanked dismally.

Wolf stiffened. His mouth went dry.

No! he thought. *Not chains!*

His heart began to thud against his ribs. He hadn't considered what he'd do if the White-eyes tried to put him in chains.

The memory of being chained swept over him with horrifying clarity. It had been in his thirteenth harvest, when his people had begun to gather the corn they'd grown during the moons of heat. Bluecoat soldiers had stormed through his village in a wild flood, sweeping everything away and setting fire to the brush wickiups.

Already a warrior, he shielded his mother as he stood his ground. Horses and men thundered forward. A red-bearded grizzly of a soldier galloped straight at him. Wolf drew his bowstring taut. The Bluecoat smiled as he leveled his pistol.

Just as Wolf loosed his arrow, his mother pushed him away. Simultaneously came the boom of the red-bearded man's gun.

His mother made a funny little noise. A bright red stain spread over her buckskins. "Run, my son!" she gasped. "Run!"

Wolf shuddered at the horror seared into his memory. He could still feel his mother's warm red lifeblood flowing across the palm of his hand, still smell the metallic scent of it. His mother sank to the ground. And all the time, the red-bearded man smiled that terrible smile.

Wolf leaped at him, trying to pull him off the horse and kill him. The Bluecoat swung his gun against the side of Wolf's head. Everything went black.

Wolf had never forgotten the red-bearded man. Nor had he forgotten the blinding, clawing panic that filled him when he regained consciousness and found he was hobbled hand and foot. Bluecoats had laughed as he thrashed about, trying to free his arms and legs from the unyielding iron manacles.

He had vowed then that never again would he be chained. Not by anyone. Ever.

The corral gate opened slowly, its hinges

squeaking in protest. Four Bluecoats faced him; two—their rifles leveled—watched alertly as the other two walked forward.

Even from across the corral, Stalking Wolf could smell the rank, unwashed odor of the bigger one. Eyes set close together as a pig's gave him a shifty look.

"I don't know why we didn't just shoot this murderin' savage when we caught him," the big one said, spitting a brown stream of tobacco juice onto the dusty ground.

"Because the Major wants to see if he can get some information from him," replied the young, sandy-haired one. The chains rattled in his hands. "You heard him say so."

"Yeah, but— Damn! The Major knows the only good Injun is a dead one. And this here one is a Chiricahua, the most dangerous kind of Apache."

Wolf eyed the heavy loops of iron. Calling on his inner resources, he retreated into the furthest reaches of his mind, willing his heart to slow its racing. The People needed the knowledge he would gain here in the enemy camp. Swallowing, he moistened his parched mouth. He stood tall, proud. He had a job to do. For The People. Even if it meant he would be chained.

He stared straight ahead as the sandy-haired Bluecoat knelt at his feet and locked iron shackles around his ankles.

"This ought to hold the thievin' bastard until the Major gets through with him," said the filthy one, as he closed heavy manacles around Wolf's wrists.

Except for a vein throbbing in his temple and a certain tension in his jaw, Wolf didn't move. Yet when the Bluecoat looked up and met Wolf's gaze, he stepped back hastily.

The Bluecoats left, except for one guard who kept his rifle leveled at Wolf. Moving carefully, so that the guard wouldn't suspect what he was doing, Wolf tested the length of his chains. There was about fourteen inches between his wrists and about eighteen between his ankles—long enough to shuffle, but not to walk.

Anger and panic welled up in him. Resolutely he pushed them down, but he knew they crouched in the back of his mind like a cougar, just waiting for him to lower his guard. Then they would spring up and attack.

He had to distract himself. Closing his eyes, he inhaled a long breath and turned his attention to the woman with hair of fire. Even when she'd frantically called her dog after it leaped off the porch, a husky quality in her voice had reminded him of a murmuring brook high in his beloved Chiricahua Mountains.

She'd knelt in the dust, her skirts billowing around her like petals of lavender starflowers. Still holding the dog, she'd looked up at him with a wide-eyed innocence, an openness, that held none of the fear and revulsion he'd come to expect from White-eyes women.

Later, when she stood on the porch and looked back at him, he'd been surprised by the feeling that something deep within each had reached out to the other. And they had touched. Not physically, but through a far more primitive sense.

He shook his head. They couldn't have! It had to be his imagination. After all, she was a White-eyes. He was an Apache warrior.

Wolf's chains rattled and clanked as he moved around, measuring how many chained strides it took to cross the corral. As he prowled, he surreptitiously strained against the heavy iron bonds, exercising his corded muscles.

The headquarters building formed one side of the corral, and Wolf shuffled over to the shade offered by the adobe wall, shoulders hunched, shambling along as though heedless of his surroundings. He sat down directly beneath an open window. Propping his arms on his knees, he rested his head on his arms, as if he were dozing.

And listened to the Bluecoat officers talking inside.

It was after seven, but the sun was still high in the heavens when Aurora left Mrs. Baker and her infant. Emerging from the hospital, she paused on the top step and peered around. No one was in sight except Pincus Jones. The photographer was setting up his bulky camera outside the corral where the Apache was held.

"Come on, Rob Roy." She snapped her fingers at the collie. "Let's see what Pincus is doing."

Her pace slowed as she neared the corral. She eyed it pensively. One part of her was drawn to the Apache; one part of her hesitated.

"Getting more pictures of the Indian, Pincus?" Aurora said, walking up beside him. She leaned against the corral rails and focused all her attention on the gaunt man fiddling with the camera.

"Not more. Some." The bags under Pincus's sad brown eyes always gave him a bloodhound look; now he looked so hangdog Aurora had to swallow a smile. "I didn't get any this afternoon, what with all the commotion your dog caused."

"I don't know what got into Rob Roy, but he . . ." Her voice trailed off as she absently glanced through the rails at the Apache. He'd ripped a sleeve off his white shirt and tied it around his forehead to keep his long black hair out of his eyes. He stood leaning against the fence on the far side, his arms crossed over his chest.

Aurora's grip on the rail tightened until her fingers went white, as she took in the heavy iron shackles at his wrists and ankles. A shiver of revulsion went through her. "Oh God," she whispered.

"What's the matter?" Pincus looked up from where he knelt beside his wooden equipment box.

"Nothing. Nothing at all."

Rising, Pincus stood behind her. "Don't try to fool me, Aurora. Remember, I traveled west on the same stagecoach as you." He squeezed her shoulder gently. "We bounced around on those hard seats for two weeks and talked as the miles rolled away. I know you too well, my girl. Now, tell me, what's bothering you?"

Aurora gulped. "I—I didn't expect to see him in chains. He may be our enemy, but it doesn't seem right." He was like a wild stallion that ran free across the land.

"I know what you mean. He's such a magnificent specimen."

She rounded on him, suddenly furious. "He's not a specimen. He's a man, Pincus. *A man.* And he should be treated like one."

"You're forgetting that he's an Apache warrior, one of the finest fighting men the world has ever known. I'd heard it said that an Apache on foot can cover as much ground as a white man on horseback, but I didn't believe it until I got a good look at our prisoner here."

"And now you do?"

"Certainly. You're a doctor; you know what makes muscles develop. Look at how deep his chest is, how heavily muscled his legs are. That's the body of a superbly trained warrior, a man who can run all day, then fight all night.

"That doesn't mean he has to be chained like a wild animal," she said stubbornly.

"Mr. Jones is right, you know, ma'am." The corporal on guard duty touched his hat and clicked the worn heels of his boots together.

The Apache had been openly studying Pincus and his camera. When his gaze slid to her, she realized his lazy stance was a facade; inside he was strung taut as a bowstring. And his lips were dry and cracked. Hadn't he had any water?

She glanced around. A water bucket sat on the ground outside the corral, where the guard had been standing. "Corporal, has this man had any water since he arrived?"

"I wouldn't know, ma'am. He ain't asked me for any." Giving the prisoner a malevolent smile, he spat a stream of tobacco juice onto the ground beside the bucket.

Aurora shuddered at his vile habit. "How long have you been on duty?"

"Since the Apache came in, ma'am."

"Open the gate, Corporal."

The guard choked and spat out his tobacco wad. He turned to her with a shocked look. "Ma'am, I couldn't do that. It ain't safe for anyone, let alone a white woman to go in there."

"For heaven's sake, he's chained hand and foot." Marching to the gate, she struggled with the heavy bolt. Finally the gate swung open with a loud screech. Aurora scooped up a dipperful of cool water and walked into the corral.

The Apache straightened up from the fence. His gaze raked her as she took a slow, careful step toward him. She held the dripping dipper out to him. He gave a single, abrupt shake of his head, and his eyes flicked to someone behind her.

She glanced over her shoulder. The corporal had followed her into the corral. "You needn't come with."

"I'm coming," he muttered, not taking his eyes off the Apache. Raising his rifle to his shoulder, he kept it aimed at the Indian.

She took another step. The Apache folded his arms across his chest. His rugged features were unreadable, except for his eyes, which said very clearly, *Stay away.*

She edged closer and lifted the dipper with both hands in silent offering. Again he shook his head.

"I just want to give you some water," she crooned soothingly. "You and I both know you need it. Everyone needs water, especially here in the desert."

He looked past her and spoke in rapid Spanish, anger and scorn filling his voice.

"Aurora?" Pincus stood just outside the gate. "He says he's not a wild beast to be tamed by the soft words of a White-eyes woman."

"He does, does he?" Frowning, she glanced down at the water, then back at him. "Why? You know you need water. Or is it that your pride won't let you accept water from a woman?"

The sun was sliding toward the horizon, and it's rays glanced off a bit of broken mirror that dangled from a rawhide thong around his neck. Above the thong the dark purple bruise made by Kreutz's noose was clearly visible. And in the hollow at the base of his throat, she could see the flutter of his rapidly beating heart. Too rapidly. He needed water—and badly.

She stopped an arm's length from him. "This water isn't poisoned." With a gentle smile, she held the dipper out.

He shook his head.

"You don't believe me, do you? I guess I'll just have to drink some to prove it." She lifted the ladle.

He slapped the dipper away before her lips touched it.

Water splashed down her dress and made a dark stain.

Shocked, Aurora stared at him, wide-eyed. "What—?"

"Miss Spencer, what are you doing?" Emmett Kreutz roared as he ran down the steps from Headquarters. Racing across the corral, he grabbed her wrist and yanked her away from the Apache.

The corporal charged past her, swinging his rifle by the barrel.

"No!" she screamed.

The wooden stock slammed into the Apache's side. His head snapped back and he went rigid. He took a single step toward the corporal, then crumpled to the ground.

"Let me go." Aurora pawed at Kreutz's hand, fighting to get free.

"No. He could hurt you." Kreutz dragged her outside the corral before he released her. "What were you doing?"

"Giving the prisoner water." She glowered at Kreutz. "And he wouldn't have hurt me. I just dropped the dipper when he reached for it." *Good Lord*, she thought, *am I crazy? I'm lying to protect an Apache warrior.*

"The Apache can have water anytime he wants.

You do not have to bring it to him. This savage is a military prisoner, Miss Spencer, and I must ask you to stay away from him."

Aurora rolled her eyes at Kreutz's heavy-handed orders. "Now, see here, Captain—"

"Shouldn't we be going, Aurora?" Pincus touched her arm. Lowering his voice, he spoke through his teeth. "You're making matters worse for the Apache. Just agree and let's get out of here."

She blinked owlishly at him. "Yes, of course. You're quite right." She rested her hand on his crooked arm. "We'll just be on our way," she said, simpering at Kreutz with what she hoped looked like an innocent smile. "I hope I haven't caused you any trouble, Captain. I was only trying to help."

"Of course not. Rest assured, the United States Army is quite capable of taking care of this savage."

"Let's go, Aurora." Pincus clamped his hand over hers, anchoring it to his arm.

"Yes, we'd better." Before she told Kreutz what she thought of him.

Pincus began to walk away, but Aurora hung back, glancing over her shoulder. Her fingers tightened abruptly when the corporal kicked the unconscious Apache.

Chapter 2

Her courage astounded him.

Wolf rested his arms on the top rail and gazed across the parade ground at the house where the flame-haired woman slept. She'd been in his thoughts ever since he'd regained consciousness. She was truly a woman of fire, a *kun isdzán*.

White-eyes feared and hated Apaches. He'd seen the terror in women's faces when he rode into towns such as Tucson and Tombstone. He'd seen them duck into a shop rather than pass him on the boardwalk. He'd seen their men watch him with hate in their eyes and guns in their hands.

But Woman of Fire walked across the corral to bring water to him, an Apache warrior. She didn't know him, yet she wasn't afraid of him. Even when he shook his head, he didn't frighten her. Instead, she offered him the dipper.

At least he'd been able to stop her from drinking the poisoned water. He'd been shocked when she lifted the ladle to her own mouth and had slapped it away before it could foul her lips. His last memory before the guard clubbed him was of her spicy flower scent, so like the rare white flowers that grew in the highest mountain meadows.

But that was yesterday. Today he couldn't allow himself to be distracted by thoughts of her. No matter how brave she was. No matter how much she intrigued him.

Turning, Wolf leaned back against the fence and tried to swallow, but his mouth was cotton-dry. The heavy, rapid pounding of his heart echoed in his throbbing head and told him more than he wanted to know.

It was two days since he'd had water, and he was in trouble. Desperate trouble. He'd hoped that when the fence rails cooled during the night, dew would condense on them and he would be able to lick the life-giving moisture off. But none had formed.

Wolf shuffled to the far side of the corral, his steps hobbled by the clanking shackles. Stiffly he hunkered down in the sparse shade of the fence rails. It was barely sunrise and already he was hot.

He wiped the sweat from his burning forehead. Not only was he feverish, but also he'd lost a lot of blood when the Bluecoat clubbed him, reopening his wound. A bullet had creased his side when he'd run into a Bluecoat patrol as he rode to meet Geronimo. There'd been no time to put a poultice on it before he allowed himself to be captured by the Bluecoats. The long red gash in his side was swollen and tender.

He fingered the bit of mirror that hung from the thong around his neck. Later, when the sun was high, he would signal Geronimo. He had to do it today; by tomorrow he might be too weak.

* * *

The air was still cool as Aurora hurried down the hall just before sunrise, her riding boots echoing on the plank floor. She tucked her white shirt into her hunter-green riding skirt as she passed the dining room.

"Where are you going so early?" Artemus lowered the cup of steaming coffee he'd been sipping.

"Riding." She leaned in the doorway, sniffing the rich fragrance of hot coffee. "I didn't get to go yesterday because of Mrs. Baker and her baby."

"Ah, yes. Why don't you join me and have some coffee?" He poured her a cup from the elegant coffeepot that was part of the Staffordshire china set her mother had treasured. "I wish you wouldn't go riding," he added, handing her a delicate rose-decorated cup.

"I need the exercise. You needn't worry about me, Pa, I'm a good rider. I rode every morning in Philadelphia." Perching on the edge of the maroon velvet chair, she sipped the fragrant coffee.

"Bah! This isn't Philadelphia, my girl. Being a good rider won't save you if there are Apaches around. Do you know, Apache is an Indian word that means enemy? They're nothing but barbaric savages."

The Apache prisoner was a barbaric savage? The memory of the intelligence she had seen in his eyes tantalized her. She couldn't reconcile that intelligence with her father's description.

In fact, she'd spent the night tossing and turning, her dreams haunted by the Apache's rugged features. She was worried about him. It wasn't natural to refuse water when you needed it.

"Aurora, did you hear what I said?"

She stared blankly at her father for a second, then admitted the truth. "No, Pa."

"Be careful when you ride. Always have an escort. And stay within gunshot-hearing of the fort, so we can call you back or you can call us. Can you handle a gun?"

"There wasn't much call for them in Philadelphia, Pa." She gave him a quiet smile.

He tried to look stern, but an answering smile spread across his wrinkled face. "You're incorrigible." He slid a small engraved silver box across the table to her. "Here. I thought it was about time you had something of your mother's."

Memories flooded her as she fingered the tarnished silver. The box had always rested on her mother's dresser, the dresser she was now using. Most of the silver had worn off the entwined initials on the top. A and E: Artemus and Elizabeth.

"Well, open it."

She already knew what was inside, but she obeyed anyway. "Oh, Pa, they're beautiful." She picked up the two-inch-wide sterling silver combs her mother had worn only on special occasions. "Thank you," she added, leaning over and giving him a quick peck on his leathery cheek. "I'll wear them at the Independence Day Ball."

Artemus plucked a cigar from the pocket of his dark blue-shirt and nipped off the end with his knife. "The initials work with your name."

"Hmm, I never thought of it, but they do, don't they." She winced as he drew a sulfur match along the edge of the walnut dining table her mother had treasured.

"Now, don't forget I'm leaving for Fort Grant this morning." He lit the cigar and puffed a few times. "I'll be gone about a week, but I'll be back for Independence Day, so I can see those combs in your hair."

"You take care, Pa. Remember, you're my only father."

"And you're my only daughter," he replied gruffly, "so you take care too, hear?"

"I will." Rising, she headed for the door, then paused and turned. "You know, I still can't get used to you without a beard. Remember when I was little and you'd come home and swing me up in your arms and your whiskers would tickle?"

"And you'd giggle and squirm until I put you down." A smile ghosted across his face at the memory. "Arizona is too hot for a beard, though. I learned that the first time I was stationed here. Now go ride before it gets too hot."

Aurora hurried across the parade ground to the stables. She paused inside, waiting for her eyes to adjust to the shadows after the glare of the Arizona sun.

The warm, earthy smells of hay and horses welcomed her. She inhaled deeply. At least the stables smelled as they did back in Philadelphia. The pungent scents of the desert sometimes made her homesick for the soft, sweet scents of roses and new-mown grass.

Halfway down the long row of stalls, a horse was cross-tied in the central alleyway. Aurora walked toward it, surrounded by the gentle snuffling sounds of horses.

"Sergeant Mac, are you here?" She peered into the shadows, searching for her usual riding companion.

"I'm going with you this morning." The gravelly voice came from a stall behind her.

Aurora whirled. "Britton Chance," she cried, giving the tall, mahogany-haired lieutenant a delighted smile. "When did you get back?" Brit and she were on the way to becoming friends, and he would understand why she objected to the Apache's treatment.

"Last night. I'm hoping you'll join me for a ride and picnic breakfast this morning."

"You're just back from riding a hundred miles, and you want to go picnicking with me?"

"I most certainly do. Your steed awaits," he said, gesturing at the brown mare in the alleyway.

"Then let's go." She untied the reins and led the mare toward the mounting block.

"Hey, what are you doing?" Brit grabbed the reins and stopped her. "I'll be glad to give you a leg up."

"That's not necessary. I'm used to the mounting block." What she really wanted to do was to ride astride, but she'd shocked everyone at the fort enough with her profession. She wouldn't add to the whispers and rumors by riding astride. At least, not yet.

"I insist." Coming around to her side, he bent slightly and cupped his hands together, then looked at her.

"Oh, all right." Aurora placed her left foot in his clasped hands, and he boosted her up onto the horse. "Thanks." She hooked her right leg over the rest and settled into the sidesaddle, arranging her riding skirt to hang in demure folds.

As Brit mounted his horse, Aurora gathered her reins and nudged the mare with her spurred left boot. She led the way out of the stable, ducking slightly to avoid the door lintel. Outside, she turned left, away from the prisoner's corral.

"Wait, Aurora. Let's go this way." Brit turned right. "I want to show you something."

Her heart leaped like a startled rabbit and she almost objected. Then she decided, why not? So what if she had to ride past the corral? She didn't have to look at the Apache. She would just stare straight ahead and pretend— No! There was nothing to pretend about. Nothing at all.

She'd merely tried to give a prisoner water and he'd refused it. That's all.

Wolf watched the White-eyes woman ride by with a Bluecoat officer. The woman didn't look at the corral when she rode past, but she sat too straight in the saddle, stared too steadily at the parade ground.

The corporal guarding him watched the flame-haired woman also. "Boy, ain't she something?" he muttered. "I wonder how she'd be in bed."

Lowering his dark lashes to hide his thoughts, Wolf turned and hobbled over to the other side of the corral. Whose bed the White-eyes woman occupied didn't concern him, he reminded himself. Only when he glanced down did he notice he'd balled his hands into tight fists.

Brit led Aurora to a trail that switchbacked up a steep slope. An hour later their horses scrambled up onto the flat top of a mesa.

"I'll take care of the horses and get our food and a blanket," Brit said as they dismounted. "You can look around."

They were high above the fort, and Aurora studied it, intrigued by the toy-sized horses and men. She picked out her father's house and the headquarters, the hospital, the corral between them, the—

Sunlight flashed off something in the corral. Aurora blinked. It flashed again. Then again. Almost like a pattern. Then the flashes stopped. She turned as Brit walked up, but didn't mention the flashes.

"Ready for some breakfast?" He carried a blanket and the wicker basket he'd tied to his saddle before they left the stables.

"Famished. I'll spread the blanket." Stripping off her riding gloves, Aurora tucked them under her belt. She laid the green and blue plaid blanket at the edge of the mesa so that they could look down at the fort.

Brit pawed through the basket and put out ham sandwiches and juicy chunks of watermelon on tin plates.

"Lemonade?" he asked, holding out his canteen.

"Sounds wonderful. I'm always thirsty here." Pulling the cork out, she took a long swallow.

"That's because the air is so dry. You need extra water to replenish what you lose in perspiration."

"Ladies don't perspire. According to Aunt Ruth, animals sweat, men perspire, and ladies get dewy." Replacing the cork, she handed the canteen to him, then sank down on the blanket.

"Your Aunt Ruth has never been in the desert in June." Brit handed her a plate.

Aurora took it, but put it down without touching the food. "Brit, I'm worried about the Apache prisoner. I took water to him yesterday and he refused it."

"You took water to him?" He stopped with his sandwich halfway to his mouth. "Where was the guard?"

"He didn't seem interested in giving the prisoner any."

"I see. Well, I'm sure the Apache's had water by now."

"I hope so." She studied the coarse-grained bread on her plate. "What's going to happen to him?"

Brit shrugged. "That depends on who you talk to. We need to find out where the Apache villages are, and he can tell us. Afterward, Kreutz wants to make an example of him and hang him. I, on the other hand, would like to use him as a go-between to reach the wild Apaches."

"Why do you want to know about their villages?"

"So we can round them up. Four years ago, we signed a treaty giving the Chiricahua Apaches land in southeastern Arizona. But now miners have found gold on their land, so our government has abolished their reservation and taken back the land."

"How can they go back on their word? It's not right."

"Right has nothing to do with it. The government wants white settlers and miners on that land, not Apaches. So we're supposed to round them up and ship them off to another reservation."

Aurora gazed at him thoughtfully. "You don't agree with the government's Indian policy, do you?"

He sighed. "No. It's as if they want to start a war. In fact, Washington, in its infinite lack of wisdom, has ordered the Chiricahua Apaches sent to the San Carlos Reservation."

"What's wrong with that?"

"San Carlos is hot, dry desert. It's only good for

growing snakes and scorpions. But Washington plans to give them seeds and plows and turn them into farmers.

"For heaven's sake, that's crazy. Even I can see the Apaches aren't farmers." Aurora's eyes widened abruptly. "What do you think the Apaches will do?"

"What would you do if a bunch of strangers stole the land you'd hunted for a hundred generations?"

Aurora gazed at the purple mountains that rimmed the horizon. "I'd fight."

"So will the Apaches."

By the time she returned, Aurora was anxious to check on the Apache as well as on Mrs. Baker and the baby. As she neared the hospital, she hesitated and glanced at the corral. Had the Apache had water yet?

The corporal who'd been on guard duty yesterday stood with his back to her. He glanced around furtively, then leaned over and spat a stream of tobacco juice into the Indian's water bucket. Aurora's eyes narrowed with horror at his vileness.

Consciously working to keep her features from revealing her feelings, she marched to the corral. When she leaned against the fence beside him, the corporal started and glanced at her, obviously surprised to find her so close. Let him worry about how much she'd seen, she thought, peering through the rails at the prisoner.

The Apache slumped at the far side of the corral. He'd pulled his shirt off as far as he could, but because of his shackles, it hung over the iron chain linking his wrists.

"Has the prisoner had any water today, Corporal?"

"I don't know, ma'am." The soldier's black-toothed smile sent chills down her spine.

"I see," she said quietly. "Has the water bucket been outside the corral since you came on duty?"

He gave the bucket a sly glance. "Yes, ma'am."

The Apache raised his head. His gaze slid from her to the corporal and on to the bucket with such contempt that she knew he'd seen the man spit in it. He knew! That was why he'd refused water yesterday.

And that was why he'd knocked the dipper from her hand! He'd known and couldn't tell her in words, so he'd done the only thing he could. And for saving her from the soldier's depravity, she thought bitterly, he'd been clubbed.

His chains clanked as he moved, but he didn't stand. Aurora's heart began to race. The Apache was a proud man. A warrior. He wouldn't be slumped like that unless he was ill. He needed water, and quickly.

Snatching the bucket, she dumped the water out, then hurried to the water wagon parked beside the stables. Turning on the spigot at the rear, Aurora rinsed the bucket, then filled it. Wrapping both hands around the handle and ignoring the water sloshing on her skirt, she carried the heavy pail to the corral. She slammed the bolt back and wrenched the gate open, then, taking a dipper of fresh water, walked into the corral.

She knew the Apache had watched what had taken place, but she wasn't certain how much he understood. Bracing his hand on the fence, he got to his feet. He stood tall, proud.

But Aurora noticed a tiny slip of his left foot and how he gripped the fence so tightly that his fingers were white. She suspected that he couldn't keep up the tall, square-shouldered way he stood much longer.

Step by slow step, she began the longest walk of her life. The searing desert wind blew a lock of hair across her cheek and she automatically brushed it back. His eyes followed the movement of her hand.

"I want you to know this is fresh water. Really fresh." His brow furrowed as his gaze moved from the dipper back to her.

"I know you don't understand English, but I want to thank you for what you did yesterday." She took another step and held out the dripping cup. "And dammit, I don't want you to think all Americans are like Kreutz and the corporal. We're not."

Every taut muscle in his chest was outlined by the harsh sunlight. His chains rattled as he took a shuffling step toward her. The breath caught in her throat. She read in his rugged features the humiliation he felt at being chained. Now that she was closer, she could see a grayish tinge to his coppery skin that indicated he was a sick man.

She stopped in front of him, so close that she could feel the heat radiating from him. "My God, you're burning up. You've got to drink." She held out the dipper.

He reached for it with both hands. His fingers brushed her palm lightly, and the touch left her flesh tingling. As he lifted the dipper to his lips, he watched her over the rim.

His gaze never wavered from hers as he swallowed the life-giving liquid. Finished, he lowered the ladle. A drop of water clung to the corner of his mouth, then slid down his whisker-darkened chin.

"*Gracias*," he said, in a voice hoarse from disuse.

Aurora's heart did a somersault at his thank you. A bee buzzed beside her ear, but she couldn't turn her head, couldn't move. All she could do was drown in the dark depths of his eyes.

"*Gracias* to you also," she said softly, hoping he'd understand, "for what you did yesterday."

The tautness around his lips relaxed into a hint of warmth. Under his wariness she sensed a strange, tentative spark of something she couldn't name.

"Pincus, would you bring the bucket here?" she called as the photographer ran up to the corral. "I want to leave it here so the Apache can get more fresh water whenever he wants it."

The Apache looked down at the empty dipper, then held it out to her with both hands, as if offering a gift. Aurora's gaze fell to his broad, strong hands, then widened as she glimpsed the long red gash in his side. "My God, you're hurt!" No wonder he was feverish and haggard. Tilting her head, she studied what she could see of his wound, trying to determine how badly infected it was.

"Pincus, would you tell him I want to examine his wound?" She didn't dare touch his bronze flesh until Pincus had explained what she proposed to do. "Tell him I want to make it"—she pointed at his side—"stop hurting."

Pincus's sibilant Spanish flowed past her in a smooth stream. The Apache shook his head and uttered something in a low growl.

"Well?" Aurora glanced at Pincus, who'd halted a few feet behind her.

"He says, Thank you, but Apaches are used to pain. He doesn't need the help of the woman with flaming hair. Apache medicine will heal him. Save White-eyes medicine for the soldiers. Soon they will need it."

"Pincus, I may not know much Spanish, but I do know he didn't say 'gracias.'" Aurora didn't take her eyes off the Apache as she spoke. "Therefore I have to wonder what other words you put in his mouth."

None, Wolf almost replied in English before he caught himself. She was right, though, he hadn't said "gracias." He found himself wanting to say it, wanting to soothe her. But he couldn't thank her now without revealing he understood English.

Her eyes were blue as the winter sky at midday. They were full of warmth and something he could only call pity. But he didn't want her pity.

She reminded him of a doe protecting her fawn. She was a gentle creature, yet when the need arose, he suspected she would fiercely defend those who needed defending.

A gray mist formed at the edge of his vision. He blinked, but the mist clouded his sight and made the woman's face waver before him. Wolf shook his head. With water he could combat the fever, but the loss of blood was taking its toll.

"Miss Spencer!" Kreutz bellowed. He leaned out a window at Headquarters. "You are doing what?"

"Giving your prisoner some much-needed water, Captain," said the woman with hair of fire, turning to face Kreutz.

He didn't need her protection. And he didn't want her pity. He wanted— Wolf blinked, trying to hold off the mists darkening and closing around him.

Hearing a heavy thud behind her, Aurora

whirled. The Apache had collapsed. His right arm was stretched toward the fence, as though he'd tried to steady himself.

"Oh no!" Aurora dropped to her knees beside him. She laid her fingers against the pulse point in his throat. His heartbeat was far too rapid.

She stiffened when Captain Kreutz ran up. His shadow fell across the bit of mirror around the Apache's neck. Suddenly she remembered the flashes she'd seen when she was on the mesa above the fort. He'd been signaling! Without questioning her reasons, she turned the mirror so that its shiny side wasn't visible.

"Miss Spencer." Kreutz grasped her arm. "Come away from that . . . that savage."

"No!" Jerking free, Aurora shaded her eyes with her hand and peered up at the Captain. "This man is dehydrated and has an infected wound to boot. We need to get him to bed and take care of him."

"Why I—he—the doctor—" Kreutz sputtered. "No. This savage is a killer. Dr. Wharton wouldn't want him in the hospital. Wounded men are there."

"He's a wounded man!"

Kreutz stroked his chin as he stared down at the prisoner. "No," he finally said.

"So what are you going to do? Leave him out here to die?" Damn! The more she saw of Kreutz, the less she liked him. "Or maybe you'd like to shoot him, like a horse with a broken leg?"

"Now see here, Miss Spencer, this man is a military prisoner and—"

"Ah, Captain?" Pincus interrupted in a mild voice. He pulled a pencil and small notebook out of his shirt pocket. Licking the tip of the pencil, he poised it over the paper. "I want to get this straight. Are you refusing water and medical aid to a prisoner of the United States Army?"

"What?" Kreutz stiffened and his eyes widened. "Why no, of course not, Mr. Jones."

"Exactly as I thought. The United States Cavalry would never do that. We're far too civilized," Pincus said dryly. "However, I can see that ministering to this prisoner in the hospital could be a problem. May I suggest that small locked storeroom in your headquarters, where I'm keeping my extra camera supplies? If we moved my boxes out, you could put a cot in there for the prisoner."

Kreutz's brow furrowed. He stared off into the distance. "Hmm, maybe that would—" He shook his head. "No. Dr. Wharton wouldn't care for a murdering barbarian."

"I'll take care of him," Aurora snapped.

"But—" Kreutz began, still shaking his head.

"What a great idea, Aurora," Pincus exclaimed. "My readers will eat up a story about a woman doctor taking care of a wounded Apache chief. Maybe the paper will run it on the front page." Flicking a glance at Kreutz, he added, "Of course, your part in capturing this wild heathen will be included, Captain, and I'll need pictures of you."

"Yes, Mr. Jones, that's an excellent solution." Kreutz's chest puffed out and he nodded. "An excellent solution. I'll have the storeroom cleared immediately."

Aurora laid a wet cloth over the Apache's brow. He was still burning up with fever. She wet another cloth and slowly drew it down the thick muscles padding his broad chest, trying to cool him.

She'd taken advantage of his unconscious state

to cut away the last remnants of his shirt, then clean and dress his wound. The white bandage she'd used contrasted with his glistening copper color. She studied him while sponging him with the wet cloth. He already seemed better, for the gray undertone in his skin was fading.

Even unconscious, there was no softness to him, only hard planes and angles, only bones and muscle and raw power.

The tension had melted out of his face, yet his features were still as rugged as the granite mountains surrounding the fort. But his lips were surprisingly full and—

Dammit! What was she doing noticing such things?

And what was she going to do when he regained consciousness and opened his mesmerizing devil-dark eyes?

Chapter 3

"**W**e'll round up the Apaches and have them at San Carlos before they know what hit them, Brit."

"How are you going to do that, Captain Kreutz?"

"Attack their villages one by one, surround them, capture them, and ship them to the reservation."

"It won't work. You'll wind up with a war."

Men's voices. Arguing in English. Wolf awoke with heart-stopping alertness. He didn't open his eyes or give any sign that he was awake, just listened and tried to determine where he was. Curling the fingers of his right hand a bit, he felt the coarse muslin of a thin mattress.

He inhaled slowly, searching the air for clues. A whiff of the flame-haired woman's wildflower fragrance taunted him, and his nostrils flared as he drew her scent deep into his lungs.

She was there! With him! His heart leaped with an unexpected ripple of pleasure. But why was she so still? Opening his eyes a slit, he gazed through the dark veil of his lashes. She and he were alone in a tiny room.

36

She sat beside his narrow cot on a rickety old rocker, looking cool and fresh in a white dress. She rested her head against the chair back, eyes closed. Her hair of fire had been piled on top of her head in a haphazard knot that had slipped down to rest over her right ear. Glossy tendrils curled along the graceful curve of her neck, inviting the whisper of his fingers. He flexed his hand, wanting to touch them. To touch her.

The clink of his chains snapped him back to reality. He was a prisoner of the White-eyes. She was one of them.

Exhausted from the heat and caring for the prisoner, Aurora had been dozing. When his chains rattled, she roused instantly. Shaking her head to get rid of kinks in her neck, she sat up straight. And found he was watching her.

"So you're finally awake," she said in a not-quite-steady voice. Now that he was conscious, his primitive maleness filled the room and left her feeling slightly breathless. Her gaze fell to the white lace handkerchief she twisted in her hands. "If only we could communicate," she muttered. "I wonder if you're ready for some water or food."

Wolf closed his eyes, afraid she would see in them that he had understood her words. *"Agua."* He ran his tongue over his dry, cracked lips.

"Water? Coming." She reached for the chipped white china pitcher sitting on the old wooden trunk she was using as a bedside table.

As she leaned forward, her rocking chair creaked, and Wolf drew a startled breath of recognition. Dimly he remembered a rhythmic *creak-creak* from deep in his dream world and a cool cloth on his forehead. Cool fingers had fluttered against his cheek. She'd cared for him when he was semiconscious.

Had he been delirious? Had he spoken English? No, if he had, she wouldn't have wondered how to talk to him. He started to sit up, but a sharp stab in his left side froze him. He ran his fingers over the thick bandages swathing his wound.

"Let me help you." The flame-haired woman put the pitcher down and standing up, leaned over to slide a supporting arm behind him.

Her eyes met his and she tensed, as if suddenly afraid. Afraid to touch him? But she'd touched him before. He pointed at the bandages, then at her. She nodded. He looked down at them, picturing her soothing hands on him.

Aurora's gaze followed the slow movement of his large hand as he felt the bandages. The memory of how smooth and warm his bronze flesh had been beneath her fingers washed over her, and her heart did a funny little somersault. It was the heat, she reassured herself. It had finally gotten to her.

Slipping her arm beneath the tattered gray ticking pillow, she lifted him and the pillow together and brought the cup to his lips.

"*Gracias, señorita.*" His voice was rusty and low.

The Apache leaned forward, as if he preferred to sit up without help. His long black hair brushed across her arm like a lover's caress, sending a rush of sensation along her nerve endings.

He clasped the cup and her hand in his and took several deep swallows of cool water. She didn't move as his hand covered hers. Then the chain shackling his hands brushed her wrist, the metal hot with his body heat. She jerked back, and her hand became tangled in the heavy links. She panicked and yanked frantically, trying to free her hand.

The Apache dropped the cup and clamped his hand around her wrist. She froze. His long fingers extended along the sensitive flesh of her inner arm, and she could feel his pulse, beating in time with hers.

"Un momento, señorita." He untangled the iron links from around her fingers. Instead of releasing her, though, he gazed down at her hand for a heartbeat, then brushed his thumb over the back lightly. *"Gracias,"* he murmured, looking up at her.

Aurora's eyes flashed in surprise. This wild Apache, this primitive savage, was thanking her for what she'd done. Flustered, she pulled away.

"Those chains are ridiculous," she said briskly. "You're ill and weak. There's no reason for them."

"Qué?" The Apache raised an eyebrow at her.

Aurora rolled her eyes and lifted her hands in a gesture of frustration. "I forgot you don't understand English. Here, have some more water."

Water from the cup had splashed the Apache's tan denim pants, and they clung to his thighs like a second skin, showing every well-developed muscle. And more. Hastily she filled the cup and held it out. A frisson of pleasure cascaded down her spine when his fingers brushed hers.

"I'll see about getting you some food." She edged toward the door.

Slipping out to the adjutant's office, she leaned back against the rough plank wall and fanned herself weakly as she tried to slow her wildly racing pulse. What was happening to her?

Captain Kreutz looked up from the outer doorway, where her father's housekeeper was handing him a tray. "Miss Spencer, are you all right?"

Dropping the tray on the desk with a clatter, he ran to her side.

"Yes, of course. I'm fine. Why?"

"Flushed you look. I knew I shouldn't let you go in there alone. You're too trusting and you can't be with these murderin' savages. What did he—?" He drew his revolver. "Never mind. No need to tell me. Just stand aside and I'll take care of him right now."

"No! I'm fine. Put away your gun." She was shocked that he'd drawn it so readily. "The Apache was unconscious until five minutes ago."

"But he's conscious now, and you can't be alone with him. I'll have Corporal Thompson guard you. He knows better than to trust an Apache."

"I'm perfectly safe, Captain. After all, he's locked in a room in Headquarters. And he's weak as a kitten. As a matter of fact, there's no reason for him to be in chains."

Kreutz snorted and shook his head. "Trust him not. He's not a civilized man and he doesn't think like one. He's a wild beast and he will remain in irons. And the corporal—"

"Can stay outside. That room is too tiny for three people. Please." She gave him a soft, placating smile as he frowned at her. "If it will make you happy, I'll take Rob Roy in. He's good protection."

He gave her a doubtful look. "All right. We'll try it like that for a day. In the meantime, your housekeeper brought some lunch for you."

"Good. I'll give it to the prisoner." She couldn't eat, not with her stomach doing flip-flops. She walked over and picked up the tray, then turned.

Kreutz blocked her way, his arms crossed over the beginnings of a paunch. "Waste of good food, if you ask me. They will eat anything that doesn't eat them."

She bit her tongue and nodded politely. "I'll remember that. In the meantime, I'll share with him. Haven't you ever heard that food is the way to a man's heart?" *My God, what am I saying?*

"Apaches don't have hearts."

"I want to try anyway." It took an iron will to smile at Kreutz before she slipped back into the storeroom.

"Food for you," she told the Apache with a genuine smile. Sliding the tray onto the old trunk, she whipped linen napkins off the two plates. The mouth-watering aromas of beef stew and hot corn bread filled the room.

"*Gracias, señorita.*" Wolf sat up and swung his legs over the edge of the cot. He'd been aware of his hunger in a distant way since regaining consciousness; only now did he realize how starved he was. He picked up the knife from beside the corn bread.

A sudden stillness filled the room. He looked up. The flame-haired woman's eyes were on the knife, her expressive face had gone gray as a winter day.

He had to stop her before she screamed. He laid the knife down and moved his hand away from it.

"I won't hurt you," he said, speaking slowly in Spanish. Her head tilted slightly as she translated word by word. She watched him warily, but she didn't lunge for the door. How could he get it across to her? Moving slowly, keeping his gaze on her, he picked up the knife and sliced the corn bread in half, then edged one piece toward her. Laying the knife down, he gestured at the corn bread. "*Señorita?*"

Only then did she exhale a deep breath, almost a sigh, and slump against the door. "Oh, you want me to share bread with you?"

"*Sí.*"

Even as the word left his lips, he knew he'd revealed his understanding of English. Reaching for the corn bread, he chewed a chunk and gazed around the room as he watched her out of the corner of his eye.

She cut a tiny piece of the bread, sat back in her rocker, and began to eat. "I really didn't fear you. I was just surprised when you reached for the knife and— Damn! What am I doing speaking English to you?"

"*Señorita?*" She hadn't noticed!

"No!" She shook her head. "No *señorita.*" Pointing at herself, she said, "Aurora." Late afternoon sun poured through the small high window and limned her in gold.

"Au-rora? Aurora." It was a name worthy of her, singing of dawn and light, of spirit and fire. He tapped his chest and told her his name in Spanish rather than Apache.

"Stalking Wolf?" She eyed him thoughtfully. "Pincus told me Apaches get their names from something they've done. I wonder how you earned yours."

"*En español, señorita,*" he reminded her. Someday he'd tell her, but not now. Not when he was a prisoner of the White-eyes.

He stirred the beef stew and began to spoon some onto the other plate.

Her cool fingers on his arm stopped him. "No."

Something in her voice made him look up. Their eyes met and held for a heartbeat, then another. Her gaze dropped to her ivory fingers resting on his dark cinnamon skin. She was as deeply aware of him as he was of her, he realized.

Abruptly she leaned forward and dug in the black doctor's bag she'd put on the floor. She fished out a small jar. "This will ease your rope burn."

"*Qué?*"

Opening the jar, she pointed to him, then dabbed her finger in the salve and smoothed it down her neck. Wolf's mouth went dry as he watched her fingers glide down the satin length of her throat. Someday his lips would trace the same path, he promised himself.

Her eyes widened as if she'd read his thought. She handed him the jar and stood up hastily. "I'd better get going."

"*Buenos días*, Aurora," he said softly. Good day.

She paused in the open doorway and looked at him for a long moment. Then she walked out.

Wolf finished the beef stew. There were so many cracks in the thin plank wall that he could hear everything that went on in the adjacent room. Soon he'd know when and where the White-eyes planned to attack The People. Then he'd escape and warn them.

He ran his hand over the cotton bandages swathing his wound. Knowing the flame-haired woman had seen him weak and helpless gave him a vulnerable feeling. And he didn't like it. An Apache warrior was trained to be strong.

That was what his mother and father, his grandmother and aunts and uncles, had taught him from the time he began to walk. He could still hear their hushed voices as they huddled around the campfire on snowy winter nights and told legends of brave Apache warriors. Except for Geronimo, they were all dead now. Killed by White-eyes.

He opened the tiny jar the woman had left him and absently smoothed salve over his rope burn. What was he going to do about her?

"Hello, Brit, what are you doing out here? Aren't you officer of the day?" Aurora paused on the porch of the headquarters building.

Brit looked up from the sheaf of flimsy yellow papers he had been reading. "It's cooler than inside." He eyed her appreciatively. "And I must say, you look bright and chipper this afternoon."

"I am. After all, it's July third. Papa is due back today. And just think, our country will be a hundred years old tomorrow." She leaned against the railing and rested her medical bag beside her.

"It'll be an Independence Day to remember, all right. I was just reading what's come over the military telegraph." He waved the yellow flimsies. "We get the news a day ahead of the civilians, you know." He smiled at her. "But that's not why you're here, is it? I suppose you want to see the Apache?"

"Right."

"He's an interesting man, let me tell you. I never realized Apaches bathed, but every time the guards take him to the latrine, he jumps in the horse trough and scrubs himself."

"That explains the mystery of how he's managing to stay clean. I had wondered about it. You know, he's recovering so fast, it's hard to believe how ill he was a few days ago." And every day she became more attracted to him. Why? Why was she so intrigued by a primitive savage?

"It's because of you that he's recovering at all.

You saved his life, you know. Dr. Wharton wouldn't have touched him. Aurora, I—'' Brit cleared his throat. "I want you to know that I really respect you for helping the Apache. It couldn't have been easy for you, knowing that the Kiowas killed your mother."

Aurora frowned at him. "The Kiowas didn't kill my mother. Where did you get that idea?"

"But your father said—"

"Oh. No, Brit. I've explained what really happened that day, but he won't believe me. He thinks I was too young to know what was going on. And I was at the time. But one day, years later, Aunt Ruth questioned me about Ma's wound. Aunt Ruth's a nurse, and she did some investigating on her own. She discovered that a drunken Army doctor killed Ma, not the Kiowas. And when I went to the Women's Medical School and learned more about medicine, I realized she was right. Ma only had a flesh wound, but when the doctor left, she was dead."

"Good God! And you've told your father the true story?"

"He refuses to listen. He says my mother was the best thing that ever happened to him and the damned Indians took her away. It's as though he has a blind spot and can't see the truth."

"He's hated the Indians for a long time. It must be devastating to think that he was wrong all these years." He patted her arm. "Don't give up. Just keep working on him. He loves you and eventually he might listen to you." He opened the door to the adjutant's office for her.

"I hope so." As she slipped past him, she felt a pang of regret. She liked Brit as a friend. He was handsome and urbane and had a promising future ahead of him. Why didn't she feel that sizzling consciousness of him that she felt when she was with Stalking Wolf?

Entering the office, she scooped the keys off the desk and crossed the room, her footsteps rat-tat-tapping on the plank floor, and unlocked the door to the storeroom. When she pushed the door open and stepped in, her eyes widened in surprise. The room was empty.

Movement behind the door snapped her head around. The Apache leaned nonchalantly against the wall, his brawny, bronze arms crossed over his bandaged chest. His gaze was dark and sensual and intense. He kicked the door shut.

Frissons of awareness fired along her nerve endings. Her unbound hair swirled around her shoulders in a fiery cape as she turned to face him. Several strands wafted across her cheek.

The Apache studied a red-gold strand that had landed on her lips. "*Boca bonita*," he murmured, lifting it off with a feather-soft touch. Beautiful mouth.

How could he affect her so with just a few words and a single touch? Aurora took a deep breath, trying to still the butterflies fluttering in her stomach. She was a doctor. He was her patient. But no patient had ever invaded her dreams as the rugged Apache did night after night. And no patient had ever made her so aware of being a woman.

Plopping her black medical bag on the old trunk, she noticed a trail in the thick dust on the floor. He'd been pacing to the window and back. She pictured his slow, shackled strides. Two up and two back, the iron chain clanking, reminding him he was a prisoner. Unexpected tears burned her eyes and she dashed them away. ·

Fishing in her bag, she pulled out a thick wad of cotton and a roll of gauze. She turned to the Apache and gasped at his closeness. He was standing directly behind her. He'd always been sitting or lying on the cot before. But now he towered head and shoulders over her, and filled the small room with his presence. Although she was tall for a woman, he made her feel positively tiny.

Wolf crooked his finger under the flame-haired woman's chin and tilted her head up. He studied the tears clinging to her eyelashes. Why did she cry?

"Have you been practicing your Spanish, Aurora?" he asked in Spanish.

"*Sí.*" She smiled mistily. "First I dress your wound," she replied in a mixture of Spanish and English as she pointed at his bandages and pantomimed cutting them off. "Then we talk?"

He nodded. With a few snips, she cut the gauze she'd wound around his chest and over his left shoulder to hold the dressing in place, and began to pull it away from his wound.

Her head was bent, exposing her nape, and Wolf fought the urge to smooth his fingers down that sensitive skin. He drew a sharp breath and held it as her fingers whispered across his flesh. It was like being tied down and teased and taunted with feathers. Hot desire stirred in him. When her hot, cool fingers brushed his ribs, he shuddered.

She looked up, her eyes wide with awareness. Then she quickly turned her attention back to the bandages. Lifting the dressing off, she examined his wound.

"You're healing well, Stalking Wolf," she said in a too-hearty, professional voice.

If she was trying to put some distance between

them, to remind him she was the doctor and he was the patient, it was too late. It had been too late from the beginning.

She arranged a fresh dressing over the gouge. Without looking at him, she caught the fingers of his left hand and pressed them against the dressing. "Hold this in place, *por favor*."

He curled his fingers around hers. She swallowed, as if the breath were thick in her throat, and he knew she realized his touch had been intentional. She didn't say anything or look at him again, just focused on the bandage.

Wolf absorbed her scent as she moved about, winding the gauze around his chest and over his shoulder. Her hair brushed his chest when she bent close to tear the end of the gauze strip with her teeth. His fingers curled into fists as he fought the need to reach for her. What would she do if he kissed her?

Aurora tore the strip back a few inches, making two ties. He watched the top of her head as she slipped one tie beneath the layers of bandage, brought it out, and knotted the ends together, securing the bandage.

As if she felt the heat of his gaze, she slowly raised her head and looked up at him. She flicked her tongue nervously over her lips, wetting them.

He was going to kiss her, Wolf knew. He had to find out what her lips tasted like. And if what he saw in her eyes was true, she wanted him to. He slowly filled his big hands with her tousled hair, relishing the feel of the silken threads flowing through his fingers.

The heavy iron chain linking his wrists came to rest against her throat. Wolf gazed at the black links pressing against her ivory skin in a perversion of a necklace. Horrified, he jerked his hands away. She was too beautiful to be dirtied by the chains he wore.

He let his hands drop and stepped back, away from her. He would not touch her again, not while he was chained.

Her brow furrowed with confusion. "Stalking Wolf, what—"

The door banged open and a Bluecoat officer burst into the room. Wolf recognized the older man who'd been on the porch with Aurora the day Kreutz brought him in as a prisoner.

"Aurora, are you all right?" Artemus bellowed, panting as if he'd run a long distance.

"Of course, Papa," she said, her face flushed. "Why wouldn't I be?"

"Why wouldn't you be?" Artemus thundered. "You're alone in a room with a wild Apache and you can ask such a question? Child, are you going soft in the head? Don't you know the chance you're taking?"

"Papa, he wouldn't hurt me. Besides, how could he do anything when he's in chains?"

"No thanks to you, young woman. Kreutz told me how you tried to get him to remove the prisoner's chains. At least *he* kept his wits about him and didn't do anything stupid."

"Stalking Wolf is weak and ill. He shouldn't be in chains."

Artemus glared at the tall Apache standing next to his daughter. "He doesn't look so sick to me. In fact, he looks too damn fit to be trusted. You are never to come in here alone with him again. Hear?"

"Is that an order?" Aurora asked in a dangerously quiet voice. She clamped her hands to her
hips.

"Damn right it is." He frowned, looking from
her to Wolf. "Stalking Wolf? How is it that you
know his name?"

"He told me. Why? Is that against Army regula-
tions?"

"He told you? And when did you learn to speak
Apache?"

"Stalking Wolf speaks Spanish."

Wolf studied Aurora's father closely. Alarm bells
went off in the distant reaches of his mind. Once
the man's hair must have been as fiery a red as
hers. And now that a broad-brimmed hat was not
hiding her father's eyes, Wolf recognized something familiar in their faded blue.

"Aurora, you are a naive child when it comes to
these savages." Artemus raked his fingers through
his hair. "You must never give them a chance to—
to—"

"To what, Papa?" Aurora prodded, furious.
"He's told me he won't hurt me."

Wolf's gaze flicked back and forth between father and daughter. Watching. Recognizing.

Artemus dragged his hand over his weathered
face. "Words fail me. You're my only daughter and
I want you to be safe. That's all I want, my dear."
He forced a smile, trying to defuse the tension
quivering between them.

Wolf tensed. That smile brought it all back. The
screams of the wounded and the dying, the orange
flames devouring the brush wickiups, the smell of
his mother's blood.

He knew. He knew. Finally he'd found the red-
bearded man. His mother's murderer!

White-hot rage exploded through him. Blood pounded in his temples, and his hands curled like eagle talons. Yelling the Apache war cry, he leaped up and clamped his hands around the man's turkey-wattled neck and began to squeeze. Slowly. Inexorably.

All his rage, all his intent, focused on Artemus.

The older man clawed at Wolf's fingers, but nothing could stop the Apache now that he'd found his mother's murderer.

Nothing.

Chapter 4

Aurora's scream echoed the Apache's yell. Her eyes widened in horror as, teeth bared in a wolfish grin, Wolf choked her father.

"No! Let go!" Grabbing the Apache's arm with both hands, she tore at his iron-hard muscles. "Let go!"

Wolf didn't look away from her father, just rolled his shoulder sharply, shrugging her off like a bothersome fly. Aurora fell back across the cot, her head banging against the wall, and she saw stars.

Artemus gave a choked cry and clawed at Wolf's hands. The bitter scent of fear filled the room.

Brit dashed through the doorway from the outer office and flung himself at the Apache, landing a heavy blow to the side of his head. The Apache simply shook his head and tightened his grip on Artemus until his fingers went white.

Artemus's hands loosened; his struggles weakened.

Brit landed another blow on the Apache's shoulder. Stalking Wolf grunted and fell against the doorframe, then with clanking chains he and Artemus tumbled through the doorway into the adjutant's office.

Aurora struggled to her feet and tottered to the doorway. Troopers poured in from outside and joined the fray. They rained heavy, thudding blows across the Apache's bronze back.

After what seemed like hours, Brit and another man tore Wolf away. Even when they pulled him off, the Apache fought to reach Artemus, shouting in Apache and ripping his blue shirt as he struggled to land another blow.

Artemus gasped and sank to his knees. Bracing himself on one hand, he rubbed his throat and took harsh, tortured breaths deep into his lungs.

"Pa!" Aurora knelt beside him, her green dress pooling around her. "Are you all right?"

He nodded weakly. She could see the dark red marks Wolf's fingers had left on his throat. The imprint of the Indian's thumbs was clear on his Adam's apple. "Oh Pa, how awful. Here, let me examine you."

"Go away," he rasped in a dry, cracking voice. "Brit, get her"—he drew a labored, whistling breath—"out of here."

"Come on, Aurora, let's go." Brit reached down to help her up.

"Leave me alone!" She scrambled to her feet, her gaze on her father. "You need medical attention, Pa."

"Dr. Wharton will see to me." A soldier helped Artemus to his feet. He swayed slightly, glaring at the Apache from beneath bushy white brows. "After I've taken care of this redskin."

Aurora's eyes widened and she shuddered, shocked by the hatred in her father's eyes.

"Bastardo!" hissed the Apache.

For the first time since the fight had started, Aurora consciously looked at Stalking Wolf. Two beefy troopers held him even though he was still in chains. His panting was loud in the deathly quiet room. She could smell the metallic scent of blood as a red trickle ran down the side of his face from a cut above one eye. His jaw was bruised and beginning to swell. But as he faced her father, his dark eyes glittered with a hatred of his own.

Anger ripped through Aurora. This man she'd cared for had repaid her kindness by attacking her father. "Papa, I apologize. You were right."

"I'm glad you're finally seeing the redskins for the murderin' savages they are."

Taking a step closer to the Apache, she glared up at him. "How could you, Stalking Wolf? You really are nothing more than a despicable wild beast. A savage wolf. A snake in the grass."

"Come on, Aurora." Brit tugged her arm. "He can't understand you."

She didn't move, just continued to glare up at the Apache, who looked past her at her father. He'd glanced down at her as she spoke, then his gaze had returned to the older man. There was hatred and death in his eyes. Waves of fury washed over her.

"Then maybe he'll understand this!" Her hand came up in a wide swing and she slapped him. Hard. He had betrayed her trust.

The sound reverberated around the room. Silence froze the air. No one moved. Everyone stared at her. The men holding the Apache tightened their grip. Wolf's dark gaze dropped to Aurora as the imprint of her hand stained his cheek.

"Damn it, Aurora, you're not helping matters."

Grasping her elbow, Brit forcibly guided her toward the door. "Let's get out of here before you do anything more."

Aurora kept her back ramrod-stiff until they were outside, but as soon as the door slammed behind them, she sagged against Brit.

"Are you going to faint?" He slipped a supportive arm around her waist. "Here, lean against me."

Shaking her head, she pushed herself away from him and turned her back, fighting tears. Her mind seethed in a chaos of fear, anger, hurt, and betrayal. She gazed out across the parade ground with a feeling of disbelief, surprised that the sun was still shining, for she felt as if she'd been in the heart of darkness.

"It was awful, just awful. The Apache went crazy. I've never seen anything like it. He took one look at Pa and the next thing I knew, he'd leaped up and was trying to kill him." Trembling, Aurora gripped the rail so tightly that her fingers went white.

"It's all right," Brit soothed, rubbing her back gently. "Go ahead and cry. You had a hell of a scare and you deserve it."

"I had just told Pa that Wolf would never hurt me when he attacked. He gave this weird yell that was enough to make the dead sit straight up in their graves. And he—" Pressing a fist against her lips, Aurora fought to hold back the sobs welling up in her.

"Don't worry; you're safe, the Apache can't get you. In fact, he can never harm you."

"He was never after me. He wanted to kill Pa. I'll never forget the hate in his eyes or the way his teeth were bared like a wolf's." She shuddered with revulsion. "Now I know how he got his name." She stared down at her hand, still stinging from the impact with Wolf's cheek. "I can't believe I hit him. I've never struck anyone."

"Well, you have now. And quite a wallop it was, too."

Wolf stared through the barred window at his beloved Chiricahua Mountains. He gripped the iron bars with both hands; they felt cool against his heated skin. Unlike his back.

Artemus Spencer had ordered him whipped. They'd tied him to a crossbar behind the stables, then the lash had bitten deep into his flesh again and again. But he hadn't allowed himself even a groan. Instead, he'd wrapped his hatred of his mother's murderer around him like a shield.

But it was no longer a shield. The lash had cut into his bandages until they'd fallen away in shreds. His back felt as if it was on fire. So did his heart. Wolf pressed his forehead against the cool bars even as the red heat of shame curled through him.

He'd betrayed The People. He'd put his lust for revenge before his responsibility to them. He'd betrayed them.

Wolf rolled his shoulders cautiously, testing the pain, then began to pace. Two shuffling, chained strides up and two back. He couldn't afford to lie down until the pain lessened, for his muscles would stiffen, leaving him too clumsy and weak to escape. And escape he would.

Two strides up and two back. He'd betrayed The People! Wolf cringed at the thought. The People needed a leader they could rely on, especially now, when they were surrounded by enemies.

He had already learned much from the meetings called by Artemus Spencer upon his return from Fort Grant. Hurt as he was, Wolf had listened as the Bluecoats plotted their treachery.

Pausing in his pacing, Wolf stared through the bars at the mountains. And the woman? a voice inside him asked. He stroked the cheek she'd struck. Even through his pain, he felt a stirring in his loins. No! He wouldn't allow himself to think about her.

Tomorrow, while the White-eyes were celebrating their Independence Day, he would escape. Tomorrow.

When he was free, he would warn The People of their danger. Only when he knew his people were safe from the White-eyes could he take vengeance on his mother's murderer.

Then he would return and finish with Artemus Spencer. The muscles in Wolf's jaw clenched. Soon his mother's spirit would walk the Underworld knowing she had been avenged. And, he promised himself, it would be a true Apache revenge.

The next evening Aurora and Brit strolled along a path lit by red, white, and blue Chinese lanterns. The sound of a waltz drifted from the open windows of the mess hall ahead of them. Red, white, and blue bunting had been wound around the porch railing and posts in honor of the Independence Day Ball. Aurora yawned.

"Don't tell me you're tired already," Brit said, smiling at her. "The dance hasn't even started." Brit tugged at the yellow cummerbund and sash on his blue dress uniform.

"I'm sorry. I didn't sleep very well last night. Thinking about the Apache, I guess. I keep asking

myself, why? Why did he attack Papa like that?"
She lifted the skirt of her blue-green ball gown a bit
to keep the hem clear of the gravel and dirt. "When
I was growing up, Aunt Ruth told me time and
again, 'See who the man is, Rory, not the color of
his skin.' I wanted to believe that. I wanted to
believe he would respond to kindness instead of
more of Kreutz's brutality; but I was so wrong. I
still can't get over how he turned into a wild
beast."

"I've thought about it, too. And something's
wrong. The whole attack is crazy, and if there's one
thing the Apaches aren't, it's crazy. They understand war and strategy, and they don't leap into
battle without a reason and without figuring the
odds for success."

"Just what are you saying, Brit?"

"I don't know." He clasped his hand over hers.
"I can't figure it out, but I do know the Apache
didn't just snap and try to kill your father. There
was more to it than that." He patted her hand
reassuringly. "In the meantime, put it out of your
mind and enjoy yourself this evening."

"That's exactly what I'm going to do," she said
as they started up the steps.

But it was hard. Since the Apache's attack, she'd
tried to calm her turbulent thoughts. She had been
attracted to Wolf, had yearned to feel his lips on
hers. Her heart had leaped when he had simply
brushed a tendril of hair off her cheek. She had
seen beneath his warrior exterior to the man
inside—or thought she had. Until Wolf had
changed into a fierce warrior bent on killing her
father.

"I want you to know I'm proud to have such a

lovely lady on my arm tonight." Brit paused in the golden candlelight spilling from the open doorway onto the porch. "Very proud."

"Thank you, kind sir." Aurora eyed the men and women thronging a room festooned with more bunting. Colorful Chinese lanterns shed their bright light over the noisy, happy crowd. "My goodness, where did everyone come from?"

"All over southern Arizona and New Mexico." He rested his left hand on his saber hilt. "Every American for miles around wanted to celebrate Independence Day here. After all, one like this won't come again in our lifetime."

"It won't come again in anybody's lifetime—the United States is a hundred years old today. It'll be something to tell our children and grandchildren."

"Our?"

Aurora snapped open her carved ivory fan and flicked him a sideways glance from behind it. "You know what I mean." She fanned herself languidly in the July heat. "There must be even more people here than were at the baseball game this afternoon."

"There's more women, that's for sure." Brit waved at a pretty redhead Aurora had never seen before.

"You haven't thanked me for rooting for your team." She nodded at Sophie Kreutz as the buxom, blonde girl whirled by in her father's arms. "Sophie certainly cheered you on."

"Sophie's just bored. Her fiance's off fighting the Sioux with Custer, and as soon as he returns, they're getting married. Now, pretty lady, it sounds like the band is striking up a polka." Brit held out his hand. "Let's dance."

They joined the other couples on the dance floor, and Brit swung her around so fast that Aurora's feet left the floor. Just when she didn't think she had enough breath left to do one more enthusiastic step, the band slowed into the "Blue Danube Waltz." As they eased into the elegant dance, Aurora checked her mother's sterling silver combs to be sure they were still secure in her upswept hair.

The evening passed in a whirl of partners and melodies. Aurora laughed and danced and flirted, determined to enjoy herself and not think about the Apache.

She was dancing with Brit again when the music suddenly degenerated into jarring squawks and squeals. Surprised, she glanced at the stage. Her father stood in front of the bandsmen. He was a sickly ashen color.

"Something's wrong, Brit," she whispered as everyone turned to her father. "I've never seen Pa so deathly pale."

The chapel bell began to toll sonorously. Like a death knell. Aurora shivered with a sudden chill.

"Ladies and gentlemen, officers, honored guests, may I have your attention, please." Artemus looked down at the yellow flimsies in his shaking hand. "I have an announcement to make. I have just received an urgent communication via military telegraph."

Pausing, he wiped a hand across his brow. A tense silence fell upon the crowd. "It says, 'The War Department informs all personnel that on Sunday, June 25th, General Custer and the men of his command were massacred at the Little Bighorn River in Montana Territory.'"

"Oh Lord, no!" Aurora swayed with shock and horror. Brit tightened his arm around her waist, steadying her. All around them there were gasps and choked screams.

"Two hundred and sixty-four brave men and officers were murdered by the Sioux and Cheyenne under Sitting Bull." Pulling out his handkerchief, Artemus blew his nose loudly before continuing in a shaky voice, "The confirmed dead include George Armstrong Custer, Tom Custer, Boston Custer . . ."

Her father's voice faded. Aurora thought of the fathers and husbands and sons who would never come home again. A lump grew in her throat and her eyes burned with unshed tears.

"No!" Sophie Kreutz screamed from the other side of the room. "It can't be . . ." Her voice melted away as she crumpled to the floor.

"I must go to her," Aurora murmured.

She edged through the crowd to Sophie's side. Kneeling beside the barely conscious girl, Aurora grasped her wrist, feeling for a pulse.

Sophie's eyes opened and she stared wide-eyed at Aurora. "Don't touch me!" she screamed, scrabbling backwards across the floor. "You . . . you Indian-lover, you."

Frozen in horror, Aurora knelt in the midst of the crowd, her hand still outstretched. "My God, Sophie, I only want to help you."

"This is what happens when people like you help the savages," Sophie's mother snapped, giving Aurora a venomous look. "Don't you dare touch my daughter with those hands."

Aurora glanced around and saw men and women nodding their agreement. Most of the women sobbed quietly, but the men were red-faced and shouting angrily.

"Damn savages, kill them all!"

"Hang the Apache!"

"Murderin' bastards!"

Suddenly Brit was kneeling at her side. "Let's get out of here. There's going to be trouble." He helped her up and they moved through the crowd, bombarded by cries from all sides.

Out on the porch, Aurora clung to a post, trembling. The chapel bell continued to toll. "Stop it!" She clamped her hands over her ears. "Can't you make it stop?"

"The bell tolls once a minute for each man." Brit gave her a somber look. "It'll toll for four more hours."

Shaking her head, she pressed her forehead against the rough wooden post, trying to shut out the horror.

"Come on." Brit wrapped an arm around her shoulders and guided her toward the stairs. "I'm taking you home."

They had barely reached the steps when a torrent of men poured out of the hall. Shouting and yelling, they jostled and shoved past Aurora, knocking her and Brit against the railing as they swept by.

"Death to the Apache!"

"An eye for an eye!"

"Brit," she cried, grasping his arm, "you've got to stop them. Whatever the Apache did, murder is murder. The killing has to stop!" He hesitated and she pushed him. "Go! I'll be all right. Just stop the killing. Please stop it."

"Go straight home," he ordered. Tilting his

saber to the side so that it wouldn't tangle with his legs, Brit ran after the mob.

Aurora picked up her skirts and hurried along the wagon road toward her father's house. As she passed the chapel, she heard a woman singing "Nearer My God to Thee."

There was only a quarter-moon, and the night was full of shadows. The pungent scent of creosote hung over the fort. A coyote howled in the distance. Aurora shivered and glanced around fearfully. Her taffeta skirt rustled loudly in the thick silence.

She had just passed Captain Kreutz's house when a tall, lean man appeared out of the shadows between the buildings and silently raced toward her.

She stared at him for a split second. Then, picking up her skirts, Aurora whirled and ran. She opened her mouth to scream, but it was too late. He clamped his left hand over her mouth as he circled her waist with his brawny right arm.

And he dragged her back, back into the deadly shadows.

Chapter 5

⌒〰〰⌒

Aurora kicked backward and felt a satisfying thump as her high-heeled shoe whacked her attacker's shin. But his grip didn't loosen. He lifted her off her feet and hauled her back against his hard chest.

Shrieking inside, she jabbed her elbows back into his belly. He grunted, but still didn't let go of her. Sand crunched beneath his feet as he retreated into a narrow passageway. Buildings blotted out the stars and loomed over them as he pulled her further into the shadows.

His hand was cutting off Aurora's air, and panic rose in her as she struggled to breathe. She clawed at his fingers. Inhaling through her nose, she drew a breath deep into her lungs.

Instantly she recognized the mingled scent of wild sage and male sweat that could belong to only one man.

Stalking Wolf!

The look in his eyes when he'd attacked her father yesterday crashed through her muddled senses. In her mind, his eyes grew larger and larger, blacker and blacker.

Turning, he backed her up against an adobe wall and pinned her there with his powerful hips and thighs.

Over the sound of the tolling bell, she could hear shouts and cries of alarm and knew the lynch mob had discovered his escape. She wanted to scream and let them know where he was, but his hand was still clamped over her mouth. Men with torches ran by the passageway. She prayed someone would look her way. No one did.

"Will you be quiet?" Stalking Wolf asked in Spanish.

She nodded. She had to breathe! He removed his hand slowly, watching her with single-minded intentness. She sagged back against the wall, taking deep gulps of air.

"You!" she hissed, putting a world of hate into the single word.

"*Si.*" His low growl rumbled through her.

Someone ran by the end of the passageway with a torch. In that flickering second, she saw that the Apache's wrist was free of the heavy iron manacles. She was still petrified, but she was beginning to think more clearly. She took deep breaths as she tried to decide if she could scream for help.

"Don't try it, Aurora," he warned in Spanish. He rested his hand on her abdomen. His long fingers brushed the lower curve of her breast, and she stiffened. "I'll do whatever it takes to stop you."

Aurora straightened to her full height and glared, her eyes flashing fire. "Don't touch me."

He didn't move. The heat of his hand seemed to sear her flesh and brand her. And he gazed down, not at her face, but at his hand, so close to her heart.

"W-what do you w-want?" she asked, trying to sound calm and in control. He might not understand English, but she felt better hearing her own voice.

His gaze roamed her features. She cringed away as he cupped her face in his large callused palms. "No-o!"

Another shadow glided up beside them. Barely visible in the faint moonlight streaming into the narrow passageway, the other man was a full head shorter than Stalking Wolf and his square face was age-weathered.

She hadn't recognized Geronimo, Wolf realized, for she hadn't stiffened in terror. Good. It was better if she didn't report that Geronimo had been there.

"We have stolen most of the horse herd and set fire to the hay behind the stables," Geronimo whispered in Apache. "As soon as the Bluecoats discover it, they'll sound the alarm and forget to look for you."

"Good. We'll sell the horses for guns and ammunition in Mexico." Wolf didn't take his eyes off Aurora.

Geronimo glanced from Wolf to the White-eyes woman. "Do you want this female?"

"Yes." Wolf studied her. She would be the instrument of his revenge. Apache justice would be done. He could never reveal who *Nantan* Spencer was, or Geronimo would wreak his own vengeance for the death of his beloved younger sister, which would touch off a far greater war than any the White-eyes had yet seen. Although Wolf didn't

care about White-eyes lives, he didn't want more
Apaches to die.

Aurora turned her head. Loose tendrils of her
hair trailed across the back of his hand like a
lover's caress. He inhaled slowly, dragging her
scent deep into his lungs, and felt a familiar stirring
in his loins. No matter who her father was, he
wanted this woman.

Aurora also felt the stirring of his manhood. She
trembled and shrank back against the rough adobe,
her pulse pounding loudly in her ears. They were
talking about her, deciding her fate, and she
couldn't understand them.

Geronimo studied Wolf intently before he asked,
"Shall we take her with us?"

Wolf eyed Aurora. It was tempting, but— "No.
Our people are in too much danger. After they are
safe in Mexico, I'll come back for her."

Geronimo nodded. "Wise choice."

Wolf shot him a wry look. "What if I'd said I
wanted to take her now?"

"You are your mother's son. I knew you would
make the right choice. After all, your heart lies with
The People."

"Yes, my heart lies with The People," Wolf
echoed. But his eyes were on Aurora.

"I'll get the horses. After we get away from here,
I will give you a salve for your back."

"While you're gone, I will see to the woman."

"*Enjuh.*" Good. Geronimo trotted away.

Aurora met Stalking Wolf's gaze and raised her
chin defiantly. Whatever he intended, she wouldn't
yield without a fight. She felt along the adobe wall
behind her, searching for a loose piece to use as a
weapon.

"*Una mujer muy bella.*" Beautiful woman.

She shivered at the intimate huskiness in his whisper. Finding a loose rock in the adobe, she brought it up in a wide-armed swing at his head. He blocked it, grasping her wrist in fingers of steel. She strained furiously against his grip.

"Drop it," he growled in Spanish, shaking her wrist.

"Damn you!" she muttered. She had no choice but to yield. The rock thudded to the ground beside them.

He looked at the large rock for several moments before his gaze slowly rose to her face. Aurora waited, trembling. What was he going to do?

His head lowered over hers, blotting out the moon and stars.

"No!" She twisted away, trying to avoid his kiss.

He pulled her against his hard warrior's body. She stiffened, determined not to respond. He paused for a moment, his hand in her hair, as he studied her by starlight.

Then his lips crashed down on hers, and his kiss was hot and hard and heavy. Aurora sank beneath its impact. Nothing she'd ever experienced had prepared her for that explosion of power and need.

She pushed frantically at his broad shoulders with both hands, but her pushing became holding, then clinging, as his elemental hunger overwhelmed her senses and left her reeling and dizzy.

His fingers tangled in her hair, and one of her sterling silver combs loosened and fell to the ground. Still dazed, Aurora absently reached up to catch the curls that tumbled over her shoulder as he pulled away.

"Sleep well, my beautiful woman," Wolf murmured in Spanish. She never saw his right hand ball into a fist or come up to tap her chin.

All she saw were stars.

Wolf caught her in his arms as she crumpled. Laying her on the ground, he gently ran his thumb over her chin. He hoped the bruise would disappear quickly. Wolf stood up slowly, gazing down at Aurora. Beside her, the silver comb gleamed in the moonlight.

He scooped it up and ran to the waiting horses.

Fort Bowie prepared for war. There were no more morning rides through the foothills. Aurora threw herself into caring for Bonnie Mae Baker. Within days, Mrs. Baker and her son were discharged and sent home.

Wherever Aurora went, she saw army wives tearing old sheets into strips for bandages. The hills rang with machine-gun bursts as troopers practiced with the deadly Gatling guns. Tucson newspapers howled for Indian blood and lots of it.

Armed patrols fanned out from Fort Bowie to round up the Chiricahua Apaches and move them to the San Carlos Indian Reservation. They all returned with the same news. The Apaches were gone. They had disappeared into the desert like ghosts. Their rancherías were abandoned, their wickiups burned, their crops of corn and squash left to wither and die. It was the same all over Arizona.

No white man knew where the Chiricahua Apaches were.

Stalking Wolf reined the bay stallion off the trail and rode to the top of a low knoll. From there he watched the long, dusty column of The People trudging south through the cactus-dotted desert. He and Geronimo had gathered over four hundred

of The People, warriors, women, and children who
didn't want to die in the White-eyes cage called
San Carlos.

Wolf had mounted the warriors on the strongest
horses and sent them out in front and behind the
column of women, children, and old people, to
protect it. The column moved slowly, for the horses
were thin and footsore. They'd fled just as their
crops neared harvest, so they carried no wickiup
poles, no stores of food. Nothing but despair.

Wolf felt the small buckskin pouch tied to his
belt, a pouch every Apache carried. He had three
handfuls of parched corn. Three days' rations, that
was all they had left.

The column was quiet except for the infrequent
bark of a dog and the sound of horses' hooves. He
understood their silence and their sorrow, for he
felt it too.

The People were leaving the land that had been
their home for hundreds of harvests. Occasionally
a woman glanced back at the rugged Chiricahua
peaks visible on the horizon to the north. Those
mountains were home to all their dreams. Now
they were leaving them to go into exile.

Would they ever see their hearts' home again? he
wondered. Would they ever again roam those
forest-covered slopes, hunt deer in that crisp, pine-
scented air, smell the wildflowers in those mountain meadows?

He had been born high in the Chiricahuas and
had spent a happy childhood among the rugged
peaks. But that had been in the days when the
White-eyes were few. In the days of peace.

Now the White-eyes were many. And peace was
no more.

As he scanned the line of march again, watching for trouble, a pregnant young woman turned her pony out of the column and rode into a clump of bright-green creosote bushes. Two withered old women turned their horses to follow her, and he knew her time had come. Although she was heavy with child, something about the proud, defiant way she sat her pony reminded him of the flame-haired woman.

The woman he'd left behind. The woman he wanted.

He reined his stallion down the slope and rode after the women. Stopping at the edge of the thicket where they'd tied their ponies, he coughed to signal his presence.

She Who Sees Babies, who was old enough to be his grandmother, emerged from the thicket and scowled. "Why are you here? Go away. We women are busy."

"Should we rest here for the night?"

She Who Sees Babies tittered. "Do you think Many Tongues is a weak White-eyes woman? We will catch up with you. We will only be a few hours behind."

He nodded. "The People will camp on the other side of the river, but I'll wait for you on this side. If you haven't come by moonrise, I will return for all of you."

It was late before Wolf hunkered down next to a tiny fire. The river was swollen from summer storms in the mountains. He had made many trips across, riding on the downstream side of the band, so that he could rescue anyone who was swept away. On his last trip he had brought across the old women, the young mother, and a new boy-child.

Now he cleaned and oiled his rifle by the flickering firelight. Soon, he decided, he would go back for Aurora.

She was always there, in the dim recesses of his mind. It was as if she rode double with him. His manhood stirred at the mere thought of feeling her supple body pressed against his, both moving with the rhythm of the horse.

He glanced up when Geronimo joined him, but didn't speak.

"When will you go back for the woman?" Geronimo asked, prodding the small fire with a stick.

"Soon." Wolf continued to oil his rifle. "After The People are safe in the Sierra Madre."

Geronimo stared into the flames. "We need to prepare our people for the time of Ghost Face." The stick broke in a shower of sparks, and he flung it into the embers. "If only you could also steal supplies and ammunition."

Wolf rubbed a spot on the silver-blue rifle barrel. "I've been thinking that, too. Although we leave the White-eyes behind, we will still be surrounded by enemies. We'll need guns and supplies to see us through the winter."

Geronimo tugged on his eyebrow as he eyed Wolf. "And?"

Wolf looked at the older man. "I have a plan."

"Aurora, I'm going to Fort Grant next week," Artemus said at dinner one night. "Would you like to come along, since there's nothing for you to do here?"

"Yes, Pa, I think it would be a nice change."

She needed one, for in the three weeks since the Apache had escaped, Aurora had found that no matter what she did, she couldn't wipe him from her mind. He was a ghost, walking with her wherever she went: she saw him in the shadows, felt his hand tangle in her hair, heard his voice when the wind whispered.

Sometimes she would awaken with her hand touching her lips, and she'd remember his soul-searing kiss.

Then the memory of his war cry when he'd tried to kill her father would knife through her, and an icy-hot mixture of fear and loathing and excitement would churn her insides.

She had tried to stay busy by throwing herself into her work, but Dr. Wharton had barred her from the hospital, and the officers' wives shunned her as an Indian lover, a traitor to their men and their cause.

Only Pincus and Brit remained her friends.

Maybe by going to Fort Grant she would be able to forget the Apache and the maelstrom of emotions that erupted in her whenever his image galloped across her mind.

They had finished dinner and were having coffee, and Pa was puffing away on a smelly cigar, when Sergeant Mac hurried into the room.

"Sorry to bother you, sir, but a messenger has just arrived from Tenehas. He's ridden hard. Says they have an outbreak of smallpox and need whatever help we can give them." He glanced at Aurora. "It must be pretty serious. They asked for a doctor."

"Hmm. I want to talk to this messenger myself." Artemus threw his napkin down on the table and hurried out.

"Where's Tenehas?" Aurora called, rushing after him.

"It's a small town on the Mexican border south

of the Chiricahua Mountains. The border towns always have problems with smallpox, because it's widespread in Mexico." Stopping in mid-stride, he turned and gave her a wary look. "Why?"

Aurora had to stop short to keep from running into him. "Because I want to go. They need a doctor and I'm available."

And she would be far too busy to have time to think of the Apache—or his kiss.

Chapter 6

〜⦿⦿〜

Sunrise was barely a peach blush on the eastern horizon when Aurora emerged from the Fort Bowie hospital, carrying the precious vaccine points wrapped in cotton. The morning breeze eddied around her, rich with the scent of well-oiled saddle leather. She walked to the gray gelding and nestled the vaccine points in her saddlebag.

She'd plaited her waist-length hair into a single thick braid that hung down her back. Settling a straw picture hat on her head, she tied its royal blue ribbons beneath her chin. Then she led the spirited, prancing gelding over to Headquarters.

Aurora nodded to the young Mexican boy who, yawning and rubbing his eyes, stood next to the hitching rail. "Did you sleep, José?" she asked in slowly improving Spanish.

"*Sí, señorita.*" Dressed in baggy white trousers and shirt, he stared down at his bare brown toes.

Had he been injured, or born with a twisted right foot? she wondered. Tenehas must be in dire straits if they had to send a lame child for help.

75

"Good morning, Pa." She waved cheerily at her father.

"Morning." Artemus stood on the top step of the headquarters' building and watched the men, horses, and mules gathering on the parade ground. "I don't know how you managed to talk me into letting you go."

"They need a doctor and Dr. Wharton can't leave the fort hospital. That leaves me. And we both know they wouldn't have sent José if they weren't desperate." She would have the satisfaction of helping people. And she'd be too tired to remember the feel of the Apache's lips on hers.

"But you'll be going through the heart of Apacheria."

"Where your own patrols have reported abandoned rancherías and no Apaches to be seen."

"Humph! Not seeing them doesn't mean they're not there, young woman."

Aurora glanced up as Emmett Kreutz joined them. "And Captain Kreutz will be leading the troops. Surely you don't think we'll have any trouble with him in charge." Personally she would have felt a lot safer with Brit Chance, but her father seemed to trust the pompous Prussian.

Aurora brightened as Pincus rode up, leading a mule heavily laden with tripods and wooden boxes full of cameras and supplies. "Pincus, I didn't know you were coming. Have you had smallpox?" The morning breeze ruffled her blue riding skirt, making the gelding snort and sidle away.

"When I was a child. How about you?"

"I've been vaccinated. Many doctors are nowadays."

Kreutz ordered his men to mount, then gave Aurora a leg up. She tightened her grip on the reins, and the gray settled down. Aurora swung into line beside Pincus as the column of soldiers trotted by twos out of Fort Bowie.

On a ridge high above the fort, Geronimo lowered the far-seeing glasses and handed them to Wolf. "You were right. They've loaded food and ammunition on the mules."

"I told you they would help the settlers in Tenehas." He scanned the column of riders and horses, searching for a brilliant mane of flame-red hair. Aurora's hair was hidden beneath her broad-brimmed hat, but she was riding sidesaddle, and her blue skirt fluttered like a flag in the morning breeze. Just the sight of her stirred the fire in his blood.

"The flame-haired woman rides with them," Geronimo said, watching him.

"Yes." Rising, Wolf strode toward the horses. "Let's prepare their welcome."

The soldiers followed a narrow canyon toward the Silver Springs Valley. As they emerged from the canyon, Aurora noticed the valley floor wasn't flat; it was a series of long, rolling ridges.

Summer rains had brought new growth, clothing the desert in soft gray-greens as far as she could see. On the horizon, amethyst mountains reached up to kiss the deep-blue skirts of heaven. Saddles creaked and bits jingled as the column trotted into the desert. Soon they snaked through horse-high stands of bright green creosote bushes.

"I don't like this," Pincus muttered.

"What don't you like?" Aurora replied. The odor of sweating men and horses surrounded her.

"All these high bushes. The Apaches could hide among them and ambush us anytime."

She glanced around fearfully at the endless expanse of cactus and bushes. "Do you think they know we're here?"

"Pray that they don't."

Aurora and Pincus rode at the front of the column of troopers, just behind Captain Kreutz. As they crested a long ridge, three Apaches trotted out of an arroyo only a few hundred feet away. Seemingly as astonished by the sight of the troopers as the soldiers were by them, the Apaches milled about in confusion.

Aurora recognized the rugged features and broad shoulders of one. "There's Stalking Wolf," she cried. Her heart leaped at the sight of him, betraying all her resolutions to forget him.

"You and Pincus stay with squad one and the pack train," Kreutz shouted. "Squad two, follow me." Spurring his horse into a gallop, he and the soldiers bore down on the Apaches.

The Apaches lashed their mounts and raced away. In minutes the troopers were simply one dust cloud pursuing another dust cloud, soon disappearing over a ridge.

The few remaining soldiers turned back with the pack train. Pincus and Aurora trailed along behind the mules. The only sound was their horses' hoofbeats.

A few pebbles rolled down a sandy ridge paralleling their path, and Aurora glanced up. She was turning away when a line of Apaches poured over the crest and swept down on them with blood-curdling war cries.

Aurora's horse reared, screaming with fright. The Apaches hurtled between the pack train and the civilians, dividing them. They split, half going after the mules, half racing toward Pincus and Aurora.

"Run for it, Aurora," Pincus yelled as he spurred his horse straight at the oncoming Apaches.

"No, Pincus!" But it was too late. He'd dashed directly into the broad line of Apache warriors.

Whirling the gray gelding around, Aurora raced along the trail. Her only hope was to reach Kreutz before the Apaches caught her.

Hooves pounded along behind her.

She leaned low over the gray's neck, lashing him with her riding crop as she'd never before lashed a horse. The gray's mane whipped her cheeks so violently that it stung and made her eyes tear. Out of the corner of her eye, she saw a brown horse moving up on her right and whipped the gray frantically. Kreutz couldn't be far!

An Apache war cry rang in her ears as the rider leaned over and reached for her reins.

"No!" She lashed his hand with her quirt.

He jerked back and yelled something at her. She didn't dare look at him. She spurred the gelding, sending it lunging toward a hillock of boulders.

In two strides he was beside her again. Their horses raced neck and neck. This time the Apache reached over and grabbed the reins even as she lashed him. Whooping wildly, he yanked the gray's head around. Thrown off balance, the gelding tumbled head over heels.

Aurora screamed as, arms and legs flailing, she somersaulted through the air. She could see the horse cartwheeling alongside her, legs thrashing wildly.

She landed flat on her back in front of the boulders. The ground shook as the gray landed beside her. She gasped when one of his hooves grazed her shoulder. Stunned by the impact, with the wind knocked out of her, she lay unable to move.

She had to move. Had to get away. Shakily she scrambled to her feet. A stocky Apache leaped from his horse and raced toward her. His hair-raising cries made her blood run cold. He was a demon and he was coming for her.

Heart thumping against her ribs, mindless with terror, she scuttled back among the boulders.

The Apache loomed over her. Lightning bolts of black paint marked his face. A long scar slashed his cheek from the corner of his mouth to his ear. He ripped her hat away so that he could see her face. She cowered back, hard against a boulder as his viper-black eyes raked her. Grasping her arm, he yanked her out of the sheltering rocks.

Beyond him, she saw another Apache on a big bay horse racing toward them.

"Oh God," she moaned.

The horse slid to a halt, then reared and pawed the sky. His rider shouted at the man menacing Aurora, and the stocky brave went deathly still.

The rider rapped out a single harsh word.

Slowly, very slowly, like a rattler pulling back from its prey, the Apache straightened up. He took a single step back.

Shaking, Aurora drew a deep, sobbing breath. At least he no longer loomed over her like the angel of death. Beyond him, the horse and rider were silhouetted against the sun. She couldn't see the rider's face; she was aware only that he was a tall man on a tall horse.

The brave who'd captured her turned and shouted at the rider. Aurora trembled at the rage in his voice. The rider's low, growled reply stiffened him.

Aurora's eyes widened, and she stiffened, too, as she recognized the deep resonance in the rider's tones. Stalking Wolf? Did she dare hope?

The Apaches argued, one in shouts, one in deadly soft tones. Her captor whipped a bloody knife out of his belt, pointed it at her, and drew the blade across his throat in an unmistakable gesture.

The rider sat like a stone statue. He spoke a single word that whiplashed through the air.

The rider's command echoed in a sudden stillness. Aurora's pulse pounded in her ears. The rough boulder dug into her back as she watched the Apaches. The shriek of a hunting hawk shattered the sky and fell over them.

Still neither man moved.

Finally her captor shot her a venomous glare. Watching her with an unblinking stare, he sheathed his knife with menacing slowness. Then he stalked stiff-legged to his brown pony. Mounting, he trotted away without a backward glance.

Bracing her hands on a boulder, Aurora levered herself up, her legs still soft as cornmeal mush. "Stalking Wolf?"

Wind whispering among the rocks was her only answer.

The bay horse danced sideways as her savior stepped off. Shading her eyes, Aurora peered at him.

"It *is* you. Oh, thank God, thank God." A wave of relief washed over her. "*Gracias . . .*"

Her voice faded as Wolf paced toward her. He was naked except for a white breechclout and knee-high buckskin moccasins. A blood-red bandanna tied around his head kept his long black hair

out of his eyes. Two cartridge bandoliers criss-
crossed his dark copper chest. The acrid odor of
gunpowder mingled with his sweaty male scent.
He stopped a foot from her. Silent. Watching.

He towered head and shoulders over her. The
power and strength he radiated staggered her, and
she took a step back.

"Stalking Wolf, surely you remember me?" She
searched his rugged features for some softening,
some sign of recognition. There was nothing.
Nothing but silence.

His primitive fierceness struck her with savage
force, shocking away every shred of courage. Her
gaze fastened on his eyes and her heart plummeted
into her boots, for she saw only the hellish darkness of an Apache. A man without mercy.

In that instant she knew he wasn't her savior.

"God help me," she whispered. Despair flooded
over her. She'd heard the stories about Apache
captives, knew what lay ahead. As he reached for
her, she leaned down, grabbed a fistful of sand,
and flung it in his eyes. Stalking Wolf staggered
back, shaking his head.

Aurora whirled and ran. If she could get to her
horse, she might still escape. If she couldn't, then
she was going to die anyway. Let it be here. And
dear God, please let it be quick.

She'd only taken a few steps when he caught
her, grabbing her wrist and spinning her around.

"No! Don't!" Terrified, in a blind panic, she
lashed at him with her riding whip.

Wolf growled as her quirt slashed his cheek. He
ripped the riding crop out of her hand and flung it
down, then watched her as he ground it into the
sand with the heel of his moccasin.

With a strength born of frenzy, Aurora tried to

wrench free. Stalking Wolf muttered something and yanked her against him.

She slammed into the stone wall of his chest. His cartridge belts pressed painfully against her breasts. She tried to push him away, but his muscles were iron-hard beneath her fingers. His rugged features were unreadable. Her whip had just missed his eyes and had left a dark purple welt down his cheek and across the corner of his mouth.

"*Dos veces*, Aurora," he said in a flat tone. He wiped away the blood trickling down his cheek. "*Dos veces.*"

Aurora's heart lurched wildly as she realized he was referring to the other time she'd struck him, when he'd attacked her father. He had known who she was all along! The icy fury in his obsidian eyes knifed through her; the bitter taste of fear bubbled up in her mouth.

Stalking Wolf grasped her hands in one of his, then drew a short rawhide rope from his belt.

"No!" Aurora screamed.

"*Sí.*" He tied her hands loosely, but not so loosely that she could slip free. Bending down slightly, he tossed her over his shoulder. His right arm locked around her knees, and he walked toward her horse, which had scrambled to his feet. Aurora was bounced, his angular shoulder jabbing her stomach with every step. She hung down, unable to see anything but the rippling muscles in his dark red-bronze back.

"Put . . . me . . . down," she gasped in Spanish, pounding his back with her fists. Her braid dragged along the ground behind them like a fiery rope. "I'll come along."

"No." When Aurora reared up on his shoulder, he smacked her backside. "Be still," he ordered in

Spanish. Before she could catch enough breath to protest again, he stopped beside her horse and set her on her feet.

"W-what are you going to do?" she asked, straining to remember her Spanish through the haze of fear.

"Take you with me. I—" he broke off as a burst of gunfire nearby made him scan the hills. Quickly he turned her around, and grasping her hips, tossed her across the gray's back like a sack of grain.

As he led her horse to his, Aurora squirmed around and sat up. Even though there was no stirrup for her right foot, she knew she'd be safer riding astride. Wolf leaped on his bay and, still leading her horse, set off at a gallop.

The Apache followed a narrow, twisting trail across the cactus-studded ridges. Aurora wrapped her hands in the gray's coarse mane as she was tossed forward and back, as the horse lunged up and down steep slopes. Taking deliberately deep breaths, she tried to slow her racing heart. She was still alive; that was the important thing. She had to keep her wits about her. That was the only chance she had of surviving.

She scanned the desert, looking for some sign of pursuit. There were no dust clouds on the horizon. No troopers rode out of an arroyo to rescue her. There was only the rapid clip-clop of their horses' hooves.

"You . . . rotten . . . bastard," she said, every word jarred from her by the trotting horse. She stared at Stalking Wolf's back with such fierce intensity that a smoking hole should have appeared in the middle of it. Maybe the way to keep up her spirits was to curse him.

"You bastard," she repeated, relishing the word.

"You lying, thieving bastard!" She paused, at a loss for words terrible enough to describe the Apache warrior who was leading her deeper and deeper into the wilderness. "You barbarian! You primitive, uncivilized savage!" She went on, calling him every name she could think of and wishing she knew more.

Stalking Wolf glanced back. She had nothing left but Aunt Ruth's favorite curse. "You son of a peach basket!" She could have sworn his upper lip twitched, but he looked away so hastily that she decided it was only her imagination. He shortened the reins, reeling her horse in until its muzzle was snubbed close to his leg.

"What's the matter? Can't hear what I'm saying about you?" He raised a dark eyebrow at her. "Well, for starters, I hope this gray horse of mine reaches over and takes a big bite out of your thigh. And I hope it's painful as heck and you need my help, because I'll never again help you." He rested the hand holding her reins on his thigh, as though tempting fate. "You know, Aunt Ruth said she never met a man she didn't like, but she never met you. I'll bet you would try her good Quaker soul to its furthest limits."

The blazing sun climbed higher and higher in the sapphire sky, and Aurora threw curses at him until she grew too parched to talk. Finally Wolf drew rein on a high mesa and scanned the surrounding desert. Aurora slumped in her saddle, wilted by the searing heat.

Lifting a deer-stomach water bag from his saddle, he untied the end and offered it to her. *"Agua."*

"Gracias," she croaked through dry, cracked lips, before remembering that he deserved no thanks. She took a big gulp. The water was warm and

tasted awful. At any other time she would have spat it out, but now she held the liquid in her mouth, savoring the moistness. She took another swallow, and as she would have taken a third he rested his hand on her arm.

"No more. The horses need water," he said in Spanish. Dismounting, he poured water into his left palm and held it out to his horse, then did the same for her gray.

Only then did he raise the water bag to his lips. Aurora watched from beneath her lashes and saw how little his Adam's apple moved, and knew he'd taken only a sip. In spite of her anger and fear she felt a flash of respect, for he'd given her and the horses far more than he'd taken for himself. He retied the corner of the bag, then mounted.

They rode on. She kept looking back, hoping against hope. They were getting further away from Kreutz and his troops. Further away from Fort Bowie and Papa.

Salty tears stung her eyes, but she refused to give in to them. Tears meant no hope—and she refused to give up hope.

"You may have captured me, but I'm going to escape. You can't watch me every minute of every day, and I swear I'll escape," Aurora warned Wolf defiantly.

Wolf ignored her.

The sun was sinking and the mountains had turned to vermilion and violet when Stalking Wolf finally turned into a canyon on the valley's west side. Aurora sagged in her saddle. Her bottom ached, a cramp in her side kept her from taking a deep breath, and her right knee was chafed raw from rubbing against the saddle. And everything that didn't hurt was numb.

She saw Apaches flitting through the grove of tall, silver-green cottonwoods that signaled water and knew he'd brought her to his camp. Wolf halted at the stream and dismounted with a pantherlike litheness that Aurora envied and hated at the same time.

"Get down," he ordered in Spanish.

If she didn't move, she knew he'd reach up with his big hands and pull her off. And she didn't want him touching her. Slowly, stiffly, like a marionette with tangled strings, she twisted around until she could slide down the horse's side. She landed in a crumpled heap at Stalking Wolf's feet.

He looked down at her for several heartbeats, then held out a hand to her. But before she could move, he muttered something under his breath and turned away abruptly to lead the horses downstream.

Aurora sat unmoving, resting her hands on her drawn-up knees. The stream gurgled over rocks just beyond her reach. She had to get her circulation going before she could move. Leaning forward, she clumsily massaged her legs with her bound hands.

Stalking Wolf returned and, barely glancing at her, hunkered down beside the flowing water. He washed his hands in the stream, then cupping his right hand, he filled it with water and lifted it to his mouth.

She watched enviously as he drank. She vowed that no matter how much she wanted water, she wouldn't ask Stalking Wolf for it. He might have captured her, but she'd never ask him for anything. Steeled by her determination, she continued to rub her tingling legs with her bound hands.

Again Stalking Wolf filled his right hand. She

watched from beneath her lashes, imagining the feel of the cool water as it slipped down her dusty, dry throat. Spinning on his heel, the Apache held out his hand to her.

"Drink."

Aurora stared, not quite believing her eyes. Then, holding his hand with both of hers, she drank gratefully. The water was fresh and cool and tasted of him. Although his hand was large, it didn't hold enough to satisfy her, so he filled it again and again until she had had enough.

"*Gracias*," she whispered, turning away in hopes of hiding from his too-perceptive gaze. Water was life in the desert, but to drink from his hand . . . There was something so utterly barbaric, so captor-captive, about it that a great awareness of him throbbed in her blood.

Standing, he lifted her to her feet, sliding his hands down until they rested on her hips, letting her feel the heat and weight of them. Aurora looked away and swallowed heavily, afraid to face a future as this primitive warrior's captive.

Wordlessly he untied her hands.

"*Gracias*," she murmured, surprised. She rubbed her hands together to get feeling back in them.

"You'll need them free to care for the horses, then see to my needs," he growled in Spanish.

"Your needs?" She glared at him, her eyes huge.

"Aurora! Aurora!" A man was calling her name from among the trees.

"Pincus?" She swung around, incredibly glad for the interruption. Joy dawned in her as she saw the scrawny photographer running through the cotton-woods.

She would have run to meet him, but Stalking

Wolf grabbed her arm. "No! You do not leave my side."

Aurora struggled to push down the tension and fear pulsing through her. Straightening her shoulders, she stood tall and silently defiant as Pincus neared them.

He was only a few feet away when he halted, noticing that she was rubbing her wrists. He realized she'd been tied. "Aurora, child, are you all right?"

"Yes. And you? Oh, thank God you're alive!"

"Not only alive, but unharmed, my dear." He glanced at Stalking Wolf, then back at Aurora. "But you—are you—"

"I'm fine, even though my horse fell and I— Oh, my God, the vaccine! With all that happened, I forgot it."

Whirling, she raced to her horse and tore at the saddlebag. Her hands were still clumsy, but she managed to get the cotton out and opened it carefully—and stared down at the smashed points. "Oh no," she whispered, suddenly overwhelmed. Losing the vaccine was the last straw. She wearily leaned her head against the horse's haunch and fought tears stinging her eyes.

"Pincus, tell Stalking Wolf about the smallpox in Tenehas," she muttered, trying not to sob. "Tell him we bring medicine for sick people. He must let us go."

Pincus spoke to the Apache in fluent Spanish. Stalking Wolf's reply was short and swift.

"He says you should tell him yourself, Aurora."

"What? He knows I make a terrible muddle of Spanish." She squared her shoulders and turned to the men.

Stalking Wolf snapped something at Pincus, but his dark gaze never left her.

"He says it's time you learned," Pincus translated in a neutral voice, "unless you want to learn Apache instead."

Aurora's stomach twisted into a tight knot. Wolf's bald statement implied she would *need* to speak Spanish or Apache, and she didn't want even to consider why. Her eyes narrowed and she glared at him, feeling the chains of captivity closing around her.

Stalking Wolf tapped his broad chest. "Ma'cho Nalzhee."

He'd told her his name in Apache, she realized. But she would never call him by his Apache name, because she would escape. She had to.

Kneeling in the dust, she busied herself with loosening the laces in her boots. "Keep up your courage, Pincus," she whispered. "At least we're not tied. Tonight after they're asleep, we'll make a run for it."

"No, Aurora, you will not," Stalking Wolf said with quiet finality.

Aurora was so exhausted that it took her a full five seconds to realize why she'd understood him so easily. She stiffened, and her fingers tangled in the bootlaces. Slowly she looked up.

He towered over her, a barbaric conqueror, his arms folded across his bronze chest, his feet spread arrogantly wide.

His dark-as-Hades eyes met hers, told her he'd understood everything she'd said as he led her into the wilderness, every curse she'd laid on his head, every vow to escape.

"You speak English?" she whispered.

Chapter 7

❝**I** can't believe I fainted.❞ Aurora lay in the shade beneath a huge cottonwood. "I've never fainted in my life."

"Well, you have now. And a nice dramatic one it was, too. You were staring at Wolf, then just silently crumpled into a heap." Pincus sat down beside her.

"Thanks for getting me out of the sun." Sitting up, she squirmed back until she could lean against the tree.

"It wasn't me, my girl. Wolf picked you up and carried you over here." Pincus glanced at the Apaches building a tiny fire just beyond the trees. "He's a strange man. Such a savage, then he goes and does something I can only call gentlemanly." He poured water from his canteen onto his handkerchief and handed it to her. "Here."

"Thanks." She wiped the dirt and dust from her face as she studied the Apaches. "What do you think they're going to do with us?"

"I wish I knew. If the stories we've heard are true, then we should already be staked out on an ant hill. But we're not and we haven't been harmed. I'd say that's a pretty strong point in our favor."

"Maybe they consider you a hero. After all, you rode directly into their line to give me a chance to escape."

Pincus snorted. "Don't overestimate me, my dear. My horse ran away with me, that's all."

"Sure, Pincus. And the moon is blue."

"I'm not a hero, Aurora. It was the strangest thing, though. I expected to go down in a hail of bullets, but none had my name on it. I simply rode between two braves and came out behind them. When I looked back, they were staring at me as though I was a ghost. Then they wheeled their ponies and came after me, but they didn't shoot; they just brought me here. They even brought the mule with my photography supplies. Crazy, isn't it?"

"Maybe that's the key. Maybe they think you're crazy—which you have to be, to ride at a pack of charging Apaches. Brit told me they think crazy people are possessed by spirits and they won't harm them." She noticed Wolf had emerged from the woods and stood near the fire, talking to several Apaches. "Stay here, Pincus," she added, getting to her feet. "I'm going to talk to Wolf. He's got to let us go."

Aurora studied Wolf as she approached. He stood a full head taller than the other Apaches. His back was to her as he spoke to the warriors. His bandoliers were gone, and in their place a tan buckskin vest was stretched taut over his dark copper shoulders.

She waited silently. The Apaches turned their unblinking black stares on her, making her skin crawl, and she edged closer to Wolf. Not that she was safer, she chided herself, but the known beast was better than the unknown.

He finally turned to her. "What is it, Aurora?" His voice was harsh with weariness and tension.

"I didn't realize you knew I was here." She wiped her sweaty palms on the folds of her blue skirt.

"I knew." His gaze went to her hair. Myriad strands had worked loose from her braid and frizzed around her face in a haze of fire-gold. "I smelled the soap you use in your hair."

"Oh." A burst of awareness spread through her. She smoothed her hand over her wild, flyaway curls. Aurora swallowed and fixed her gaze on the bit of mirror hanging from the thong around his throat. She had to remember why she'd approached him. "What I tried to tell you earlier was that Pincus and I were on our way to Tenehas with medical supplies. They've had an outbreak of smallpox and—"

"Wait." Resting his hand on her shoulder, he looked at each of the braves clustered around them and said something in Apache, then waited until they'd gone before he nodded at her. "Go on."

She drew a deep breath, startled by the way her heart had skipped a beat at his touch. "Tenehas has smallpox, and we need to get there as quickly as possible. You've got to let us go."

He crossed his arms over his chest and shook his head. "No."

Her eyes widened in surprise. "But they need us! They sent a messenger begging for a doctor and supplies." She glimpsed the little lame child from Tenehas through the trees. "Look—that's the boy who brought us the message."

Wolf called him over. "Is this the one?" He rested a arm over the boy's thin shoulders.

Aurora felt a surge of sympathy for the child. His white shirt and pants were gone. He was now dressed like a miniature Wolf in a buckskin vest, white cotton breechclout, and knee-high moccasins. "Are you all right, José?" she asked, smiling reassuringly at him.

"*Sí.*" He stared at the ground.

"Poor child." Aurora raised her eyes to Wolf beseechingly. "Can't you let him go? He isn't a threat to you, and his parents must be worried sick about him."

"I would like you to meet my newest warrior, Blue Hawk." Wolf squeezed the boy's thin shoulders and looked down at him with pride.

"What are you talking about? He's only a child."

"He's thirteen and he did a warrior's work today. He went into the enemy camp and gave them a message and slept in their wickiups and rode with them when they took the trail to Tenehas."

Aurora was so tired that it took her a moment to figure out who the enemy was. "Oh, my God! You mean the message from Tenehas was a fake? They don't have smallpox?"

"They didn't send the message. I did." He said something in Apache that made the child smile as he ran off.

Her hand rose to her throat in a protective gesture. "But why?"

"The people of Tenehas don't want you." He moved closer until he stood mere inches from her. She could smell his male scent mixed with the acrid odor of gunpowder. His gaze focused on her hair as he reached out and rubbed several strands between his thumb and finger. "I do."

For once in her life, Aurora was speechless. She stood, opening and closing her mouth like a fish as the meaning of those two words sank in. Then she picked up her skirts and fled.

"Well, how did it go?" Pincus asked as she plopped down beside him.

"Not well." She drew up her knees and wrapped her arms around them. "The message from Tenehas was a fake. He sent it." Wearily she rested her forehead against her knees.

"Hell and damnation!" Pincus leaned back against a tree trunk and studied the setting sun. Finally he patted her back in a fatherly gesture. "Don't worry. Somehow we'll get out of this mess."

As the sun sank, the Apaches gathered around the small fire. Using supple green branches as skewers, they set rabbits to roasting over the flames. The ugly brave who'd first captured Aurora drifted in after nightfall. He crouched by the fire, tore a haunch off a rabbit, and began to gnaw it. He glanced at the prisoners, then made some comment that made the other braves guffaw and look at them also.

Aurora shuddered when two Apaches rose and walked toward her and Pincus. "My God, what do you think—?"

Wolf appeared from the darkness and stepped in front of the braves, halting them in mid-stride. Whatever he said, it satisfied them, for they turned back. Following them to the fire, he ripped a couple of chunks of meat off a rabbit, then left the circle of light and walked through the darkness to Aurora and Pincus.

She didn't know how he could see so well in the

dark, but he crouched directly in front of them and handed each a piece. "Eat."

He sat down beside Aurora. The scent of horses and smoke clung to him. The meat was hot and juicy and she bit into it, surprised by her sudden appetite. After she had finished, he led her down to the stream for another drink. When they returned, Pincus was gone.

"Where's Pincus?" She glanced around, hoping she'd simply missed him in the darkness.

"He will sleep at the other side of the camp."

Aurora gripped the folds of her skirt tensely as she scrutinized her tall, broad-shouldered captor, trying to make out his expression. The stars shed some light but still left his eyes shadowed and unreadable.

He shook out a rawhide rope.

Her knees turned to mush and she began to tremble. "What are you going to do?"

"Tie you so you can't escape." He pointed to one of the cottonwoods. "Sit with your back to the tree, White-eyes."

"I promise I won't try to escape. You don't need to tie me." She rested both hands on his arm. "Please, I give you my word, Wolf." He stiffened, reminding her of the power in the muscles rippling beneath her fingers.

Turning his head slowly, he gazed down at her. "The promise of a White-eyes to a despicable wild beast?"

Aurora remembered exactly when she'd screamed those words at him. After he'd attacked her father—and just before she'd slapped him. "I was distraught," she cried, whirling away. "You'd just attacked my father." Even as the words left her lips, she knew she shouldn't have mentioned him.

"With reason," he shot back, his voice harsh.

She took a step away from him, rubbing her hands over her upper arms, fighting the icy fear knifing through her. "Isn't there anything I can say to convince you I won't try to escape?" she asked quietly.

"Do you think I forget the vows you made today?" he replied just as quietly.

Trembling so badly that she could barely move, she sat down by the tree. Wolf knelt beside her. He looped a length of rawhide around her wrists and tied them. Then he wound another rope around the tree and her body several times until she was securely tied.

"Now I know you will be here when I return." He crouched beside her and tucked a thick lock of hair that had fallen over her cheek behind her ear. "And be glad I left you your clothes, White-eyes. I could have cut them off and left you waiting for me naked."

He paced away, leaving his words thundering like war drums in her ears. Aurora could feel every jagged pebble beneath her. She tested the ropes, hoping he'd left her some slack. He hadn't. She was well tied and helpless in the dark. A captive of the Apaches. Alone.

She mustn't give in to despair, she told herself. She was alive, and where there was life, there was hope. But even as she fought her tears, determined to be brave, they spilled over and rolled down her cheeks.

She was so alone. Utterly alone.

Wolf walked back to the fire, surprised and impressed by Aurora's courage. Most White-eyes women would be reduced to gibbering hysteria at the mere thought of capture by the dreaded Apaches. But she'd kept her wits about her. He was proud of her and the way she'd kept up her spirits by heaping insults and curses on him.

When he'd first galloped up after her capture and seen Bear Killer towering over her, threatening her, he had been shaken to the core. He had never expected to feel such protectiveness for her, a White-eyes woman. But in those vital moments when he faced Bear Killer, something had blossomed deep within him. And he knew he would fight—and kill—Bear Killer to protect Aurora Spencer.

He shook his head as he walked through the cottonwoods. A blood lust had gripped him that was equal to the one he'd felt when he'd recognized his mother's murderer.

He glanced over his shoulder, gazing into the darkness where Aurora was. How could she intrigue him so?

Geronimo sat beside the tiny fire. Wolf hunkered down across from him, balancing his weight on the balls of his feet. The other Apaches were already asleep in their blankets. Geronimo poured bits of turquoise, "pieces-of-sky," through his fingers, watching closely as the blue stream mixed and eddied on the ground. Wolf waited, knowing he was seeing the future.

Geronimo finally looked up. "She is indeed brave. She will make you a good wife. It is time you took a woman."

"I will never take a White-eyes woman for my wife!" Wolf leaped to his feet and paced around the dying fire. Geronimo crossed his arms over his red cotton shirt and watched, but said nothing. Finally Wolf broke the long silence. "What is it, Uncle?"

"I'm surprised." He poured the pieces-of-sky back into their pouch and placed it in his medicine bag. "I have never known you to make such a rash statement."

"It's not rash. I will never take her as my wife."

"You are wrong. The blood of many warriors flows in your veins, and she lights a fire deep in you. I have never seen you burn for a woman like this. You will take her."

"But not as my wife." Yet even as he spoke, he glanced at the woods where Aurora was tied.

Geronimo appeared not to hear as he tied his medicine bag shut with a rawhide thong. "And when you take her, she will capture you."

Wolf glided silently through the cottonwoods. When he'd captured Aurora, he'd thought to wreak his revenge on her father—and to satisfy his desire for her. Then he would be free of the spell cast by the bewitching woman with hair of flame.

But he was finding that it would not be quite so easy. When she'd drunk from his hand that afternoon, a wave of emotion had washed over him, unlike anything he could remember, a yearning for something he couldn't even name.

But he mustn't ever forget she was a White-eyes, he chided himself. A hated, never-to-be-trusted White-eyes. He halted beneath the trees, watching her.

Gradually Aurora sensed rather than saw a shadow, darker than the others, that towered over her and blotted out some of the stars she'd seen earlier. Her heart pounded against her ribs. She tested her bonds. They were still tight, for, she thought with a despairing sigh, she'd been tied by an Apache.

"How long have you been there?"

"Long enough."

She pulled at her bonds frantically when he shook out a blanket and spread it on the ground. She tensed when he turned toward her.

"It is time, White-eyes. Our bed waits." His low voice echoed with promises of the night. Promises she didn't want to contemplate.

He loosened the rope that tied her, coming to stand before her as he slowly coiled it in his hand. Was he going to use it to tie her down? Fear paralyzed her muscles so that she couldn't even scream. He finished coiling the rope and laid it beside her.

"P-please," she pleaded. "No."

"Come, White-eyes." He held out his hand, palm up. She stared at it, afraid of what would happen if she took it. He didn't move. Finally, as though he was willing her to do it, she placed her hand in his. His fingers closed around hers, and he drew her to her feet in a smooth motion singing of power.

"What do you want?" She trembled as he studied her in the starlight.

"You." He backed up, drawing her with him. Her legs were soft as porridge, yet she matched him step for step until they stood beside the blanket. "Lie down."

Aurora faced him squarely, determined to be brave. "It doesn't matter what you do to my body, Wolf. You'll never have my—" She broke off, not wanting to say *heart*. "You'll never have the part of me that makes me what I am."

He raked his hand through his hair, then exhaled a long sigh. "I will not hurt you, Aurora. I promise you that."

Aurora swallowed a sob as she knelt on the

scratchy wool blanket. He loomed over her, blotting out all the stars. No matter what happened, she would survive.

He knelt on one knee beside her, watching her. "Turn on your side, facing away from me." His voice was low, with an undercurrent she couldn't quite identify.

"What?" Good God, what was he going to do?

Wolf wearily rubbed the back of his neck. "Obey me, White-eyes." Crouching, he cupped her face in his callous-roughened palms. "Woman," he growled, leaning so close that his warm breath feathered across her cheek, "I promise you, I want more from you than a hurried coupling on the hard ground in the midst of a war party. You will perform many services in my wickiup, but right now I simply wish to sleep. Now roll on your side."

Aurora rolled to her side a good foot away and watched him warily over her shoulder.

Wolf pulled her back against himself, spoon-fashion. He slipped one arm beneath her head and closed it over her breasts, locking her against him. "Just so you don't try anything during the night," he murmured.

Aurora lay motionless, achingly aware of the Apache warrior who was imprisoning her in his arms. She jumped when his knee brushed her thigh. And her heart raced madly.

Lifting his head, Wolf leaned over her. "Sleep, White-eyes." He gloried in the feel of her soft curves pressed against him. "We'll be back in the saddle before daybreak."

"How do I know I can believe you?" There was a definite quaver in her voice. She could feel his manhood pressing against her thigh.

"You don't. You'll just have to trust me." He

lifted her braid, which was caught between them, and buried his face in it, reveling in the silken strands that slid over his lips. Then he carefully laid it over her shoulder so that it wouldn't get caught again. "Just as I trusted you when you brought me water."

Wolf settled down, feeling the thudding of her heart beneath his hand. He'd wanted her for a long time. Holding her in his arms would be enough for now. It would be sweet agony waiting until she came to him with a softness and a wanting equal to his.

That would be the ultimate revenge.

Chapter 8

❧⎯⎯∽∾⎯⎯❧

Wolf and Aurora rode out of camp before dawn. He'd saddled both horses with cavalry saddles, so Aurora rode astride instead of on that god-awful sidesaddle. To her surprise and relief he didn't tie her hands, as he'd done the day before, but he still led her gray gelding.

By the time the summer sun exploded above the horizon, they were far from the war party. Soon the hot wind was like a dragon's breath licking at her flesh. Perspiration rolled down her face. She kept wiping her forehead on her sleeve, using the movement to hide her frequent glances back, hoping against hope she'd see soldiers on their trail. As the hours passed and Wolf led her deeper into the wilderness of desert, she began to despair. Where was Kreutz?

Finally, when all hope seemed gone, she glimpsed a dust cloud on their back trail. Turning quickly to face front, she edged the gray gelding closer to Wolf, not wanting to give him any reason to look back.

He flicked her a suspicious glance. "What is it?"

"Nothing. Why?" She lowered her lashes, veiling her eyes, afraid he'd see her glee at the thought of the pursuing troopers.

"I can't see you riding near me out of attraction."

"Believe me, I'm not." She sighed loudly, feigning despair. "I'm utterly lost, so I guess I better stick close to you."

He lifted a disbelieving eyebrow at her. "Am I supposed to believe that, White-eyes?"

"Believe what you want," she snapped, at the end of her patience. "You will anyway."

He halted on the next ridge and, drawing a pair of binoculars out of his saddlebag, scanned the trail ahead and behind. Aurora stared straight ahead, not daring to look back, for she knew he would watch where she looked.

Wolf exulted at the sight of the dust rising behind them. The Bluecoats had taken the bait and were following the tracks of the shod horse. Soon they would be in sight. Leading Aurora's horse, he headed southeast toward the Chiricahua Mountains and the pass into Mexico.

Whenever she thought Wolf's attention was on the trail ahead, Aurora glanced back. To her dismay, the dust cloud wasn't getting any closer.

What was the matter with Kreutz? Wolf wondered, as he slowed the horses. Kreutz was falling further and further behind, even though he had practically left trail markers for him. He would have to stop until he was sure Kreutz had come close enough to see them. He wanted the Bluecoat to carry the news back to Fort Bowie that Aurora was alive—and Stalking Wolf's captive.

Soon the sun was a burning ship sailing a turquoise sea, and Aurora began to wonder if she'd

survive another day in the searing heat. She heaved
a grateful sigh of relief when Wolf drew rein
beneath a stand of cottonwoods growing beside a
dry streambed. Slipping off her horse, Aurora
stood thankfully in their shade.

Wolf led the horses into the streambed and
taking a folding shovel out of the bedroll on his
Army saddle, began to dig a hole in the sand. At
first she watched simply because he was her captor,
then because she was fascinated by the flexing of
the muscles in his mile-wide shoulders. What
would it feel like to touch those muscles, to stroke
those shoulders? she wondered, aware of a butter-
fly fluttering in the pit of her stomach.

When the hole was over two feet deep, Wolf
stepped back. Water seeped into the hole, and the
horses drank their fill.

"How did you know there was water there?" she
asked. Such knowledge might come in handy
someday.

He nodded at the leafy green cottonwoods arching above them. "These trees tell me that there is a
steady supply of water here. If the streambed is
dry, the water has gone underground, so I know I
must dig to find it." Climbing the bank, he braced
his hand against a tree trunk and watched her. "We
will rest here."

"How long?" She needed to delay him only for a
short time. He stood so close that she could feel his
heat and smell his male scent. She looked away,
too aware of him as her captor and as a man.

"Not long." He stretched out in the sun-dappled
shade and patted the ground beside him. "Come
here, White-eyes."

Aurora hesitated. He sprawled on the ground
like a copper-skinned Adonis, his broad chest

rising and falling steadily with his breathing. His white breechclout was bunched between his sinew-corded thighs. The air thickened in her lungs. She tensed, hating herself for responding to him on a primitive level. He was her captor and a savage, her inner voice cried.

"Come here." His command was quiet but unmistakable. Her heart pounded. Could she reach her horse while he was relaxed?

Her eyes met his. Oh God, he knew what she was thinking, and he was waiting for her to try it. She approached warily, watching him all the while as she sat down at the outer edge of his reach, ready to retreat at his first move.

She looked wary as a wildcat, Wolf thought. He took two strips of deer jerky from the small deerskin pouch tied to his belt and held one out to her. "Eat."

She started to reach for it with her left hand, but winced and hesitated.

"What is it?" Wolf sat up in a single fluid motion, watching her intently.

"Nothing!" She rubbed her upper arm.

"Let me see." There was a small tear at the top of her sleeve, and Wolf reached over, hooked his thumb in it, and ripped the sleeve open. He drew in a sharp breath when he saw the ugly purple bruise on her upper arm. "Damn it, woman! Why didn't you tell me about this?" he growled.

"It's all right." Oh God, she didn't want him touching her. Not when she was so conscious of him. "Leave me alone."

"When did it happen?"

He brushed his thumb over the bruise in a whisper-soft touch. Even so, she twitched away from the contact.

"Yesterday."

Wolf muttered something menacing in Apache. "Did Bear Killer do this?" His hard gaze demanded an answer when she hesitated. "Did he?"

"It happened when my horse fell. He was thrashing when he landed beside me. One of his hooves struck me."

"Why didn't you tell me?" His voice was harsh.

"If you'll remember, a bruised shoulder was the least of my worries at the time," she snapped. The memory of the terror she'd felt when she looked into his merciless eyes and realized who he was sent a shiver through her.

His lips thinned and he shook his head. "I don't understand you, White-eyes woman. You were hurt, yet you didn't tell me."

"Would it have made a difference?"

Something flashed in his eyes, as if he were hurt and angered by her question, then it was masked.

Rising, he paced over to his horse and fished in his saddlebags, then returned and hunkered down alongside her. He unscrewed the top of a tiny jar and opened it.

"What are you—?" She glanced at it and inhaled sharply. "That's the salve I gave you."

"Yes." Their eyes met as both remembered the rope burn left by Kreutz's noose. "Now it's your turn." He dipped his fingertips into the jar.

"You don't have to do that. I can take care of myself."

"I will do it." His low voice wrapped around her like a shawl on a summer night. He paused, his fingers a hairsbreadth from her flesh. "Tell me if I hurt you." He gently smoothed the salve over her shoulder. His touch was icy and hot and soothing all at once.

She studied him openly, for his whole attention was focused on her shoulder. A tiny scar crossed one eyebrow, and crow's-feet were beginning at the corners of his eyes. It was impossible to miss the dark red slash her whip had left on his cheek yesterday.

His fingers slowed, and his gaze lifted from her shoulder to meet her eyes. "I did not intend for you to get hurt," he muttered.

Startled by his low-voiced admission, she stared at him. He was just inches away. His lips were full and enticing. His gaze catalogued her features in a slow-as-molasses-in-January look. "You are so beautiful." She blinked, aware of a waiting stillness in the air.

She looked at him with eyes so blue that Wolf felt as if he were falling into the sky. The memory of the kiss they'd shared the night he escaped flashed across his mind. The memory sent molten gold rushing through his veins, and he inhaled deeply as he pictured her in his arms, her hair tumbling over her shoulders like satin flame. He imagined the silken strands running through his fingers, her warm lips soft beneath his.

It had been a shared kiss, he reminded himself, for whether or not she wanted to admit it, she'd responded to him with budding passion. He brushed his thumb over her soft, warm lips.

"Don't," she gasped, jerking away.

"Why not?" he asked in a husky tone.

"Because."

"Aurora?" Her name was honey on his lips. "Why not?" He leaned toward her.

Wolf watched her eyes widen and darken. The pink tip of her tongue circled her lips. He knew he'd soon trace the same path with his own. As she looked up at him, her hair curled around her face in wild tangles. He slowly filled his hand with the silken strands, letting them flow through his fingers in rivers of flame.

"So you remember, too." He lowered his head.

"No!" Aurora screamed, wrenching her head away, letting her hair fall like a curtain between them. Stiffening, she spread her hands over his broad chest, trying to push him away. She was afraid of him, of his kiss, of the way he made her feel.

"Don't touch me. I don't want you to ever touch me, damn you!"

"You lie, White-eyes." He turned her face to his and his mouth came down on hers in a conqueror's kiss, hot and hard and full of fire. Taking, not giving. Demanding. Stamping her senses with his scent and feel and heat. Her head began to spin, and deep within her a primal tension blossomed.

She pounded his shoulders, but gradually her blows softened until she felt the warm smoothness of his flesh beneath her fingers. She heard a moan and dimly realized it came from her.

Then his hot, masterful tongue invaded her mouth. She tried to fight him and was drawn into a pitched battle, one that left them both triumphantly breathless when Wolf finally raised his head.

Aurora simply gazed up at him, too weak and confused to move. There was confusion in his eyes too, she realized, with a dart of satisfaction.

"Are you done?" she tried to ask icily, but her voice was a bare breath of sound. And her hands still clung to his broad shoulders.

Instead of being quelled, Wolf just shook his head. "Only for now, my fiery captive." He dropped a quick, hard kiss on her mouth, then released her and sat up.

Aurora stared past him, trying to ignore his nearness, struggling to understand what was happening to her. What was he doing to her? She knew she should move away from him, but she didn't have the strength. Her heart was still pounding madly and her blood racing.

Wolf sat with his hip against her thigh, scanning the surrounding hills. "Do you wait for me to return to you, woman?" he asked, slanting her a sideways glance.

She bolted up like a jack-in-the-box and scrambled to her feet. "No, thank you, I wish to forego that . . . that . . ."

"Pleasure?" He rose to his feet also.

"Hah! You have a vivid imagination." She busied herself vigorously brushing dirt off her skirt.

"Really?" His voice was soft, but he eyed her with a speculative glint she didn't like one bit. Waving at their back trail, he added, "I think we've given Kreutz enough time to catch up, don't you?"

Aurora froze in the act of picking a dried brown leaf off her skirt. "You knew Kreutz was following us?"

Wolf crooked a finger beneath her chin and tilted her head up. "Of course! I am Apache," he growled, "not a blind White-eyes. The blind Kreutz seems slow to follow, although I've left as plain a trail as I could without making him suspicious. He ought to be close enough to see you by now."

"To see me?" She pulled away, trying to put some distance between them. She couldn't think when he was so close. "Why?"

"So he can go back to your father and tell him that I have his daughter and that she is alive."

"What? That's what this is all about?" Her voice rose with each word. "Why? Why are you doing this?"

"Your father and I have unfinished business."

Her eyes widened and she clapped her hands to her cheeks as understanding dawned. "My God, you're using me as bait! You're going to draw my father into a trap, aren't you?"

"I—" A low rumble of thunder drew his attention to the Chiricahua Mountains. Iron-blue clouds boiled over the granite peaks, sending lightning shafting down. "Come on." He grasped her elbow and hurried her toward the gray gelding. "We have some hard riding to do."

As they galloped away from the cottonwoods, Aurora was still stunned. He'd captured her to use as bait. And his kiss? What was that?

By the time they crested the next ridge, she was furious. He'd been toying with her, amusing himself with her. She rubbed her palm over her mouth, trying to rid herself of his taste. Never again would he kiss her, she vowed. Never again.

She had to escape. Then Pa would have no reason to come seeking her and he wouldn't fall into Stalking Wolf's trap.

Lightning danced over the jagged peaks, and thunder shook the ground as the storm began to swirl down the mountain flanks. Wolf urged the horses on. If he didn't reach the river before it flooded, they'd be trapped between a wall of water and the Bluecoats.

Aurora threaded her fingers through the gray's coarse mane and hung on as they raced across the desert. A rifle boomed behind them and dirt spurted up beside Wolf's horse. Without looking back, he leaned low and urged the horses on.

Aurora glanced over her shoulder and cheered loudly when she saw the column of cavalry chasing them. Crouching forward over the gray's neck, she tried to grab his reins from Wolf's grasp, but she couldn't quite reach them. There was more gunfire, and dust spurted up around them. A quick glance back showed the soldiers gaining; she could even make out Kreutz's stocky form in the lead.

"Hang on," Wolf shouted as he and his horse disappeared over the edge of an embankment.

The gray followed and Aurora screamed when she saw how steep the slope was. She whipsawed back and forth like a rag doll while the gray skidded down the bank.

Wolf paused at the river's edge. It was higher than he'd ever seen it, but the horses could still make it across if he was quick.

Aurora kicked the gray's side and shifted in the saddle, trying to get the horse to act up. It whinnied in protest and reared, almost yanking Wolf out of his saddle, but instead of releasing the reins, he pulled the gray's head down and lashed both horses. Neighing, they leaped into the water.

Behind them Kreutz and his men poured over the bank, shooting and shouting. Water fountained around Wolf as bullets tore into the river. Wolf kneed his horse forward, dragging Aurora's horse behind him.

Aurora felt the gray lose touch with the riverbed and begin to swim. She turned in her saddle and waved at the soldiers. "Hurry! Hurry!"

They had almost reached the other side and her gray was pawing for a toehold in the slippery mud when he stepped in a hole and fell away from beneath her.

It happened so swiftly that she barely had time

to kick free of the stirrups as she went down. Her horse shrieked and disappeared under the water.

"Help," she screamed, icy water rising to swallow her up. "Hel—" Water filled her mouth.

She kicked frantically, trying to stay afloat while her heavy skirt pulled her down. She glimpsed Wolf reaching for her upraised hand through the foaming water. Their fingers touched . . . slid . . . slipped . . . slipped away.

He'd missed her!

The churning green waters closed over her head.

Chapter 9

〰️

"**A**urora!" Wolf shouted, his heart pounding with fear unlike any he'd ever felt. "Aurora!"

He'd lost her. He'd lost her!

He glimpsed her hair floating to the surface. He reached out to grasp a handful, and pulled as hard as he could. She came up sputtering and choking, but she came up. His stallion staggered, fighting to stay upright as it was pushed sideways by the rushing current and by Wolf's weight as he hung from its side.

He had to get her to the horse quickly, before it toppled over. Fighting the current sucking at her, he pulled her toward him.

Aurora choked back a scream. Her scalp hurt like the devil, but she could breathe again. She could breathe!

Her face barely out of the water, she could see Wolf leaning dangerously far out of his saddle, reaching for her with his free hand. She clutched his arm as the swift current threatened to tear her away. He finally got an arm around her shoulders and slowly pulled her clear of the water sucking at her legs. Throwing her arms around his neck, she held tight as he straightened in the saddle.

"I've got you." He clamped her against his side.

Aurora clung to his broad shoulders, terrified that he wouldn't be able to hold onto her. The stallion staggered, fighting to keep from being swept away by the force of the water, then finally scrambled up the bank.

Wolf halted at the top and gently eased Aurora down the horse's side. When he let go, she crumpled to the ground in a silent sodden heap. He leaped off and knelt beside her.

"Aurora, are you all right?" he asked breathlessly. Wrapping his arm around her shoulders, he tilted her head back. She was ice-cold and shivering, but she was alive, he exulted. Her blouse clung to her like a second skin, outlining her breasts and cold-hardened nipples. A breathtaking wave of protectiveness crashed through him.

Wolf hugged her, needing to hold her tight as much as to stop her trembling. How could he expect her to be all right, he raged, when he was still shaking from the thought of losing her?

"Yes. I just need to catch my breath." She coughed weakly, her head drooping against his shoulder. "Thanks. I would have died in that water if you hadn't—" A whirlwind of emotions surged through her, giving her desperate strength. She reared away from him and scrambled to her feet, albeit wobbly. "Why am I thanking you? I wouldn't even have been in that water if it wasn't for you!"

"Don't you think I know that?" He stood up and put out a hand to steady her.

"Don't touch me! Haven't you done—?"

Sand and pebbles spattered them as a bullet plowed into the earth next to Wolf's moccasin.

"Damn Bluecoats!" Wolf dropped to the ground, pulling Aurora down with him.

She lifted her head just high enough to see over the bunchgrass, aware of a strange, deep-throated rumble coming from upriver.

"Aurora." Kreutz's voice was faint over the roar of the water. "Hang on. We're coming."

His men were trying to force their horses into the rushing river, but the animals were balking and rearing and giving terrified neighs. Suddenly a seething wall of water and debris swept around the bend and surged toward them. Men and horses scrambled up the far bank, the river snapping at their heels.

Numb with despair, Aurora watched them retreat. They'd come so close. Big, cold raindrops plopped down on her as the sky hardened to steel-blue. Then lightning tore the clouds open. A moment later, curtains of rain hid the troopers on the far bank. "So close." Oh God, they'd come so close.

"Come on, we're getting out of here." Rising to his feet, Wolf pulled Aurora up beside him. He took a stride toward his horse, but halted when Aurora didn't move.

"Leave me here! You know they're coming for me. The river won't hold them up for long, then they'll be on your trail again. Leave me, and they won't come after you."

His stormy gaze raked her. "I didn't save you to give you up."

"Damn you! I wouldn't have needed saving if it wasn't for you!" Her eyes widened with dawning horror. "Oh, my God! They were watching, so you couldn't afford to let me drown. You needed me alive so they could tell my father you had me. That's why you saved me."

Let her think that, Wolf decided. His other need, the ever-growing desire for her, the consuming want—that didn't count, anyway. "Don't think they'll rescue you. They could barely follow our trail when I was leaving markers for them. Now that they've seen you, we will disappear."

Grabbing her wrist, he dragged her along as he ran for his horse.

She hung back, fighting him every step of the way. "Damn you, Wolf!"

Halting beside the steaming horse, he shoved her against the bay's haunches. "Don't try to run, don't even move, White-eyes." Watching her as he worked, he loosened the saddle girth.

"What are you doing?"

"We're both going to ride him, because your horse is gone. It'll be hard enough for him to carry double without the weight of the saddle also."

Aurora stood in the pouring rain, her gaze down, afraid that if her eyes met the Apache's, he would realize she was plotting her escape. All she had to do was get the horse away from him. Without a horse, he couldn't catch her.

Wolf stripped the saddle off and dropped it in the sand, then grabbed the canteen and rifle.

"Let's go." Wolf's abrupt command startled her out of her planning. "I'll give you a leg up." He clasped his hands together.

Aurora's heart thudded against her ribs as she realized this was the perfect opportunity. "All right." She casually gathered the reins in her left hand and prepared to step into his hands. She'd whirl the horse away as soon as she settled on his back, and—

Wolf pulled the reins away from her and dropped them, ground-tying the animal. Then he bent slightly and clasped his hands together again. Thwarted but not defeated, she stepped into them and he boosted her up.

Aurora gripped the horse's hot, rain-slick ribs with her knees and legs and quickly leaned forward, grabbing for the reins.

"Oh, no you don't." Wolf jerked them out of reach. He watched her warily as he slung the canteen over his left shoulder and the rifle over his back. Resting one hand on the horse's withers, he swung up behind her in a lithe leap.

She choked down a gasp when he wrapped his right arm around her waist. He slid forward slightly, adjusting his seat until his hips pressed against hers and his thighs cradled hers. Holding the reins in his left hand, he kneed the bay on.

The great beast leaped forward, throwing Aurora back against Wolf's broad chest. She grasped the flowing black mane and tried to lean forward, away from Wolf, but his hand tightened, holding her to him.

The forward and back rocking motion drove his hips against hers with every stride. One part of her recognized it as the natural suppleness of an expert rider, the other part cringed at every contact between them. She held herself stiff and aloof, trying not to feel every inch of him pressed against her back. Every inch.

She tried not to notice that his heart was thudding against her shoulder blade, that his bronze arms imprisoned her, but she did. He guided the horse with his legs, and she could feel every ripple of his thigh muscles as they pressed against hers.

"Relax," Wolf growled. "I feel like I'm riding with a wooden board."

"I wish *I* did," she muttered under her breath.

Wolf gloried in the feel of his captive. She was his now, caged in his arms. Several strands of her hair slid across his chest like silk flames, and he lipped those the wind tossed across his mouth. The forward and back motion drove her against him in a rhythmic movement that added flames to the fire in his blood.

In less then a mile he slowed the stallion to a walk. "Too hard on the horse to carry double," he explained gruffly.

"Then why don't you get off and give him a rest," she suggested, her voice so full of sugar it could have choked him. A frisson of awareness washed through her as his warm breath stirred the wet hairs along the back of her neck. She shivered as his long fingers splayed over her stomach, leaving five trails of heat across the cold, wet cloth.

"The rain will wipe out our tracks. The Bluecoats won't be able to follow our trail."

Wolf was right, Aurora realized. She couldn't depend on Kreutz to rescue her. And if she didn't get away from the Apache, Pa would come for her and ride into a trap.

The rain stopped and the sun came out. Within minutes their clothes began to steam in the heat. Aurora scanned the country continuously, trying to memorize landmarks for her return journey, for she was sure an opportunity to escape would occur. And she was going to take it.

They were both on foot now, with Aurora in the

lead. As her boot came down between two low silvery-gray bushes, she saw a yellow and black snake stretched across the path directly under her foot. Twisting, she leaped sideways, landing several feet away.

"Snake," she yelled, backing further away.

"Rattler." Stalking Wolf stood firm and held onto the reins as the horse caught a whiff of snake and reared. When he'd calmed the animal, he added, "It's out early."

"What do you mean?" Aurora watched the snake slither into the shade beneath a prickly pear.

"Snakes hunt at night in the summer, because it's too hot for them in the sun, so it's unusual to see one when the sun is high." He led the horse up the trail.

"Aren't you going to kill it?" Giving the snake a wide berth, she fell into step behind him.

"No. It isn't bothering us." Wolf glanced over his shoulder. "I am not a White-eyes, killing creatures for the sake of killing. I am Apache."

And that said it all, she thought. They came from different worlds. He slept on the hard ground. She slept in a soft bed. At night he sat by a campfire; at night she sat by an oil lamp and read. His skills helped him survive alone in this great savage land. Her skills helped her survive in cities, among people. His world was primitive and uncivilized. Hers was modern with gas lights and railroads. His experience was war and taking life. Hers was saving it.

Yet in spite of all their differences, she was attracted to him. Even now, she tingled with that wild awareness that only happened when she was with him.

They climbed out of the desert into the lush

green grasslands skirting the Chiricahua Mountains. Aurora was riding and Wolf walking when they crested a hill and she spied a stream in the grassy swale below. As they descended, she saw the water was running fast and high. The stream wasn't as wide as the one that had stopped Kreutz, though.

"We'll camp on the other side," Wolf said, breaking the silence that had stretched between them for miles. He led his horse straight into the water downstream from a dogleg bend in the creek.

Although her fingers were wrapped in the bay's coarse black mane, Aurora was ready to slide off if the horse stumbled. She glanced upstream just as a tree, its tangled roots riding high out of the water, swept around the bend. Wolf's back was to the tree as he held the horse's head and murmured reassuring words to it. He hadn't seen it!

Sunset was close, and this might be her only chance. All she had to do was keep quiet.

But he'd saved her from drowning, her inner voice said. Could she let him drown?

"Wolf, watch out!" she cried, making her choice.

He turned, but it was too late. The roots hit him full in the face and wrapped around him, dragging him under.

As soon as the Apache let go of the reins, the stallion turned back to get out of the rushing current. Aurora gathered the flapping reins as the horse scrambled up the bank, and lashing him across the withers, galloped up the hill.

At the crest she halted the horse and looked back. Had Wolf survived? She couldn't go on without knowing. She watched for long minutes before she finally saw him crawl out on the near bank and collapse, unconscious but alive.

Only then did she send the bay stallion galloping back the way they'd come. She'd done it! She'd escaped the Apache. He was afoot; he'd never catch her.

She headed north, using the landmarks she'd memorized. The sun went down, the last light faded, but she rode on.

When the horse tired she slowed to a trot. They had crossed the desert, and the river that had stopped Kreutz earlier was now a gentle, knee-deep stream. She and the horse drank, then she headed on in the darkness, sighting by the North Star. Kreutz and the troopers couldn't be far. They couldn't travel during the storm and they would have camped before sundown.

Cresting a ridge, she scanned the desert, looking for a campfire. But there were no blazing fires, there was only darkness. Her heart sank.

No! Wait! She squinted at a flickering spot of golden light on a ridge not far away. Relief flooded her. She'd found them!

She urged the horse forward at a canter, letting it pick its way around the clumps of cactus. She never took her eyes off that golden light. It got brighter, as if the troopers were piling on more wood, which reassured her, for she'd seen how small Apache campfires were. This one blazed high, a beacon guiding her home. Home to safety.

As she neared, she grew ever more anxious to be safe. "Hello? Hello?" she called, knowing there would be sentries posted. "I'm Aurora Spencer. Don't shoot." She slowed to a walk. No use scaring everyone by galloping in. "This is Major Spencer's daughter. I've escaped!"

She dodged around some high feathery bushes

and reached the edge of the haven of golden light. Aurora's eyes widened as she scanned the camp. Except for the fire, it was empty. There wasn't a soldier in sight.

"Hey, where is—?"

Out of the corner of her eye, she saw Wolf rise from the bushes beside her.

"No!" she screamed, beside herself with despair and dashed hopes. Sawing on the reins, she tried to turn the horse away. This couldn't be happening!

Wolf leaped up to sweep her out of the saddle. She lashed his face with the ends of the reins. It slowed him for only an instant, but it was enough for her to slip off the horse's far side and run.

"Don't run, Aurora. You can't escape."

She dodged behind some bushes. Then, crouching low, she raced from mesquite to mesquite, from shadow to shadow, always looking over her shoulder. The sandy gravel crunched beneath her boots, giving her away as she ran for her life. She could hear the Apache pounding along after her.

"Aurora, don't be foolish." He was close. Too close.

Desperation lent wings to her feet. She sprinted ahead, then darted behind a huge clump of prickly pear. Wolf kept going.

She waited, heart pounding in her ears. She clamped her hands over her mouth and breathed through her nose, determined to make no sound that would give her away. The sound of his moccasins faded.

She was alone. It was silent except for the hoot of an owl.

Suddenly a black shadow coalesced out of the darkness on the other side of the prickly pear, about twenty feet away. She watched as Stalking Wolf turned this way and that in the starlight, listening.

Finally he looked straight at her across the prickly pear. "Stop running, Aurora. You can't get away."

He was bluffing. She knew it. He couldn't see her. There was no way he could know she was there.

He started to walk around the clump of prickly pear. Aurora backed up and glanced around, looking for another hiding place. A rattle like dry mesquite leaves rustling in the wind startled her, and she jumped.

Even as she realized what the rattle was, she felt a sharp pinprick on her ankle.

"Wolf!" She had taken only three strides when she ran into a warm wall. In her panic, she ricocheted back and would have fallen if not for the two strong hands that grasped her shoulders.

"I've got you now." Stalking Wolf's arms wrapped around her and he swept her against his chest.

"Sn-snake b-bite." Aurora sagged against him, aware of a burning feeling as the poison moved up her leg. She had to stay calm, she told herself—but she was already dizzy. Her pulse hammered wildly. Her fingers curled around Wolf's cartridge belt. Darkness flowed at her from all sides. Talons of icy fear clamped around her heart. "Help . . ."

"I will, I will." Bending, he swept her up with one arm beneath her knees, the other behind her back.

Aurora's memory of the trip back to the campfire was hazy, for she floated on a cloud of pain. She wasn't aware of Wolf running, yet within minutes he laid her close to the fire's golden light.

"Aurora." Wolf shook her roughly, bringing her out of the black hole she'd fallen into. "Aurora, you've got to help me. Where were you bitten?"

Her eyes half-opened, then began to close. He felt her fading away. There was no time. No time. He shook her again. "Answer me! Where were you bitten?"

"An-kle . . ."

His heart thudded against his ribs. He had to find the bite quickly. Pushing her dusty blue skirt up, he slashed her laces with his knife and yanked her boots off. He reached up her white thighs and yanked her cotton stockings down. Turning her left ankle in the firelight, he examined it for the telltale mark. Nothing!

He dropped that foot and picked up her right ankle. Immediately he saw the blue-purple swelling. He glanced at her ghastly white face. For her sake, he was glad she was unconscious.

He used his knife to make two cuts across the bite, then knelt down and sucked out as much of the poison as he could. When he had finished, he leaned back on one knee, studying her ashen face. Had he gotten enough of the poison out?

"C-cold," Aurora moaned. Tremors racked her slim form.

Wolf spread a blanket, moved her onto it, then lay down beside her and wrapped it around them both. "Sleep, brave one, sleep," he whispered, drawing her close. Brushing her tangled curls away from her face, he stroked her cheek. She shook violently with a chill, but her skin was hot.

"You'll be all right," he murmured over and over

through the long hours of darkness. "You'll be fine, my brave *kun isdzán*—my brave woman of fire."

But would she? Would she even survive the night?

Chapter 10

⁓⁓

Aurora was aware of a bright emerald light even before she opened her eyes and stared up at the fernlike mesquite leaves. Where was she? Why did her leg hurt like the devil? What had—? Her delicate features twisted into a grimace as the memory of the snake crashed into her consciousness.

"I tell you, Captain Kreutz, I saw a fire on this here hill last night," a gruff voice said nearby.

"I don't doubt you, Thompson, but it could have been Apaches."

She was hallucinating, she decided, hearing voices speaking English. The poison had affected her mind.

"No, sir. It was too big. The Apache don't make no fire that can be seen from afar. And I seen this here one from a long ways away."

A horse stamped close by and Aurora felt the vibrations through the ground. Saddle leather creaked, spurs jingled.

Her blue eyes flared. She wasn't hallucinating!

"I'm here," she called, but her voice came out as a rusty croak. "I'm—"

Broad shoulders blocked out the sun, and a large dark copper hand came down over her mouth. She stared into black, black eyes. Hard eyes. Warrior eyes. Apache eyes.

"Did you hear somethin', Captain? Maybe over here?" Sand crunched as footsteps came toward them.

"Only the wind. Don't bother going up there, Thompson. We can pick up their trail on the other side of the river."

The footsteps halted. "That storm yesterday wiped out every trace. We'll never be able to trail them now."

Wolf knelt on one knee beside her and peered through the bright-green mesquites toward the voices.

"Hell and damnation!" Kreutz cried. "That little bitch has cost me my promotion. How am I ever going to go back and tell Spencer that damn Apache, Stalking Wolf, has his daughter—and that she's alive?"

"She's probably dead by now, if I know the Apache. Better for her, too." The footsteps began to recede.

No, I'm not! Aurora wanted to scream. *Don't stop looking for me. I'm alive!* They were so close. She stirred and tried to lift her hand to claw at Wolf's, but her arm seemed held down by lead weights.

Wolf leaned so close that his warm breath feathered against her ear. "They wouldn't hear you anyway."

Helpless, she stared up at him and listened as the cavalry horses trotted away. Only after the metallic clink of horseshoes on rocks had faded did he lift his hand.

"Let me go," she whispered weakly. "All you have to do is fire your rifle, then you can disappear into the desert. They'll come back and find me."

He rocked back on his heels and studied the mountains rising high above them. He was silent so long that Aurora began to hope. Maybe he would listen to reason after all.

Finally he shook his head. "I can't."

"You'll be rid of me, and no one will come after you." Every word was an effort, yet she had to try to persuade him. "I promise I won't tell them which way you went."

"I am Apache. I know how much White-eyes' promises can be trusted. Especially to a rotten bastard," he said, throwing her own words back at her.

She groaned. "Do you remember everything I said?"

"Yes." He had to remember. He had to be reminded that she was a White-eyes and never to be trusted.

The finality in his voice crushed her. Chewing her lower lip, Aurora looked away, fighting not to let despair overcome anger. As long as she was angry, she could keep the tears at bay. But if she once gave in to despair . . .

"Do you want water?" Wolf's low voice wrapped around her like a velvet chain.

"Yes. How did you know?"

"You have a fever. It was higher during the night, but it's not completely gone." Slipping his arm beneath her, Wolf cradled her against his shoulder as he held the canteen to her lips. She took a few swallows, then he pulled it away. "See if you can keep this down. I'll give you more later."

She nodded, slumped weakly against him. Sweat was pouring off her.

He felt her forehead. "You're burning up again. I'll make you a prickly-pear poultice tonight."

"Tonight?" she asked weakly. She was so tired, yet his cool hand on her forehead was strangely comforting.

"Now we will go. There are too many Bluecoats around. Some might come back."

Wolf stroked her forehead, brushing her tousled curls away as he assessed her fever. He had to get her out of the desert heat, he decided; she was getting weaker by the minute. Kneeling, he gently scooped her up in his arms.

Aurora's eyes had been closed, but now they opened wide as white-hot agony shot up her leg. "Oh-h." She gripped his shoulder tightly, fighting the waves of pain threatening to swamp her consciousness.

"The pain will soon be over," Wolf said, carrying her to his bay stallion. "I will hold you once we're mounted, but I have to put you on the beast first. Can you sit up? It'll only be until I swing on."

"I'll be fine." She clamped her jaw tightly to keep from crying out as he set her sideways on the horse's broad back, moving slowly and smoothly to lessen her pain. Just having her ankle dangling down, rather than flat on the ground, increased the searing agony. Aurora gripped the stallion's black mane tightly and tried not to groan.

Wolf rested a hand on the stallion's withers and lithely swung up behind her. When he lifted her across his thighs, Aurora tensed and gripped his arm tightly. He gently cradled her against his broad chest. A muscle in his jaw throbbed.

"We have a long way to go," he said, his voice a deep rumble beneath her ear. "Try to sleep."

She rested her head against his solid body and listened to the soothing beat of his heart and inhaled his masculine aroma of sage and sweat.

He started the horse off at a walk, and she choked back a groan as her leg was jolted by the movement.

They had left the desert and were in grasslands among juniper trees when Wolf finally halted. He dismounted, then lifted Aurora off.

Taking one look at her white face and pain-pinched lips, he demanded roughly, "Why didn't you tell me the pain was so bad?"

She didn't have enough energy to answer after fighting the pain for so long.

"Stubborn woman," he muttered. He carried her over to a juniper and laid her on the ground in the shade of the pungent green needles. "So stubborn."

She lay back, exhausted, pillowing her head on her arm and closing her eyes. "Where are we going now?"

"To a place I know of high in the mountains. It will be cool and sheltered, and I have supplies cached there. You will be able to rest and recover."

"If I do," she murmured. Her doctor's instincts told her the infection in her leg was spreading.

"You will." He lifted a fiery tendril off her cheek and tucked it behind her ear. "Now rest." There were blue shadows beneath her eyes, and her clammy skin had taken on a transparent look that worried Wolf.

He gathered dried twigs and built a tiny fire.

While the coals were burning down, he gathered juniper berries and mixed them with an herb he took from his medicine pouch. He steeped the berries and herb in boiling water, then poured the liquid into the canteen. He wanted enough tea to keep Aurora asleep until they reached the cave.

Crouching beside her, he woke her and held the canteen to her lips. "I made some tea for you."

She took one sip and immediately spat it out. "Ugh. That's awful."

"Drink more. It'll make you sleep."

"I don't need a sleeping potion."

"I do. I need a rest from your sharp tongue." And a rest from her pain. He raised the canteen to her lips.

"Then you drink it." She pushed his hand away.

He rocked back on his heels and sighed loudly. "Why must you always be so obstinate? We will be traveling through rough country. Drink this so you'll sleep and won't feel the pain."

"Oh." For once Aurora was at a complete loss for words. He'd stopped to make her a painkiller. This uncivilized barbarian, this demon of the southwest, had made her a painkiller. "Well, if you insist," she muttered.

"I do." He held the canteen to her lips again. "That's good. Take another sip for me."

He waited until the tea had made her drowsy before lifting her onto the horse, then remounted and settled her against his chest. Aurora dozed as they climbed higher into the towering mountains.

Wolf enjoyed the feel of the woman sleeping in his arms. He glanced down at her delicate features often. They gave no hint of her strength and determination, yet she had as much courage as the wounded mountain lion cub he'd found one summer. At first the cub had spat and clawed him every time he came near, but gradually it had been tamed until he could stroke its fur. Then, when it was well, he'd freed it.

Aurora moaned softly as she stirred, and he knew she was beginning to awaken and feel the pain. He tightened his arms, as though to keep the pain from touching her. He held the canteen to her lips, and after a few sips, she slowly relaxed.

It was late afternoon before Aurora yawned and looked around sleepily at the pine trees that surrounded them. "Where are we?" Wolf's arm was strong and warm as he cradled her against his chest. The pain in her leg had subsided to a dull throb, and she felt immeasurably better. She sniffed the crisp, pine-scented air.

"Almost there." They emerged from the forest at the foot of a granite cliff over three stories high.

Aurora gazed at the sheer wall barring their way. "I think you've reached the end of the trail, Apache," she said, with some of her old spirit.

"Almost." Instead of dismounting the normal way, he swung his leg over the horse's withers and slid down with his precious burden. Now that they'd reached the end of their journey, he didn't want it to end, for he wanted to go on holding her.

Aurora gazed up at him from beneath her lashes. For hours her head had rested against his broad chest and the steady beat of his heart had been part of her dreams. The strength of his arms had made her feel safe and secure.

He carried her to a boulder near the bushes that screened the beginning of the trail to the cave he was making for. "Are you strong enough to sit up by yourself for a minute?"

"Of course." Her hands slid down over the taut muscles of his chest as he settled her on a rock. As soon as he let go, her shoulders rounded and she slumped, not as strong as she'd thought she was.

He slipped the canteen off his shoulder and swished it, watching her closely. Almost empty, but there was enough for one more drink, he judged.

"Drink up," he said, handing it to her.

"I don't need it. I feel better." She shoved it back into his hand. "The pain in my leg is down to a dull roar."

"It won't be by the time I get us up that cliff."

Aurora looked over her shoulder and stared at the cliff. "We're going up that?" Her voice ended in a squeak.

"Yes." He braced one moccasined foot on the rock beside her and leaned forward, resting his forearm on his knee as he studied the cliff. "But the trail is steep and I need my hands free to grip the handholds." He paused a beat to let that sink in. "That means I can't carry you."

Her eyes were as big and blue as the sky above when she turned to him. "My leg may be better, but . . . ah . . . I don't think I can—"

"You won't have to. I'll take you up with me, but not in my arms."

Tilting her head, Aurora eyed him warily. "Just how?"

"Over my shoulder. That's the only way."

Aurora eyed the cliff again, then held out her hand. "Give me the canteen."

"How do you feel?" Wolf sat cross-legged beside Aurora on the ground, resting his hands on his knees.

"Better." Glancing around, Aurora realized that she lay on a bed of blankets near the back wall of a large cave. "How long have we been here?" she asked, her voice weak and thready.

"Two days, but the fever's finally broken." He reached for the canteen. "Drink?"

"Please." Aurora gave him a wary look when he held the canteen to her lips. "Is this more of that awful tea you fed me?" She could have sworn laughter glinted in his devil-dark eyes; then it was gone and so quickly that it must have been her imagination.

"Water. You don't need the tea, now that your leg's healing. But while you're awake, I want you to eat some of the venison and acorn stew I made." He walked to the fire he'd built just inside the mouth of the cave, where it was hidden from outside, yet the smoke could flow out without making a telltale column. Ladling the stew into a wooden bowl that had been among the supplies cached in the cave, he carried it to her.

Wolf sat beside Aurora, then lifted her carefully and cradled her in his lap, supporting her with his left arm. "All right?" She nodded.

Pulling the bowl within reach, he began to feed her, using a piece of dried gourd for a spoon. She had lost weight fighting the fever and felt almost weightless in his arms. Yet never had he met a woman so full of spirit and fight. He'd feared for her life during the days of fever and delirium, but now her eyes were clear and he knew she would survive.

"It's delicious," Aurora said, chewing slowly and trying not to notice his sinew-corded thighs beneath her. Nor did she dare turn her head, not when her ear rested against his thickly muscled chest and she could hear the deep, steady beat of his heart. How could she feel so safe when she was held in the arms of her captor?

"No more," she said, pushing his hand away after four spoonfuls. Her eyes were already closing when she felt him tuck the indigo-blue wool blanket over her shoulders.

Over the next few days, Aurora felt stronger each time she awakened. When she opened her eyes on the third day, she saw Wolf standing on the ledge outside the cave, combing the surrounding mountains with binoculars.

She took the opportunity to study him, intrigued by all the contradictions in him. From the turned-up toes of his moccasins to his dark-red headband, he was Apache warrior, proud and powerful. Yet he'd held her, taken care of her when she was ill and helpless. He was uncivilized, a primitive barbarian, yet he'd saved her life. According to all she'd heard, the Apaches were ruthless killers— yet this man was neither ruthless nor killer.

She stirred, moving her legs cautiously, not wanting to awaken the pain demon. Although her movement was slight, Wolf glanced over his shoulder at her.

"You are awake again." When he knelt beside her, his tan pants drew taut over his muscular thighs. "Good. Are you ready to eat?"

"If it's more of that delicious stew you've been feeding me." Aurora wondered whether there really was a note of warmth in his voice, as if he was glad she was awake, or whether she was imagining it. "What is it?"

"*Chichil bitoo*. Acorn stew." He ladled the stew into the wooden bowl and carried it to her.

Aurora braced her hands and sat up by herself, proving to both of them that she really was getting stronger. "I'm a lot stronger today; I can feed myself."

Wolf sat down Indian-style beside her. Instead of wearing his usual buckskin vest, he was naked above the waist, and his broad chest glistened like polished bronze in the late-afternoon sun. The slanting rays outlined each thick pad of muscle in fascinating detail, awakening a funny little flutter in her stomach. She inhaled slowly, drawing his male scent deep into her lungs.

"What's wrong?" His dark voice wrapped itself around her.

Aurora looked up from his chest guiltily. "I—I was wondering where you learned to cook. This is so good." He quirked a disbelieving eyebrow at her. "I mean—I guess I didn't expect cooking to be among your skills." And what did she expect his skills to be? She was getting herself in deeper and deeper.

"A boy of The People is apprenticed to older warriors for his first four war raids. He must keep their weapons clean, care for their horses, and cook for them."

"I see." She'd never thought of him as a child. In her mind's eye, he'd sprung from the earth as a full-grown warrior. What had he been like as a boy? Had he been a happy, smiling child? And what had changed him into the grim man she saw?

"Are you done?" He nodded at the empty bowl.

"W-what? Oh, yes. *Gracias.*" She watched him take the bowl over to the other side of the cave. "Stalking Wolf, what about Pincus?"

He glanced back over his shoulder. "He went

with Geronimo's men. He should be at Juh's Stronghold in Mexico by now. Where we should be also."

Aurora ignored his last comment. The important thing was that Pincus was all right. She flung back the blanket and plucked at her blue skirt. "Now I want to see my wound."

Striding over, he rested his hand on hers, stopping her. "It is healing. The Apache medicine is working." He wanted her to know it was The People's medicine that had saved her.

"I want to see it."

"It isn't pretty," he warned, "when it's your own flesh." His hand manacled her wrist gently but firmly.

Aurora gazed down at that large, strong hand. It was the hand of the man who'd twice saved her life. His thumb brushed the sensitive flesh of her inner wrist, and the breath thickened in her throat. She resolutely pushed his hand away. "I'm a doctor. I can take it."

"Stubborn woman." With a sigh, Wolf pushed her skirt up, then unwrapped the strips of bark he'd used to bind the poultice to her wound.

Aurora tried not to notice his palm cupping her heel and his long fingers flexing along the back of her calf, but she couldn't help gasping and curling her foot when his thumb and finger circled her ankle.

Wolf froze. "Did I hurt you?"

"No. No, it's nothing." Nothing but a consciousness of him that she didn't want. She straightened her shoulders and watched intently as he pulled away the last strip of bark and revealed the green pulp covering her ankle. "Yikes! What is that?"

"Poultice of *nopal*. Prickly pear." He knelt back on one knee, resting his arm on the other.

"You can't use that. It'll infect the wound."

"My people have used it for generations, White-eyes. Need I remind you that it has drawn the poison out?"

Her eyes flicked from him to her wound several times. Finally she nodded. "Whatever you did, it worked. *Gracias.*" She touched his arm tentatively as she added, "And I owe you a much larger thank-you." She took a deep breath. "Twice now you've saved my life."

His dark eyes met hers, then he silently turned away. The slanting rays of the late-afternoon sun shafted through the entrance and washed across his back, highlighting a nightmare tangle of white, snaking scars.

Aurora gasped. "My God, what fiend whipped you like that?"

Wolf froze. Then slowly, as though against his will, he looked at her over his shoulder. His eyes had gone obsidian-hard. "Your father."

"You lie!" She flinched as if he'd struck her. "My father would never do such a—a barbaric—"

"He would and he did." Turning, he crossed his arms over his chest and gazed down at her arrogantly.

"No, I can't believe Papa would— It must have been Kreutz. Yes, of course, that's it; I can believe he would do it."

"It was your father. He had me tied to a cross-beam behind the stables. Then he watched."

"No!" She covered her ears with her hands, trying to blot out his voice. But she couldn't blot out the memory of the hatred in her father's eyes when he had looked at Wolf. Could Papa really have done such a savage deed? "I can't believe— Maybe it— Yes, it must have been after you tried to kill him," she rushed on, trying to defend her father. "After all, your brutal attack was unprovoked and insane."

He stalked back to her with a menace that was palpable in the suddenly silent cave. Not even the fire crackled. But Wolf did. His gaze chained her in place as he hunkered down and leaned close.

"Not unprovoked and not insane," he gritted. "Your father has much to answer for. He—" Wolf broke off at the look of stunned disbelief on her face. Why tell her? She'd never believe an Apache's words against her father.

"Don't try to justify your attack," she raged. "It was cowardly, and nothing you can say will make me believe you."

"Right. Why believe an Indian when you can believe a White-eyes?"

"A lie is a lie, no matter what the skin color of the man who tells it. You do know what a lie is, don't you?" she added in a scathing tone.

"Bah! You White-eyes are all alike. You hear only what you want to hear, see only what you want to see. You know nothing of truth or honor. Nothing." Grabbing his rifle, he stalked out of the cave.

Aurora sat stiff and proud until he was gone, then she slumped against the rocks. Never had she met anyone who could make her so angry. Still, she couldn't help wondering why he had attacked Pa. It didn't make sense.

Her own experience showed that he wasn't a ruthless killer. So why, when he'd been chained and in the midst of hundreds of soldiers, had he attacked?

What would Aunt Ruth have done? she wondered. She would have stayed calm and said there had to be an answer. And, Aunt Ruth would also have said, she should give Wolf the benefit of the doubt until she found the answer.

"Good advice, Aunt Ruth," she murmured. "I will watch and wait and see what's what. Then I will escape."

At that moment Wolf walked in carrying a cleaned rabbit. She started, for she had heard no footsteps. Had he heard her mutterings? Silently he added wood to the fire. Then, as it flared up, he began to strip the pelt from the rabbit.

"Wolf," she began, twisting her hands together tightly, "I have been thinking since you left, and perhaps I was wrong."

He looked at her, his rugged features unreadable as the granite mountains that surrounded them.

"I—I—" She steepled her fingers and stared steadfastly at them. "Perhaps you don't think it was an unprovoked attack on my father. Perhaps you really believe that you know him."

He turned his attention back to the rabbit.

"I have to admit, Brit said that he didn't think you'd attacked Papa out of the blue. He said you Apaches are good tacticians; that you don't do things without a reason, and that you always calculate the odds and aren't foolhardy."

He pulled the pelt away from the rabbit. "So?"

"Maybe you think you know Papa, but you must've confused him with another cavalry officer. You see, he's just come to Arizona. He's been here less than three months."

Wolf didn't look up, but he stopped working. "*Nantan* Spencer was in the land of The People many harvests ago."

Aurora's head snapped up and her eyes narrowed. He was right; Pa had been in Arizona back in '63, soon after Ma died and— No, it was impossible that they would have met then.

"Yes, he was," she admitted quietly. "But it was many years ago. You couldn't have been more than a child."

"A child in years. A warrior in experience. I—" Wolf paused, eyeing the rabbit in his hands. Abruptly he threw it onto a round of wood he used as a plate and stood up. There was no use in telling her what had happened. Not when the murderer was her father.

Wolf stalked through the cave into the tunnel at the back, where The People had cached supplies.

Aurora's eyes widened as he disappeared, seemingly into solid rock. "Wolf, where have you gone?" she called.

"There is a passageway that runs through the mountain and comes out far from here." His voice had a hollow sound. "The People cache supplies here, so that in an emergency we can retreat to this place and resupply our warriors."

Could she escape through it? she wondered, even as he stalked back into view, holding a handful of brass cartridges.

"Do not think you can follow it and escape, woman. You would never find your way through the twists and turns."

"Just where are we?" she asked casually, as though she didn't have the slightest interest in escaping.

"In the Chiricahua Mountains." He loaded the bullets into his cartridge belt.

"We're not in Mexico?" Good Lord, if she was

still in the United States, maybe there was a chance the soldiers would find her.

"No. The Apache stronghold in Mexico was too far away, and you were too ill." He came to stand over her, his arms crossed over his chest and his feet spread wide. "Do not look for the Bluecoats to rescue you. They think The People are desert-dwellers. They don't understand that we live in the desert during the moons of cold and the mountains during the moons of heat. They will not look high enough in the mountains to find you."

"I see." Beyond the cave's gaping mouth, the twilight sky was blood-red. Were they still looking for her?

Silence settled over them. Wolf returned to the fire and stirred the coals again. He skewered the rabbit and braced the stick so that it hung over the coals, not the flames. Then he went outside and sat on a ledge until the last lingering blaze of red had faded into the navy-blue night sky. When the rabbit was done, he shared it with Aurora, but still didn't speak.

Aurora finished gnawing on her leg of rabbit, then laid the bones down on the round of wood she was using as a plate. She watched Wolf as he moved around the cave restlessly.

"If you hate my father so, Wolf, why did you save me? I don't understand. You could have just left me to die."

"I didn't choose to let you die." He broke a thick branch into pieces over his bent knee.

"But I was your prisoner; you didn't owe me anything."

His eyes met hers from across the cave. "You're still my prisoner," he replied, purposely jolting her with the reminder. He added the wood to the fire and stared down into the dancing flames. "Maybe I remembered a White-eyes woman giving me water." He glanced at her over his shoulder. "I am a man of the desert; I know how desperately I needed it at that moment."

"But I'm a doctor. My job is to save lives. You're different. Your job isn't to—"

"Save lives?" He thought of the four hundred Chiricahua Apaches who had followed him into exile. And of the White-eyes who wanted to steal the land that had been theirs for generations. "You're right. I do not choose to save White-eyes lives."

"Then why me?"

He turned then, and his eyes flashed with dark fire. "Is it not enough that I did?"

She plucked at the indigo blanket, which had *U. S. Army* stitched along one edge in thick white thread. "I understand why you saved me when the soldiers were watching. After all, my father wouldn't come after me if he knew I was dead. But when the snake bit me, you could have just left me, and no one would have known."

"I would have known."

She studied his harsh features for several heartbeats before she shook her head. "That's not good enough. Why did you save me?"

"You ask too many questions, White-eyes," he snapped, at the end of his patience.

"And you answer too few, Apache," she shot back.

Chapter 11

The next day they were once again captor and captive, separated by a gulf as deep as the deepest sea.

"You will remain here while I'm hunting, White-eyes." Wolf buckled his cartridge belt around his narrow waist, grabbed his rifle, and headed for the mouth of the cavern.

"Aren't you afraid I'll escape?" Aurora jibed, from her nest of blankets. "Better take the bridle. Otherwise I might climb down the cliff and steal the horse."

He stopped in mid-stride and slowly turned around. "No, I'm not." His hot-eyed look singed her nerve endings and set her pulse to pounding. "If you were not hurt, I wouldn't trust you, Aurora. But you are neither stupid nor foolhardy, and right now, you're too weak to try anything. This is something we both know."

Pacing across the cave, he knelt, crooked his finger under her chin, and tilted her head up. "And when you are well again, I will not trust you. Remember that, woman." Then he was gone.

145

Aurora slumped on her blankets, exhausted by the tension flaring between them. She closed her eyes, just for a moment, she promised herself.

When she awoke, it was dark outside. The fire had burned down until only a tiny circle of flickering light fought the darkness crouching all around.

"Wolf?" When he didn't answer, she realized he was still gone. Her first thought was escape. Her second was reality. She was too weak to stand. At the moment, she had no hope of escape. But soon. Soon.

Dry leaves littering the back of the cave started rustling as if something moved through them. She craned her neck, trying to pierce the murky darkness. The leaves crackled. The sound seemed to be coming from the tunnel. Trembling with weakness and fear, she sat up and scanned the shadowy cavern for a weapon. There was nothing but the firewood Wolf had piled along one wall.

Clinging to the rough rocks, inch by labored inch, Aurora pulled herself to her feet. Bracing her back against the wall and trying to keep her weight off her ankle, she eased herself along with tiny hop-steps.

The rustling among the leaves grew louder.

Whatever the creature was, it was getting closer—and was too big to worry about being heard. Still easing along, she bumped into the pile of firewood. Not daring to take her eyes off the gloom at the back of the cave, she reached down and grasped a chunk of wood. Hefting it with both hands, she prepared to use it as a club. She wouldn't go down without a fight!

"What are you doing?"

Wolf's deep voice was so close that Aurora gave a choked scream and dropped her club. She whirled, and her ankle gave way, throwing her against the tall Apache.

Aurora clung to him, feeling the powerful muscles of his broad shoulders ripple beneath her fingers. He was back, she thought, weak with relief. There was something so reassuring about his deep voice, so protective about the way his arms closed around her. No matter what happened, she knew he would be able to deal with it.

"Thank God, you're back." Her heartbeat began to slow and she took a deep breath, no longer terrified. She was safe. He was back and she was safe.

His grip tightened momentarily, as if he wanted to hug her. Then he set her back a half-pace, although his large hands remained at her waist, steadying her. "Who was the club for?" he demanded.

"What—not who. And where have you been? You've been gone for hours! I could have been killed—did you ever think of that? You'd better, because there's something big at the back of the cave!"

Wolf pulled her back against his chest as he peered over her head, trying to pierce the shadows. The leaves crackled.

"Stay here." Gripping her waist, he lifted her and set her near the wall. Watching the rear of the cave, he threw wood on the guttering fire. Then, cougar-like, he glided forward, moving from shadow to shadow, his rifle at the ready.

Aurora lost sight of him. A high-pitched chatter erupted from the darkness.

The wood began to catch and the flames grew. She glimpsed Wolf frozen in mid-step, staring down. Slowly, very slowly, he took a gliding step

back. The angry chatter continued and claws
clicked on the rocks. Aurora frowned, unable to
imagine what was threatening enough to make the
Apache warrior back up. It didn't sound like a bear.
Wolf took another careful step back.

Then she saw the creature emerging from the
gloom—a small black creature with white stripes
running along its back. The fat skunk danced on its
front feet, its rear raised high in the air, threatening
smelly disaster.

"Don't move." Wolf's words were a mere breath
of sound. 'I don't want to scare it any more than it's
scared already."

"Don't worry. I'm not crazy."

Seemingly reassured by their stillness, the skunk
lowered its dangerous end and began to snuffle
across the dusty floor, stopping to inspect a bowl
that held a bit of stew.

"They don't see very well," Wolf murmured.
"They rely on their noses to warn of danger."

"That's a wonder," she said wryly. He glanced at
her with a smile that lit the red-bronze darkness of
his features. "You can smile! I didn't think you
could."

"Of course." But the light was gone from his
face, and his voice was curiously flat.

The skunk angled across the cave to Aurora's
side of the fire, and when it came to her bare feet, it
stopped and sniffed each toe. Taking a deep breath,
she gripped the wall behind her, determined not to
do anything to scare it. But when its whiskers
tickled her toes, she couldn't help jerking her foot
away.

The skunk looked up, up, up. Aurora held her
breath. It returned to examining her little toe, then,
seemingly satisfied, it waddled outside, still chat-

tering. Aurora exhaled a pent-up breath and slumped against the rocks.

"Well, there goes your monster." Wolf paced across the cave to her side.

"From the way you got out of its way, it was your monster, too." She felt lightheaded with relief, now that the skunk was gone. "I can't tell you how scared I got when you backed out of the shadows. I couldn't figure out what was so big that you, the great Apache warrior, would back away."

"I know what they can do. I had my first experience with a black-and-white cat when I was two." He watched the cave mouth to make sure the skunk didn't return.

"A cat?" Aurora frowned, then smiled as she pictured an inquisitive two-year-old playing with the strange "cat." "You didn't pick it up, did you?"

"I tried."

"You didn't!" Aurora clapped a hand over her mouth to hide her smile. She would never have expected this grim warrior to admit to such a childhood mishap. "I'll bet your mother knew as soon as you got home."

"She knew long before I arrived. The odor carries for great distances." He stroked his jaw absently as he looked across the years to a happier time. "The whole village emptied out as I ran through."

She giggled at the picture he painted of people running away from a two-year-old child. "You must have made quite an impression on them."

"It was a long time before the elders stopped calling me Skunk Boy."

His voice didn't give her a clue to what he was thinking. As Aurora studied him, though, she became aware of a twinkle sparkling in his so-dark eyes. So he did have a sense of humor!

"From Skunk Boy to Stalking Wolf," she said dryly. "Quite a name change, isn't it?"

"Skunk Boy is not the kind of name that would strike fear into my enemies' hearts." Although his tone was solemn, his upper lip twitched.

"I see." She nodded. "Wolf is a warrior's name." It didn't matter what his name was; he would always strike fear into his enemies. But what she was feeling now wasn't fear, she realized with a dawning sense of wonder. It was a desire to know this mysterious man better, to explore the mystery of him. She wanted to touch him, to smooth her fingers over his flesh, to learn what was in his heart.

He nodded and a lock of his long midnight hair fell across his forehead. She reached up to brush it away.

He jerked back and clamped his hand around hers. Surprised by his reaction, she froze. She could feel his racing pulse drumming against her fingers.

"I . . . you . . . you startled me. I didn't . . ." Slowly he released her, his fingers sliding over the back of her hand in a caress as light as a morning breeze.

He was apologizing, she realized—as much as he was capable of. "I was just going to do this," she said softly, again reaching up to brush that lick of hair off his forehead. This time he didn't move, although she saw his Adam's apple go up and down as he swallowed. His skin was warm with life as her finger trailed over it.

What had made him so wary of a woman's touch? she wondered.

"I was most worried when the skunk looked up at you." His voice broke the spell that had begun to weave itself between them, and she knew he'd felt it also and had broken it on purpose.

"So was I. I tried not to move, but its whiskers tickled." He stood so close that his body heat enveloped her, and an odd breathlessness stole over her.

He looked at her bare feet. "You're ticklish?"

The whole situation was getting ticklish, she decided, drawing her feet back under the edge of her tattered blue skirt. "You really should have left me a gun to protect myself," she said, going on the offensive. "I was alone and it could have been another snake." Not for all the tea in China would she admit how relieved she'd been by his return. "What if it had been a bear? Or a wolf?"

"And what would you have done if I'd left you a revolver?" he asked, knowing the answer full well. She would have shot him.

Would she have shot him? Aurora wondered. She hated him, didn't she? After all, he'd carried her off, taken her away from everyone she knew and all that was familiar. But then she pictured him being driven back by a bullet she'd fired. She imagined the I-knew-you'd-do-it look in his eyes before they closed for the last time.

A vise of overwhelming melancholy tightened around her heart. The little voice inside her was silent and she knew her heart had spoken. Her head rose. Her eyes met his.

"I promise I won't shoot you." It was an easy promise to make. "But I need a gun for protection when you're gone."

An unfamiliar emotion, one he couldn't name, surged along Wolf's veins like hot lava. Could he believe her? Did he dare? After all, she was the daughter of the man he'd sworn to kill. "I would have to be soft in the head to trust the promises of a White-eyes who tells me she hates me," he growled.

"Damn you, Wolf. When will you learn that I keep my promises?" She turned and tried to stomp away on her good foot. She'd only taken one step when Wolf swung her up in his arms.

"What are you doing?" Aurora threw her arms around his sturdy neck.

"Taking you to bed." Her ear was pressed to his chest and his words reverberated through her bones.

"What?" She gripped his shoulders tautly. As he paced across the cave, she felt his powerful muscles flexing beneath her fingers.

"You heard me." He knelt by her blankets and laid her down as carefully as if she were a fragile, spun-sugar confection. Aurora's hands trailed down his sinew-corded arms as he leaned over her.

One long curl clung to her cheek and Wolf lifted it off with his thumb. Slowly, allowing himself the luxury of touching her as he hadn't in days, he wrapped the lustrous strands around his finger. Did she know how sensuous and inviting she looked with her tousled hair billowing around her delicate face like copper flames? A hot wave of desire washed over him. His nostrils flared as he breathed deeply, inhaling her unique woman scent. His hand tightened in her curls.

"W-Wolf?" she murmured uncertainly, her eyes becoming darker as she gazed up at him.

Wolf rested his hands at the sides of her head as he gazed deep into her eyes, searching for the answer to his unvoiced question. Abruptly he spun away and paced across the cave. *"Ha she!* Damn White-eyes woman!"

Aurora lay in the dark, mystified by the Apache. His skunk story had revealed him as a curious, trusting child. What had happened to make him such a grim man? What had turned him into a man who never laughed? Who couldn't trust? That, most of all, she thought, aware of a chill in her bones. A man who couldn't trust.

Wolf rolled himself in his blankets and lay with his back to Aurora. A searing image of her, naked and sprawled wantonly on the blue blanket, her slim ivory arms held out to him, was too strong, too strong in his mind and in his loins.

As soon as she was out of danger, he'd moved his blankets to the other side of the cave, as far away from her sleep-softened sighs as he could get. It was the only way he could rest. But tonight he pillowed his head on his folded arms and stayed awake long after the fire had died.

She was right. He had forgotten how to laugh, even how to smile. He had had a happy childhood, petted and cherished as only a child of The People could be. But his childhood had ended one cold winter day, when his mother's bright red lifeblood flowed over his hand.

Then came the long years of exile in Boston, the years when he knew only loneliness and the hatred of his relatives. Afterward, with his white father not yet cold in his grave, had come his uncles' betrayal.

Shanghaied onto a clipper ship as a nameless prisoner, he'd finally managed to escape in San Francisco. Hiding by day, traveling at night, he'd set out cross-country to find his people. When he returned to The People, he'd found them beset by the invading White-eyes. There had been little to smile about for many years.

But, he realized, thinking back over the past two months, when he met Aurora he came to feel truly alive again. A single shy glance from her could awaken his blood and send it rushing through him. And her hair, her sparkling crown of copper flame—just to touch it or see it swing down around her like a curtain, hiding the mystery of her—drove him wild and loosed a glorious need in him. She was fire lighting his darkness.

Tonight she'd touched him. She'd brushed the lock of hair off his forehead. Not as a doctor touches a patient, not as she'd done when she'd been fighting for her life and had struck him. No, tonight she had been simply a woman touching a man. That was all.

Or was she a woman touching *her* man? Were her feelings for him changing?

He glanced over at her. Could her feelings for him change? Could the fire ever want the darkness as much as the darkness seeks the fire?

Aurora awakened to the golden light of sunrise. She glanced around and saw that Wolf and his rifle were gone. As she braced her hand to help herself sit up, it brushed cold metal. For a long time, she eyed the revolver he'd left at her side. It signified so much. Wolf's trust was only one part. Twice before, he'd refused to believe her promises. And those promises hadn't had any bearing on his life.

He was concerned about her. He wanted to protect her, she thought with a sense of wonder. And he believed her—enough to put his life in her hands.

It was well past noon. Aurora had heard no steps on the gravel ledge, but suddenly Wolf stood in the entrance, silhouetted against the iron-gray sky, his thumbs hooked over his cartridge belt, his feet spread wide. His stern features were shadowed and hidden.

They assessed each other during a long heartbeat of stillness. Wolf moved first, stalking into the cave and crouching by the fire to stir it.

"Thank you for the protection." Her voice sounded rusty in the thick silence.

Rising, he paced over and hunkered down beside her. His eyes were puzzled and wary, as if surprised that she hadn't shot him. "I'm here now. You don't need it." He held out his hand, palm up, silently demanding the gun.

She studied his hand. There was a rein-caused callus at the base of each finger and a puckered white scar from a knife slash across the palm. Her gaze rose slowly. He was watching her, not the gun. She picked up the heavy revolver and laid it in his hand.

"Thank you, Wolf." But she wasn't sure whether she was thanking him for the gun or the trust.

He nodded sharply. His long fingers closed around the wooden handle and he slipped it inside his belt. He'd bathed while he was gone, and smelled of pine. She pictured him scrubbing his powerful, ruddy-bronze body with wads of pine needles, and felt a delicious flutter in the pit of her stomach. His long black hair was still wet, and when he shook his head, water drops flew off, landing on her clasped hands and sparkling like diamonds. Each was warm with his heat. Wolf gazed at the drops a moment, then brushed them away.

Aurora swallowed heavily, afraid of the electricity arcing between them. A sudden crash of thunder made her jump. She glanced outside. The sky had darkened to an ominous blue-black, and fat raindrops spattered on the ledge.

"I think it's raining," she said, needing to say something, anything, to shatter the tension.

"It's just a summer storm." He straightened and turned away. Was he going soft in the head? Wolf blasted himself as he paced over to the fire.

He could lust after her, want her, take her; that was safe. But to have tender feelings for her; to want to feel her hands wandering over his body, touching, stroking? No, that would be the death of him.

He cursed silently as he stirred the fire. It was dead, as he would be if he allowed himself to become soft and tender with this woman.

Wolf drew his knife and began shaving wood curls off a piece of pine. Putting them aside, he gathered dried leaves from the back of the cave and piled them in a small mound on a slab of bark. Taking two straight sticks out of his saddlebags, he powdered a dried leaf into a hole in one stick, then stood the other stick in the hole.

"What in the world are you doing?"

"The fire's gone out. I will start a new one with this fire drill." He began to twirl the upright stick between his palms. A thin spiral of smoke soon rose from the area where the two sticks rubbed.

Keeping the drill going with one hand, he nosed another leaf up to the base of the smoke, and a tiny flame flared for an instant. As it did, he realized with a sense of shock that the fire inside him, the fire for the White-eyes woman, no longer smoldered—it was full-blown flame.

He pushed another leaf up to the drill, and another tiny flame flared. He dropped the smoldering leaf onto the pile of dried leaves that he had prepared on the bark and blew on them very gently. "If I blow on them too hard," he explained, "I'll blow the flame out and will have to start over." Perhaps if he took her and slaked his need, the flame burning in him would go out.

"Can I help?"

Wolf shook his head. He continued to blow, and the tiny flame grew larger. "Now I add wood shavings and when they catch, I'll add kindling." And he was keeping busy instead of touching her.

"Whew! I never realized it's so hard to start a fire if you don't already have a flame."

He glanced at her, his brow furrowed in surprise. "Haven't you ever started one from scratch?"

"Sure, but I use a sulfur match, or a flint, or a glowing ember. You didn't use any of those."

"I had matches, but they got wet when that tree dragged me underwater at the stream." He didn't look at her as he laid thin slivers of kindling on the flaming wood shavings.

"Oh." Aurora drew up her knees beneath her skirt and wrapped her arms around them.

Silence rang between them as they remembered the flooded river and her escape. Lightning flashed outside. The kindling crackled and sputtered as Wolf slid the whole piece of bark into the firepit like a pan of fire. The fire in him flared higher.

"I waited on the ridge until you got out," she said quietly. Good God, what was she doing admitting that?

"I know." Wolf piled firewood over the kindling. "I saw you before I collapsed." He paced across the cave and stood over her. His hands curled into tight fists as he willed himself not to take her. Not yet. He had only to remember her touch last night to know why. He would wait for the fire to come to the darkness.

Aurora didn't have to look up to know that he stood tall. She stared steadfastly at his knee-high moccasins. "Why do the ends of your moccasins turn up?" she asked, trying to distract them both.

"To protect my toes when I run in the desert." His deep, dark voice wrapped itself around her. "As I did that night."

The memory of that night shivered between them.

He was doing it to her again, making her aware of him in every bone in her body. She turned her head slightly, letting her long, tangled curls fall forward over her shoulder and shield her from his gaze.

"You use your hair like a curtain." An undercurrent of tension vibrated in his voice. "Do you think to hide from me that way?"

"I would be a fool to try that," Aurora said softly. She looked up at him. "And I'm no fool."

Something flickered in his eyes and was gone. "I agree."

A cold wind gusted through the cavern. Aurora tucked her bare feet underneath her skirt and watched the storm outside, unable to meet his too-intense gaze.

"Your feet are cold?" Wolf savored the growing tension sparking between them. He would wait for her to come to him, he vowed, but it was damned hard. He'd taken a lot of baths in the icy creek during the last few days.

"Yes, but I—"

"Your wound is healing. Perhaps it's time you

had moccasins," he said gruffly. What was he thinking of? he castigated himself, as he headed into the tunnel where the supplies were cached. With moccasins, she could escape.

Aurora smiled a secret smile when he disappeared into the tunnel. With moccasins, she could escape.

He returned in a moment. Rather than touch her, he dropped the moccasins in her lap. "Here."

Aurora eagerly pulled them on, glad to wrap their knee-high warmth around her cold feet and legs. Now all she had to do was get away, she thought, as she laced up the buckskins.

Wolf stood over her, his thumbs hooked in his cartridge belt, watching. She kept her eyes downcast, afraid that if she looked at him, he would see her plans to escape. Suddenly he crouched and crooking his finger beneath her chin, tilted her head up until their eyes met.

"You'd never get away. I'd never stop looking for you and I'd find you, no matter where you went."

"I don't know what you're talking about," she said quickly—too quickly, she realized. "Just how is it that you have woman-sized moccasins here? Or is this where you bring all your women captives?"

He raised a dark eyebrow at her, then spun away and stalked over to the fire. "We have supplies for warriors, women, even children, in case The People have to hide from enemies here. And women warriors would need new moccasins if they rested here."

Aurora's head snapped up and her eyes narrowed. "Your women go to war?"

"A few. If a woman loves a man very much, she may decide to ride the war trail at his side."

She clamped her hands to her hips. "What kind of woman goes to war! I can't imagine—"

"How can you say that when you've gone against the code of your own people and become a doctor? Or are there so many women doctors among you White-eyes?"

She gazed out at the storm for a long time before she turned to him. "You're right. I am being narrow. It's just that I'm so surprised; I thought your women only gathered food and cooked."

"Gathering food and cooking is important work. It is the heart of a family." He crossed his arms over his broad chest. "But unlike the White-eyes, The People don't say a woman can do this, but she can't do that. In our world, a woman is free to do whatever she wishes. If she is a good saddle maker or arrow maker and wants to do that, she does. If she wants to stay unmarried and be a woman warrior, she is free to do that. She can choose."

"I had no idea Apache women had such freedom." It was far more than the freedom granted to many women she'd known. Only because she'd grown up among the Quakers, whose men admitted that women had minds, had she been able to choose her work.

"It is the way of The People." He stalked over to the fire, knelt on one knee, and stirred the embers.

After that, the words between them were few, the touches even fewer. Only the glances and the quick turning away when their eyes met were frequent.

All evening Wolf stayed on the other side of the fire, far away from her. They both knew why.

Chapter 12

〜〜〜⌒◯◯⌒〜〜〜

One afternoon several days later, Aurora sat outside on the ledge, looking out over the dark-green pines that blanketed the mountain slopes.

"Do you watch for Bluecoats?" Wolf emerged from the cave and leaned against the boulders behind her. "They will not look for you so high in the mountains, White-eyes."

"I wasn't." She swung around. He was naked except for tan denim trousers, and she caught her breath, struck by his savage ruggedness. He raised a disbelieving eyebrow at her.

Her gaze wavered. Actually she'd been puzzling over the enigma that was Wolf, although she wasn't about to admit it. "I've been combing my hair," she said, intentionally changing the subject, "but I'm afraid fingers aren't very good."

"Perhaps this will help?" He reached deep into a fold of his moccasins and drew out a deer rib with teeth notched into one edge. "Come," he added, sitting down on a boulder. He spread his legs and patted the ground between them. "Sit here and I will comb your hair."

"That's all right. I can do it." She was conscious enough of him. It was disturbingly sensual to think of sitting between his legs as he combed her hair, running his fingers through it. Touching her . . . softly . . . gently.

He didn't move, just rested his big hands on his knees and waited. "I want to," he finally admitted quietly.

She wanted that also, enticed by the thought of his powerful hands in her hair. Her eyes met his. No words were needed, she realized, as she sat down between his legs.

He was incredibly gentle. Her hair was waist-length, and he started at the ends, combing a tangle out, then moving up slightly and combing out a higher tangle. His hands whispered through her hair. Again and again and again. Hypnotizing her with his gentleness.

No one had ever brushed her hair like that. No lover. No one. Aurora closed her eyes, drowning in his touch. She drew a deep breath, inhaling the warm, rich scent of horses clinging to his pants. She relaxed, letting her head fall forward. His breath stirred the fine curls along her nape and sent a shimmer of sensation down her spine. Smiling softly, she tilted her head. Her cheek brushed the inside of his thigh.

Startled back to reality, she jerked bolt upright, yanking the comb out of Wolf's hand.

"Be still, woman." But there was a smile in his voice as he retrieved it.

The spell was broken, though, and Aurora was determined to see it didn't return. She couldn't let him hypnotize her with his gentleness. She had to keep talking; that would keep her alert, keep her awareness of his touch at bay.

"You know, I don't think Kreutz would ever have captured you if you hadn't wanted to be captured. So I've been sitting here asking myself why you would want to be captured." She had asked herself that question a thousand times.

"And you know what?" she continued. "I think you wanted to get into the fort and knew a strange Apache would be noticed but not a prisoner. No one would think twice about what they said in a prisoner's hearing. And you never revealed that you spoke English, not even when I was trying to talk to you."

"It was very hard with you." He lifted a lustrous lock of her long hair and draped it across his thigh, then set to work combing it until it glowed in the sunlight. "I wanted to talk to you and I almost did several times. But then I'd remember my reason for being there."

"But you almost died for lack of water," she said sharply, angry with him for taking such risks.

"I wasn't delirious yet. I could still think and I could have drunk the water Thompson had poisoned"—he paused, then continued—"if I had gotten desperate enough."

She slammed her hand down. "Oh, come on! You were already in terrible shape when I walked into that corral. You're just too stubborn to admit it."

"Perhaps." He leaned over her and combed her hair back from her forehead. "When I woke up in the storeroom, though, I knew that everything had worked out better than I planned."

"Because what you wanted was information, and I had put you in the perfect place to get it?" His knee brushed her shoulder.

"Yes. I could hear what the Bluecoats planned to do and when and where they would attack my people. That was what I needed."

"What did you do after you escaped?" she asked, tilting her head and glancing back at him from beneath tawny lashes.

"You mean after I kissed you?"

"After you knocked me out!" She rubbed her chin, remembering the sudden void she'd fallen into.

He looked a bit shamefaced. "That was one of the hardest things I had to do. I wanted to go on kissing you and I couldn't."

"I didn't notice that stopping you. Do you know my chin was black and blue for weeks where you struck me?"

He shot her a hot-eyed look that set her alarm bells ringing. "Perhaps I can make it up to you now."

"Never mind." She faced forward and crossed her arms over her bosom. "Just keep combing. Besides, you still haven't told me what you did when you escaped."

"I told Geronimo what I had learned about the Bluecoats' plan to move The People to the San Carlos Reservation." He snorted derisively. "He and I rode to warn them. Over four hundred warriors, women, and children chose to follow us to Mexico and live, rather than die at San Carlos."

"You led four hundred Apaches into Mexico?" Once again, she turned, eyeing him with astonishment.

"Why do you sound so surprised?"

"I was right. You're not just a warrior. You're a

chief, aren't you? And the message from Tenehas may have been a fake, but you wanted those supplies for your people, didn't you? That's why you asked for them."

He gave her an approving nod. "My people will need the supplies during the winter. Even the medical supplies will be used."

"How did you know I would come?"

"I knew Wharton would not leave the safety of Fort Bowie. He is terrified of Indians."

"But I could have decided not to come. As it was, I almost couldn't . . . didn't go." She stopped before she mentioned her father. In these past days, Wolf had begun to trust her, to talk and explain, and she didn't want to jeopardize that hard-won openness.

"I knew you would want to. You want to help people. That's why you came into the corral when an Apache prisoner needed water. That's why you stomped around the fort when Wharton wouldn't let you into the hospital."

"You know about that?"

"Of course. I knew I was coming back for you, so I left a man to watch you."

"I see." He knew he was coming back for her. That simple fact echoed in her mind like the beat of a drum. He'd known he was coming back for her when he rode to warn the Apaches, when he led them into exile in Mexico.

He fumbled in a fold of his moccasin. "Would you like to use this to secure your hair?" Reaching over her shoulder, he held out her silver comb.

"That's mine!" She twisted around, bracing one arm on his knee for balance.

"I know." A thread of something deep within him colored his voice.

"I thought it was lost. I couldn't find it after the dance and—"

"I took it with me." To have something of hers until he returned for her.

Her eyes met his obsidian gaze as they remembered that night. That kiss. A muscle tightened in Wolf's jaw.

Aurora turned her attention to the comb, running her fingers over the tarnished silver, but she was still aware of him with every particle of her being. "Thank you, Wolf," she said softly. "This was my mother's. She died when I was very young and this is so precious to me."

"It had meaning for me also." His words floated between them, whispering of unexplored promises, of wild horizons.

Slowly, giving her time to move or protest if she wanted to, he leaned toward her.

He was going to kiss her. And she wanted him to. She wanted him to. A shiver of primitive consciousness sparked through her as she looked up at him. Other men had wanted her, but she hadn't wanted them. He was different, she realized with age-old instinct. Rising on her knees, she turned to face him, to meet him. She gripped his broad shoulders, not to push him away, but to pull him closer.

Wolf paused, studying her expressive features, waiting for a hint of fear or horror to cross them. But there was none, only her warm, full mouth inviting him closer. With a sigh, he touched her lips with his.

This time his lips were soft and warm. His kiss was gentle, singing of sun-washed days and moon-kissed nights. Enticing. Beckoning. Promising so much.

Heat pooled in her, making her go soft inside. She leaned into him, arrowing her fingers through his silky black hair, letting her tongue touch his, meeting him touch for touch, magic for magic.

Slowly he lifted his head and looked down at her. His eyes reflected the same confusion and wonder that she felt.

"I—" Breaking off, he surged to his feet and stood for a second looking down at her, kneeling between his legs. "I shouldn't have—" Turning, he stalked into the cave.

Aurora watched him walk away, understanding the confusion he was feeling, for she felt it too. He was a savage, she reminded herself, yet sensitive and perceptive. And there was something so boldly exciting about him, that she felt awake and alive as never before.

Limping badly, with loud sighs that were supposed to show how painful walking was, Aurora slowly followed Wolf through the forest. Her ankle was actually healing rapidly, but she didn't want him to know that. The longer they remained in one place, the better the chance of her father's troops finding them. Once over the border in Mexico, rescue would be much riskier, especially if Papa was involved.

In the meantime, she would slow Wolf down as much as she could. She inhaled the fragrance of the pines towering over them in a dark-green canopy. The woods were alive with brilliant blue jays, scolding them, then flying ahead to perch and scold them again.

"We're almost there." Wolf glanced over his

shoulder, saw how far behind she was, and slowed his pace.

"Good." She paused at the edge of the sunny glade, leaning against a pine. The stream broadened into a pond, where the water slowed and whispered, as if reluctant to leave.

Grass rimmed the sun-drenched pool in a lush, green embrace. Sinking down on it, Aurora pulled up a tuft just to touch something soft. The sweet scent of crushed grass brought back all the times she'd sat on the grass in Aunt Ruth's yard inside its white picket fence, smelling the roses and soaking up the warmth of a much weaker sun.

But that was before she came out west. And instead of being safe in Aunt Ruth's yard, she was the captive of an Apache warrior. Instead of smelling roses in civilized Philadelphia, she smelled wild pines in a wild place, and the sun could be both friend and foe in this forbidding land.

Aurora fingered the collar of her filthy blouse, then smoothed a hand over her tattered riding skirt. Her boots were gone completely. And she was alone. Utterly, completely alone. She blinked hastily, fighting the tears that stung her eyes.

"Stop feeling sorry for yourself," she admonished herself under her breath as she took off her moccasins. "You're alive. You will not cry. You will not cry," she repeated over and over. For if she started, she might not be able to stop.

She stood up, savoring the feel of the cool, soft grass between her toes. Anxious to bathe, she undid the top button on her blouse, then paused, looking around for Wolf.

A huge rock slab slanted down into the pool. He stood at the top, six feet above her, his feet spread wide, his rifle, as always, cradled in the crook of his right arm. Sunbeams splashed across his taut sinews in a golden glaze. And he was watching her.

"I'll be all right. You don't have to stay."

His gaze skimmed her, firing her flesh. "I will stay."

Aurora's eyes narrowed dangerously. She'd been looking forward to bathing, to feeling squeaky clean, but no one had seen her naked since Aunt Ruth had taken care of her during a bout of tonsillitis when she was eight. She glared at Wolf, wishing lightning would flash out of the cloudless sky and strike him. Aurora closed her eyes, hoping. When she opened them, he was still there, still watching.

"You don't understand."

"I do understand. But you said you fear the wild beasts. I will stay and protect you."

"A fine time for you to think of protecting me," she jeered in her most withering tones. He didn't move. "Barbarian!" Turning, she strode into the sun-warmed water, which welcomed her with open arms. As she waded farther out, sand squished between her toes.

"That's far enough, Aurora," Wolf warned.

"Afraid I'll swim away and escape?" she taunted, wading further out to where the water was shoulder-deep. Hiding beneath the glossy blue surface, she slipped out of her clothes and let them sink to the bottom.

Taking a deep breath, she ducked under the surface and scooped up a handful of sand. She began to scrub herself. The sand was rougher than any soap and left her skin reddened and tingling, but for the first time in days, she felt clean. "Clean,

clean, clean," she hummed. Combing her fingers through her hair, she shook it, anxious to wash it, but sand wouldn't do the job.

"Catch." Wolf threw her a small piece of shriveled brown root. "Use this on your hair."

"What is it?" She eyed it warily.

"Yucca root. Soapweed. Try it in your hair."

Sinking down, she rubbed the yucca through her tresses. Pleased by the thin, soapy lather, she washed and rinsed once, then again.

Then she swished her shirt and skirt and petticoats around in the water. No matter how poor her laundry job was, they were bound to be cleaner than before.

Finally. she turned and shaded her eyes against the sun, squinting up at Wolf. "Would you please turn away so I can get out and get dressed?"

"It's not a good idea in the forest. You never know what kind of wild animal might come along."

Silently Aurora looked at him. After an eternity, he turned away, although a grin lit the darkness of his features first. Rather than wading all the way back across the pond to Wolf, she splashed over to the far bank, wrung out her clothes, and pulled on her cold, clammy skirt.

A low growl made her look up. Aurora's eyes saucered as she stared at the huge bear that stood less than twenty feet away. She froze, her numb fingers dropping the shirt. Watching her and growling loudly, the bear bent to sniff the soapsuds freckling the water.

"W-Wolf," she whispered through barely moving lips. She caught a whiff of the bear's fetid breath, and her heart hammered against her ribs.

"I see it. Don't move." His voice was a deep well of calm, and from it she could tell he still stood on the rock. Not close at all.

"I-I won't." She couldn't; her muscles were paralyzed. Her pulse was thundering so loudly in her ears that she barely heard the metallic click as he cocked his rifle. The bear slapped the water with her huge paw.

"Sh-shoot. Shoot it," she pleaded.

"Not yet. She's a sow. See how swollen her teats are?"

This bear was getting ready to eat her, and he was worrying whether it was male or female? She wanted to turn and scream at him.

At the barest movement of her head, Wolf hissed, "Don't move, *isdzán*."

The bear flicked him a glance, then her small piggy eyes returned to Aurora. Her massive head tilted to the side as if she was calculating how much meat covered Aurora's bones.

"Shoot," Aurora screamed in a whisper. "What are you waiting for?"

"There's time. She hasn't decided if she's going to charge."

At that moment, two squalling, wrestling cubs tumbled out of the berry bushes behind the bear. With a roar that shook the trees, the bear stood up on her hind legs.

Aurora screamed.

Wolf's rifle boomed behind her, and chunks of wood flew from a tree beside the bear. The cubs skidded to a halt. The sow galloped toward them, shooing them back into the forest. At the edge of the trees, she paused and turned to Aurora. A second shot dropped a pine bough on her broad

back. Growling ferociously, she swatted it into
toothpicks, then followed the cubs, crashing
through the undergrowth like a runaway steam
locomotive.

Aurora raced around the edge of the pond,
across the grass, and straight into Wolf's arms.
They closed around her, nestling her against his
wide chest. For the first time in long minutes she
felt safe, and she savored the feeling, wrapping her
arms around his waist as she pressed against him.

"Oh, Wolf," she gasped, trembling like a quak-
ing aspen. He still gripped the rifle with his right
hand, and she could feel the length of warm barrel
jammed against her back.

"It's gone." Threading his fingers through her
wet hair, he cupped her head with his left hand.
"Don't worry; you're safe now." He caressed her
temple with his chin.

"No thanks to you," she yelped, rearing back
against his arm so that she could look up at him.
"Why didn't you shoot as soon as you saw it? What
were you waiting for? For me to die of fright?"

"Hush, woman, you talk too much," he rumbled, but there was no anger in his eyes, only
smoke and flame.

Her eyes widened as he lowered his head. His
broad shoulders blotted out the golden sun and the
green pines and the blue skies. "I do not!" she
breathed against his lips.

His kiss was demanding and triumphant, and it
took her breath away. Aurora's fingers speared
through his long, midnight hair, absorbing the
silkiness even as she kissed him back.

He stiffened for an instant, as though surprised,
then his hold on the rifle loosened and it slid down

her back and landed with a soft thud on the grass. She shivered as he slid his hands lower, filling them with her lush curves and urging her into the hammock of his hips.

His tongue invaded her warmth and she touched it tentatively with hers. He growled far back in his throat as his hands crushed her to him. His tongue dueled with hers, advancing and retreating, touching and touching again. She grew dizzy and locked her arms around his neck to keep from falling.

When he finally lifted his head, her heart was pounding like a kettledrum and she was breathless. Wolf swept her tangled tresses back over her shoulders and studied her wordlessly. She gazed up at him, drinking his rugged features into her senses.

Her breasts were pressed to his smooth, granite chest and she could feel his racing heartbeat. Her naked breasts?

In one panicked moment of horror, Aurora remembered she had dropped her shirt. She pushed herself out of his arms and whirled away. Standing with her back to him, she crossed her arms over her bare bosom. "Go away. Don't look at me."

"Don't turn away from me, Aurora." Wolf's hands were gentle on her shoulders, and his breath was a whisper across her nape. He kissed the sensitive spot behind her ear with a fierce tenderness, and her heart skipped a beat.

"Please let me go," she whispered, afraid of him, afraid of the way her heart was hammering, afraid of the heat pulsing in her blood. "Please."

"I can't." He punctuated each word with a kiss as soft as a dandelion puff. "I won't."

Aurora could hear tiny plops of water dripping

off her skirt. She watched, as though her body belonged to someone else, as his large, callus-roughened hands cupped the fullness of her breasts. His thumbs brushed over her nipples. She trembled as his hands spread honeyed warmth into her bones.

A sunburst of need bloomed in her. She wanted him. Deep down in the pit of her stomach, where butterflies fluttered wildly, she wanted him. Slowly, hesitantly, she turned.

Shyly she studied the ground, veiled by the curtain of long hair falling over her shoulders. Wolf's hands stilled for an eternity as he gazed at her.

"You're so beautiful." Awe deepened his voice. "So very beautiful." Sweeping her up in his arms, he carried her into the cool shadows beneath the pines. There he knelt and gently laid her on a bed of moss. Aurora smiled, surprised by its soft springiness. She rested her arm over her forehead, shielding her eyes even as she watched Wolf through her lashes.

He stood looking down at her. Dark and light shadows played over him in ever-shifting camouflage, giving him a mysterious quality. Aurora drew a sharp breath, torn between fear and awe at the strength and power of this primitive warrior.

"I've pictured you sprawled at my feet, holding out your ivory arms to me," he said in a husky whisper. Slowly, drawing out the anticipation of what was to come, his hands went to his belt. "I've pictured you opening for me, inviting me into your warmth." He unbuckled his belt. "I've pictured you wrapping your long legs around me, Aurora. I want you to want me the way I want you."

Aurora closed her eyes, mesmerized by the pictures he'd painted in her mind. This joining between them was right. Inevitable as sunrise and sunset. The culmination of a look from a man with dark-as-Hades eyes to a woman whose heartstrings hummed in response.

It was their destiny.

His belt thudded softly on the ground, followed by the dry rustle of his pants. Kneeling beside her, he slipped his large hand beneath her hips and skimmed off her tattered blue riding skirt.

Aurora shivered in the chill mountain air, but an instant later Wolf's heat cocooned her as he stretched out beside her. Wrapping his arms around her, he drew her close. "Warm enough?"

"Yes." He was burning up, but this time it wasn't a fever. At least, not one that medicine could cure.

He leaned over her, cradling her face in his palms and brushing silken kisses over her forehead and eyes and cheeks. Tantalizing her with whispering touches.

Just as she lifted her head, reaching for him, his lips came down over hers in a soft, tender kiss. Surprised and intrigued, she clasped his broad shoulders and met his gentleness with a promise of her own. Their tongues danced together instead of dueling, and when she finally broke away, she was breathless and exhilarated.

Wolf trailed a necklace of fiery, stinging kisses down her throat. Raising his head, he studied her with such intensity that she wondered if he could see into her soul. He touched her only with his heat.

She stiffened when his gaze focused on something beyond her and he reached for it.

"Let it be a surprise, *isdzán*," he murmured, as she would have turned her head to see what he was doing.

"Should I close my eyes?"

"It's not necessary." The warmth in his voice caressed her.

He scattered a handful of tiny lavender flowers over her. "These flowers are very rare and beautiful," he whispered, picking one up and drawing it over her breasts in intricate twirling designs. "Like you."

The petals were cool velvet trailing across her flesh. Aurora gave herself over to pure feeling as he drew the velvet flower back and forth over her. Then his fingers followed the same paths, leaving her skin tingling and alive as never before.

He drew his fingers down her ribs in an almost-hard touch that sent a shiver cascading through her. Once. Her breath was coming faster now. Twice. Her heart thrummed against her ribs. A third time.

"Oh, Wolf." She sighed. She drew her fingers down his back in a hard-light touch that made him twist violently and groan far back in his throat. "Did I hurt you?"

"No." He dropped a quick, tingling kiss on her breast. "I like your hands on me." He dropped another kiss on her other breast. "All over me."

Then his mouth settled over her rosebud of a nipple, and he flicked his tongue over and around it. The breath thickened in her throat as a wave of feeling swept out from her breast.

Aurora ran her fingers down his back again, drawing another groan and shudder from him.

"Two can play that game," he murmured as he drew his teeth across her sensitized nipple.

He sent another starburst of sensation sweeping through her. Aurora moaned softly and gave herself up to the tension and need blooming deep within her.

He suckled at her breast, drawing her pebble-hard nipple into the moist, heated interior of his mouth. New sensations swept her, leaving her hands and feet tingling in their golden aftermath. When he let go of her nipple, he blew a whisper-soft teasing breath across it, lifting her higher and higher.

"Wolf—I need you," she gasped, arching her back.

"Be patient, my beautiful flame." His fingers sought the curls at the joining of her legs.

Frightened in spite of her need, she brought her knees together, catching his hand. He brushed his fingers along the sensitive insides of her thighs until she quivered and sighed with pleasure. Slowly, so slowly, she relaxed and spread her legs. When she finally lay open to him, he bent down and kissed her—there—in her most secret place.

Aurora's eyes widened with shock, and she threaded her fingers through his hair to push him away. But he did it again, and suddenly she was pulling him closer. His hair feathered across the sensitive flesh of her inner thighs as he kissed her time and again. Each stroke, each touch, ignited new sensations.

"Wolf, please," she whispered tautly. Need grew in her, and an awareness of an aching emptiness only one man could fill.

"That's exactly what I want, my *kun isdzán*, to please you." He kissed her. There.

"You are." He was making her mindless with pleasure.

"Then say you want me. Tell me you want me as much as I want you." He moved up, raining kisses all over her. Slowly he filled his hands with her tousled hair and gazed down at her in the sun-dappled shadows.

"Oh . . . yes . . . I want you."

He slid between her legs, and his throbbing manhood pressed at the entrance to her warmth. Instinctively she stiffened, wanting him, but afraid, so afraid.

"It's all right, *querida*. We'll go slow and easy," he promised. He prodded her moist entrance with his manhood, knowing that every moment of delay just made everything better when they finally climbed the last peak together. He eased forward.

She stiffened and choked back a cry.

Wolf froze as he felt a barrier tear. "Why didn't you tell me?" he whispered as he gathered her close and kissed her fiercely. "Why didn't you tell me?"

"Would it have made any difference?" Wrapping her arms around his neck, she reached up and kissed the pulse point beating in his throat.

He shivered at the feathery touch of her lips. "Only that I would have gone slower," he rasped, taut with trying to control his need for her.

"Then I would have gone crazy faster. No, don't pull away." She wrapped her arms around his shoulders, holding him close.

She was so tight, so incredibly tight. He waited, giving her time to adjust to him.

"Don't be afraid. We'll climb the highest mountain peaks together." Wolf pushed her tangled hair off her brow and rained kisses over her face. He began to thrust, cautiously at first.

"Ohh. Ohhh." She gripped his massive shoulders tightly and met him thrust for thrust. Deep within her, the delicious tension coiled tighter and tighter. She clung to him as the pines began to spin around them. He stroked harder . . . faster . . . deeper. . . .

She raked her fingers down his back and felt him writhe with pleasure.

Harder . . . faster . . . deeper. . . .

Waves of sweet rapture swept her higher and higher, carrying her above the pines, above the mountain peaks, above the clouds.

"Aurora!" Wolf crushed her in his embrace as he gave one final shuddering thrust.

And she soared with him.

Chapter 13

Aurora slowly became aware of her surroundings. She was still locked in Wolf's arms. Birds were singing in the pines overhead, and the sweet smell of crushed grass mingled with the erotic scent of their lovemaking. And she was no longer the person she'd been an hour earlier.

Unlike most maidens, she'd known what the physical act consisted of, but all her medical knowledge hadn't prepared her for the tumultuous emotions that had seethed within her and the incredible experience of joining with another human being.

She had become one with Wolf. Just the simple thought left her heart turning somersaults. Although he rested most of his weight on his forearms, Wolf still blanketed her, and she welcomed his warmth. She ran her hands over his sweat-slick shoulders, savoring every precious moment of their oneness. They were slowly becoming two again, and she felt a touch of sadness that their closeness was slipping away.

The memory of the first time their eyes had met

floated through her mind. Even then, she'd felt as though they'd touched. Only now did she understand what that primal awareness had foreshadowed. So much had come between them, yet it was as if their destiny was to join together and become one.

Good God, was she falling in love with him? Aurora's eyes flew open and she stared at the turquoise sky. Love? Utterly impossible! It was just the heightened awareness that came with shared danger, then being in each other's arms, a few fiery kisses and—

No, she didn't want to think about it. It was too farfetched, too unimaginable.

Wolf rested his head on the grass beside hers, and when she turned, she found he was watching her. Her heart leaped like a startled gazelle at the smoky fires in his eyes.

"*Enjuh*," he murmured in a deep tone of satisfaction.

He rolled to his side, taking her with him. "Very *enjuh*." He trailed his fingers over her breasts lazily.

Aurora trembled beneath the icy-hot whisper of his possessive hands. Oh, so possessive! She closed her eyes, unable to meet his gaze, as he rested his palm on her breast. His thumb brushed her already-taut rosebud nipple. A shimmer of anticipation washed through her.

"W-what does *enjuh* mean?" she asked, trying to keep her wits about her.

"Good. Did I hurt you?"

"No, I'm fine." She stretched tentatively and found no aches yet. "At least, I think I am."

"Then was it *enjuh* for you?" His voice was black velvet, wrapping around her like a summer night.

"Yes." *Enjuh* didn't begin to describe the won-

drous feelings that had filled her. "Is it always so—
enjuh?" she asked hesitantly.

He leaned over her, filling his hands with her
flowing locks and dropping fiery kisses on her
breasts. "No, my little inquisitor. It's rarely this
enjuh."

"Oh." She gazed at him for several heartbeats,
then a very womanly smile lit her features. *"Enjuh!"*

"Ah, I hear triumph in your voice." He kissed
her nose. "See how easy my language is? You've
already learned your first word of Apache."

"No, it's my second. You called me *isdzán* when
the bear threatened me. What does that mean?"

"Did I? It means woman." Rolling away from
her, he sat up. Facing her, magnificent in his
nakedness, he pulled on his pants. "Come, *isdzán*,"
he said, holding out his hand to her, "it's time we
returned to the cave. The sun is low, the shadows
grow long."

Later, after a meal of corn tortillas and piñon
nuts, Wolf disappeared into the supply tunnel,
reappearing with two metal cartridge boxes.

"What are you doing?" Aurora sat on her blanket, brushing her hair with the deer-rib comb. Wolf
had made love to her with exquisite gentleness that
afternoon. He'd led her into a new world. A world
of sensuality and passion and oneness with another human being.

"I'm reloading my cartridge belt, the one good
thing the Bluecoats brought to this land." Hunker-
ing down beside the fire, he filled the loops on the
canvas belt with long brass bullets. "It is time I
returned to my people. They need me. We will
leave tomorrow."

She stopped in mid-stroke. "But my ankle is—"

"Healing very well, as we both know." He shot her an unreadable glance from beneath his dark brows.

At a loss for a reply, Aurora decided to ignore his comment. Time and again he'd surprised her: his twenty-four-hours-a-day alertness, his knowledge of English, his knowing how to give a lady a leg up, his reluctance to shoot the bear. "I've been thinking about this afternoon," she said as she slowly drew the comb through her clean tresses. "You wouldn't have killed that bear, would you?"

"It was not necessary." He looked up from tying his saddlebags, and his voice hardened. "You are like all the other White-eyes. Kill all animals you don't understand. Kill all people who aren't White-eyes."

"That's not true and you know it! But that bear threatened me and—"

"She was simply being a good mother." He looked up from where he sat at the other side of the fire. "She put on a bluff-threat to keep you away from her cubs. You would have done the same thing to protect your cubs."

"But what if she'd charged?"

He didn't hesitate. "Then I would have killed her." He stirred the fire before he continued in a deeper, more thoughtful tone, "Killing bears is not something my people do if we can avoid it. Bears are like people: they walk on their hind legs; they eat the foods we eat. My people believe some of our dead may return from the Underworld and walk Earth Mother again as bears."

"So killing one would be like murder?"

"Something like that. And if they are evil ones, then we might unleash great evil on the world."

She pulled one section of hair forward over her shoulder as she finished combing it, then went on to the next. "You said the warrior who captured me was called Bear Killer." She shuddered, just thinking of the filthy brute.

"Yes."

"Well? Is he proud to have killed a bear?"

"My people are named for things they have done. It does not matter whether they are proud of it or not. They have done it. When he was young, Geronimo was called *Goyahkla*, He Who Yawns. Then the Mexicans came and they killed his mother and his wife and his sons and his daughter. That is when he stopped yawning. Now he fights."

"What a violent life. It's a wonder any of you survive."

"It is the life of my people. We have always fought our enemies." He exhaled a long, deep breath, then added slowly, almost reluctantly, "As a child, I didn't know people died of old age. I was nine before I saw anyone die other than by violence."

The deer-rib comb clattered to the dirt, and Aurora blinked owlishly as the horror of his words sank in. "My Lord!" She studied him as he stalked to his blankets at the other side of the cave. He'd lived through violence she couldn't even imagine. Yet that afternoon he had made love to her with excruciating gentleness. Just thinking of the places his hands and mouth had been made her heart thrum with a wild beat.

As if he read her thoughts, Wolf shook out his blankets, threw them over his arm, and paced toward her.

Aurora's eyes widened. "Wolf?"

"We will sleep together tonight, White-eyes." He spread his blankets beside hers and patted them. "Come, do not look so frightened. Lie down here beside me."

"But—"

"No buts tonight, *kun isdzán*. Come here."

She lay down on her side and he pulled her against him, spoon-fashion. His hand cupped her breast.

Aurora's head was pillowed on his arm. "Wolf, what does *kun isdzán* mean?"

He was silent so long that she thought he wasn't going to answer. "Woman of fire."

A soft warmth washed over her. With a deep sigh of contentment, she closed her eyes.

And so that night, when the fire died and the cold crept out of the rocks, Aurora lay locked in Wolf's arms, appreciating his virility and vitality in a new way. Something had happened that afternoon. Not only had he protected her from the bear, but also she'd run to him, run to her kidnapper.

And she'd found strength and safety in his arms. That was what stunned her. She'd felt safer than ever before—in his arms.

Then had come their lovemaking. No matter what happened, she would never regret it, for it had been a special time, a time out of time.

The next morning, Aurora watched Wolf rise from their blankets. She'd never seen him naked in full daylight. He turned away and bent down to pick up his pants.

Aurora's gaze slid down the long curve of his dark copper back to his white buttocks gleaming in the morning sun. She blinked. *His white buttocks?*

An Apache would be the same rich copper all over. Unless—unless he wasn't an Apache. Unless everything he'd told her was a lie and he was— Aurora gasped.

"What is it?" Wolf demanded, glancing over his shoulder.

Aurora sat up. "Who are you?" she cried.

"Are your brains addled, woman? You know who I am."

"You're not an Apache." Desperately needing to shield herself, she drew up her knees and wrapped her arms around them. She'd seen plenty of white men at the fort who were as dark as he. "You're a white man—which means that every single thing you've told me has been a damn lie!"

A muscle pounded in his temple, but he said nothing as he pulled his breeches up and tied them. The silence grew as he buckled his cartridge belt around his narrow waist.

Aurora's mind was racing. If he was a white man masquerading as an Apache, then that would explain many of the things she'd noticed, things that didn't add up to a wild Apache.

The fire had died down in the night. Wolf hunkered down beside it and stirred up the embers. While his back was turned, Aurora hastily threw on her clothes, feeling utterly naked and degraded, knowing she'd slept with a man who told her only lies.

His eyes met hers as he laid fresh wood on the coals. Aurora crossed her arms over her bosom protectively. "Who are you really, Wolf? Although I doubt that's even your name."

"My name is Ma'cho Nalzhee."

"No, it isn't." Why did he pretend to be what he wasn't? Good God, was that why he wanted to kill her father? Because her father knew the real identity of this man?

Wolf stood up, rising higher and higher until his head seemed to touch the roof. His broad shoulders were enormous, and the morning sun etched the harsh planes and angles of his face. Aurora felt a twinge of apprehension as his hands balled into tight fists.

"You are wrong. Do not get your hopes up, Aurora. I am an Apache, one of The People."

"I don't believe you, Wolf, or whatever your name is. You know things no wild Apache could. You know how to give a lady a leg up onto her horse. You speak English too fluently, as if you've spoken it all your life. And when we were in the storeroom, you told Pincus you knew about trains. But the train hasn't come to Arizona yet, so I know you've traveled a great distance from here. And last, run your hand over your cheek. Your beard is too heavy to be an Indian's."

"Look around you," Wolf growled, sweeping the cavern with his hand. "This is the cave where I was born. Does this look like a White-eyes house to you?"

Aurora shuddered at the idea of going into labor and bearing a child in this barren place. "How awful."

"It is the way of Apache women. It is what their mothers and their mothers' mothers did."

"That doesn't make it right. If your mother was Apache, then your father had to be white. Was he a rancher or a soldier? Am I right?"

"Yes and no." Wolf studied the clump of dirt he'd crushed in his fist. Slowly he let the soil sift through his fingers and return to earth. "He was the eldest son of a Boston shipping family."

"Good God! How did he ever come to marry an Apache?"

He flashed her a surprised look. "Why do you think that?" White-eyes lay with Indian women; they didn't marry them—although his parents had been married in The People's way.

"I don't know. I guess I assumed that since you speak English so well, you'd learned it as you were growing up, which means your father didn't abandon your mother."

"He didn't know he spoke English. He had no memory of his life before he woke in my mother's village." Speaking of his father had awakened long-buried memories, and they held a warmth he'd forgotten. "It was many years later that we learned his father had sent him out west to check on a family gold mine in Mexico. He caught the manager cheating, and the manager's thugs beat him unconscious and left him in the wilderness to die. Instead, my mother found him."

"And nursed him back to health. How romantic! He must have had amnesia. How did he regain his memory?"

"The People do not speak of the dead."

"But you just did, which shows you're not one of The People," she persisted, unwittingly reopening an old wound.

Bear Killer had taunted him with those same words when he was six. He'd given the older boy a bloody nose.

"I am Apache," he growled, striking his dark copper chest. "My skin may betray me with whiteness, but in my heart I am Apache. My blood runs hot with the blood of Apache warriors. My heart and my blood cry that I am one of The People."

She studied him with a concentration that made

him wary. "What about your mind? What does it say?"

He rested a hand on the boulders and gazed out at the pine-covered slopes. "It, too, says I'm Apache."

"I don't believe you. If you were a ruthless Apache, you would have left me to die. You didn't."

"Perhaps I saved you because I have a use for you."

"Your use for me was fulfilled when the soldiers saw I was alive and your captive."

He gave her a slow, white-hot up-and-down look that left her flesh tingling. "I have other uses for you."

Aurora felt a frisson of fear mixed with a strange excitement. "I can't imagine what," she snapped.

"Can't you?"

"Did your father regain his memory? He must have, since you speak English." She was babbling, but she couldn't stop. "You don't have any accent and—"

"He finally remembered he was Timothy Tobias Winthrop, and as soon as he did, he returned to Boston with me." He picked up the stick he'd used earlier and stirred the fire again.

Aurora knelt and tightened the laces on her moccasins. She was aware of a change in him she couldn't quite define—but there was a harshness in his voice, a stiffness in his shoulders.

"I'll bet his family was happy to see him," she said brightly, "returned from the dead as it were."

"Hardly. His brothers would have preferred him to stay among the dead. His father was dying, and his brothers had already decided how they'd divide up the family shipping business. Then he came back—the oldest son, the one who would inherit everything. As if that wasn't bad enough, he'd returned with a half-breed son!"

Aurora looked up from where she knelt in the dust. "I get the feeling they didn't exactly welcome you with open arms."

"They had closed arms. Closed minds. Closed hearts."

"What about your mother? Did she go with you?"

Wolf walked outside into the sunlight. As if that could melt the ice in him, he thought scornfully.

"She was dead, murdered by a Bluecoat." A sharp crack made him look down at the branch he'd broken.

"Oh, Wolf," Aurora murmured weakly, "how terrible."

He flung the pieces of wood over the edge of the cliff and watched them fall. "You see," he continued, as if he hadn't heard her, "Bluecoats attacked my village during the moons of Ghost Face. My father and the other men were out hunting. The Bluecoats stormed through, burning our wickiups, shooting and killing everything that moved. They killed women, children, even the babies," he whispered hoarsely. He stared out across the valley, seeing only the horror of that long-ago day.

When he glanced at her, she drew a sharp breath at the agony etched on his rugged features. "I was thirteen, already a warrior." A muscle throbbed wildly in his tightly clenched jaw. "I tried to defend my people. I drew my bow taut as a Bluecoat officer rode straight at me with his gun leveled.

"I wanted to kill him and he wanted to kill me.

Just as I loosed my arrow, my mother shoved me out of the way and the Bluecoat fired. She took the Bluecoat bullet meant for me." He exhaled slowly, deeply. "Her last words were 'Run, my son. Run.' But I held her, and her life's blood flowed across my hand as she died."

"When my father returned from hunting and saw my mother's body, he was so shocked that he cried out in English. He remembered who he was, and took me back East. I lost my mother and my people together."

Filled with a need to touch him, to share his grief, she rested her hand on his arm, iron-hard with tension. "I'm so sorry."

He looked down at her hand, so small and white against his dark bronze flesh. "I vowed then that I would kill that Bluecoat officer. Even during the years in Boston, even when I was shanghaied onto a sailing ship, I never forgot that vow."

"You were shanghaied? Why? How?"

"On the day of my father's funeral, my uncles got rid of me. They thought I'd never survive the voyage. But I did, and when the ship docked in San Francisco, I escaped and headed home to my people."

"And they welcomed you." Aurora said with a sudden understanding of his love for his people. What a contrast to the betrayals he'd suffered from white men.

"Yes, they opened their arms and hearts to me. And when I recovered my strength, I began searching for the Bluecoat who murdered my mother." He turned to her as he continued, "I rode the length and breadth of Arizona and New Mexico, searching for that red-bearded Bluecoat."

An icy shaft of fear knifed through Aurora. Papa had a beard in those long-ago days, and he'd been stationed in Arizona. Surely he couldn't—

"A red-bearded man with blue eyes."

Wolf's low voice was like the sound of doom as a thousand thoughts whirled in her head. She had to swallow twice before she had enough saliva to speak. "Did you ever find him?" Even as she asked, she already knew the answer.

He looked at her, and the fires of hate blazed high in his eyes. "You know I did, Aurora."

"You lie! Papa would never shoot a woman!" She whirled away, unable to face the tension and fury in him. Pacing to the other side of the cave, she rubbed her arms against the chill in her heart. "Besides, he doesn't have a beard. You can't be sure."

"But he did when he rode against my people on that day many harvests ago."

"I know my father. He's a decent man. He wouldn't do such a thing." She faced him, head held high. "You're wrong, Wolf. He might have whipped you, but he wouldn't kill a woman. You've recognized the wrong man."

"He's the right man. His hair was the same color as yours. That's not a common color. Besides, I knew who he was when he smiled at you in the storeroom. It was the same false smile he smiled when he shot my mother."

Aurora turned slightly, letting her hair shield her from his gaze. "He's a decent man; he wouldn't do such a thing," she repeated weakly.

"I speak true, Aurora."

She looked up. He watched her intently. Suddenly the icy horror of it struck her. The cave spun around her, and her knees gave way. She sat down abruptly. "Oh Lord, no," she moaned. "It can't be true."

What was she going to do?

Chapter 14

"That's the mesa where we go," Wolf said, pointing ahead to a flat-topped mountain. They had emerged from a mountain pass into a grassy valley and were walking beside the horse to rest it.

They'd been traveling hard for five days, following faint trails and no trails at all, through mountain pass after mountain pass.

Shielding her eyes with her hand, Aurora squinted at the distant purple peaks. "I can't see anything but mountains," she finally said. "Always mountains."

"Good, White-eyes. That is what the Mexicans see also. Nothing." Although they search for our stronghold, they can't find it. It takes Apache eyes to see it."

"And how did you find it, Apache?"

"My grandfather's grandfathers found it. Now it is Juh's Stronghold. He is *nantan* of the Apaches who live in Mexico."

Aurora was aware of the man walking beside her in every fiber of her being. She knew that his lips

194

tightened when she stumbled, that the brackets around his mouth had deepened as they progressed further into Mexico. She knew how long his stride was and that he would shorten it when she walked beside him.

She knew how often he glanced at her, and how often he reached out to touch her, then stopped. Since they'd left the cave, he'd made a point of not touching her except for unavoidable, quick, efficient touches. They'd walked beside each other, slept beside each other, eaten beside each other on the long trek, but there had been only rushed monosyllables—and silence.

"Juh has offered refuge to my people," Wolf continued.

"You make it sound as if you've been forced into exile. After all, you chose to run away." Though she would have done the same thing, she admitted to herself.

His eyes went iron-dark, iron-hard. "Your father would have rounded my people up like animals and sent them to San Carlos. He would have made the earth into a cage!" His voice was harsh with hate. "They chose to follow me. Yes, it is exile. We live far from our home, the home we've known for hundreds of harvests, the home you White-eyes have stolen."

"Damn it, my father doesn't want to hurt your people. He's just doing what he thinks is right." Why was she defending Pa when she didn't agree with what he was doing?

"Bah! He would slay my people until we were only a memory, lost in the dust."

"No, he wouldn't." She tugged at his arm, making him stop and face her. "Listen to me! You don't know Pa at all!"

"It is you who don't know your father." He stalked toward the plateau. A wall of silence fell between them.

Aurora walked beside the horse, wondering once again if Wolf spoke the truth about Pa. The whole time they'd ridden south, the question of whether her father had killed Wolf's mother had plagued her. Part of her said Pa was a decent man, he'd never shoot a woman; part of her said he hated Indians and could have done it.

Time and again she told herself it couldn't be true. Time and again she realized it explained Wolf's attack on her father when nothing else could.

"We're going up that?" Aurora exclaimed, looking up at the sheer two-hundred-foot cliff they'd reached. "It's twenty stories tall."

"It is easy. There is a trail."

She raised a disbelieving eyebrow at him. "You forget, Apache. I've seen what you call a trail."

"Nevertheless, it is the only way to get to the top." He started up the narrow path, leading the horse. She followed, slipping back one step for every two she took.

Finally they topped out. Panting, Aurora took that last step onto level ground and gazed around. The mesa was much larger than she'd expected. Horses and mules grazed belly-high in lush green grass. The breeze carried the scent of roasting meat, and beyond the horses, she saw an Apache village with many dome-shaped brush shelters hidden beneath towering oaks.

Wolf swung up on the bay stallion. Aurora held out her hand, expecting him to swing her up behind him.

"You will walk behind my horse."

"I will what?" Aurora stared at him.

"You heard me. It is important that The People see that I have returned unwounded. And that I return with a prisoner. Therefore you will walk."

A flush of anger swept her. "And if I refuse?" she asked as her chin came up.

"That is your choice. I will leave you here and go on to the village. And you will be fair game, available to any warrior who chooses to capture you." He turned the horse and set off for the village at a walk.

Aurora followed, eyes narrowed and blazing with fire. "I'll get you for this," she muttered under her breath.

They followed a wide, well-trodden path toward the village. Dogs barked an alarm. Women and children stared at them from among the wickiups. Warriors watched them, their rifles glinting in the sunlight.

A flashy black-and-white-spotted pony raced toward them, a slim Indian woman on its back. Slowing the pony only slightly, the dusky-skinned maiden leaped off and ran to Stalking Wolf. Clasping his moccasin in both hands, she held it to her breast and gazed up at him with adulation.

"Finally you're back, Ma'cho Nalzhee," Destarte gushed, smiling up at him. "When Geronimo returned without you, I feared for you."

"It wasn't necessary, Destarte." Disliking the way she was holding his foot and simpering up at him, Wolf lifted his leg over the horse's withers and slid off. "How is Blue Hawk?" he asked, resting an arm over her slim shoulders in brotherly fashion as they walked beside the horse.

"My brother's leg has bothered him since he

came back from the raid you led." She flipped her long, shiny black hair back over her shoulder so that it brushed across his arm when she moved her head.

"You should be proud of him. He did a warrior's work and led the Bluecoats straight into the trap we'd set for them. He has proved himself a man."

"I didn't ride out here to talk of Blue Hawk." Destarte threw him a flirty little sideways look.

What had gotten into her? he wondered. Apache maidens were chaste and well-mannered, and rarely spoke to a single man who was not a relative. It was rare for one to be as forward as Destarte.

"Who is your captive?" she asked, glancing back at Aurora, who was silently following them.

"The woman I sought." His plans were his business.

Although he didn't seem to watch her, Wolf was aware of the calculating look Destarte shot him. "It's good you brought her back instead of killing her. We need another slave to help with the harvest. Geronimo has looked into the future and says the months of Ghost Face will be long this year. He says we must store much food."

"I will decide what the woman does," he replied stiffly.

Aurora watched the exchange, understanding all too well the way the girl looked up at Wolf. But it was the baleful looks the Apache girl shot her that put Aurora on guard. Her own eyes went to Wolf's broad back. As though he felt her gaze, he glanced over his shoulder.

Destarte's dark eyes narrowed at the look that passed between Wolf and his captive. "What does this woman mean to you?" she cried.

He would have to be careful with Destarte, he realized, and never let down his guard. She was like a viper, slipping in and striking under cover of darkness. Although she wouldn't attack him, she wouldn't hesitate to attack someone weaker than her—someone like the flame-haired woman.

"She is my hostage, Destarte. Her father will pay many rifles and bullets to get her back." He realized it was the first time he'd thought of Artemus Spencer in days. Aurora had filled his thoughts instead. The memory of the passion they'd shared in the sunny glade lingered in a place in his heart he hadn't known existed.

But now, for The People's sake, he'd have to put all thoughts of Aurora aside. The People needed guns and ammunition, which were essential for hunting during the time of Ghost Face and for defense against enemies, both Mexican and Bluecoat.

Destarte halted and faced him. "And what if her father doesn't?" she hissed like a snake.

"That is a choice he will have to make. His daughter or his guns." The choice would be doubly cruel for *Nantan* Spencer, for he had to know the guns would be used against his men. Satisfaction surged through Wolf. Let Spencer be slashed by his own sword. "Either way, I have uses for her."

"You would spend your seed in her? We need warriors, not weaklings. You are strong and brave, Ma'cho, you can give us many warriors. But not if you spend your seed in a White-eyes such as her." Turning, she spat at Aurora.

"That is for me to decide, Destarte"—his mild voice hinted of steel—"not you."

Destarte's shoulders straightened and she pinned him with eyes narrowed in fury. "You will regret bringing this woman into our stronghold. Mark my words, Ma'cho Nalzhee, you will live to curse the day you brought her here." Whistling to her spotted pony, Destarte swung up and galloped off.

Aurora quickened her pace. "What did she say?"

"Nothing that concerns you." He mounted the horse and left her to follow on foot.

Boys rode to meet them, circling as if they were a wagon train. Their wild cries were the heart-stopping cries of young warriors.

"They practice their attack," Wolf called as clouds of dust rose around them.

"But some can't be more than five or six," Aurora exclaimed, dismayed.

"Apache children must grow up quickly if they are to survive." As they neared the village, he added, "Stay close to me, White-eyes."

The village was much larger than she'd thought. Some wickiups were visible in the clearing, but many more were hidden beneath the oaks and maples. All faced east and the rising sun.

The warriors smiled and called to Wolf while giving Aurora appraising looks that made her feel naked. The women smiled at Wolf, but when they gazed at Aurora there was no welcome in their square, mahogany faces, only menace.

As Wolf and Aurora began to pass between the wickiups, she edged closer to the horse. A stone struck her in the back. Then a large rock. She winced, but didn't look back, just walked on, head held high. The hot bite of a lash wrapped around her shoulders. Shocked by the pain, she stumbled and went to her knees. Glancing over her shoulder, she saw a withered old crone smile evilly as she lifted her whip again.

"Wolf," she cried.

Leaping from the stallion, he was at her side in an instant. Reaching down, he grasped her around the waist with his powerful hands and lifted her up like a rag doll. He crushed her to his side, his long fingers resting possessively on her breast.

Aurora stiffened and took a deep breath, but knew this was neither the time nor the place to object.

He spoke quietly yet authoritatively to the women who crowded around them. She scanned them. Their expressions ranged from dislike to hatred. She leaned against Wolf, suddenly glad for his protection.

"Don't give me any more trouble," he muttered as he shoved her in front of him.

"Who? Me?" She had to trot to stay ahead of his long-legged stride. "Where are we going?"

"To Geronimo's wickiup. Then mine."

He halted before a wickiup facing a cleared area in the center of the village. The stocky, gray-haired man she'd seen on the night of Wolf's escape stood outside.

"This is Geronimo." Wolf shoved the horse's reins into her sweaty hands. "Wait here."

Geronimo stepped forward and hugged Wolf. "We have watched for you for many sleeps. What held you up?"

Wolf nodded at Aurora. "The woman was bitten by a rattlesnake. I waited until she was strong enough to travel." He didn't mention that she'd been trying to escape when she was bitten. That was between him and her.

Geronimo lifted a questioning eyebrow at him. "Does my sister's son grow weak in the head that he would wait for a captive to regain her health? Why not just leave her?"

"It was important, Uncle. Her father will not trade the guns and ammunition we need if all we have is a body."

"He would not have known until it was too late." Geronimo crossed his arms over his barrel chest.

"She saved my life when I was a prisoner of the White-eyes," Wolf replied stiffly. "I am an Apache warrior. Could I do less?"

"Humph! Chili Eater went back to look for you." His arms still crossed over his chest, Geronimo circled Aurora, studying her. "He said the desert swarmed with Bluecoats looking for you and the woman. Where did you hide?"

"I took her to the cave where my mother gave me life." Wolf rested his hand on Aurora's shoulder in a gesture both possessive and protective.

"*Ha she!*" Geronimo's brow furrowed and his gaze went from Wolf to Aurora. "Already she means much to you."

"She means guns and bullets. That's all. Has her father sent a reply to my message?"

"Not yet. But Pony That Talks tied the paper with your scratchings around a rock and threw it through the window of *Nantan* Spencer's wickiup in the Bluecoats' fort."

"*Enjuh.*"

Geronimo glanced at Aurora again, pulling on his eyebrow, as he often did when deep in thought. "Come inside," he finally said, brushing aside the deerhide covering the entrance to his wickiup. "We will talk."

As he ducked through the opening, Wolf glanced

over his shoulder at Aurora. "Stay with the horse, White-eyes, and don't try anything."

"In the middle of an Apache village?" Aurora said, desperately trying to keep up her courage.

Closing her eyes, she leaned her head against the horse's warm neck and inhaled the familiar aromas of hot horse and leather, and told herself she wasn't really a captive in an Apache village. She was just having a nightmare. Soon she'd awaken, safe in her bed in Fort Bowie. The horse snorted and sidled away, killing her dreams.

Her shoulders still stung from the whip, and she rolled them gingerly. Keeping her head down, she looked around through the veil of her lashes. A silent throng of women surrounded her, staring at her. Although they were shorter than she was, most weighed more, and the young ones looked as muscular as the men.

A cackling old crone moved closer, her eyes narrowed with hatred, and jabbed Aurora in the shoulder. Another woman grabbed a hank of Aurora's flaming hair and jerked hard, as if to see if it was real. The women were fascinated by her hair, and first one then another pulled it, jerking her head this way and that.

A man's low, guttural voice came from the back of the crowd. His voice cut across the women's silence like a knife, and they parted and fell back, revealing Bear Killer. Aurora tensed, instinctively afraid.

Another brave stood beside him. They sauntered toward her and stopped just inches from her, one on each side. Aurora backed against the horse. Bear Killer's viper eyes moved over her slowly. The other brave also studied her as they talked, and

Aurora didn't need to understand Apache to know that they were discussing her and that she wouldn't like what they were saying.

She shuddered as an evil smile creased Bear Killer's ugly features. With no warning, he grasped her breasts through her shirt and squeezed painfully hard.

"Wolf," she screamed.

She didn't know how he could move so fast, but he ducked out of the wickiup while her cry still hung in the air. Even so, Bear Killer's hands dropped away from her, although he still stood close.

Wolf straightened slowly, letting the deerhide slide down behind him with a rustle. "Are you all right?" he asked, watching Bear Killer.

"Y-yes." Wolf would protect her.

Bear Killer smiled evilly. "Does she squirm good under you, Ma'cho Nalzhee? Or have you had to take a whip to her?" His eyes narrowed. "You know, I think I'd take a whip to her anyway to teach her who owned her. Then I'd keep on taking it to her."

"Get away from her," Wolf growled. "She is mine."

Aurora glanced from one to the other. Bear Killer met Wolf's hard-eyed stare. The tension between the men was palpable, and her heart thudded against her ribs.

Slowly Bear Killer raised his hands and took a single step away from Aurora.

Wolf had all he could do not to walk over and snatch Aurora from between Bear Killer and his partner. "Drop the reins, White-eyes," he said quietly, "and come over here behind me." Aurora glanced fearfully at the brave on each side of her. "It's all right. They won't hurt you."

While Aurora crossed the open space to stand behind him, Wolf watched Bear Killer. Giving him a hatred-filled look, Bear Killer turned on his heel and strode away, as though she meant nothing to him. Suddenly he paused and spun around. "Better use her while you can, Stalking Wolf."

"Go back to your *tizwin*," Wolf snarled, referring to the corn beer that Bear Killer loved. He didn't move until Bear Killer had melted away among the wickiups.

When he turned, Aurora stared up at him, a hint of moisture in her enormous eyes and her lower lip quivering. He ran his thumb over her lip, as if that would stop her trembling. She blinked, and he could see tears hanging on her lashes like diamonds. He wanted to kiss them away.

"Come," he said gruffly. "I can see you'll cause less trouble if you're inside with me."

Instantly her chin snapped up. "*Me* cause trouble?"

Good, the threat of tears was past. "Come, I have work to do." He lifted the deerhide for her, then as she passed him, smacked her rump possessively. "Move."

She gave him a killing glance as she ducked inside. He followed, but she didn't move as fast as he'd expected, and when he stood up in the dimly lit interior, her lush bottom pressed against him. It was only for an instant, then she moved forward, but it was enough to leave his manhood rising to the occasion.

"Kneel behind me," he ordered, drawing her past Geronimo. Sitting down cross-legged and

resting his right arm on his knee, he prepared to
resume his conversation with Geronimo, Juh, and
several subchiefs.

Aurora knelt quietly behind Wolf, grateful for his
protection, yet part of her seethed at his brusque
orders. His broad back blocked her view of the
wickiup. She could smell his male scent mixed
with smoke. His buckskin vest was stretched tight
over his shoulders.

Besides Wolf and Geronimo, there was a very fat
man and four younger warriors, and except for
Wolf, they were all looking at her. She clasped her
hands in her lap and looked down demurely.

She looked up when a beautiful young woman
and Destarte entered with steaming bowls of stew.
Just as the other woman would have served Wolf,
Destarte elbowed her aside and knelt before him.

He stiffened, surprised and wary.

"I apologize for my harsh words earlier,
Ma'cho," she whispered, handing him tortillas and
a wooden bowl of stew. "I didn't mean them. I was
upset because of Blue Hawk's leg. I worry about
him so."

"Don't worry, Destarte. I knew it was not really
you speaking." But was it?

As the other girl moved around the fire, serving
the delicious-smelling stew and tortillas to each of
the men, she glanced at Aurora, giving her a shy
smile and a quick nod. Aurora smiled back, heart-
ened by the girl's fleeting contact.

The conversation between the men didn't slow
as they began to eat. No one offered Aurora
anything. As though rebelling, her stomach
growled loudly.

Without looking, as if he assumed she was

where he'd told her to kneel, Wolf reached back and handed her a tortilla.

"Thanks."

"Come up here, White-eyes." He patted the ground beside him. "We'll eat together."

She sat beside him, being careful not to touch him. He moved restlessly until his knee pressed against her thigh. She looked at it, then slowly raised her head. His eyes met hers and she realized his touch was deliberate.

Wolf took a mouthful of stew, then handed the bowl and spoon to Aurora as he turned to talk to another brave. Hungry, she took a large spoonful. She began to chew, expecting something like the acorn stew Wolf had made. Too late, she realized it was chili-seasoned and it was hot, hot, hot.

She could do nothing but finish chewing and swallow. Tears streamed down her cheeks, and she felt as if her mouth was on fire. Trying not to call attention to herself, she set the bowl down and raised her hand to cover her mouth.

As though sensing something was wrong, Wolf glanced at her. "What's the matter?"

"Hot," was all she could say in a choked, wispy voice she didn't recognize as her own.

Geronimo said something and handed Wolf a gourd full of liquid. "Here." Wolf handed it to her. "Geronimo took pity on you. He says, 'Drink this and the fire will die.'"

Aurora took a long swig of watery, sweet-tasting beer, and the burning sensation began to fade. She took another swallow. "*Gracias*," she said, looking at the gray-haired man, who was about her father's age.

He gave her the barest nod, then began talking to

the fat chief. Had she done something wrong? She glanced at Wolf. He seemed deep in conversation, but he shot her an approving glance. His gaze went to Geronimo then returned to her, and she realized he was telling her she'd done the right thing.

The sun had set by the time Wolf stood up. Rising, she followed him outside. "Where are we going now?"

"To my wickiup." He grasped her elbow in his large hand and guided her toward the edge of the village. "You have duties to perform there."

Her heart began to drum, but in the changing shadows, she couldn't see the expression in his eyes.

The violet blush of twilight slipped toward night as they followed an overgrown path up a slight rise toward a wickiup set back from the others. The aromas of smoke and roasting meat mingled with the rich earth scent of an oak forest. Dogs barked nearby. An owl hooted in the distance.

A shimmer of awareness swept through her as Wolf's long fingers stroked the sensitive skin on the inside of her wrist. She glanced at him as they walked side by side.

"Wolf, I—" Something whistled by her head.

Wolf jerked her back against him. She looked down. A bone-handled knife was embedded in the path in front of them.

"Good Lord, what's that?"

"It's all right, Aurora. I've been expecting it." He turned slowly as though he knew what he'd find.

Bear Killer stood in the path behind them, arms crossed over his chest, his legs spread in an arrogantly challenging stance. He was naked except for a dirty white breechclout. Beneath his heavy brow his eyes were narrowed and hate-filled.

Wolf said something in such an iron-hard tone that Aurora whipped around to stare at him. His lips had thinned to a straight line slashing across his grim features. A vein throbbed in his temple. It was the first time she'd seen him truly furious, and in the next heartbeat she was thankful his anger wasn't directed at her.

Bear Killer stiffened and grinned a mockery of a smile filled with cruelty. Aurora noticed many warriors emerging from their wickiups and drifting toward them.

Wolf shoved her behind him. Picking up the knife, he contemptuously tossed it to the ground in front of Bear Killer. Although he appeared to throw carelessly, the blade plunged into the hard-packed earth all the way to the hilt.

Bear Killer's evil grin grew wider. All the Apaches headed toward the center of the village.

"Come." Wolf paced back toward the village.

"What's happening?" Aurora ran to keep up with his long strides. "Why are we going back into the village?"

"I've decided to fight Bear Killer."

"What?" She grabbed his arm with both hands, trying to slow him. "But you can't. We've been traveling since before dawn. You're exhausted."

"Not too tired to fight Bear Killer." His glance sent a shiver of apprehension though her.

"Why now? Why not tomorrow?"

"Tomorrow would be too late. We must fight tonight. He has claimed you by right of first capture."

Chapter 15

"**N**o!" Aurora stopped dead, as if a giant fist had slammed into her. Her heart began to pound at the thought of Wolf fighting in his exhausted state. "Wolf, you can't. You're too tired, you'll get hurt. Please, no."

He looked back over his shoulder. "I must."

He kept walking and she ran to catch up with him, following him to the center of the village. A large circle had already been drawn in the dirt. It seemed as if every warrior, woman, and child was gathered around with torches.

"Here, Chili Eater, guard this woman well." Wolf thrust her toward a stocky brave.

Aurora realized he had used Spanish rather than Apache so that she'd understand. He took off his buckskin vest and handed it to Chili Eater.

In the meantime, Bear Killer had strutted to the center of the circle and said something that left the Apaches muttering among themselves and throwing sideways glances at Wolf. He stiffened. His head lowered slightly. His eyes hardened. Bear Killer's words had angered him even more. Was that what the man meant to do—anger Wolf into making a careless move?

As Wolf turned away, Aurora gripped his arm with both hands. "Please," she whispered. "You've got to be careful. I—I—" She broke off before she could say *I need you*.

His gaze held hers for a long heartbeat. "I will."

Wolf paced to the center of the ring and spoke to Bear Killer. A taut silence fell over the assembled Apaches.

"What did he say?" she asked Chili Eater in Spanish.

"He asked if Bear Killer is prepared to walk the Underworld before this night is done."

Bear Killer went into a menacing crouch. Firelight glinted off the long knife he tossed back and forth between his hands. Aurora sucked in her breath at the evil in his eyes.

Geronimo called to Wolf and threw him a knife. Wolf crouched, eyes on Bear Killer. He held the knife loosely, almost carelessly.

Bear Killer darted forward and slashed viciously. Wolf danced back, out of reach.

Aurora clamped her hands over her mouth as a scream rose in her. Wolf was fighting this savage for her. For her. She'd been thrust into a savage world where warriors fought for women.

The men feinted and dodged back and forth, slashing at each other. The clash and clang of their blades rang loud in the silence. Their grunts and gasps filled the air.

Bear Killer gave a cry of triumph as a long red ribbon of blood trailed down Wolf's right arm, his fighting arm. Aurora's stomach lurched as she caught the metallic scent of blood. Fear for Wolf made her heart pound, and she wrung her hands helplessly. She had to do something to help him! Unconsciously she took a step forward, but Chili Eater's hand on her arm stopped her.

Wolf countered Bear Killer's lunging knife with his own—and the blade broke off. Ducking away, he tossed the knife aside, then leaped at Bear Killer. They went down in a tangle of arms and legs, and choking clouds of dust billowed up as they rolled back and forth.

Aurora couldn't see them clearly; all she could hear was grunts and heavy thuds. Suddenly Wolf was on top, and time stood still as he raised his right arm high. Torchlight glinted on the knife he held. Bear Killer's knife. He looked at Bear Killer, then his arm plunged down.

Aurora screamed.

Breathing hard, his copper skin glistening with sweat, Wolf stood up. He looked down at the man he'd conquered.

Aurora's eyes widened with surprise as she realized that the knife wasn't buried in Bear Killer but plunged to the hilt in the dirt next to his head. Bear Killer sat up slowly, shaking his head to clear it. Wolf said something in a low tone only Bear Killer could hear.

Then, spinning on his heel, Wolf headed for Aurora, gazing at her with a fierce intensity that stole the breath from her lungs. She tensed, suddenly afraid of the uncivilized barbarian pacing toward her.

He moved with taut menace, like a lion that had killed a rival and was about to seize its lioness. Her heart galloped raggedly. She backed up. Something told her the battle between Bear Killer and Wolf wasn't over yet—and she was part of the final act.

She heard the Apaches murmuring in the background, but their voices faded as Wolf reached her. She lifted her head defiantly, meeting his hot, hard eyes.

Grasping her wrist, he spun her around and swept her back against himself. She cried out in alarm and pawed at his arm with as much effect as a fluttering moth. Lifting her off her feet, he held her against his hip and strode back into the circle.

He had acted so quickly that she didn't even have time to protest. He set her on her feet but kept her against him with one arm wrapped around her just beneath her breasts.

She could feel the heavy pounding of his heart against her shoulder blade. His chest rose and fell with each panting breath. Most of all, she was aware of the weight of her breasts on his arm.

Wherever she looked, Apaches gazed back impassively. Panic rose in her throat like a living beast.

"Wolf, let me go!" She twisted violently, frantic to loosen his grip.

"Be still," Wolf ordered. He spoke over her head to the Apaches facing him. He made a quarter-turn and repeated his words. Again Wolf made a quarter turn and spoke over her head. The faces were a blur except for Destarte, who smiled at her with unmistakable hatred.

Again they turned. This time Wolf spoke in Spanish. "Look closely at this woman. She is mine. She sleeps in my wickiup. To want her is to fight me."

She knew he'd spoken in Spanish so that she would understand. Boneless with despair and shock, she sagged against him. All that held her up was his blood-streaked right arm. Never had she felt so far away and lost to everything she'd ever known.

Wolf released her and grasping her elbow, guided her toward Chili Eater. Flushed with triumph, he glanced at her. His eyes widened when he saw her too-white face. Stopping, he crooked his finger under her chin and lifted her bowed head until their eyes met.

"I had to protect you, my *kun isdzán*. It was the only way."

Her brow furrowed. "What are you talking about?"

"Bear Killer would have been only the first. You attracted warriors today as honey attracts bees."

His face swam before her as understanding swept over her. She rested her hand on his forearm as she swayed, suddenly dizzy. He'd been protecting her. "My God," she murmured weakly. He'd fought to protect her.

His arms locked around her. "You're not going to faint, are you, *isdzán?*"

She gave him a faint smile. "No, my warrior," she said on a bare breath of sound.

He eyed her for several heartbeats. *"Enjuh."* But he kept her pressed against him as they walked toward his friend.

"Chili Eater, I—" Wolf broke off. His friend's gaze was on Aurora. White-hot anger surged through Wolf, taking him completely by surprise. His mouth grimmed to a thin line. He'd had to fight Bear Killer to establish his right to her, now he realized he was also very willing to fight his best friend merely for looking at her.

Wolf pushed Aurora behind him. Startled, Chili Eater glanced at him. His eyes widened with shock at Wolf's hard-eyed glare.

"A man can look, can't he?" Chili Eater gave a nervous laugh.

"No! Where's my vest?" Ripping it out of Chili Eater's hand, Wolf turned and slipped it over Aurora's shoulders. "Here, wear this over your shirt." The vest, made for his broad shoulders and deep chest, was huge on her, but he tugged the soft buckskin forward on her shoulders and pulled the front halves together.

"Come. We will go to my wickiup." Grabbing a torch from a warrior, he wrapped his large hand around her elbow and guided her through the Apaches. Aurora held her head high, even as the implications of Wolf's words echoed in her mind.

As they left the village, the path narrowed and Wolf dropped behind. Her awareness of the man who paced behind her grew with each step. She could hear his light breathing and feel his warm breath wafting past her cheek. The leather vest she wore was branded with his scent.

When he reached past her to push a branch out of the way, his fingers grazed her shoulder and left a tingling trail. They were alone in a primitive world, two people with an uncanny consciousness of each other.

He'd fought to protect her. He'd protected her at risk of his life. The knowledge sang in her blood like fire-warmed wine.

Wolf followed Aurora, his blood still pulsing with the heat of combat. His nostrils flared as he inhaled her woman scent mixed with his own from the buckskin vest. It was a potent aphrodisiac, he thought—as if he needed one. He wanted his scent all over her.

In the circle, as he'd spoken to his people, another part of his mind had been aware of the

curve of her bottom pressing against his thighs, the
sweet smell of her wind-tossed hair, the gentle
weight of her breasts on his arm. He'd been aware
of all those things and a thousand more he couldn't
even name. Swallowing heavily, he tamped down
the power and need that surged through him with
volcanic force.

He wanted to sink into her softness and lose
himself in her warmth. He wanted her to wrap her
legs around his waist. He wanted her to cry his
name in the helpless urgency of passion. He
wanted . . . her.

At the wickiup, he threw back the wolfhide that
covered the entrance and motioned for her to
enter. Aurora glanced up at him, at this warrior
who'd risked his life for her. The flaring torch lit his
rugged features and showed her the flames in his
eyes.

She ducked inside and paused, waiting for her
eyes to adjust themselves to the dim light. The
wickiup was bare except for a couple of baskets
and a single cast-iron cooking pot, visible in the
flickering torchlight. Looming large on the other
side of the firepit was a pile of brown buffalo robes.
His bed, she thought. Their bed. She looked away
hastily.

Wolf entered and let the wolfhide slide down. He
tossed the torch in the firepit and halted behind
her. Silent. Not touching her. Still.

Aurora stopped breathing, aware of a savage
silence. This man had protected her from horrors
she could barely imagine. He'd fought for her.
He'd risked his life for her. She was his prize. He'd
won her.

His male scent mingled with the pungent scent
of pine pitch from the torch. She could feel the

thrumming of her pulse throughout her whole body.

She was a civilized woman and she'd been thrust into a primitive world. A world where a man fought to protect what was his. And now he would claim her.

When he rested his large hand on her shoulder, she jumped. She'd known he was going to touch her, yet still she was unprepared, and her heart leaped at the sensation of his long fingers brushing the hollow of her shoulder.

The fire began to catch, lighting the wickiup.

Her blood was racing, pulsing, thrumming. She shivered.

Wolf's hand tightened on her shoulder, and he turned her to face him. She stared up at him in the flickering light, alive as she'd never been alive. His primitive maleness set her heart to hammering against her ribs.

"My woman of flame," he murmured, wrapping his hand around the slender column of her throat. His thumb brushed the hollow where her pulse pounded.

Instinctively she reached up to clasp his hand, and felt warm, sticky wetness. Shocked, she pulled his hand down and studied it in the flaring light.

"My God, you're still bleeding." Her eyes widened as she took in the long bloody trail down his arm. Her nostrils flared at the iron scent of blood. His blood, shed for her. "Why didn't you tell me? Come to the fire where I can see it better."

"It's nothing." But he let her lead him closer to the fire. "It'll stop bleeding soon."

"If it was going to stop bleeding, it would have stopped already. I need some water and a cloth to clean it."

"There's water in the *tus* over there." He indicated a tightly woven, bottle-shaped basket sealed on the inside with pine pitch. "But it's not bad, it's only a scratch."

"Ha! If it was a mere scratch, it wouldn't still be bleeding." She ripped the tail off her shirt to use as a swab. Tipping the *tus*, she wet the cotton, then gently wiped the blood away.

Aurora was well aware of him watching her, but she didn't look up. Her brow furrowed as she cleansed the long gash in his arm. It was far deeper than she'd first thought. He must have been in pain, but not once had it shown on his stern features.

"It looks as if he missed all the tendons, but not for lack of trying."

"Enough, woman," he growled, pulling away from her.

She looked up and immediately regretted it. He was so close, so male, so powerful, so primitive. But she was a civilized woman, used to civilized men.

He reached for her.

"No!" She ducked away from him. "You may have defeated Bear Killer, but you haven't won me." She had to fight the thrumming of her blood; she couldn't let him think he'd won her just by fighting for her. It was too primitive, too savage, too shocking. "You'll—you'll never have my heart," she finished in a rush.

Pine scented the wickiup, but beneath it, he could smell her woman scent. His gaze touched the swell of her breasts, visible beneath her shirt. He reached over and brushed his thumb over the dark circle of her nipple, barely visible through the thin cotton. "I don't need your heart." *Liar*, he thought, and was shocked by the realization. He wanted her heart above all else. "I have your body and it says you want me."

"My body lies." It was she that lied, she chided herself. She trembled, aware of a hot need throbbing deep inside her. Ever since they'd left the village, a need to touch and be touched by this man had been building.

She drew a single finger down one of the deep brackets edging his mouth. It was firm now, but she'd seen it when it was soft and sensual, had felt his soft, sensual lips all over her body in places she hadn't known could feel. Until he showed her.

He turned his head and scraped his teeth over her finger. She drew a sharp breath, wanting him.

"Oh, Wolf," she whispered.

He pushed the leather vest back, then slowly, deliberately, unbuttoned her shirt. He pushed both off her shoulders, the slither of soft leather combined with the dry rustle of cotton. His hot gaze swept her like liquid flame.

"My Aurora, you are so—" His brow furrowed and he peered intently at her breast. "There is blood on your breast. Are you hurt?"

"Blood?" She felt as though she was speaking in a long tunnel. She looked down at the reddish-brown streak. "No, it must be yours." Her breath thickened in her throat.

"I'll wash it off," he said in a voice deeper than the deepest well. He took the wet cloth from her hand.

It was cool on her heated skin, and his touch soft as the finest silk. She trembled as the cold cloth circled her nipple and he washed his blood from her breast.

Without taking his eyes off her, he threw the

cloth over his shoulder into the fire, where it sizzled and spat steam.

An eternity passed. She waited, wanting him.

He swung her up in his arms and stalked across the wickiup to the buffalo robes piled on a bear grass mattress. There he let her legs swing down, but he kept her against him, fitting her softness to his hardness. His gazed moved over her features slowly, cataloguing them. Then his lips crashed down on hers, and his kiss was hot and hard—a victor's kiss, a triumphant kiss full of want and need.

And she recognized it and met it and knew it with a shivery sense of wonder as her lips bloomed for him.

Wolf's mouth was hungry, searching, demanding. She met him with her own hunger and demand. He sank to his knees, taking her with him. Gently he laid her down on the buffalo robes, so gently that she was startled by the feel of the woolly fur against her back. With a last kiss to her breast, he untied the waistband of her skirt, then pulled it away along with her underdrawers.

He stood over her, tall as a lodge pole and just as stalwart. The dim golden light burnished his rugged sinews.

Her heart leaped into her throat, and she rested her arm over her eyes, suddenly shy. He stretched out beside her and studied her from the tousled locks curling around her face to the darker curls where her legs joined.

Finally Aurora couldn't stand it. "Please," she whispered, "don't look at me. It embarrasses me."

He trailed a tantalizing finger across her breasts. "Aurora, don't you know it's natural for a man to want to look at his woman? Don't be ashamed. It's part of what happens between a man and a woman. And I am only a man."

"I thought you were an Apache warrior," she shot back.

"In other times and other places. But in this time and this place, I am only a man. A man who wants you." He dropped a kiss soft as a snowflake on her breast.

He leaned over her, resting his weight on his hands on either side of her head as he gazed down at her. "You have such blue eyes. Sometimes I feel as if I'm falling into the sky."

"And your eyes are so endlessly dark. At first I thought I was looking all the way to Hades." She combed her fingers through his silky black hair.

"And what do they remind you of now?" he murmured as he flicked his tongue over the red raspberry of her nipple.

"They're just as dark, but now I know that I'm looking into a well." A delicious shimmer of tension radiated out from her breasts. "A well hiding so much of the man."

Lifting his head, he gazed at her for the longest time. His eyes searched hers. The corners of his mouth tilted up. "I believe you mean that, my fire woman." He bent to blow a gentle breath over her breast, still moist from his tongue.

"Let me pleasure you," she breathed on a bare wisp of sound.

Wordlessly he rolled over on his back, taking her with him. She sprawled over him, her legs tangled with his. Bracing her hands on his chest, she lifted herself enough to look down into his eyes. Her long hair flowed over them, veiling them in their own world.

"Now I have you in my power," she murmured, brushing her thumb across his sensual lips.

"You've had me in your power for a long time," he admitted softly.

Slowly she lowered her head until her lips touched his. She had intended to make it a quick, teasing kiss, but the instant their lips met, she was lost. His long fingers wove through her hair and he pressed upward, seeking more of her passion, drinking it from her lips.

Finally she reared back, gasping. Wolf reached for her, trying to fill his hands with her firm, high breasts, but she batted his hands away. "I'm in charge here," she reminded him, then dropped a tiny kiss on his dark nipple.

Leaning over him, she moved her head back and forth slowly, drawing her tresses over his chest in silken, feather-light brushes. Wolf lay back, watching, absorbing, feeling. Taking several strands between her fingers, she drew intricate, teasing patterns on his chest. And in between those so-soft touches, she rained kisses over him. Wolf held himself utterly still as she teased and taunted him, but his smothered groans told her he was enjoying the game as much as she.

Slowly, building up her courage, she let her hand drift lower and lower. She watched his half-closed eyes as she wrapped her fingers around his manhood.

His slow, heavy sigh told her that he liked her hand there. "Do you like this?" She moved her hand up and down.

"Umm. Too much."

He groaned with pleasure as Aurora moved her hand along his length. She did it again and again, watching the strain of fighting drain out of his rugged features until the delicious anticipation of their joining was the only tension left in him. That was when Aurora leaned over him and took him in her mouth.

He jerked violently at her warm, moist touch. Instinctively he grabbed her shoulders, then, as he gazed at her poised above him, he knew it was no mistake. "Thank you," he said simply. His fingers loosened until he was rubbing her shoulders.

"Now it's my turn," he said a few minutes later, pushing her over onto her back. Bending over her, he kneed her legs apart and settled between them.

Even though she wanted him, she tensed when his manhood pressed against her. He didn't move. His eyes were shadowed, but she could have sworn a tiny smile softened his sensual lips.

"Beautiful *kun isdzán*, this is our destiny," he whispered. He shook his head, brushing his long hair over her sensitive breasts with the finesse of a painter's brush.

He rolled her nipple between his forefinger and thumb with gentle roughness. Aurora closed her eyes and drank him into her senses. Then slowly, so slowly, his hand wandered lower over her belly and lower still. His finger brushed across her wet curls.

"Oh, Wolf, you make me want you." Even she could hear the soft throatiness in her voice.

"Not half as much as I want you." He rained fiery kisses over her. Slipping his hand between them, he entered her with two fingers, stroked her secret place. Aurora bucked as her heart thudded against her ribs.

"I want you to feel everything I'm going to do to you."

"And what are you going to do?" She raked her

fingers down his sweat-slick back with not-quite-painful pressure, making him shudder violently.

"First I'm going to do this," Wolf muttered. He entered her slowly, giving her time to adjust herself to his presence.

She was ready for him and wrapped her long legs around his waist. "Then what?"

He told her in explicit words as he surged into her time and again.

"Show me," she taunted, returning his movements with her own in a fierce dance of life.

And he did.

Their need was great, their blood hot. Each demanded much. Each gave much.

Within minutes, Aurora tensed. "Wolf!" she cried as he forged into her again, driving her over the edge.

"Yes!" Wolf cried as the spasms of her body embraced him. "Aurora! Yes!" His voice was tight with tension as he gave one more powerful, shuddering thrust. He crushed her in his arms as he reveled in victory.

Aurora drifted back to earth gently, too satiated to move or think. Locked in Wolf's brawny arms, she had found all she needed to make her world complete.

He was sprawled over her, blanketing her, and she basked in the knowledge that he, too, had been carried away.

Wolf stirred and drew a long breath. He started to lift his weight off her, but she grasped his shoulders and pulled him back down. "No. Don't. I like feeling your weight on me."

"That was *enjuh*, my *kun isdzán*," he said, dropping a tiny kiss on her cheek. "Was it *enjuh* for you also?"

"Very." She explored his sinew-corded shoulders with gentle fingers. "Very *enjuh*."

When Aurora awakened, it was the middle of the night. The moon shone through the smoke hole, lighting the interior of the wickiup with a soft, silver light. She glanced at the man who slept beside her. He lay on his stomach, one arm thrown possessively over her.

She snuggled closer, wanting to touch him and hold him and never let him go. Never had she been as happy as she was at that moment. Her heart was full of a warmth and joy unlike anything she'd ever felt.

Could she be falling in love with him? she wondered. Smiling, she remembered that as a romantic child she'd dreamed of being carried off by a prince on a white horse. Never in her wildest dreams had she pictured an Indian chief on a bay horse!

Wolf tightened his arm around her and dropped a butterfly-soft kiss on her breast. "Are you warm enough, *isdzán*?" he asked, pulling the buffalo robe up over her shoulders.

"Umm." She didn't want to talk. She wanted to think about this incredible, magic fire that flared between them. Was this what love was?

As she gazed at him in the silver moonlight her eyes met his, and she knew he had to feel something also. He had to. This fire wasn't hers alone.

"Sleep, *kun isdzán*," Wolf murmured, wrapping his arms around her and drawing her close. "This night is ours."

But was it? And what would the day bring?

Chapter 16

A week later, Aurora knelt beside their fire making tortillas. Her hand still ached from grinding the hard, dried corn between two stones. Earlier, before sunrise, the other women had roused her and taken her berry picking.

She wore the turquoise cotton skirt and white peasant blouse Wolf had brought her. The blouse's round neck and long sleeves were gathered by drawstrings, and she'd adjusted it so that she was covered as primly as any schoolteacher in Philadelphia. Well, almost as primly.

"She Who Sees Babies is doing a good job teaching you to cook. It's a good thing, too. Geronimo's wife was tired of seeing us at their campfire." Wolf sat cross-legged at the other side of the fire, watching her. "She's complained to me that you don't work fast enough picking berries."

Aurora decided to ignore his last comment. "Is that what she's called?" In her mind she'd been calling the crabby old crone more descriptive names.

"Yes. She's a midwife. You and she ought to

compare notes on birthing techniques." He wore only blue denim pants, and his mahogany shoulders gleamed in the late-afternoon sun.

"Fat chance," Aurora muttered. Taking a ball of cornmeal dough, she worked it between the heels of her palms, flattening it into a lumpy square that barely resembled the round tortillas She Who Sees Babies made. Peeling the sticky dough off her palm, she dropped it on the hot stone she'd placed at the edge of the fire. So what if it wasn't round, she thought, eyeing it balefully as it sizzled and spat steam.

She was making progress. Two days earlier she'd added too much water, and the cornmeal had become a soupy glop. Wolf had given it to the camp dogs, then mixed up fresh dough and made the tortillas himself. As he'd worked, women had wandered by, tittering shyly behind their hands when they saw their chief cooking dinner for his captive woman.

The edges of her tortilla began to curl up. Now came the hard part—trying to grab an edge and flip the tortilla without burning her fingers. After several passes, she caught it and flipped the tortilla. Only half flipped. The other half stayed glued to the hot rock and was rapidly charred to a blackened mass that not even the dogs would eat.

"Try again," Wolf offered. "You're getting better." He stretched out on his side in the sweet-smelling grass and propped his hand on his bent arm.

"Are you sure you don't want to make them? Yours taste so much better than mine."

"Yours are getting better—or I'm getting used the taste of burnt corn."

Aurora rolled her eyes and tried again, wondering if she'd ever get the hang of it. "Who's that beautiful young girl with the boy baby?" she asked. The girl had touched her hand and smiled encouragingly while the old crone was haranguing her as if she understood Apache already.

"Izzago Lanni, Many Tongues. She had her baby on the trail when The People fled from our land."

"She's so beautiful." Aurora dropped a thick tortilla on the hot rock. "And proud of her baby."

"He's her first. Her husband was killed fighting the Bluecoats, and the baby is all she has, so she—"

"Aurora! Aurora!"

At the familiar voice, she glanced over her shoulder and spied a cadaverously thin, gray-haired man laboring up the slight slope.

"Pincus!" Picking up her skirts, she flew to greet him. "I'm so glad to see you." She hugged him close. "Are you all right? Where have you been?"

"My dear child," he said, giving her a great big bear hug, "you can't imagine my joy at seeing you alive and well. Have you been here long?"

"I've been waiting for you a week, but I—" She broke off as Wolf slipped his arm around her waist and jerked her to his side. Aurora glanced up and found him dark-countenanced and threatening as a summer storm. "What's the matter?"

He ignored her as he spoke to Pincus. "You're lucky you're an old man. A young one would not live to see the sun set today."

"Why are you getting all huffy? You know Pincus is an old friend."

"And you! You do not go around hugging other men in my village. Once a woman cleaves to a man, she doesn't run around with other males. Apache women are chaste."

"But I'm not an Apache woman," she replied in a sweet tone dripping with enough sugar to choke an ox. "Remember?"

"I remember." His dark eyes raked her. "I remember exactly who you are, Aurora Elizabeth Spencer." His deep, gravelly voice held an undercurrent of tension that she hadn't heard in days. "Even so, I'll let you speak to this old man because you knew him in your other life." He strode away before she could give him a piece of her mind.

When she would have run after him to argue, Pincus stopped her.

"Don't, Aurora. He was just warning you. Remember, he's a chief and his people look to him for a lot of things. Now, come along to my wickiup, child, and fill me in on what's happened to you."

"Your wickiup?"

"Yes. Geronimo had the women put one up for me. And I'm beginning to think they actually want me to take pictures of their way of life: they saved my photographic supplies when they captured us. From what Geronimo has grunted from time to time, I think Stalking Wolf had a lot to do with it." They walked toward the village beneath shimmering oak leaves.

"When you and Wolf didn't arrive at the village, the Apaches were very upset," Pincus continued. "They had search parties scouring the desert for you."

"Humph! The soldiers and the Apaches both sent out search parties looking for us, but neither found us."

"Where were you?" He dodged around two

naked little boys playing in the dirt between the wickiups.

"Wolf took me to a cave high in the Chiricahua Mountains to recuperate."

He glanced back at her over his shoulder. "Why did you need to recuperate?"

"I was bitten by a rattlesnake. That's what held us up."

"But you're all right now?"

"Yes. I'm fine."

"You're sure? Ah, here we are at my wickiup." He stopped at a shelter beneath a huge old oak and ducked inside.

Aurora pushed aside the deerhide and bent to follow him into the dim interior, but Pincus shook his head. "No, Aurora, I think you'd better stay outside. I have a feeling chaste Apache women don't go into single men's wickiups."

"Oh, pooh, it'll be all right." But Aurora paused and glanced around anyway. Three women were watching her. She straightened and let the deerhide fall back into place. "Maybe you're right, Pincus. I'll just wait out here."

He returned in a moment with a stack of photographs. "Come, sit down and look at these, Aurora. Pictures like these have never been taken before. Some of them are truly remarkable, because I've been able to show the Apaches in their normal home life." He grimaced. "Or what passes for normal. It's such an incredibly hard life, I don't know how any survive.

"Here, look at this." Pincus handed her one from his stack. "This is Geronimo's wife making *tizwin*." He showed her a stocky woman stirring a large kettle. "The warriors say that's why he married her. He loves her *tizwin*.

"You're amazing, Pincus. How did you learn so much about these people? Do you speak Apache already?"

"Not yet, but I'm learning—and improving every day. I just speak Spanish to whoever's guarding me. Almost all of them understand it." He shook his head. "I'm beginning to wonder if there isn't something wrong with our Indian policy. We call them stupid savages, yet most of them speak two languages, and many speak English also. How many Americans speak two, let alone three, languages?"

"Do you realize you sound as if you're enjoying this, as if it's been an adventure?"

"I guess that's the way I've treated it so far. And remember, neither of us has been harmed."

"No, thank God, that's true. Have you shown these photos to anyone?"

"You're the first. But with pictures like these, I'll have enough material for at least five or six front-page stories when I get back to Washington."

"Or a book. You've taken enough."

"A book?" He shuffled the photos slowly, studying each. "Hmm, I never considered that."

"It's just a thought." Aurora rested her hand on his. "Pincus, thank you for charging the Apaches that day. It was the bravest thing I've ever seen anyone do." He gazed at her hand for a long moment, and when he raised his eyes, Aurora was surprised to see a hint of moisture in them.

"It was nothing, really," he said gruffly. "You know I don't have any family except for my brother and his children, and I've come to look upon you like a daughter. Besides, I probably never would have photographed these people if it hadn't been for you. So it's worked out for me, but that doesn't mean it has for you. Are you truly all right, child?"

Aurora felt her cheeks redden as she realized what he meant. Of course he'd know what happened to a woman in captivity, yet it gave her a strange feeling. "Oh yes, fine. Really, I'm fine. Perfectly fine."

"Methinks the lady doth protest too much."

"No, I don't." Aurora met his droopy brown eyes. "I owe Wolf my life," she burst out. "I was trying to escape when the rattler bit me."

"Ah ha. So, there is more to the story. Tell me all that's happened."

She was sitting Indian-style on the thick, sweet-smelling grass, just finishing her tale, when a man's dark shadow fell between her and Pincus. She gazed at it for a moment, thinking it was like a knife cutting her off from her old life. Then she looked up—not that she needed to.

"Hello, Wolf." She tried to remain relaxed and nonchalant in the face of his wide-legged, arms-crossed-over-the-chest stance.

Wolf inhaled, drawing her scent deep into his lungs. Would he ever get enough of her? Just watching her sitting here, talking to another man, had driven him crazy. He'd wandered around the camp, ostensibly talking to warriors about laying in extra stores for the coming winter, but he'd always managed to stand where he could watch his woman of fire.

She'd gone up in flames in his arms last night. Just the memory created a magnificent tension in his loins and sent the blood rushing through his veins like a storm of hot sunlight. It seemed always to be that way when he was around her. She glanced at him, and her eyes widened. Then she stared steadfastly at his face, and he knew it was because she'd seen his arousal.

Turning, she practically dove toward the stack of photos piled beside the old man. "Wolf, you've got to see these pictures Pincus has taken. They're wonderful, a whole fresh view of your people."

"You mean they're not killing White-eyes?"

She looked up at him as he towered over her. "Is that the kind you want? Killing and more killing?"

"No, you're right." He hunkered down on the grass beside her. "I would like to see my people shown as they are. People. Not savages. Not animals. Just people whose lifeway is different from the White-eyes way."

"Then look at these, Apache." Her voice was low and throaty and resonated through him.

"That's the hoop-and-pole game." Her fingers brushed his palm as she handed him the photo. "Ah, these are *enjuh*," he said, studying the pictures. He looked up at the old man. "You are a good photographer. You've caught more than flat images. You've caught the spirit of my people."

"Why, thank you, my boy."

Wolf's eyes hardened. "I'm not your boy."

"No, no, of course not—I didn't mean to imply—I just meant to say thank you." Pincus bent over the pictures and thumbed through them furiously before he selected one to hand over. "Here's a good one of Blue Hawk and his flute."

"It is. It's too bad you can't record his music, too. The music is so pure, it flows from his flute directly to the hearts of those who hear it." Wolf handed the photograph back. "Do you have a picture of an Apache prisoner with his hair held back? You know, the one you were going to send back to the people in Washington so they could see what their boys in blue were doing to protect the West."

The photographer paled, but he answered quietly, "It's back at Fort Bowie. I didn't bring the exposed plates with me."

Wolf eyed Pincus for a moment that seemed to stretch as tautly as a bowstring before he nodded sharply. "You have courage, old man. That is what has kept you alive."

"And you too, I think," Pincus replied with a tone of respect in his voice.

"Perhaps." He turned to Aurora and she felt as if a light had focused on her. "It is time to eat, woman. You need to prepare our meal." He looked over her head at Pincus. "Join us, old man, if you like your food charred black on the outside and raw on the inside."

"Sounds better than my cooking." Pincus shot Aurora an encouraging smile. "Besides, I can't believe Aurora doesn't know how to cook."

"You will after you taste my disasters," Aurora said.

They talked as they wound their way through the village. Wolf held her elbow or rested his hand in the middle of her back or on her shoulder, but Aurora found she didn't mind. There was something about having his hand on her that made her feel protected and safe. She glanced up at him several times, trying to understand the attraction she felt for him.

Attraction, she thought wryly. What a weak word for the all-encompassing awakening of her senses when she was with him. Being with him was like being in a different world, a world with jewel-like colors and rainbows of scents.

As they walked through the trees, a ghostly

melody drifted by on the breeze. At first Aurora thought it was the wind whistling through mountain passes, but gradually, as she listened to the notes floating on crystalline air, she realized the haunting music was man-made.

"Where is that music coming from, Wolf?"

"It's Blue Hawk playing his flute."

"The little lame boy? My goodness, where did he learn to play like that? It's so ethereal. It's as if the music came from the mountains themselves."

"It's a special talent he was born with. Or perhaps the mountain spirits are playing the flute through him. The People feel Earth Mother has blessed Blue Hawk's music."

"I can see why." She stood there, head tilted, listening to the sparkling notes. "I may not understand your language, but his music quivers in my bones and calls up echoes in my soul."

"It is like that for The People also. We call it blood memory." He gave her an intense look. "Come, it is time we returned to our wickiup."

When they climbed the slight slope to their campsite, Aurora found Wolf had left a rabbit roasting, so at least their meat was cooked properly. And even her tortillas didn't burn badly.

"Where have you been for the last week, Pincus?" Aurora asked when they had finished eating and were lounging against backrests of firewood. Thank heavens, he hadn't been there to see Wolf fight Bear Killer for her. The memory shivered through her. She flicked a glance at Wolf, and his gaze met hers, then fell to her breasts. She drew a sharp breath, feeling her nipples tighten as though he'd caressed her.

"We went north to the Mexican side of the border near Tenehas. I only took a few pictures."

Wolf's head snapped up and his eyes narrowed. "How far north?"

Pincus shrugged. "I don't know. The warriors told me we were about a half-day's ride from Tenehas."

Wolf gazed absently in the direction of the village. "I told them not to go into that area because of smallpox."

"We didn't really talk to anyone, Wolf. The Mexicans fled as soon as they saw us coming, and your people only stole horses and cattle." Pincus rolled his eyes. "Listen to me! I go raiding with an Apache war party, and say they 'only' stole horses and cattle."

After that, the conversation lagged. Wolf seemed preoccupied, staring into the fire as Aurora and Pincus talked. Finally, after several yawns, Pincus stood. "I guess I'll be getting back to my wickiup. Good night."

After his steps faded, Wolf stood and stretched. His muscles flexed in the golden firelight, reminding Aurora of statues she'd seen of Greek gods. She tensed as he circled the fire to stand behind her. Clasping his hands around her waist, he drew her back against himself.

His heat enveloped her and warmed her far more than the fire. She inhaled deeply, absorbing his scent deep into her bones. She could feel his heart beating steadily against her shoulder. Arching her head back against his broad chest, she closed her eyes.

"It is time for bed, *kun isdzán*," he murmured, his warm breath caressing her cheek.

"So soon? I'm not tired yet." Not when her whole body tingled with awareness and her senses sang a song of Wolf.

"Neither am I." He dropped a tiny, soft kiss in the hollow of her shoulder. "That's why we're going to bed." He palmed the fullness of her breasts through her soft cotton blouse.

Her heart leaped like a startled doe. "Don't. What if someone should see?"

"I would hear them before they could see anything. Besides, no more village women will be coming up here tonight. They only come when we're eating to see what a bad cook you are." He twisted a tendril of her hair around his finger.

She glanced at him over her shoulder. "Is that why they wander by?"

"Yes. And to see me cook. They can't figure out why I keep you when you can't cook or even collect berries." He raised his bushy black eyebrows and leered at her. "In fact, they wonder just what you're good at."

"Medicine."

"That, too. Now come inside." He led her into the wickiup, then let the wolfhide slide down behind them.

Aurora studied him in the molten firelight filtering through the brush walls. He was a golden statue, gilded by the light, his muscles rippling with power.

He rested his hands on her shoulders and gazed down at her with eyes that were shadowed and unreadable. "Do you know how many men in the village envy me?"

"Even though I can't cook?" Her blood was beginning to rush with hot lava.

"Yes." The single word was hot flame, licking at her. He untied the drawstring at her throat. Hooking a single finger through the gathered material, he loosened it slowly. "Do you know how much I look forward to undressing you every night?" He nuzzled her throat, sending a shimmering flow of sensation down her spine.

"Do you know how much I look forward to having you undress me?" she asked on a bare wisp of sound, startling herself with her boldness. What had happened to her? she wondered. Then he filled his hands with her tousled locks and his lips came down on hers, and she forgot to wonder about anything.

He pushed the loosened blouse down over her shoulders, pinning her arms to her sides as he showered hot kisses over her like stars. Her head lolled back and she sighed deeply, giving herself up to the delicious spiraling tautness within her.

Suddenly Wolf lifted his head, listening.

"What is it?"

"Someone is coming up the slope toward us." He set her aside and grabbed his rifle. "Stay here." He ducked outside and waited for their visitor.

Aurora peered through a crack in the brush wall. Geronimo appeared out of the darkness and waited at the edge of the firelight, his arms crossed over his red calico shirt, until Wolf nodded and set his rifle down, leaning it against the wickiup.

He and Wolf stood near the fire, talking. Although neither spoke fast or gestured, Aurora received the impression that something was wrong.

A woman ran out of the darkness into the firelight. She was breathing hard and wringing her hands. "You come," she cried to Geronimo. Then her Apache became too rapid for Aurora to understand, though it was obvious that she was very frightened. Geronimo nodded abruptly and ran after her down the slope.

"What's wrong?" Aurora asked, emerging.

"Her son was in the same raiding party as Pincus. He returned this afternoon and has become sick." Wolf walked over to the woodpile and picked up several pieces of firewood.

"So she came to the witch doctor for help?"

"He's not a witch doctor," he said wearily. "He's a shaman. You White-eyes are all the same. You belittle anything you don't understand. Geronimo has a special ability he will use to make the boy well." As he laid the wood on the dying fire, he glanced down at the village.

"Are you and Geronimo through talking for the night?" She tugged at her blouse sleeves, straightening them.

"Are you asking if I'm coming to bed?" He gave her a blow of a look, one that left her knees knocking together.

She straightened to her full height and crossed her arms over her breasts. "I most certainly am not! Why would I care if you came to bed?"

"Why, indeed?" Sitting down cross-legged, he rested his forearms on his knees as he stared into the fire. "Go on to the buffalo robes. I'll stay up for a while."

She moved to stand behind him, resting her hands on his shoulders and looking down at the top of his head. He leaned back against her legs, but didn't say anything, just stared into the fire.

"Wolf?" She fingered his long hair, combing it back off his forehead. "Can I help?"

He shook his head, his hair brushing across her knees. Then, as she turned to go, he reached back and wrapped an arm around her legs. "Stay."

He needed her, she thought. Whether or not he would admit it, he needed her. She stayed, silent, sharing the flames with him, combing her fingers through his hair. Suddenly she felt him tense. Looking up, she found Geronimo had emerged from the darkness and stood watching them.

Wolf nodded at Geronimo, and he moved forward and took a seat at the other side of the fire. He and Wolf ignored Aurora as they talked. Aurora glanced from one to the other. Whatever the problem, it was grave enough to worry both men. Several times she heard the word *viruelas*, but she didn't know what it meant.

Finally Wolf turned to her. "Geronimo says the boy is very ill, but he has no Apache medicine to combat this sickness since it is a White-eyes sickness."

"I see." She glanced at Geronimo, but his features were inscrutable. "If it's a White-eyes disease, maybe I have something for it. May I see the child?"

Wolf spoke to Geronimo, who grunted as he tugged at his eyebrow.

"Come." Rising, Wolf held out his hand. "We will see the child now."

Aurora grabbed the saddlebags containing what was left of her medicines, and followed him into the darkness. She heard Geronimo's footsteps rustling through the leaves behind them. They wended their way through the village to the far side, where a fire still burned strong. Pacing beside it was a man Aurora recognized as one of Wolf's most trusted warriors.

"In here." Wolf lifted the deerhide for her, then he and Geronimo slipped in behind her.

The woman who'd come for Geronimo earlier stood to one side, clasping her hands tightly in front of her. In the shadows, a thin boy who couldn't have been more than thirteen lay on a blanket, moaning and thrashing in his sleep. Aurora knelt beside him and felt his forehead.

"He's burning up with fever," she murmured to Wolf. "I'll need a torch so I can see him better."

"I'll get it." He went outside and returned in a moment with a long flaming piece of wood. "Pony That Talks is getting a another torch, but in the meantime use this."

"Thanks. Just bring it over here and hold it up high."

As soon as light fell across the boy's face, she saw the telltale splotches. Aurora stiffened and looked up at Wolf. His gaze met hers, and she realized that he knew exactly which White-eyes disease this was. And its deadliness.

She examined the child carefully, hoping against hope she was wrong in her diagnosis. She wasn't. She glanced at Geronimo, who stood at the edge of the light, his arms crossed over his chest, watching her. No wonder he'd said it was a White-eyes sickness.

Rising, she turned to Wolf. "This boy has smallpox."

Chapter 17

66 **W**hat can you do for him?'' Wolf crossed his arms over his chest. Aurora had confirmed his worst fears.

"There's little we can do once the disease develops. Some people think alcohol baths help bring down the fever.''

"We don't have any alcohol except firewater.''

"That'll do, he'll just smell like whiskey. And we need to know who's been in contact with him. Do you think he caught it on the raid?''

"Probably.''

"My God!'' she cried, realizing Wolf had now been exposed to the deadly disease. Grasping his arm, she tried to drag him away from the child. "If you haven't had smallpox, get out of here. You haven't been vaccinated.''

"Yes, I have.''

Her brow furrowed and she tilted her head as she eyed him. "You have? How? Where?''

"In Boston. But the rest of the village hasn't.'' He stepped to the entrance and spoke rapidly to the Apache who waited outside. "I've told him to assemble everyone so I can tell them the White-eyes sickness has struck again. We must make preparations in case others sicken."

"They will." Her lips tightened as she glanced at the boy, who was scratching his blisters in his sleep. "If only we had some vaccine. Vaccination is the key to beating smallpox."

"What about the vaccine you were taking to Tenehas?"

"Don't you remember? The vaccine points were crushed when Bear Killer made my horse fall."

"Do the Bluecoats have more at Fort Bowie?"

"Of course. Every Army hospital keeps a supply on hand in case of an outbreak." Her eyes widened abruptly. "My God, are you thinking of vaccinating your people?"

Grasping her shoulders in his large, square hands, he stared into her eyes. "If I can get the vaccine points, could you do the vaccinations?"

"Yes, but—"

"No but's, Aurora. This is life or death for my people. Can you do it?"

She stared at him for a long moment. "Yes."

He gave her an assessing look, then turned and spoke to Geronimo. The older man frowned and shook his head, but Wolf continued talking until Geronimo gave Aurora the same thoughtful look. He stalked to the wickiup entrance, glanced at her again, then ducked out.

"Well, did you convince him?"

"Convince him of what?" Wolf replied warily.

"Whatever it was that you wanted."

"Vaccination is a foreign idea to my people. To put a strange material into the body and be guarded against a White-eyes sickness before it

strikes—that isn't something they understand."
He pinched the bridge of his nose and sighed
wearily. "Even Geronimo has a hard time with it.
He's gone to think about it."

"Do you need his permission to vaccinate your
people?"

He gave her a level look that would have put
frost on an iceberg. "Permission has nothing to do
with it. His support would be helpful in convincing
my people. Geronimo is a war chief now, but he is
also a shaman, and the people respect his ability
both to set broken bones and to see into the future.
Now come. We will talk to my people."

Grabbing her medicine bag, Aurora hurried after
him. They zigzagged between wickiups to the
village center.

Wolf built up the fire and passed out torches to
the Apaches who were already there. By twos and
threes, others emerged from the shadows and
joined the growing crowd. They appeared without
a sound to warn of their coming. There would be
only shadows and darkness, then suddenly the
short, sturdy Apaches were there.

The women wore blouses in all colors of the
rainbow and full skirts that never matched their
blouses. The men wore voluminous knee-length
breechclouts. The Apaches murmured among
themselves, sounding like leaves rustling in the
wind.

Aurora looked at Wolf, but he shook his head
almost imperceptibly as he scanned the crowd.
"Not yet."

Geronimo joined them and moved to Wolf's left,
where he stood with arms crossed over his chest.
"Stand on my right, Aurora," Wolf said. "That will

show my people that I honor you and they'll be more apt to listen to you."

Finally Wolf began to speak. With his first words, silence fell across the crowd. They listened attentively, occasionally glancing at Aurora. When Wolf finished, Geronimo spoke for a few minutes.

"I've told them that once again the deadly sickness has struck. It is a White-eyes illness, brought to us by the White-eyes. Maybe White-eyes medicine is the way to fight it. I've told them that among White-eyes you are an *izze nantan*, a medicine captain, and you wish to help us. Nod."

Aurora nodded vigorously. She could see fear on some of the women's faces, but the warriors seemed impervious to it. She picked out Destarte, but fear, not hatred, filled her eyes as she rested her arm over Blue Hawk's thin shoulders. On her other side stood Bear Killer, his black reptilian eyes shooting hatred at Wolf.

"What do you want me to say?" she murmured.

"Just tell me how my people can fight this White-eyes sickness. I will translate for you."

"All right." She nodded as her gaze connected with various Apaches in the crowd. "The first thing everyone has to realize is that nothing is gained by running away." She waited while he translated. "They've already been exposed to smallpox, to *viruelas.* That means no one may leave the village." Again she waited. A burst of chatter told her when he got to the part about not leaving. "Wolf, explain that if they go to another village, they will spread the disease, and more Apaches will die. And anyone who comes to this village must stay here. Everyone must remain here until there are no more new smallpox cases."

The torches flared and sputtered, throwing their fitful light over the Apaches. Bear Killer no longer stood in the front row, aiming his hatred at them. In fact, he was gone from the crowd altogether.

"Will they agree to the quarantine?" she asked when Wolf finished translating and turned to her.

"They are Apache. They will do whatever is necessary for The People. Now give me the rest of your instructions."

She did, then stood at his side while he translated. Wolf kept his voice calm and reassuring, looking directly at one Apache after another as he spoke. After a moment, each would nod, and Aurora knew he'd enlisted one more in his campaign to quarantine the village. Aurora moved closer to Wolf, letting him feel her support. He didn't glance at her, but his hand brushed her shoulder as he gestured to his people and she knew the touch wasn't accidental.

When he finished, he waited a moment to see if there were questions, then turned to her. "All right, now let's go back to our wickiup." He rested his hand in the small of her back as they walked through the crowd.

As they neared the trail to their wickiup, Wolf exhaled deeply. "You spoke well tonight, Aurora."

"I didn't do anything, Wolf. It's you that your People trust. That's why they will do as you ask."

He raised a dark eyebrow. "A compliment? From you?"

"Don't look a gift compliment in the mouth, Apache," she warned softly. A passing warrior jostled her, knocking her against Wolf. Automatically he grabbed her arms to steady her, and as he set her back, their eyes met. He held her a heartbeat too long before he slid his hands down her arms, and they both knew it.

At their wickiup, as Aurora would have ducked inside, Wolf rested his hand on her shoulder. "No. I'll stir up the embers so that we can see, and then I want you to draw me a map so I know where the vaccine is kept at Fort Bowie."

"No!" Aurora's heart pounded raggedly as she fought the sudden terror that crashed through her consciousness. "You can't mean to get it yourself!"

"Who did you think would go for it?"

"I—I don't know." Ducking out from beneath his hand, she began to pace around the fire in a panic. "I guess I expected to. After all, I know where they keep the vaccine points and I know Papa would give them to me and—"

"Your father wouldn't give you a single vaccine point if he knew it was for Apaches."

"Yes, he would, especially if I told him they were for women and children."

Wolf froze in the act of adding a piece of wood to the fire. Slowly he looked up, and his features had hardened until they seemed chiseled from granite. "You still don't believe me, do you?"

She circled the fire to stand beside him. "Wolf, let's not argue about this now," she implored, resting a hand on his arm. "The important thing is to get the vaccine. And Papa will give the points to me. I know he will!"

"I know him better than you do, Aurora." He gazed at her small white hand for a long moment. "And that's all the more reason I should go," he added, his voice harsh with tension. "I can get the vaccine, and you can keep your illusions about your father."

"You can't." She grabbed him with both hands and shook him. "Don't you understand, Wolf? You can't go back into Fort Bowie. Let Pincus go. He can get it."

He shook his head. "Won't work. Pincus is an old man. He can't ride that hard or that far." He gently pulled her hands away. "I have to get my horse."

"Then I'll go," she cried, panic squeaking in her voice. "I'm young and I'm strong and I can do it. Don't look away from me, Wolf. I mean it. Look at me!" She reached up and held his head between her palms.

"You don't know the trail. I do." He grasped her shoulders, then his hands slid down her back, his fingers kneading her taut muscles. He filled one hand with her wildly tousled mane as he urged her against his hard body. "I'm the only one who can go. The People will need a doctor. They'll need you, not me."

"B-but they'll recognize you. And this time they won't take you prisoner, Wolf. They'll just shoot you." She could barely speak for the fear that boiled in her stomach and swamped her senses.

"They won't recognize me. All Indians look alike to White-eyes."

"I recognized you!"

"You don't look at me with the eyes a Bluecoat does," he replied gently. He led her closer to the fire. Picking up a twig, he handed it to her. "Draw me a map so I know where to look for the vaccine."

"And if I won't?"

He eyed her in the golden firelight. "You will. You can't stand by and see people suffer. That's why you dared come into a corral with a savage Apache prisoner. I needed you then, Aurora." He reached over and took her hand and dropped a tiny kiss on the back. "I need you now."

"Damn you, Wolf," she whispered. He'd once again touched that harp string buried deep in her, the one only he could touch. She inhaled deeply and with a long sigh, knelt in the dust and began to draw. He knelt beside her, studying her drawing as she explained where he would find the vaccine points.

He repeated her directions. She listened and savored the deep, rich sound of his voice, storing its resonating echoes in her heart.

"Is that right, woman?" Wolf asked.

"What? Oh, yes. Right." She stared at the dust as he stood and drew a moccasin through her drawing, obliterating it with one stroke. One bullet. That was all it would take. She rubbed her upper arms as a chill settled in her heart.

Wolf wrapped his arms around her. "I'll be all right, *isdzán.*"

She locked her arms around the sturdy column of his throat and hugged him tightly. "How long?"

"At least ten days. Five up and five back." He brushed a kiss over her freckle-dusted nose. "And that's assuming nothing goes wrong."

She groaned and stared at the ground, afraid she was going to burst into tears.

"Aurora" His voice dropped, became rough. "Look at me, please, my *kun isdzán.*"

She buried her face against his warm throat. "I can't. I'm a coward."

"Far from it." He gently pulled himself away from her. "Stay here. I want to get something for you." He ducked into the wickiup and almost immediately returned with a magnificent, intricately carved silver and turquoise necklace. "I had this made for you. I was going to give it to you later, but now I want you to have it before I leave."

"It's gorgeous." She ran her fingers over the heavy carved silver, warm from his hand. Polished turquoise was inlaid in flower designs.

"I had the Apache silversmith make it with pieces-of-sky because it means good luck and because your eyes are like pieces-of-sky." He paused, gazing at her mouth hungrily. "I want to put it on you before I go. And I want to see you wearing it when I return."

"I will wear it," she murmured with a catch in her voice. The thought of his fingers looping the heavy silver around her throat made her heart thrum softly.

Wolf's eyes locked with hers as he brushed her long, fire-gold hair up. "Hold this for me," he murmured. She caught the long strands in her hands, swept them up over her head, and held them. His rough-tipped fingers caressed her satin skin as he slowly fastened the necklace at her nape.

His silky black hair grazed her cheek as he dropped a tiny kiss on her shoulder beside the necklace. She let her hair slide through her hands until it hung down her back in a sheet of flame. His hands settled over her shoulders, and he drew her close and kissed her—slowly, hungrily, thoroughly.

She clung to him as her bones began to melt. Her tongue touched his in invitation.

A gunshot shattered the night. Wolf and Aurora broke apart and stared through the darkness, waiting. There were no more shots, just a terrible stillness.

Wolf reached into the wickiup to lift his cartridge belt off the cactus-thorn hook, and buckled it around his waist. Stepping into the shadows, he scooped up his rifle from where it leaned against a oak. All the time, he watched the path.

"Aurora, pack dried berries, jerky, and parched corn in the deerskin pouch for me."

Her eyes widened with surprise. "You're not going tonight, are you?" She'd thought they would sleep together one last time.

"Yes. Get the food. Now." He focused his attention on the trail as they heard horses' hooves.

Chili Eater rode into the circle of firelight, leading a horse on which Bear Killer slumped, semiconscious. Behind him three other warriors rode into the light, one holding a yawning four-year-old boy in front of him. The last one led Wolf's bay stallion.

Chili Eater and Wolf spoke rapidly in short bursts of sound like Gatling guns. Aurora could feel the tension in the riders as they looked to Wolf for some sort of decision.

Aurora waited silently until Wolf glanced at her. "What is it? What's wrong?"

"Bear Killer attempted to slip away with his son." Wolf glanced at his enemy with a look of sadness and compassion. "He thought to go to another village where there is no *viruelas*. He didn't make it."

"But doesn't he understand he could already have smallpox and he could spread it to other Apaches?"

"He isn't thinking that clearly right now. He's terrified. All he wants is to get his son away from the sickness. The boy is everything to him."

"I see." Aurora was impressed by Wolf's compassion for Bear Killer.

Wolf paced over to Bear Killer's horse and shook

the man until he straightened in his saddle. Whatever he said to Bear Killer, it made the other Apache stiffen. Bear Killer spoke rapidly, and Aurora was shocked by the pleading tone in his voice. Wolf stepped back and shook his head. He turned and started back toward her.

Bear Killer's rifle glinted in the firelight as he raised it.

"Behind you!" Aurora screamed.

Whirling, Wolf said something low to Bear Killer. Their eyes met for a lifetime. Then Wolf turned his back and walked toward her. Bear Killer pointed his rifle skyward and fired it. With a wild cry, he galloped away.

"Are you going after him?" Aurora asked. *Please stay with me. Let someone else go after him. I need you. Oh God, I need you.*

"No. He won't leave the boy; he just has to ride off some of his frustration and fear. I'm going to ask She Who Sees Babies to care for his son."

Wolf took his stallion's reins, then his deep voice resonated around the circle of horsemen. In seconds the riders were gone.

They were once again alone. Alone and already apart, Aurora thought sadly, as Wolf stopped several feet from her. Too far away for she wanted desperately to rush into his arms and have him hold her and kiss her and tell her everything would be all right. Only it wouldn't. Not until he returned.

"Where's the food?" He stood tall and stiff, the reins in his left hand.

"It'll only take a minute." She ducked into the wickiup and brushed a tear from her cheek. Grabbing the butter-soft deerskin pouch, she began stuffing it with every bit of jerky and dried berries and corn she could find. At the doorway she paused and hurriedly brushed more tears away.

"Here." She didn't dare look at him or say more as she shoved the bag at him. His fingers grazed her palm as he scooped the pouch up and slung it over his left shoulder.

"Look at me, Aurora." Slowly she raised her eyes. His eyes were bottomless wells of darkness. He held his rifle in the crook of his right arm. "I'm leaving you the revolver. You know how to use it, don't you?"

"Yes." Her throat was so tight that she could barely get the word out.

"You'll be all right?"

"Yes." She clasped her hands behind her back to keep herself from grabbing him and trying to stop him.

"If anything should happen, go to Geronimo. He'll take care of you."

"Yes." *Go. Go quickly.*

"I'll be back as soon as I can." He twisted the reins in his hand.

"I know." *Go, damn you, don't keep standing there, torturing me! Go!*

"And I—" He dropped the rifle and the reins and the pouch and took a stride toward her, and wrapped both arms around her and pulled her against him hard. "Kiss me," he whispered fiercely, filling his hands with her unbound hair. "Kiss me before I go."

"Oh yes," she murmured, clasping his shoulders tightly.

Before she had enough of his hot mouth and his hard, searching hands, before she'd tasted enough of his taste or inhaled enough of his scent, he raised his head and gently set her back from him.

He ran his fingers over her necklace one more time. "Wear this for me."

Then he turned and swung up on the horse. He didn't look back as he reined it toward the path. He'd almost reached the edge of the circle of firelight when she called to him.

"Wolf?" He glanced over his shoulder. "Take care."

"You, too." And he was gone.

She stood by the fire, listening to the sound of his horse's hooves. All too soon they faded away. She was alone. So alone.

"Take care, my love," she whispered. "Take care and come back safely."

Chapter 18

$\sim\!\!\infty\!\!\sim$

Aurora gazed into the dying fire. Never in her whole life had she been so alone. Not even when her mother had died and she'd gone to live with a stranger named Aunt Ruth had she felt so alone and so lonely. Two different emotions, but that night they added up to a trembling lower lip and eyes brimming with unshed tears.

Footsteps on the path made her start and stare fearfully into the trees, trying to pierce the darkness.

Chili Eater emerged into the firelight. "Stalking Wolf has asked me to sleep by your fire until he returns." He carried a tattered wool blanket.

"Enjuh." What a thoughtful thing for Wolf to do. With all that he'd had to think of, he'd still made sure she had someone to protect her while he was gone.

His dark eyes went to her necklace. "My friend has given you a beautiful collar."

"Yes. It is beautiful, isn't it." She fingered the heavy silver links. "I would see the sick boy now, Chili Eater. Will you come with me?"

He nodded and followed her down the path into the village. Aurora found the boy's mother bathing him with cheap whiskey. His condition was unchanged, though he was less restless. She stayed until she was sure there was no more she could do for him.

"Have you known Wolf long, Chili Eater?" she asked as she followed him up the slope to Wolf's wickiup.

"Many harvests. Ma'cho Nalzhee and I grew up together and were trained as warriors by Geronimo." He added wood to the fire, then spread his blanket on the far side of the fire.

Reluctant to enter the lonely wickiup, she sat by the crackling fire and wrapped her arms around her knees. "How did he get the name Stalking Wolf?"

"We have children's names until we earn our adult name. Ma'cho earned his in his fifth harvest. He wanted Geronimo to start his warrior training, but Geronimo was busy training older boys. To prove he was old enough, Ma'cho took a mouthful of water and ran to the top of a nearby ridge, just as Geronimo had the older boys do." Chili Eater stirred the fire. "It is how we learn to breath through our nose when we run. He was supposed to return and spit the water out to show Geronimo he hadn't swallowed it, but he didn't come back."

"What happened?"

"Finally Geronimo climbed the ridge to look for him. In the valley on the other side, he saw a wolf pack had killed a deer and were feasting on it, and there in the tall grass, creeping toward them on his belly with his child's bow and arrow, was the boy. When Geronimo saw him, he named him Ma'cho Nalzhee, He Stalks Wolves."

"And he was only five?"

"*Sí.*" Chili Eater rolled into his blanket. "It is time to sleep, *isdzán* of my friend."

"You're right. There will be much to do tomorrow to prepare for the White-eyes sickness." Pushing aside the wolfhide, she ducked inside. She burrowed deep into the buffalo robes. They still held Wolf's scent, and she inhaled deeply, filling her lungs and her lonely heart.

She lay on her back, stared at the stars sparkling through the smoke hole, and thought about her equally sparkling discovery. She was in love with Wolf.

Her finger traced the turquoise necklace with a sense of wonder. The Apache warrior who held her captive had given her a glorious gift. Was it a token of his love?

When had her awareness of him flowered into love? With each breath, an inner voice answered. With each sip of water they'd shared in the desert, with each touch of their bodies as they rode double, with each kiss, with each sharing of the heart and mind. That was how love blossomed between two people.

Her fingers were still touching her necklace and her eyes were still wide open when the new day dawned. And she treasured her discovery in her heart.

As the sun rose, she forced herself to put aside thoughts of Wolf. Right now she had work to do. These were his people, the people he loved and felt responsible for, and she would use every bit of her medical skill to help them.

"Pincus, I need your help," she called as she approached Pincus's wickiup.

"Certainly, my dear," he said as he pushed aside

the deerhide and emerged. "What brings you over in such a rush?"

Quickly she explained what had happened and what she needed him to do.

Aurora spent the day checking the Apaches' stores of firewater and anything else she could use when the virulent disease struck again. And it would, she knew.

All too soon, her days became an endless round of sick people. Sick children. Sick adults.

Many Tongues came to her, wanting to help, but Aurora warned her to stay away from the sickness for the sake of her infant son. After that, whenever she returned to the wickiup, she would find cooked food and she knew it was Many Tongues' way of helping.

At night, she would snuggle into the buffalo robes, seeking the last remnants of Wolf's scent, and sleep the sleep of exhaustion. She preferred that—then she didn't have time to think of Wolf or of the emptiness of the buffalo robes and the chill of the night.

Too often for her peace of mind, Aurora found herself walking to the edge of the mesa, where she would watch the trail from the north, seeking a dust cloud, seeking a rider on a bay horse galloping toward her.

Day after day, there was nothing, nothing whether she watched in the morning or afternoon or evening. Nothing but her fear. Had he gotten inside the fort? Had he found the vaccine? Had he been discovered? Had he confronted her father? Had he gotten away or was he lying somewhere, wounded and— No! She wouldn't allow herself to ask that question.

"Wolf, where are you?" she whispered one afternoon as she stared down into the valley and fought tears.

She was about to leave when she glimpsed a rider in the valley. He wasn't riding the bay stallion, yet something in the breadth of his shoulders and the way he sat his horse, like a centaur, sounded a chord deep in her.

The horse began to stagger, and as she watched, it crumpled to the ground. Aurora choked back a scream as the rider went down with it. The rider slowly sat up, pulled his rifle close, and used it as a crutch as he struggled to stand. Sinking to his knees, he rested his forehead against the rifle stock as he paused.

Finally, with a rush, he staggered to his feet and limped over to the motionless horse. He stripped the saddlebags off the brute, hefted them over his left shoulder, then began walking. Gradually he increased his pace until he was trotting toward the plateau.

Aurora twisted her hands as she tried to decide if this truly was Wolf. She drank in the strides of his long legs, the pumping of his brawny arms. On and on he came. Step by ragged step he came. He was clearly weary, stumbling more and more often, but still he came. This was a warrior with the great heart of a lion, she thought. Or a wolf.

So she watched, and hoped, and prayed—and finally was sure.

She lost sight of him when he reached the base of the mesa. Heart fluttering like a caged bird, she hurried toward the trailhead. Gradually her steps slowed. If she was waiting for Wolf at the top, he'd know how much she'd missed him, how worried and frantic she'd been.

Now that she'd recognized her love for him, she felt oddly vulnerable. She needed to cherish her discovery by herself, to hold it to her breast and treasure it. She couldn't declare her love aloud, not yet at least. After all, he'd never mentioned love to her.

No, she decided reluctantly. It was better not be be waiting for him at the trailhead. There was no need for him to know he'd captured her heart. For the time being, it was better if he thought he'd captured only her body.

She turned back to the village and gave Geronimo the news. As Apaches began streaming toward the trail, she joined them. Several warriors raced by on their swift ponies.

"Ah, there you are, Aurora," Pincus said as he fell into step beside her. "Would you help me with my equipment?" He carried his camera on its tripod on his left shoulder and held a large wooden box under his right arm, while a smaller box dangled from his fingers.

"How could I refuse when you look as though you couldn't stagger another step? Here, give me that box."

"I'm anxious to get pictures of the villagers greeting their chief when he brings the lifesaving vaccine."

"Don't you think that's a bit melodramatic?"

"Whatever sells newspapers," he replied with a wink. "I'm excited, though. Aren't you? Now you'll be able to vaccinate the Apaches."

"Maybe I'll be able to start today." She cast a calculating eye toward the late-afternoon sun.

"And Wolf's back," he said, eyeing her craftily. "Aren't you excited about that?"

"Why should I be? All I'm interested in is the

vaccine." She completely ignored the way her heart was thudding against her ribs.

"Hey, this is me, Pincus, you're talking to. Don't try to pull the wool over my eyes, my girl. I know better."

"I'd rather not talk about it right now." She shifted the heavy box in her arms. "I'm tired, you're tired, and Wolf is probably exhausted."

"All right, we'll pretend Wolf doesn't mean anything to you." He waggled his thinning gray eyebrows at her. "Far be it from me to pry and give advice where it isn't wanted."

"I'll remember that next time you give me advice."

Wolf staggered the last few steps onto the mesa, and she forgot all about Pincus. Apaches clustered around him, but she could still pick him out, standing a head taller than the others. Her heart skipped a beat. Wolf was back.

He was home!

She smiled and her blood began to pulse as it hadn't since he'd left. Thank God, he was back.

"Here, give me that box, Aurora. I want to set up here."

She barely heard Pincus as she focused on Wolf. He paced along the dusty path surrounded by Apaches—his people. Aurora clenched her hands in the folds of her turquoise skirt and schooled her features to reveal none of her inner turmoil. She waited, head held high.

Wolf looked ahead and his gaze locked with hers. He stopped about five feet away. "Hello, Aurora." His voice was hoarse and raspy from trail dust. "How are you?"

"Fine." She was shocked by the deep, grim lines

etched into his rugged features. His eyes were sunken and red-rimmed with fatigue. She longed to touch him; she couldn't. She wanted to be alone with him; instead she was hemmed in by Apaches crowding around. Her heart cried out to him—so much needed saying.

His gaze snagged on the necklace. She smoothed her fingers over the heavy turquoise nervously. He pushed through the crowd to her. "You wear the necklace," he said in a low, gravelly voice meant only for her ears. His intent gaze probed deep into her soul. "I'm glad, White-eyes."

The people around them faded away and she saw only Wolf, heard only Wolf. She flicked the tip of her tongue over her lips to moisten them. "I wore it the whole time you were gone, Apache."

"Enjuh."

His gaze fell to her breasts and she felt a distinct shimmer of awareness, as if he'd touched her. Instinctively she crossed her arms over her bosom. "Tonight, my woman of fire," he whispered, and the warm tone in his voice wrapped around her like a buffalo robe.

Chili Eater tugged at his arm and spoke. Wolf's gaze remained on her for several heartbeats, and the promise in it took her breath away. Then he turned to the stocky warrior and listened attentively. Aurora felt drained, as if she'd been released from a secret spell Wolf had cast over her.

"Come on," Wolf said as he started to walk away. "We'll do the vaccinations in the center of the village."

At the center of the village, Chili Eater placed the saddlebags on the ground. Wolf knelt and unbuckled one, and pulled out a buckskin pouch. Aurora moved to stand behind him, her shadow falling across him.

"This was what they had." He drew out a handful of vaccine points.

"These will be fine."

"I'll tell Chili Eater to have everyone gather here. Then you can get on with the vaccinations." As he stood up, his gaze again met hers and this time there was nothing hiding his thoughts. The need and want in his eyes were naked and searing. "While we wait for The People to gather, we will talk." He wrapped his large hand around her elbow and guided her away from the Apaches.

Wolf could feel the smoothness of her arm as her pulse hammered beneath his fingers. He inhaled deeply, drawing in her scent, savoring it like a starving man savoring a feast, trying to clear his lungs of the scent of horse and leather and sweat.

In the weeks since he'd captured her, she had become part of him. Her spirit and her courage and the soft welcome of her body—all had become part of him. Every second he'd been gone his body had missed her. But even more, his mind and his heart had missed her. She was the flame who brought light and warmth into all the dark places in his heart.

Aurora walked beside him, aware of his long, rein-callused fingers stroking the sensitive skin of her arm. As they reached the edge of the trees, he stumbled over a tree root, but caught himself. Still, she reached out to steady him. "Are you all right?"

"Tired, that's all."

She gave a choked gasp as he swayed. "Wolf! You're not just tired." Her eyes widened with horror. "Surely you don't have—"

"I'm vaccinated, remember? I just need to sit for a moment. It's been a hard ride." He slumped on a fallen log, hands on his knees, and took several deep breaths. "Stand in front of me so no one sees me."

Aurora felt his forehead. "No fever, or very slight if there is one."

"I told you I'm fine," he growled, pushing her hand away.

Oh God, she should never have touched him. She'd been doing all right until her fingers stroked his warm flesh. "No, you're not," she snapped, "so don't pretend with me." Needing to touch him, she began to knead the tight muscles in his shoulders.

"I don't pretend with you, White-eyes. And I need your strength right now." His voice was low, as if he was reluctant to admit it. Wrapping his arms around her waist, he drew her close and buried his face against her breasts. "I need you, Aurora," he whispered.

She continued kneading his shoulders as he slumped against her. "Just rest, Wolf. We don't have to do anything for a few minutes." Exhaling a long, pent-up breath, he closed his eyes. Bending down, she rubbed her cheek across his dust-stiffened hair. "Rest."

All too soon, she felt the change in tension in his neck muscles as he slowly straightened up. "Stay, Wolf. Rest."

"I can't." He looked up at her with bloodshot eyes. "My people need the vaccine. But you need to remember that vaccination is strange to them. Be patient if at first they are reluctant. I'm sure they'll come around, but we'll have to move slowly in the beginning. It is important for my people to see that

I support your White-eyes medicine, so I will assist you."

"You will?" She'd been worried about getting a helper. She hadn't wanted to use Pincus, because she'd wanted it to be a joint Apache–White-eyes project, but her short time in the Apache village had shown her that men did not act as helpers. "Thank you. I was worried about who to get."

"We will discuss your thanks later. Now it is time to go back." Instead of springing up lithely, he visibly gathered himself and pushed himself up from the log with his hands.

"You're exhausted!" She rested her hand on his arm. "How can you keep going?"

He straightened to his full height. "I am Apache."

And that said it all, she mused, as she followed him back to the village center.

When the Apaches had gathered, he spoke in firm, resonating tones. The voice of a leader, Aurora thought as she stood quietly beside him.

"Wolf," she said, jogging his arm. "Be sure to tell them it takes time for the White-eyes medicine to grow strong in their bodies. Some of them might still become sick. But once the medicine is strong they never have to fear smallpox again. But each must have the medicine. No one can take it for another."

"Good thinking, my little *izze nantan*, especially about no one taking it for another." He turned back to his people, and whatever he said made the Apaches murmur and cast suspicious glances at her.

"What did you say?"

"It isn't translatable." The People shuffled

around, but no one got into line. "You will do me first," Wolf said.

"But you've already— Oh, I see. You're showing your people what it is and that it doesn't hurt."

"Whether it hurts or not doesn't matter to an Apache," he growled, "but they need to see how it is done."

"I'd like you to hold the points for me while I do you—if you can, that is?"

"Woman, you try my patience. Give them to me." Snatching the pouch out of her hand, he drew out a point and held it out to her.

"Here we go." Moving to his side, she grasped his left arm with her left hand. For a moment she froze, too aware of the powerful muscles rippling beneath his warm copper-hued skin. Then she scratched an X into his arm with the point, leaving a tiny streak of blood. "That's all there is," she said, stepping back.

Wolf spoke to his people again, and they began to line up. Geronimo's wife was first in line.

"Is this a good sign?" Aurora asked as she scratched the woman's arm. Wolf stood close beside her, his moccasin brushing hers, as he handed her the vaccine points.

"It shows that Geronimo believes you have good medicine. Put the used points in here." He held a hollow gourd in his other hand.

"Has Geronimo been vaccinated?" she asked as Wolf motioned the next woman forward.

"Don't push your luck." He flashed her a wry smile.

The inoculations went smoothly. When an adult held a child, Aurora would do the child first. Aurora's eyes widened as she vaccinated child after child and none cried out. Several of the youngest grimaced, but not one made a sound.

"It seems so strange," she murmured. "Not a single child has cried yet."

"No Apache child would. From the time they are in cradleboards, they're trained not to cry."

"That's impossible." Aurora didn't look up from the warrior she was vaccinating. "How can you train a child not to cry?"

"You forget, my people are surrounded by enemies. A wailing child can betray the hiding place of a whole village. So when a child cries, he is ignored. But when he's quiet, a fuss is made over him. By the time he's six months old, he's learned that only by being quiet does he get attention."

"You actually train babies not to cry?" Shuddering, Aurora glanced at him. "What a dangerous world your people live in."

"It is what we must do to survive."

She was motioning to the next warrior in line when she actually looked at him. And froze. Bear Killer swaggered toward her, head held high. He held his four-year-old son in his arms.

"The boy's name is Peaches, because he is so light-skinned," Wolf said in a low voice.

When Aurora reached for the boy's thin arm, Peaches slapped her hand away. Bear Killer bent over and with his head close to the child's, murmured something, but Peaches shook his head. His head up, neck stiff, Bear Killer snapped something at Wolf.

Aurora tensed, expecting Wolf to snap back, but he just nodded.

"He says do him first"

"Is that all he said?"

"It's enough for you. Do him quickly before he changes his mind and leaves."

Aurora grabbed Bear Killer's arm and scratched it with a fresh point. She could feel his gaze hot with hatred on her. Out of the corner of her eye, she saw Peaches watching warily.

"All right," she said with a bright smile, "it's your turn now. Here, do you want to hold this?" She handed him an unused point and took another from Wolf. Peaches' face screwed up and he let out a loud wail at the scratch. Startled, Aurora glanced at Wolf.

"It's all right," Wolf answered her unspoken question. "His mother didn't train him very well."

"That explains it," she said dryly. "After all, it's always the mother's fault." As she watched Bear Killer walk away with his sobbing, light-skinned son, her brow furrowed in thought. Something was bothering her. Something wasn't quite right.

Suddenly, with a deafening click, all the pieces fell into place. "My God," she cried, whirling to stare at Wolf, "his mother was a white captive, wasn't she?"

Wolf rubbed the back of his neck wearily as he tried to choose his words. He was in no shape to fend off her questions. "She is dead now. Mexicans raided their village and killed her. Peaches is all he has left."

A horrifying image of Aurora fleeing Mexican soldiers flashed through his mind. He inhaled sharply and turned away. Even knowing the image existed only in his imagination, he shuddered at the fear that knifed through him.

"Are you all right?" Aurora asked from behind him. "Should I get someone to relieve you? I'm sure Geronimo or Chili Eater could take over if you wanted to lie down."

"No." Wolf cleared his throat. "I'm fine." If only he could clear his mind of that terrible image. "Your next patient is waiting," he added gruffly.

After that, they were wrapped in their own thoughts and spoke to each other only when necessary. The fiery orange sun edged toward the horizon as the line of over six hundred Apaches from Juh's and Wolf's villages marched past Aurora.

"That's the last one," Aurora said as Many Tongues walked away with her infant son. She packed all the leftover points in the saddlebags. "Thanks."

"Let us go to our wickiup and you can thank me properly," Wolf growled in a rough, intimate tone meant for her alone.

Chapter 19

When Aurora threw aside the wolfskin and entered their wickiup, her body sang a song of welcome for the man who paced behind her. As they'd walked through the village, their hands and their hips and their minds had touched. And every touch had awakened her senses more.

"Who started the fire for us?" Wolf said as he followed her into the golden light.

His deep, dark voice wrapped around her like a velvet cloak. She turned, absorbing that beloved, missed voice with every particle of her being. "Probably Many Tongues. She leaves me food every day so I have something to eat when I return from treating the sick."

"*Izzabo Lanni* is a good woman. I will thank her tomorrow." Clasping her shoulders in his powerful hands, he gazed down at her for several heartbeats. "But now it is another woman I want."

She wrapped her arms around his waist and clung to him, unable to get enough of touching him. He smelled of horses and gunpowder and dust and sweat, and he smelled wonderful.

"I want only you," he murmured, nuzzling the side of her throat. "Day after day as I rode, I could only smell death. Now I smell you, and you smell of wildflowers and life."

"Oh, Wolf." Aurora locked her hands around the back of his neck and pulled his head down as she stood on tiptoe. But before she could kiss him, he took control. His lips ravaged hers in a hungry kiss, a hard, demanding kiss, wild and uncivilized as the Apaches. And Aurora reveled in it.

When he finally raised his head, a tiny smile lifted the corners of his mouth. "I've been wanting to do that since I arrived and saw you waiting for me."

"Then why didn't you?" she asked throatily, still trying to catch her breath. Her breasts were pressed to his chest and she could feel the thudding beat of his heart.

"The People don't kiss." He slid his hands down her back, relearning her curves. "It is a White-eyes vice."

"What?" She pushed herself out of his arms. "You call what we've just done a vice?" she demanded, hands on hips.

His smile turned positively wolfish. "No. I'm afraid this is one place where my White-eyes blood comes out. I learned this vice in Boston and find it pleasant and—"

"Pleasant? How—"

"Hush, *kun isdzán*. My woman of fire. This is not a night for fighting." Pulling her back into his arms, he brushed a quick kiss across her lips. "I will return to you when I've bathed, but right now I stink of horses and days in the saddle. I couldn't come to you without cleansing myself." He nodded at the pile of buffalo robes. "Wait for me there, woman."

His low command throbbed in her blood. She wanted him to come to her clean, smelling of the pungent soapweed, not of gunpowder and sweat, but at the same time she didn't want him out of her arms. She wanted to go on touching him and holding him and feeling the beat of his heart beneath her fingers.

"I could bathe you here. There's water in the *tus*, and I have soapweed."

"Here?"

"Then you wouldn't have to walk all the way down to the stream. You could save your strength."

His hot gaze settled on her white blouse. "I can think of better ways to use it."

"So can I," she murmured throatily.

"Perhaps we should consider these other ways of using my strength?" His hands slid down over her bottom.

"Perhaps." Aurora slipped out of his arms. "Get undressed, Wolf." She picked up a buffalo robe from their bed and flung it down near the fire. "You can lie here."

"And you will bathe me?" His gaze held hers captive as he stripped off his filthy shirt and pants.

"I will bathe you." Aurora drew a sharp breath, struck as always by his awesome power and strength. Even dirty, he was a statue of Apollo, his taut muscles rippling in the firelight as though gilded. And tired as he was, his body shouted that he wanted her.

Wolf lay down on the woolly brown robe and folded his arms beneath his head. "I'm ready."

"So I see," she murmured dryly.

"I'll be even more ready by the time you finish."

"That's hard to believe."

His eyes were red-rimmed, his rugged features haggard and drawn. Yet a smile, slow as molasses, lifted the corners of his mouth. "I'll show you when you finish, my *isdzán*," he promised.

"Never mind." She tipped the *tus* and poured water over a piece of dried soapweed and a square of doeskin. "I said I'd bathe you. That's all."

"Hmm. Maybe I can change your mind."

"I doubt it," she teased, even as his voice pulsed in her blood. She knelt and began to draw the soapweed down his broad chest. Would it be too unseemly to just fall on him and hold him forever?

"I almost didn't recognize you on that strange horse this afternoon," she said, by way of distracting them both. "Where's the bay?"

Wolf dragged his fingers through his dust-stiffened hair. "He's dead. He ran until his great heart gave out and he could run no more. He gave all for The People."

"I think it was you who gave all for The People." She rubbed the soapweed gently over the long scar on his side.

Her loose hair tumbled down over her shoulders and brushed Wolf's flesh with silken flames. He shivered beneath the haunting touch. Idly he combed his fingers through the luxurious cascade, watching the long, gleaming strands flow across his hand in a river of fire. "I dreamed of doing this day after day as I rode." His hand trailed down, brushing across the fullness of her breast. His thumb flicked across her pebble-hard nipple. "Your clothes wouldn't get wet if you took them off."

Aurora flashed him a smile. "My, aren't you practical tonight."

His hand tightened on her shoulder. "Take them

off." His voice was hoarse from days of inhaling dust, yet she felt the warmth in it. "I would see you naked, Aurora, my woman of fire."

Her heart did a somersault and a throbbing began deep inside her. She stepped out of her moccasins and stood up slowly, her eyes challenging his. She watched him as she took her time loosening the ties at her wrists and throat. Then, a taunting inch at a time, knowing how the movement raised and shaped her breasts, she pulled her blouse off over her head.

She paused and smiled, then let her blouse float down onto his chest. His gaze didn't waver as he crushed it in his hand and flung it into the shadows. His nostrils flared as he inhaled her scent, like a predator scenting his prey.

"Now the skirt," he rasped.

She untied the strings at her waist, then let the skirt slip down over the curve of her hips and pool at her feet. His hot gaze raked her nakedness, touching her breasts and her waist and the curve of her hip and the curly thatch between her legs, and she trembled.

He rolled to his side and brushed a soft kiss over her ankle. "My God, how I missed you." Lying back, he smiled up at her. "Now finish bathing me, my woman of fire."

His voice, his touch, combined to heighten the tension so deep within her. She knelt and grasping the long soapweed stalk with both hands, drew it down the taut muscles of his chest with a pressure that might have been painful—but wasn't. "Like this?"

"Yes." He watched her as she bent over him, then firmly yet gently clasped the fullness of one breast in his callous-roughened hand. "Exactly like this."

Aurora drew a sharp breath. Instinctively she knew each was challenging the other, drawing out the anticipation of what was to come in delicious torture. Her bones were so soft she could barely stand. She decided Wolf was going to be in the same state by the time she finished, and gave him a cat-that-swallowed-the-cream smile.

Soaping both hands, Aurora slowly scrubbed every inch of his shoulders and chest, taking special care with the tight dark nubs of his nipples. She ignored his sudden gasps and violent twitches, except to smile.

Wolf groaned deeply, feeling nothing but the taunting touch of her hands. He reached up and trailed a finger along her necklace. "I dreamed of you leaning over me, wearing the pieces-of-sky necklace and nothing else. And you know what?"

"What?" What would he do if she threw herself on him?

"Seeing you is better than the dream."

His voice throbbed deep inside her as she again soaped her hands and worked her way down his taut abdomen and through the midnight thatch at the juncture of his legs, being especially careful not to touch his rigid staff.

Wolf drew a deep breath and held it, not exhaling until she began bathing his sinew-corded thigh. Then the breath whooshed out of him, leaving almost all of him limp.

Aurora didn't dare look at him as she continued washing his knee, then his leg and foot. Her mouth twitched when he jerked violently or when he groaned. She washed his other foot and began to work her way up his other leg.

"You've become a tease while I was gone," Wolf said in a strangled voice as she soaped his upper thigh.

"Am I bothering you?"

Wolf grumbled under his breath, while gripping the buffalo robe tightly with both hands.

Aurora knelt back and rested her soapy hands on her thighs. "All right, I'm done with this side. Now roll over."

"Don't you think you missed something?" he gritted through tightly clenched teeth.

She looked him up and down, as if puzzled. "Oh—that. I'll get it last."

"You speak true," Wolf promised. He tangled a hand in her hair, pulled her across his broad chest, and planted a resounding kiss on her mouth.

When he released her, Aurora sat up slowly, stunned by his power, even in his exhausted state.

Their eyes locked as he slid his large hand between her thighs and felt the warm moisture. "Ah, that's good. You're torturing yourself as well as me." A lazy smile lifted the corners of his mouth, and he flopped over onto his stomach. "Finish bathing me, White-eyes."

Aurora's mouth gaped. Her brow furrowed and she eyed him thoughtfully, for much as she'd taunted and teased him, he'd just regained control of the situation. It was up to her to make him lose it again, she decided as she soaped her hands. And by God, he would.

She massaged the tight muscles in his back, feeling them slowly loosen beneath her soapy fingers, then moved on to his buttocks and legs. And all the time her heart was drumming against her ribs. She took her time, rinsing him thoroughly with the soft doeskin, then drying him.

Finally she knelt back. "I'm done. You can roll over now, Wolf."

His head pillowed on his folded arms, Wolf had been silent as she washed him. Now he didn't move.

"Wolf?" He still didn't move. "All right, you win. Now stop fooling around or I'm going to tickle you." She prodded his side with her finger.

Nothing.

"Hah! This'll get you." Leaning close, she blew a soft breath in his ear. He still didn't move. As she sat back on her heels, she realized he wasn't teasing her.

He was asleep.

"Well, I'll be," she murmured. "Looks like I outsmarted myself." Aurora smiled, then she chuckled. Stretching out, she wrapped her arms around Wolf and rested her head on his broad back. He might be exhausted, but at least he was back in her arms. He smelled of pungent yucca soap rather than his normal male scent, but it didn't matter; he smelled wonderful.

"Thank God you're back. You're back!" She rained kisses across his skin.

Her lips brushed across the raised flesh of a scar, then she found another and another and another and she kissed them all. And gradually her kisses became sobs as she wept for the pain he'd endured with each bite of her father's whip.

"Oh, Papa, how could you do this to the man I love?" she whispered. Her hot, salty tears washed over the wild tangle of scars, as if she could wash away his pain. "How could you?"

* * *

Dawn's light already pinked the eastern sky when someone coughed softly outside the wicki-up. Aurora awakened instantly. She lay on the buffalo robe bed and realized that sometime in the night, Wolf must have carried her over to it. He lay beside her on his stomach, his arm resting across her breasts, his eyes closed. She started to ease away. Instantly his arm tightened around her. Surprised, she glanced at him and found his eyes wide open and questioning.

"Someone's sick, Wolf. I have to go."

His nostrils flared as he inhaled her scent, but he released her. "Go. I had you all night."

Aurora threw on her clothes. Ducking outside, she found Pincus nervously shuffling his feet.

"Sorry to bother you," he said, looking every-where but at her. "Bear Killer's son is feverish and I think you'd better take a look at him."

She couldn't help groaning. "Oh no! Of all the children who could have gotten sick. All right, let me grab my medicine bag and we'll go."

Wolf had rolled over onto his back. Now he rested his head on his clasped hands and watched as she edged past him to get her bag. "Who's sick?"

"Peaches."

Aurora followed Pincus through the village. Bear Killer's wickiup was set back from the others, as if he wanted to be alone. She pushed aside the bearskin covering the entrance and ducked inside.

A small fire burned in the center, dimly lighting the interior. Peaches sprawled on an untidy pile of deerskins. His light complexion had a pallor Auro-ra didn't like. As she would have knelt by him, Bear Killer stepped from the shadows.

"No!" he hissed in Spanish, glaring at her.

"Don't touch him." Rounding on Pincus, he cried, "I told you not to bring the witch here."

"Your son is very ill, Bear Killer. Let me examine him and see what I can do for him."

"Haven't you done enough, Witch? You poisoned him last night. My son is very brave and that is why he cried out when you touched him. He knew you were evil and that you carried death." He came toward her slowly, clenching and unclenching his fists.

"No! That's not true!" She moved back, only to come up against a stone wall of a body. A glance over her shoulder reassured her. "Wolf!"

His gaze didn't waver from Bear Killer, even as his large hands settled around her waist and he lifted her to the side and put her behind him.

"Bear Killer," he said in Apache, "you heard me tell The People that some could still become ill before the White-eyes medicine would grow strong."

"Bah! What kind of medicine can it be, that it has to grow strong in our bodies? White-eyes lies. You're under the woman's spell, Ma'cho Nalzhee. She's come between you and The People. She poisoned my son and you helped her!"

"You are a fool if you believe that." Wolf's eyes were cold as black ice and as hard.

"No, you are the fool. She is a White-eyes, an enemy. What kind of potion does she feed you to bewitch you so?"

"I know exactly what she is. I knew when I captured her and I know now. Her father is the man who—" Wolf broke off. No Apache but he knew that Artemus Spencer had murdered Geronimo's beloved younger sister. No other Apache must ever know. "Her father will pay a huge ransom of guns and ammunition for her," he finished, using his avowed reason for kidnapping Aurora.

"Bah! Where are the guns? Where are the bullets?"

"He is collecting them now. I saw them while I was at Fort Bowie getting the vaccine." A tiny gasp behind him told Wolf that Aurora had understood his words.

He glanced at Peaches, who slept fitfully, moaning and scratching at the red splotches on his body. "Bear Killer, she is a skilled medicine woman," Wolf said. "For your son's sake, let her see if she can help him."

Bear Killer studied his son for long moments. Abruptly he nodded. "For today only she may make medicine over him. But if he is not better by tomorrow—"

"We will talk again." Turning to Aurora, Wolf added, "You can see to the child, but don't make any quick moves or give him anything without first showing it to Bear Killer."

She peeked around his broad shoulders at the still-glowering Apache. "He thinks I'm a witch, doesn't he?"

"He doesn't like either of us, but he loves his son and will do anything for him. Now, the question is, can you do anything for him?"

"Let's hope so." Kneeling beside the boy, she felt his forehead, then uncovered him to check the progress of the smallpox. He had a high fever and was painfully thin, with matchstick arms and legs. In fact, he didn't look as if he had any reserves of strength to fight the deadly disease. Aurora would have sighed with despair, but knew all three men were watching her every move. "Wolf, there's one dose of quinine powder left in my bag. Would you mix it up in some water?"

Wolf fished in her bag and drew out a packet of white powder wrapped in glassine paper. "This?"

She glanced over her shoulder. "Yes. And bring me some wet cloths and alcohol so I can bathe him. Maybe that will bring down the fever."

In moments he handed her a gourd full of bitter quinine water. She awakened Peaches, fed him some, then let him go back to sleep.

As she bent over Peaches, Aurora was aware of the way Wolf watched her. What would it be like to have a child with him? She pictured a toddler running to greet him, throwing his short chubby arms around Wolf's leg as he looked up at his father. Would he love their child even though it was part hated White-eyes?

Wolf watched as she bathed the boy, drawing the wet cloth over his whip-thin limbs. Her luxurious mane tumbled over her shoulders, reminding him of its feathery touch the night before. A flash of heat surged in his blood. What would it be like to have a child with her? Would she bend over their child, cuddling and crooning to him as tenderly as she crooned to Bear Killer's son?

Would she love a child who came from their joining?

Not likely. She'd told him she hated him. He frowned pensively. Did she indeed still hate him? She'd told him so often enough in those first days, but lately there had been other words between them, words of passion and want and need. Could her feelings for him be changing?

What did it matter? She was the daughter of his mother's murderer. He'd kidnapped her for revenge and to slake his desire for her. He didn't need soft words from her, only her body.

But what about her heart and her mind and her mouth? a voice asked from deep inside him. And he knew he needed and wanted all of them from her, more than he wanted her body.

He became aware of the scrutiny of the other men and he stiffened. His gaze pinned Bear Killer, then Pincus, and he realized both men had been watching him as he watched Aurora.

He squared his shoulders, silently daring either of them to say anything. Then he spun on his heel and stalked out of the wickiup. Outside, he stared into the scarlet flames of the morning campfire, his thoughts still with Aurora. Last night they'd both reveled in her teasing and taunting, for it had been the greeting of a strong woman to her man.

What babies they would make in the coming years! Creatures of flame and passion and courage. Brave warriors. Women brave enough to be warriors' women.

The bearskin slid back and someone emerged from the wickiup, but Wolf didn't look up. He stared into the flames and saw the coming years. He saw Aurora and his children running across flower-filled mountain meadows in the Chiricahuas. He saw—

"She cared for your people while you were gone, Wolf." Pincus's voice ripped his vision of their children to shreds and dragged him back to an Apache village hidden on a mesa in Mexico.

"I know." Wolf drew a smoke-tanged breath deep into his lungs. "My people have told me what she did."

"But now the vaccinations are done and there's no more she can do. She's no further use to you."

Oh yes, she was. He needed her! He needed her courage and her spirit and her passion. Crossing his arms over his chest, he looked up, piercing Pincus with his steely gaze. "Be careful where you tread, old man."

"I am an old man, and that's why I'm not afraid to say this to you. Let her return to her own people, where she belongs. Let her go."

"Never." Wolf stalked away.

Yet he knew that he and Aurora would share no future, that he would have no children with the woman who set fire to his loins. He had found the woman he would want and need forever, but destiny had made her the daughter of his enemy.

Once in the sheltering forest, hidden from everyone's view, he braced a hand against an oak. All around him were sounds of life: jays scolded, squirrels chattered, quail called. All had mates. All had young ones to nurture and raise. He ran his fingers over the rough bark. He, too, had a mate.

But she was a White-eyes. White-eyes had shown him nothing but betrayal and hate, nothing of honesty, nothing of trust. How could he think she was different?

The rustle of footsteps on dried leaves made him look up. Through the trees he glimpsed Aurora coming up the trail. Her head was down as she picked her way through the tangled undergrowth.

A tidal wave of desire washed over him. He stepped onto the trail in front of her.

She looked up and her eyes widened at his sudden appearance. "Wolf?" That was all she had time to say before he backed her against a tree.

She was his mate and he'd waited a lifetime for her. In spite of everything, she was his mate!

He sank his fingers into her glorious silken

mane, holding her head still for his kiss. Did she feel anything for him? he wondered as he drank from her lips. She must, for their joinings were times of wild beauty. Surely even a White-eyes couldn't fake that.

Lifting his head, he catalogued her chin and mouth and nose and eyes. "I want you," he murmured as he swung her up in his arms and carried her deeper into the forest.

"The thought of you waiting for me kept me going through dust and darkness and death," he said as he stopped and slowly let her legs swing down until she could stand. "I wanted to stroke you . . . like this." He drew a single finger down her arm. "I wanted to kiss you . . . like this." He ravaged her mouth with tender fierceness. "I wanted to touch you like this . . . and this . . . and this."

His lips were hot against her throat and her head fell back across his arm. "Please, Wolf," she whispered.

"That's exactly what I intend to do."

He laid her down on a bed of springy moss, then threw off his clothes and joined her, drawing her into his arms and kissing her tenderly, enticingly. She writhed beneath him, calling to him with her tongue and lips and hands and body.

Then he came to her. She sighed and clung to him as she stretched to accommodate him. He drank tiny cries of passion from her lips. "Ohh, yes." She wrapped her long legs around his waist and moved with him

They united in passion and desire. Wolf could feel her heels digging into the backs of his thighs as he thrust against her tightness. He could smell her wildflower scent. He drove into her harder and harder, goaded by anger and sorrow at what could never be, by anger and sorrow at the destiny that had brought them together—and would leave them forever separated.

She stiffened in his arms and gave a wild cry of joy. Then he soared into the sun.

Later, as he held her, Wolf wanted her again. Union had made them one, but it hadn't eased his anger or grief or need.

He gazed at her and knew he would never get enough of his woman of fire. His *kun isdzán*.

Chapter 20

Aurora lay in Wolf's arms, boneless and satiated. He still blanketed her, and she savored his warmth, wrapped in her love for him. She caressed his back and felt the ridged scars snaking across his flesh, and once again she felt his pain, pain that her father had inflicted.

"Wolf, I—" Turning her face against his throat, she began to sob bleakly.

Wolf tightened his arms around her. "What is it, *isdzán*? Did I hurt you?"

"No. It's just that Papa—" Pulling back in his arms, she gazed at him with tear-filled eyes. "I'm so sorry for the pain Papa gave you. So sorry. If only there was some way I could take that pain away."

He went very still. "So you finally admit that it was your father who killed my mother?"

She gasped. "No! I was talking about when he lashed you."

Yet he was right; she was beginning to believe that her father had killed Wolf's mother. And that had given Wolf far more pain than any lashing ever could. What her father had done that day, so many years earlier, would come between them for the rest of their lives. She felt her heart break, for she knew there was no hope for a future with Wolf.

A terrifying vision opened before her. She was sitting in the parlor of a lovely two-story house, but it wasn't Wolf's house. Her husband was upstairs, but he wasn't Wolf. Two toddlers came running to her, their faces smeared with strawberry jam. And though she loved them, they were not Wolf's children.

The pain of her future, a future without Wolf, clawed at her. She tried to take a deep breath, but she couldn't. The agony was too sharp. She had to get away from it. She had to.

Turning, she dashed into the forest, dodging the bushes that reached out to grab her. Her heart wept for a love that would never blossom.

"Aurora, wait!" Wolf pounded along behind her, adding wings to her feet, for she didn't want him to catch her, didn't want to face him, not when all her pain was still visible.

She couldn't outdistance him, though, and his strong hands settled on her shoulders and he whirled her around.

"Let me go!" She kicked him on the shin. She couldn't breathe. The pain was too strong, like a vise around her heart, squeezing tightly.

"No! What is wrong, woman?"

"Damn you, Wolf!" She pounded his chest with her fists. 'Damn you! Damn you! Damn you!"

Though she was strong for a woman, her strength was no match for his. Wolf held her loosely, waiting for her fury to pass. Each blow was like a leather gauntlet striking his face, reminding him of the future and the children that would never be theirs.

When she finally stared up at him, wild-eyed but silent, he said the first thing that came to mind. "Why did you run? I told you never to run from me."

"That's right, I forgot. Running prey brings out the predator in you, doesn't it?" she sneered, even as she fought the pain deep inside her, the pain for what might have been, but never would be.

Is that what she thought? That she was prey to him? How could he tell her he needed her, that she was the woman he'd searched for all his life? Why would she believe him? "If you're going to call me savage, then I will act the part," he growled.

His lips came down on hers and he ravaged her mouth quite thoroughly. Aurora struggled, first to get away, then not to respond to him. She lost both battles.

She arrowed her fingers through his hair and pulled it hard, even as she kissed him back. How many times more would she be able to hold him like this and kiss him like this? What hope was there for them?

Wolf groaned far back in his throat and pulled her down beneath the ancient oaks. They rolled over and over, passionately fighting and making love at the same time, each driven by anger at what could never be, each grieving for a future that would never be theirs. Each full of need for the other. When it was over, they lay locked in each other's arms, gasping for breath, unable to speak, unable to move.

Wolf was the first to recover. He brushed a sweat-dampened curl off her forehead. "I'm sorry." His voice was low, contrite. "Did I hurt you?"

"No." Aurora shook her head. "Yes. Yes, you did. Must you always humiliate me like this?"

Wolf raised his head so he could gaze at her. "Humiliate you? How?"

"By making me want you!" She turned her head, as though she couldn't stand the sight of him.

"Ah, my woman of fire." He dropped a kiss at the corner of her eye. "I did not know. How would you suggest I avoid this humiliation of you?"

"Leave me alone." With a sudden rush of strength, she tried to push herself out of his arms, but he tightened them.

"I can't, my *isdzán*," he admitted reluctantly. "I like feeling your naked body pressed to mine. I like the feel of your breasts pressed to my chest. I like filling my hands with your curves. I like sinking into your welcoming warmth."

"I don't like it."

"That's not what your body says."

She turned away, letting her hair fall between them like a curtain. "My body lies," she mumbled.

"You tempt me to show you once again what your body says." He flicked his thumb across her nipple and watched it harden to his touch.

Distant shouts made them look up.

"Someone's coming." Aurora pushed at him frantically. "Get off. Please, Wolf, move!"

"No, they're not." Tilting his head, Wolf listened to the shouts.

"Yes, they are. Let me go." When Wolf released her, she rolled away, scrambled to her knees, and glanced about for her clothes. "Quick, help me find my clothes."

Wolf scanned the clearing, then dragged a hand through his hair. "They aren't here. They're up by the trail."

Aurora moaned and sat down suddenly. "Are you telling me I ran through the forest naked?"

"So did I," Wolf said dryly.

"It's different for you. What will I—"

He motioned for silence as the shouts resumed. "There's illness in Destarte's wickiup."

Aurora snapped to alert. "Destarte?"

"Blue Hawk. Come on, let's go." He helped her to her feet, then started off through the forest.

"But"—she had to run to keep up with his ground-eating stride—"our clothes."

"I'll go ahead and get them before anyone sees you." He lengthened his stride and moved away from her with astonishing speed. A few minutes later he returned and tossed her clothes to her. He began to pull on his breeches.

"That poor child." Aurora pulled her blouse over her head. "Do you know that from the first day of sickness, Blue Hawk played his flute for the village. Every day his music soared over the village and lifted everyone's heart."

Wolf led the way down the trail. "Don't forget that he's gone on a war raid and proved himself a warrior. He's important to me, Aurora, for he's a warrior like no other."

"You know I'll do my best," she replied stiffly as they approached the village.

"That's all I ask."

Inside the wickiup, she was surprised to find that Destarte didn't face her with hatred. This time she wrung her hands and looked helplessly at her younger brother. Blue Hawk was in a coma and running one of the highest fevers Aurora had yet encountered.

"He needs to be bathed in cool water until the

fever comes down." She waited for Wolf, who paced restlessly, to say something.

"You heard her, Destarte. Get some cloth and cool water," he snapped. After Destarte left, he asked. "Will he survive?"

"I don't know; his fever is so high. It'll depend on his care."

"I will see to it."

"You'll do it?"

"Of course. He's one of my warriors." When Destarte returned, he took a cloth and dipped it in the water she'd brought. Wringing it out, he began wiping Blue Hawk's thin, childish chest.

Aurora watched him for a moment, then quietly left. So much had happened that morning. She felt wrung out and exhausted, almost shaky.

By the time Aurora finished her rounds, the sun was close to setting.

At their wickiup that night, there was a stiffness to their talk and tension between them. Neither mentioned what had happened that morning. Neither forgot.

When Aurora checked her patients the next day, she found Blue Hawk was better while Peaches had worsened. She bathed Peaches, then held him, crooning soft words to him. But all her skill wasn't enough, and she could tell he was slipping deeper and deeper into a coma.

Peaches had been holding her hand, as if he could hold onto life that way. As his tiny hand relaxed and his grip loosened, she began to weep. Bear Killer gave an inarticulate cry and fled into the woods.

Aurora stood up slowly, grieving for the life cut so short. Only when Wolf rested his hands on her shoulders did she look up, startled. "I didn't know you were here," she murmured.

"I just came in. Come, we must leave and let Bear Killer see to his dead." He guided her outside.

By the time she and Wolf reached their wickiup, she saw a fiery glow coming from the village. "What's that?"

"Bear Killer is burning his wickiup. It's what we do when someone dies."

She looked at him, dull-eyed and exhausted. "I know, I saw many wickiups burned while you were gone. I didn't expect it now, though, after we'd done the vaccinating."

"You said it would take time for the vaccine to grow strong in our bodies."

"Yes, but I really didn't expect more deaths, I guess. And he was so young."

The days and nights that followed blurred into an endless round of patients. Aurora began to fear the vaccinations hadn't worked. Wolf, with quiet strength, kept her going time after time when she wanted to quit.

At night she would stumble back to the wickiup, exhausted. Often she would find a haunch or rack of venison roasting over the fire. Wolf hunted every day, bringing back meat which he shared with the widows, orphans, and sick Apaches, anyone who had no one to hunt for them.

Aurora was impressed by the way the Apaches took care of one another. Other warriors followed Wolf's lead and hunted for those who couldn't, while the women left baskets of food at the wicki-ups of those who were too ill to cook.

All through those exhausting, frantic days, there was a tension, a wariness between Wolf and Aurora. Often she would look up from her work and find him watching her. Sometimes she felt as if they were two lions circling each other, wary, waiting for an attack each believed was coming from the other.

Only at night, when their hands and lips and bodies spoke another language, a language of the heart, were they free with each other. But even then there was an undertone of urgency, as if they knew their nights together were numbered.

Every day Aurora was torn between her love for Wolf and for her father. She had to stop Wolf from killing her father. But how?

Finally there came a day with no new sickness, then a second, and a third, and Aurora began to hope that the epidemic was over.

Wolf was hunting and she was alone. She hadn't seen Pincus in days, except for hurried moments, so she took the opportunity to visit him.

The deerskin covering his wickiup entrance was up. He sat inside, studying a stack of photographs.

"Have you got some new pictures to show me?" she asked, bending to look in.

"No." He emerged and shoved his hands into his pants pockets. "There won't be any more photographs, I'm afraid. I'm out of developing chemicals. It's time to return to civilization."

"Civilization? I haven't thought about it for so long." She looked around at the leaves that turned each oak into a golden pyramid. "You know, it's strange, but I almost feel as if I've always lived here."

"You haven't and, believe me, you don't want to, unless you want to grow old before your time. Look around you. These people live an incredibly hard life. They barely survive. It was a nice adventure while it lasted, but enough's enough." He glanced around, as if making sure no one was close enough to overhear them. "I'm ready to get back to civilization, Aurora, and soft feather beds and sturdy walls that keep out winter winds. How about you?"

"Yes, I guess so." Tilting her head, she frowned at him. "Just what do you mean?"

"They've stopped guarding us. If we planned carefully and bided our time until the right moment, we could get away."

"You mean escape?"

He glanced at her, obviously puzzled. "Are you being deliberately obtuse, or have you been drinking this morning?"

"No. It's just that the idea is so startling." She rubbed her hands over her arms, feeling chilled.

"Why? You tried to escape before. What's different about now?"

Crossing her arms over her breasts, she leaned against an oak, thinking. How could she explain that she'd fallen in love with Wolf? She flicked Pincus a quick glance. Surely he suspected. "I couldn't leave now, Pincus. Too many people are still recovering from the smallpox and I—"

He walked over to stand directly in front of her. "I won't leave without you, Aurora. You know that, don't you?" He was telling her that if she didn't come, he would be stuck there also.

"You really think we could make it?"

"I think we'd have a damn good chance. I watched the trail closely when the Apaches brought me here. But we're going to have to go soon, before snow blocks the mountain passes. What do you say? I've been putting aside food and I've already got my pictures packed in saddlebags.

Just say the word and we could be out of here tonight."

She began to pace, rubbing her hands over her upper arms. "I can't go on a moment's notice, Pincus. Wolf's people need me." How could she leave Wolf? That would be like tearing out her heart.

"Don't lie to yourself. They don't need you." His eyes searched her mobile features. "Neither does Wolf."

She spun away from him, heart thumping like a startled doe's. "Don't say that! Wolf does need me. He told me so."

"You're blind to the truth." Pincus grabbed her arm, bringing her to an abrupt halt. His eyes were harder than she'd ever seen them. "Don't torture yourself. There's nothing here for you, and I mean nothing. Not Wolf or anything else. Don't you realize nothing can come of this infatuation between you and Wolf? You come from two different worlds."

"I can't. Wolf's people need me," she whispered.

"No, they don't. Bear Killer is telling everyone you're a witch and that you murdered his son and saved a useless cripple. And he isn't the only one that hates you."

"Don't wait for me. Just go."

"And face your father when I get back to Fort Bowie and tell him I left his little girl in the clutches of an Apache chief? No, thank you. I may be foolhardy, but I'm not crazy." He spun away, then faced her from across the small clearing. "Do you remember Wolf mentioning that your father was collecting the guns and ammunition for your ransom?"

"Yes, but—"

"What if your father is already on his way south? All we'd have to do is ride away from here and we'd meet him."

When she didn't say anything, he continued, "Damn it, Aurora, don't let romantic dreams chain you here. Wolf is an Apache chief. His loyalties, his responsibilities, are to his people, not a White-eyes woman. "Don't wait for him to—" He gave her an intent look, then turned away. "What's the use?"

She rubbed her forehead pensively. "I have to think about this. It's all coming so fast. Besides, you don't know Wolf as I do. He's an honorable man."

"Apache honor isn't the same as what we call honor."

"Oh? How about when he asked Chili Eater to sleep at my fire and protect me when he was gone?"

"Are you sure he was there to protect you? What if he was guarding you to make sure you didn't escape? Have you ever wondered if that necklace Wolf gave you, the one you wear so proudly, could actually be a collar, marking you as his property?"

Aurora stared at him as she remembered Chili Eater's words the night Wolf had ridden away. He'd called her necklace a collar. "No, you've got it all wrong."

"And what if I haven't? Don't let love make you blind to the true situation here. Wolf is holding you for ransom from you father."

She squared her shoulders resolutely. "I don't think we're getting anywhere. Why don't we just drop it? I'll talk to you in a few days."

But as she walked away, she couldn't help looking back. Was there a chance he was right?

* * *

That evening she sat by the fire, waiting for Wolf. Was Pincus right? Was she living in a dream world? Time and again in the days since Wolf had returned, she'd almost told him she loved him. Time and again she'd wondered whether he would believe her if she did tell him she loved him. And could she find some words, some plea, that would make him give up the idea of killing her father? For if she couldn't, there was no hope for them.

She stared into the flickering flames, but they had no answer for her that night. When the fire died, she crawled into the buffalo robes. Long after she'd gone to sleep, Wolf joined her and wrapped her close.

"Where were you?" she murmured drowsily.

"I had to hunt far away. The deer are disappearing. And Ghost Face will be long and hard this year."

"Oh." The smell of horses and leather mixed with his own scent told her he'd ridden far that day. "Wolf, I—" She paused, wondering how to ask the questions she needed to ask. "Are you asleep?" A soft, muffled snore answered her.

A hard frost came to the mesa that night, and when Aurora awoke, a thin sheet of ice covered the water in the drinking gourds. She threw on her thin blouse and skirt, then added a deerhide poncho for extra warmth. The frozen grass crackled beneath her moccasins when she stepped outside.

She'd taken only a single step when she spied a neatly folded deerskin beside the entrance. Puzzled, she knelt to examine it. She unfolded an intricately beaded deerskin shirt. Beneath it was a pair of butter-soft moccasins covered with yellow, white, and blue beadwork. "Wolf, what is this?" she asked as he stepped out of the wickiup. She held the shirt up to him, measuring it against his broad shoulders. "This is too small for you."

"It's for you, not me. So are the moccasins." He glanced down at the village, visible through the oaks now that they were losing their leaves. "They're gifts. Women have left them to thank you for what you did for their families."

"But I didn't do anything special. I was just being a doctor." She smoothed her hand down the velvet-soft deerhide.

"My people think you did." He toyed with her fire-gold hair, winding it over his finger. "I don't know how many would have died without your vaccinations. Keep these gifts and honor the women who made them by wearing them."

"Are they both from one person?"

His bittersweet smile was a white slash across his copper features. "No Apache woman is that rich."

She clutched the shirt and moccasins as she glanced at him. "I'm touched. I never expected your people to—" She ran her hand over the shirt again. "I didn't even know if they liked me. I'll wear them today." She ducked inside and in a moment came back out. "This is so beautiful." The top half of the shirt was bead-covered, like a magnificent jeweled breastplate.

"Yes, it is." His eyes flashed, warming her far more than the buckskin poncho. He walked over to the woodpile and picked up a chunk of firewood. "I think you have another gift over here."

Aurora stiffened when she saw the cast-iron pot behind the woodpile. "What's this? A cooking pot? Is someone telling me to improve my cooking?"

"You don't understand. That's not it at all." Gathering an armful of wood, he walked over to the firepit and dropped it close by. "Someone has just given you the most precious thing in her wickiup. You should feel very honored. Other than her jewelry, a cast-iron pot is the most valuable thing an Apache woman owns. We can't make them so we have to trade for them, and they're handed down from generation to generation. Without one, a woman is reduced to cooking in pottery, but clay breaks easily, and often the food is lost into the fire. Then a family goes to bed hungry."

"That's terrible! I can't take it, I'll give it back."

"You must not. You would dishonor the woman who gave it to you." He stirred the fire until it began to catch. "Besides, you don't know who left it."

"I can find out easily enough. All I have to do is walk around until I find someone cooking with pottery instead of an iron pot."

"You will not have time for that. We are leaving here in a few hours."

"Leaving? Why?"

"The deer grow scarce. There aren't enough to carry us through the moons of Ghost Face. Juh's people and mine make over five hundred to feed. And the people who were ill aren't regaining their strength." He glanced up at the iron-gray clouds scudding across the sky. "Those look like snow. If the time of Ghost Face is as bad as Geronimo predicts, the weak ones won't make it."

"It doesn't snow here, does it?"

He gave her a startled look. "Yes, it snows here. It snows in the desert, too, but there it isn't as cold as the mountains." He scooped the ice out of the water gourd and drank deeply. "Pack everything you can. We're moving to the desert today."

"But isn't that dangerous? What about the Bluecoats and the Mexicans?'' She sounded like an Apache, talking about Bluecoats.

"Yes, but my people have been too weakened by the smallpox.'' He shook a handful of dried berries out of a deerskin bag and began to chew them. "Many are still recovering, and now the game grows scarce. They will have a better chance of surviving in the desert, where it is only cold at night.''

"Are we going back to Arizona?'' She, too, shook out a handful of berries and began to eat, trying to seem unconcerned.

He turned and gave her a long, unreadable look. "There is much desert in northern Mexico. We do not have to return to Arizona.''

"But you'd like to, wouldn't you? That's where your people's home is, isn't it?''

"You ask too many questions, White-eyes.'' He stalked past her.

She grabbed his arm. "That's what you told me in the cave. It didn't stop me there, and it won't stop me now.''

Anger flashed in his eyes. "Maybe this will.'' He cradled her cheeks in his palms and his mouth came down over hers, quite effectively silencing her. Abruptly he released her and turned away.

"That's only a short-term solution,'' Aurora snapped.

He kept walking. "I'll be back with a pack mule within the hour.''

As she packed their few belongings, Aurora tried to decide what she'd do if they should meet her father coming south to rescue her. She loved her father, but she loved Wolf, too. She tied the rawhide thongs around their buffalo robes even as she brushed moisture from her cheeks.

What cruel twist of fate had led her to fall in love with the man who wanted to kill her father?

And how was she going to stop him?

Chapter 21

Aurora coughed as clouds of dust and grit rolled over her. They'd been traveling for three days, and she could feel the sandy grit between her toes and her teeth and even on her tongue.

She walked in a long column of over five hundred Apaches. The women led horses and mules loaded with their meager supplies as they snaked across a grassy plain dotted with lonely mesquite trees. On all sides, distant snow-capped mountains trumpeted the coming of Ghost Face.

Wolf had wanted her to ride, but she'd insisted on walking as the other women did. It would be hard, but she knew there was much grumbling among the men about his treatment of her. Bear Killer wasn't the only one who hated her.

Aurora glanced around. Except for Destarte, the women seemed to have accepted her. She smiled at Many Tongues, who walked nearby, carrying her infant son strapped in a cradleboard. Aurora had discovered that it was Many Tongues who'd given her the cast-iron pot.

Seated on a huge black stallion, Wolf cantered out of the dust. Drawing rein, he stepped off the horse and fell into line beside her. She could smell his sweat mixed with the scent of his horse.

"How are you holding up?" He'd ridden up and down the line of women and children all day, watching for problems. Each time he'd passed, he had wanted to stop, but he'd made himself wait. Now it was late afternoon and the sun was a blood-red globe in the sky.

"Dusty. Dirty. Tired." She flicked her braids back over her shoulders, but didn't look at him. She had searched for a way to reason with Wolf, to make him see he wouldn't accomplish anything by killing her father. As they marched north, she watched the horizon ahead intently, ever fearful of meeting Papa riding south. How would she stop Wolf from killing him if that happened?

"We'll stop soon." Each day that they marched northward he could feel the tension rising between Aurora and himself. "See the mountains straight ahead?"

Shading her eyes with her hand, Aurora studied the three almost equal peaks on the horizon. "Yes?"

"We'll camp at the base of the middle peak for a few days and let everyone rest up. There's a stream there."

"I'm glad. You're moving too fast, Wolf. I worry about the ones who were sick. They don't have the energy to keep up this kind of a trek."

He gave her a guarded look. "We have to. We're too exposed crossing this plain."

The tension in his voice made her look up. The brackets around his mouth had deepened and his eyes were red-rimmed with fatigue. "What are you worried about?"

"There is always danger for my people." Months earlier, he'd led his people on another journey as they fled the White-eyes. That one had ended at the hidden mesa, where they'd been safe. He hoped this one would end as safely.

Sunlight flashed off something on the crest of the low ridge that flanked them on the right.

"Did you see that?" He went on full alert, squinting at the boulder-strewn slope, trying to make out details among the confusing elongated, late-afternoon shadows.

"What? I didn't see anything. Why are you so jumpy?"

"I need to check something. I'll see you before we camp." Swinging up on the stallion, he cantered nonchalantly along the column of women. If someone was watching, Wolf didn't want him to know he'd been spotted.

Calling over a warrior, he sent him to circle behind the ridge. It was the second time he'd seen sunlight glint off something there. The man he'd sent out before had returned after finding only unshod pony tracks where Wolf had seen the first flash.

But he couldn't rid himself of a prickly feeling along the back of his neck. Something wasn't right.

He glanced back, checking to see where his few men were. Geronimo had seen a large cattle herd earlier and had taken many warriors to bring it back. Wolf studied the men he had left. Bear Killer and his young, hot-headed followers, Juh and his sons, and a few more, were the only ones left to guard the women.

A faint, sweet, smoky scent drifted on the breeze. Wolf sniffed, trying to place it. Burning tobacco. A pipe. None of his warriors would smoke when on the march. That meant—

"*Rurales!* Soldiers!" Whirling the stallion, he raced along the line of women and children. "*Rurales!* Take cover! Hide!"

Instantly the column degenerated into chaos as the women turned the pack horses and mules loose. He looked for Aurora, but couldn't find her in the dust and confusion.

A long line of Mexican soldiers in blood-red uniforms poured over the top of the ridge and headed straight for the women and children. The sharp, cracking boom of rifle fire drowned out the soldiers' battle yells.

"Aurora," he shouted, scanning the women running past. "Aurora!" He couldn't find her and there wasn't time—there wasn't time!

Wolf saw the warriors at the front and rear of the column race to cut off the Mexicans before they reached the women and children. A shallow arroyo cut across the plain directly in front of the Mexicans, and there the warriors tumbled off their horses and prepared to make a stand.

Wolf galloped to join his warriors at the wash. They'd have to hold the Mexicans at the arroyo to give the women and children a chance to escape. Leaping into the shallow ditch, he rested his rifle on the sandy rim and aimed and fired, aimed and fired, again and again.

They had to give the women time to get away. That was the most important thing.

He was aware of a warrior firing beside him, but only when the gunfire lessened could he glance over to see who it was. "Blue Hawk, you're shooting as well as you play the flute." He clapped the boy on the back. "Keep it up, warrior."

As he spoke, Blue Hawk raised his rifle and shot over Wolf's shoulder. Wolf whirled to see a Mexican with a heavy sword sink to the ground barely an arm's length away.

"I owe you my life," he cried over the deafening roar of gunfire. "Here they come again."

He aimed and fired, aimed and fired. And all the time he prayed that Aurora was all right. During a lull, he scanned the plain, trying to pick out her flaming hair among the women. He couldn't.

The cries of fleeing women and children drummed against Aurora's ears in an unholy cacophony. A thick yellow fog of sulfur and gunpowder spread over the fugitives, and her mouth was filled with the bitter taste of fear.

As she ran she kept looking back, trying to make some sense of what was happening. She'd seen the warriors ride to meet the Mexicans, but where was Wolf? She'd lost sight of his big black stallion.

A stampeding horse galloped toward her, its eyes white with fright. The reins flapped loosely against its neck. If she could just grab one of the reins! As she raced to meet the horse, out of the corner of her eye she saw a crying infant in a cradleboard, half covered by its mother's lance-pierced body. Slowing and swerving, she scooped the baby up from the cradleboard.

At that moment, the horse galloped past.

Clutching the wailing baby to her breast, Aurora glanced around, looking for an escape route. Smoke and dust clouded the plain, occasionally clearing enough for her to see running horses or men struggling with one another.

She ran toward the low, melting adobe walls of an abandoned hut. It was the closest thing to a refuge she could find in the satanic red glare of the setting sun.

Thundering hooves drew closer and closer, and she looked back over her shoulder.

A Mexican soldier in a blood-red uniform leaned low on his charging horse and aimed his lance straight at her. Aurora screamed and dodged left.

He overran her. Reining his horse in a wide circle, he came around and leveled the lance at her again. There was no place to hide. Her heart pounding like a steam engine, Aurora dashed for the adobe ruins.

Suddenly, through her haze of fear, she glimpsed another Mexican in front of her. He'd ridden from the other side of the hut. His lance was pointed at her heart. She skidded to a halt, panting, trapped between them.

"Americano," she cried, pointing at herself. "Americano."

An evil smile played across the lancer's dark, mustached face. "Lying whore," he replied in Spanish. "I will collect a bounty on your scalp and that of the Apache bastard in your arms." Spurring his horse into a trot, he lowered his lance a notch.

"Wolf!" Aurora screamed as she ducked sideways and ran. *Hear me, Wolf! I need you—hear me!*

Wolf and Blue Hawk had pinned down a group of Mexicans. Wolf had just lowered his hot rifle to reload when he thought he heard Aurora scream.

Whirling, he searched the chaotic plain. A few Mexicans had broken through their line and were now loose among the women.

Suddenly he glimpsed Aurora's crown of flaming red hair trapped between two men on horseback.

"Bear Killer, help Blue Hawk," he cried as he swung up on the black stallion. Spurring the horse mercilessly, he was already racing toward Aurora when she screamed again.

It seemed to take him forever to cross the battlefield. He saw Aurora dodge toward an low adobe wall. One of the horsemen cut her off.

He had to reach her in time! He had to!

Raising his rifle, he began shooting long before he had a chance of hitting either lancer. One glanced at Wolf, then calmly raised his own rifle, sighted, and pulled the trigger. The bullet whistled over Wolf's head.

As he neared the closest lancer, his rifle jammed, so he sent the black stallion barreling straight into the Mexican's horse, knocking it off its feet. As the man rolled free, Wolf leaped off and reversing his rifle, clubbed him. He turned to the other. And froze.

The Mexican had jumped off his horse and grabbed Aurora, and he held her in front of him as a shield. Wolf saw it all in a split second. The Mexican's long bloody knife was pressed to her throat, keeping her from crying out a warning to him. She clutched a naked infant to her breast and stared at him, her eyes huge with terror.

His eyes locked with hers. *I'm here. I'll save you. I'm here.*

I know. I trust you. I love you.

"Hombre," the Mexican hissed from behind her.

"*Qué, hombre?*" Wolf growled as he took a step closer.

"Do you want your whore to live?" He pressed his knife harder against Aurora's throat.

Wolf stared at the lancer, his iron-hard eyes drilling into him. "The question is, do *you* want to live?" he said in a steel-edged tone. "Let the woman go."

"No! Don't come any closer," the Mexican ordered as Wolf took another step toward him. "Or I swear I'll—"

"You'll die!" Wolf's words lashed the Mexican.

"If I let her go, how do I know you'll let me go?"

"You don't. But if you harm her, then I swear that you won't live to see the sun set." His hands were tight fists and he balanced on the balls of his feet.

Neither man had to look at the sun to know it was sinking beneath the horizon.

The baby in Aurora's arms wailed. She cuddled it as she shushed it. The Mexican shifted to the right slightly. As he moved, he lowered the knife an infinitesimal bit. That was all Wolf needed.

He sprang at the Mexican, grabbing his knife arm and wrenching it away from Aurora. Simultaneously he shoved Aurora away with all the strength he could muster.

Turning, he grappled with the Mexican. In the back of his mind, Wolf knew Aurora had fallen and rolled away from them, but he couldn't help her. Not while the Mexican lived.

His eyes met the Mexican's. "My woman lives, *hombre*," he growled. "But you will not."

Aurora got to her feet slowly, breathless and shaking, still cradling the infant in her arms. She wanted to cover her ears so that she wouldn't hear the thud of the men's fists, their grunts and groans.

The metallic scent of blood mixed with the aroma of crushed sage as the men rolled over and over. There was a sharp thud, and the Mexican groaned and went limp.

Wolf flopped off him. Braced on his hands and knees, he took deep, labored breaths. He gazed numbly at the perspiration dripping off his nose and chin and sinking into the sand.

Cool hands touched his shoulder. "Wolf?"

He swung around and Aurora leaped back out of reach. "Are you all right?"

He nodded, too out of breath to speak.

"You killed the Mexican."

He shook his head. "He's unconscious. He hit his head on a rock. And you?" He scrambled to his feet.

"All right." She cuddled the baby.

He took a single step and wrapped her and the baby in his arms. "Thank God, I—"

Gunshots reminded Wolf that they weren't the only ones on the battlefield. He glanced over her shoulder and saw that the Mexicans had overrun the warriors and were loose among the women and children, like wolves among sheep.

His warriors were fighting them hand to hand, but they were terribly outnumbered. A massacre was in the making.

"Hide in the ruins. Keep your head down. I'll come back for you." He threw her his revolver. "Keep this. If I don't come back, don't come out for anything. No matter what you hear, Aurora, don't come out!" Swinging up on his stallion, he rode straight into the melee.

Only when she was safely behind the adobe walls did Aurora look at the baby closely. She gave a start of recognition, for she held Many Tongues' son.

Night fell and Aurora could still hear gunfire. She huddled in the shadows behind the low walls, trying to shut out the awful noise of battle. Wolf's last words echoed and reechoed in her mind. *No matter what you hear, don't come out.*

Gradually the gunfire stopped and the cries of the wounded faded. The plain became deathly quiet. Standing up, she peered around, trying to see into the darkness. She heard the steady clip-clop of a walking horse long before she could make it out, a dark shadow among dark shadows.

Who was coming? Wolf? Or an enemy?

She waited, hiding against a wall, silent as a wraith.

"Aurora?" Wolf's low voice came out of the darkness.

"Thank God." She sagged against the adobe as she began to tremble with relief.

He stepped off the horse and enfolded her and the baby in his arms. He smelled of the acrid, biting scent of gunpowder and blood and sweat, but he was alive. Leaning her head against his wide chest, she held him close.

He held her as tightly. "It's over. You're alive and I'm alive and it's over."

But inside he knew it was only beginning. It had been a massacre. His people had suffered terribly.

The baby began to cry again, and she cuddled him. "Poor little tyke," she crooned as tears of relief filled her eyes. "He's Many Tongues'."

"She's among the dead." Wolf held her as her hot tears fell on the baby.

"I-I-I'm all right," she finally got out, trying to

still the sobs. Swallowing noisily, she straightened and wiped her hand across her eyes. "What about Pincus?"

"He's all right. He was with Geronimo." He rubbed his chin against her tangled curls. For a moment he closed his eyes and just absorbed her into his being. He needed her this night.

Reluctantly he loosed his arms. "Can you come now? There are many wounded. Geronimo needs your help."

"Of course." She put aside her relief and grabbed for her self-confidence. She edged toward the horse. "Let's go."

He rested his large hand on her shoulder. "I needed you. I—" He coughed. "Never mind. You're right, let's go."

Aurora gasped as they rode into the Apache camp. The campfires lit a scene from Dante's *Inferno.* The wounded were everywhere. Slipping off Wolf's horse, she handed the sleeping baby to a young girl and set to work.

Wolf had found the pack horse that carried her medical bag. Taking it, she knelt beside She Who Sees Babies, who sat by her grandson, holding his hand. Even as she knelt, Aurora could see the boy wasn't breathing. Gently she took the old woman's withered hand in hers. The woman's leathery face crumpled and she clamped her hand over her mouth as she began to cry silently.

Aurora moved on, helping a warrior with a broken leg, a woman who'd been lanced. Wolf had warned her that wounded Apaches were trained to be silent and not give away their location to the enemy. Still, the utter silence unnerved her. There wasn't a moan from any of them. Only silence.

"Aurora." She spun around at Wolf's hoarse, almost unrecognizable call.

Out of the darkness his figure slowly materialized into the firelight. Wolf walked toward her, carrying Blue Hawk. The child's arms and legs hung limp and still; his head lolled back over Wolf's arm.

"He's dead," she said, even as she knelt beside the boy's still, slight form.

"I know. I felt his spirit fly away." Although his voice was steady, the anguish in his dark eyes staggered her. He turned and silently melted into the darkness.

Aurora went on, tending the wounded, doing what she could for the dying. Once she glanced up and saw Geronimo doing the same. Finally she retreated to a small fire at the edge of camp and slumped down beside a boulder. Drawing her legs up, she wrapped her arms around them and rested her forehead on her knees.

Someone came and sat beside her. She didn't have to open her eyes to know it was Wolf. He smelled of blood and sulfur and gunpowder . . . and pain, she realized. Concerned, she rested her hand on his sweaty arm. "Are you all right?"

"Yes." There was an emptiness, a deadness to his voice she'd never heard before.

"No, you're not. You're wounded." She trailed her finger across the back of his hand, tracing a still-bloody knife slash.

"It's nothing." He drew his hand away.

She wondered if he'd leave, but he just sat there and gazed at the fire. "What is it, Wolf? Can I help?"

He flashed her a look of black despair. "No. No

one can." He leaned his head back against the boulder and stared up at the stars for a long time. "Blue Hawk was special. He wasn't a seasoned warrior, yet he was important to my people. His music sang the song of the Apaches. And I killed him."

Aurora's brow furrowed. "Nonsense. How could you have killed him?"

"When I heard you cry out, I told Bear Killer to fight beside him and I left." He picked up a dry stick and ran his hand up and down it absently. "Bear Killer and he couldn't hold off the Mexicans, and they killed him."

"But you knew those soldiers would kill me." A cold chill slithered down her spine. Was he sorry he'd come to her aid? It was a question she didn't dare ask. She turned away, afraid he'd see the trembling of her lower lip.

He broke the stick and flung it away. Reaching out without looking at her, he grasped her shoulder and pulled her close. "Don't think I'm sorry for coming to you. You needed me." Turning slightly, he wrapped his other arm around her and rubbed his chin on her hair, now white with dust. "Be glad you have flaming hair, *isdzán*. That's how I spotted you. Strange, isn't it? That's also how I recognized your father."

She could feel the stiffness in him, the awful tension. His hands were on her, but his mind was somewhere else, somewhere she couldn't reach.

He gazed at the fire for a long time before he cleared his throat. "I need you. But my people need Blue Hawk, perhaps more than they'll ever know. His music was a bridge to other people, even to White-eyes."

"You have other bridges. Don't forget Pincus has

taken pictures of the Apache lifeway," she murmured.

He shook his head, his dust-stiffened hair sliding across her breasts in a rough caress. "But his pictures are flat images, dead moments frozen in time. Blue Hawk's music was alive, as full of life as water in the desert."

He'd betrayed The People, Wolf blasted himself. He'd put his needs above theirs. They needed him, but he'd run away from battle to save his woman.

After this attack by the Mexicans, he knew that his people could no longer survive surrounded by enemies. No safe place was left for them.

Could he lead The People into the world that was coming? For, he admitted with a heavy heart, the world of their fathers and grandfathers was gone. The lifeway The People had walked since the time before time began was ending.

Wolf tightened his arms around Aurora. Would he have done anything differently? No! In his heart he knew he'd had to go to her, for life without her would have been nothing. He realized he couldn't remember much of his life before her. She had the power to make him smile and, yes, even laugh. She brought fire and light where before there had been only cold and darkness.

He drew a deep breath, inhaling the scent of her, the fear and perspiration and blood and last hint of yucca root that lingered in her hair. He had kidnapped her for revenge, but something else had happened along the way. She'd captured his heart.

"I have to go back to the wounded," she said softly, pulling away from him. "Maybe I can do more."

"Go. They need you." *I need you also, but they need you more.*

As she walked away, a tiny ember of hope glowed deep inside Aurora. Maybe she'd been wrong about Wolf. Could he love her? Only a man who cared for her would have heard her cry for help in the din of battle. Wolf had heard.

She looked around at the Apaches. He was a *nantan*, a chief, and these were his people, the people he loved and felt responsible for. Yet he'd left them to come to her. Surely that was proof he loved her. The more she thought about it, the more she was sure. Only someone he loved could have drawn him from the defense of his people.

As she ministered to the wounded, she thought back to other times when she'd been in danger. When she'd come close to drowning, he'd saved her. When the rattlesnake left her delirious and near death, he looked after her. He could have let her die either time, but he hadn't.

Could he have cared for her even in those early days? Was that why the ruthless Apache had refused to answer her questions in the cave? Because he cared for her and didn't want to admit it?

Then had come the duel with Bear Killer, the fight in which he shed his blood for her, protected her. The memory made her heart leap wildly.

Straightening from bending over a wounded Apache woman, Aurora rubbed the small of her back. The more she thought about it, the more she was certain. That was why there were such fireworks when they made love. They came together as two people who loved each other.

All the signs had been there, but she hadn't seen them. What if she told him she loved him? She paused, struck by the idea. That was what she'd do as soon as the right opportunity came along.

Surely he'd believe her. And if he loved her, that meant he trusted her.

Exhausted, she slumped down between two boulders and rubbed her eyes wearily. Once Wolf knew she loved him, that they could have a life together, he would realize their future was more important than killing her father. She leaned her head against a boulder and breathed deeply.

Maybe there was hope for them after all.

After Aurora left, Wolf leaned back and studied the distant stars. Never in his life had he felt so torn. The People had claimed his loyalty from the time before he could walk. Then, after his mother's murder, his father had wrenched him away from all he'd known.

Many years later he'd returned to The People, an orphan. They had accepted him as the White-eyes had not. But what would life be if the woman of his heart was dead?

He felt as if he were being dragged in two directions by wild ponies. Could he survive?

A discreet cough warned him of the approach of one of The People. He looked up and found Geronimo entering the small circle of firelight. The older man squatted near the fire and drew aimless lines in the dust with his finger.

"What is it, Uncle?" Wolf asked, knowing Geronimo was waiting for his question.

"There is much talk. Many warriors are shocked that you left the battle line to go to the White-eyes woman."

"Is that all they say?"

"No." Geronimo pulled on his eyebrow. "Bear Killer is agitating the young bucks. Twice now you have scorned Destarte, and she will never forgive you. Blue Hawk's death is an excuse for her to hate you. Now they've joined forces. They say you have been bewitched by the woman, that you are no longer one of The People. They say that you are no longer fit to lead and that she is an evil witch."

"After she helped fight the White-eyes illness? After what she's done tonight?"

"When we fled the White-eyes three moons ago and joined Juh's village, the two villages were over six hundred strong, Stalking Wolf. Two moons ago you brought her to our village, and the White-eyes illness struck and we lost seventy of The People. Today she journeys with us and we are attacked by the *Rurales* and lose over a hundred. In the two moons you have had her in your wickiup, we have lost almost two hundred of The People. Are you sure she is not evil?"

Wolf stood slowly, aware of a chill that had nothing to do with the night air. "Who speaks these words, Uncle? You, or Destarte and Bear Killer?"

Geronimo also stood. "I speak them."

"Do you also think I was wrong to go to her?"

"I wasn't here, and for that I have regrets. I should have stayed with you instead of taking so many warriors on a cattle-stealing raid. But at least we heard the gunfire and returned."

"Yes, your arrival was what routed the Mexicans. But you haven't answered my question."

"I can't. I have never been bewitched by a woman as you apparently are, so I can't understand your thinking."

"What about Gay Woman? How did you feel when the Mexicans killed her twenty harvests ago?"

"I grieved. After all, she was the mother of my

sons and daughter. But you have no children with
this woman; you're not bound to her; she is nothing but a White-eyes. How do you think our people
feel? They look to you for leadership, and see a
warrior obsessed with a White-eyes woman."

Wolf stroked his jaw thoughtfully. "I am calling
a war council. Assemble the warriors."

Geronimo's head snapped up. *"Enjuh."*

Chapter 22

Aurora stood outside their wickiup, fighting a suffocating feeling of panic, as she watched Wolf throw the saddle on his black stallion. In the days since the massacre there had been no opportunity to tell him she loved him. Now he was preparing to ride away, and she still hadn't told him.

"How can you go raiding when we've only been back in Juh's Stronghold for a day? Your men are exhausted. They need rest and food, not a war raid, not more fighting."

"We must go to avenge our dead, and to stop the Mexicans. They are calling in more troops and when they think they have enough to massacre us, they'll come again. Today, tomorrow, next week, next month, they'll come again, unless we stop them now." He took a buffalo robe out of the wickiup and kneeling on the ground, rolled and tied it.

"Fighting and more fighting. Is that all you know?" Aurora drew her buffalo robe up around her throat to ward off the morning chill. She had to stop him; he was too exhausted to lead a war party.

"We go because we must. We've fought the Mexicans for over two hundred years." He tied the sleeping roll to the back of his saddle. "Now we fight the White-eyes, also. And we will go on fighting, for it's the only way to survive."

"You're wrong." She shivered, aware of a chill in her heart far colder than the fall morning. "It's not a way to live, only to die. What do you have to show for all your years of fighting the Mexicans? Have you won any peace?"

"We get supplies. They raise horses and mules and cattle, and we take them."

"And smallpox. Don't forget you got that from them, too. Wolf, hear me out, please. Your people need food and rest, not more fighting. You know there isn't enough game up here to feed Juh's people and yours through the winter, and you know they're too weak to survive on starvation rations. Take your people back to the San Carlos Reservation."

His brow furrowed and he glared at her from beneath his eyebrows. "Have you lost your mind? Go to San Carlos? Return to a land where we are surrounded by White-eyes? That would be the way to certain death."

"It's the only way. The People will have food and shelter. They can rest and regain their strength. Most of all, they'll be safe from enemies."

"How can they feel safe encircled by White-eyes, people who have always met us with treachery and betrayal? We could not sleep at night if we had to trust White-eyes for our safety." The autumn wind stirred the fallen leaves into a scarlet and gold blizzard as he walked toward his horse.

"You're wrong, Wolf. There are other White-eyes like me who want to help the Apaches. Britton Chance would help you. And my father. And many others."

"Your father? He would see us all dead," he snarled as he whirled and paced toward her. The tension he radiated struck her with almost physical force. He halted, towering over her. "Do not ask me to trust White-eyes, Aurora. I cannot; I have seen too much treachery from them."

"But—"

"Enough words. I must go." He plucked a golden leaf out of her hair and crumbled it between his fingers as he studied her. "Will you kiss me before I go?"

"I—" This couldn't be it. He couldn't be leaving so quickly. She began to tremble.

He frowned. "Why do you shake so? Are you cold?"

"Yes. Because inside I'm so afraid." She grabbed his hand and pressed it to her breast. "Feel how my heart's pounding. I'm terrified you'll be hurt. Please don't go."

His fingers spread out over her breast and she inhaled deeply, savoring his beloved touch. She saw his Adam's apple move as he swallowed. Then he wrapped her in his arms and his mouth came down over hers swift and hard.

She clung to him, drinking him into her senses.

Too soon he let her go, spun on his heel, and strode toward his horse.

Aurora gasped as anguish knifed through her. He could be riding to his death, and she couldn't stand it. She fought to drag air into her pain-seared lungs. She had to stop him; she couldn't just let him ride away.

"Wolf, wait." She ran after him and threw her arms around his narrow waist. She pressed her cheek against his back and listened to the steady thrum of his heart.

She took a deep breath. "Wolf, I—" It wasn't as easy as she'd thought it would be to say those magic words. Even knowing he must love her, it wasn't easy. Still, she couldn't let him leave without telling him.

"I love you! Don't you understand? I love you! Don't go. Please."

He stiffened and his hands clamped down over hers, anchoring them to his waist.

"You know I want you." But he didn't turn. "I can't seem to get enough of you," he murmured in a surprised tone. "I can't—" He broke off and shook himself, as if ridding himself of something. "I must go, White-eyes." He gently pulled her hands from his waist. "My men wait."

He stalked away without looking back. Gathering the reins, then bracing his hands on the stallion's withers and the Apache saddle, he swung up on his black stallion. When the beast reared, he sat like a centaur, gazing at her. "I will be back."

Then he turned the horse and galloped into the forest.

Aurora stood there under the barren oaks, listening until even the beat of his horse's hooves faded. Feeling abandoned and alone, she slipped back into their wickiup and folded the remaining buffalo robes and tried not to remember what they'd shared on them hours before.

Why had he stiffened when she told him she loved him? Why hadn't he whooped with joy and turned and taken her in his arms? Instead he'd been distant, almost formal. She'd never before told a man she loved him, so she didn't know what men did, but it seemed to her that something was wrong.

Too restless to sit, she grabbed a basket and set out to see if there was any fruit left in the berry thickets. It was late afternoon by the time her basket was full and she started back.

The undergrowth was so dense that she didn't see Destarte coming toward her until they were almost upon each other. The Indian woman's hatred of her and Wolf had grown more and more vicious, and Aurora turned away as they were about to pass each other.

The Indian maid grabbed Aurora's basket. "Ho, White-eyes, did you see that your great *nantan* has enough bullets with him?" she asked, hatred blazing in her eyes. "That's what a good Apache wife does."

"But I'm not an Apache wife," Aurora shot back icily.

"Not worth much as a hostage, either. Your father took so long to leave the White-eyes fort, he must not want you."

Her words slammed into Aurora like a battering ram. "My father has left Fort Bowie? When?"

"Yesterday. When Ma'cho Nalzhee returns from avenging our dead, he will meet him and take the guns and bullets."

Aurora clenched her fingers around the reed basket. "Did Wolf know this when he left this morning?"

Destarte smiled nastily. "Of course, White-eyes."

Aurora glared at her and walked on, head held high. As soon as Destarte was out of sight, Aurora turned off the trail and leaned against an oak. Why hadn't Wolf told her about Papa? It didn't make sense.

She thought back over their conversation that morning. Could he have meant to tell her and forgotten? No, Wolf didn't make mistakes like that. Which meant he'd chosen not to tell her. Which meant that he didn't tell her because he didn't trust her.

She straightened with shock and her fingers tightened on the rough tree bark. He didn't trust her?

In the beginning he'd made it plain he didn't believe her promises, but in the cave he'd left a gun for her protection. It was there she'd thought he had started to trust her.

But could trust have been beyond him? Could she have been wrong all along?

Had Chili Eater slept at her fire not to protect her, but to guard against her escaping, because Wolf didn't trust her?

Just that morning he'd told her not to ask him to trust White-eyes, because he couldn't. And then he'd called her White-eyes. How much clearer could it be?

Without trust, there could be no love. No wonder he'd never spoken to her of love. He'd said he wanted her, he needed her, but never had he said he loved her. Never. The knowledge swept away every shred of air in her lungs.

Slowly she sank to her knees amid the bright-green bushes, feeling shaky and faint. Her heart was racing, her hands were icy, and she couldn't breathe. The pain in her heart felt as if it was tearing her apart.

Pincus had tried to warn her, but she'd refused to listen. Wolf had even told her in his own way.

"And I told him I loved him." No wonder he'd stiffened when she told him. It had been plain old shock. He'd told her he wanted her, but even then he hadn't turned and swept her up in his arms. Now she knew why.

A ray of sunshine splashed over her, but didn't warm her. She would survive this, she vowed. Damn it, she would survive, if only to show Wolf what she thought of him.

She had to talk to Pincus. Sniffling, she willed herself not to cry. Resting the basket against her left hip, she strolled down the path into the village as if she didn't have a care in the world.

"Pincus?" she called softly from outside his wickiup. The deerskin was down over the entrance and she couldn't see if he was inside.

"Hello, Aurora," he said, emerging. "What can I do for you?"

She glanced around to see if anyone was in hearing distance. Even though they spoke in English, she wanted no one to overhear. "I've just met Destarte. She told me Papa had left Fort Bowie with the ransom."

He nodded sharply. "I heard the same thing this morning from Pony That Talks. I went looking for you, but couldn't find you."

"I was collecting berries. Do you think it's true? How did the Apaches know so quickly?"

"Didn't Wolf tell you he'd set up a chain of warriors with signal mirrors on mountaintops? He probably knew your father had left Fort Bowie before the last trooper had ridden off the parade ground."

She pursed her lips. "It's just another thing he forgot to tell me."

Pincus gave her a strange look. "Something wrong?"

"Pincus, I want to apologize. I was wrong. You were right about"—she swallowed twice, trying to wet her dry mouth—"Wolf."

He peered at her. "You look as if you've had a shock. Would you like a shot of firewater?"

She clasped her hands tightly and eyed him. "That's all you're going to say? You're not going to crow and say I told you so?"

"Would a friend do that?"

She gave him a wobbly smile. "Thanks, friend."

He ducked back into his wickiup and came out with a canteen and a hollowed-out gourd. "How many fingers?"

"What?"

"I can tell how often you drink. I think a finger will be enough." He splashed a little whiskey into the gourd and handed it to her. "Here."

She sipped and shuddered. "Ugh, this tastes awful."

"If you can still taste it, you haven't drunk enough. Drink it all down quick."

Pinching her nose closed with one hand, she gulped the whiskey down. "Ugh, how can you like that stuff?"

"It's an acquired taste."

"Pincus, do you think we could escape tonight?"

They talked over several plans and worked one out.

"And you're sure you can find the trail we came down from Arizona?"

"Yes. When Wolf retreated and brought his people back here, we crossed it. It's not far, and we'll just take it and head north."

"I thought I was doing a good job of memorizing

landmarks, but you've done far better, Pincus.
Tonight, then, two hours after midnight, we'll go."

Back at the wickiup, she sat Indian-style on the
buffalo robes. Taking off her turquoise necklace,
she rubbed her thumb over the intricate carvings.
She had thought it a token of his love. She'd been
wrong.

He'd used her.

The words struck her again and again, like a
mallet hammering on an anvil. Everything they'd
done, everything they'd shared, had been a lie. A
lie! Because Wolf couldn't trust White-eyes. Not
even one who loved him.

Choking back a sob, she flung the necklace into
the dust. No, she wouldn't cry. Not one damn tear
for him! Not one!

At least now she was no longer tortured by
wondering how to stop Wolf from killing her
father. She would ride to warn her father and get
him to turn back before Wolf returned from his
raid. And wouldn't Wolf be surprised when he
returned and found the White-eyes woman was
gone.

She dressed in her finest beaded deerskin clothes
and moccasins that moonless night. The women
had been honest in their gratitude and acceptance
of her, and she treasured their gifts. Stealing out of
the wickiup after midnight, she took one buffalo
robe for the journey home.

It was a frosty night, and their breath steamed in
the air. When she and Pincus reached the trailhead
at the edge of the mesa, she glanced back, but the
wickiups were hidden beneath the oaks.

In spite of her resolve, memories of the fierce
tenderness of her Apache warrior tugged at her,

calling her back to their wickiup. She muttered curses under her breath so that Pincus wouldn't hear her and be shocked.

Dismounting, she led her mare onto the narrow trail. Several times during the night she imagined strong hands on her. Each time she cursed and brushed the feeling away.

They traveled hard that night and all the next day. There was no telling when Wolf would return, and Aurora wanted to put as much distance between her and the Apaches as possible, just in case Wolf came after his hostage.

Aurora had learned much in her captivity, and as twilight neared on the second day, she spotted a cave in the walls of the canyon they were passing through. She and Pincus tethered the horses deep inside, then slept near the entrance. The next morning they were on their way long before sunrise. And always they traveled north.

Wolf stood in the empty wickiup. The afternoon sun shone through the smoke hole and spotlighted the pieces-of-sky necklace lying in the dust. She'd left. Everything she'd said, everything she'd done, had been a lie to get him to let down his guard. And he'd fallen for it.

She'd told him she loved him, and he'd believed her. He'd believed her! he raged inwardly. He raked his fingers through his sweat-damp hair. He'd trusted her!

Once again, a White-eyes had betrayed him.

He'd come back weary and heartsore, needing her soothing hands and her voice and her body. Needing the warmth he found in her arms. But she was gone.

How could he have trusted her? Had he forgotten she was a White-eyes? When had they ever kept the promises they made?

He gave their buffalo robes to widows who would need them during the time of Ghost Face. He gave their cast-iron pot to She Who Sees Babies. The old woman took the pot and started to say something, then looked at his eyes and grew silent.

He returned to the shelter they'd shared and removed the wolfhide from the entrance. Then, taking a flaming torch from the fire, he touched it to the wickiup in a dozen places. When a person died, his wickiup was burned. Well, what they'd shared in that wickiup was dead.

After the flames burned down, there was nothing left but ashes. Wolf stood there, looking at them. He felt as burned out as that circle of ashes.

"Wolf, why do you burn your wickiup? What's wrong?" Destarte swung her hips seductively as she walked toward him in the fading light. "Has someone died?"

"No." He wasn't in the mood to listen to Destarte and her hatred and false smiles. "Do you want something?"

"A new rifle. When the *Nantan* Spencer delivers the rifles, I want one. Now that Blue Hawk's dead, I have to hunt for myself and I could use one of those fast repeating rifles."

"You don't need to hunt for yourself, Destarte, and we both know it," he snapped, out of patience with her scheming. "All you have to do is accept one of the warriors who would bed you."

"As you do the White-eyes woman?" She glanced around. "By the way, where is she?"

His head snapped up. There was something in

her tone, something that wasn't quite right. "Why do you ask? Do you know anything about her leaving?"

"She's gone?" Destarte gave him a wide-eyed look.

Too wide-eyed, he realized. His hands closed around her upper arms like eagle talons. "Hear me, Destarte. I have never in my life struck a woman, but never has a woman tempted me as you do. I will ask you only once, maiden. Did you have anything to do with her leaving?"

"No." She pulled at his hands and he let go, too heart-weary to touch her. She walked to the other side of the fire before she continued, "I merely told her that her father was on the way."

"*Nantan* Spencer has left Fort Bowie?" His deadly soft tone should have warned her.

"Yes. Didn't you know?"

He whirled away from her and stalked down the path into the village. Warriors looked at him and got out of his way. Women watched him silently. He stopped in front of Geronimo's wickiup, towering over the older man, who sat staring into his fire and didn't greet him.

"When did you find out that Spencer had left the White-eyes fort?"

Geronimo didn't look up, just gazed at the flames for long moments before he replied. "Not long after you left."

"Why didn't you send a runner after me? Or send a message with the signal mirrors?"

"I didn't want you distracted by thoughts of the woman or her father."

"That is not for you to judge, old man. She is as important to me as the guns and ammunition. You should have let me know."

Geronimo stirred his fire and didn't look at him. "Do you go after her now?"

"Yes. My warriors and their horses are too exhausted to ride with me. Let them rest for a full sleep before they follow my trail."

Wolf saddled the black stallion and took along a second horse for when the black gave out. Then he galloped north.

Through mountain passes, beneath pines and junipers and oaks, through canyons, down into the desert, across ridges, around huge stands of cactus and mesquites, he rode north.

When the powerful stallion began to falter and stumble, he halted. Stripping off the bridle and wooden Apache saddle, he turned to the gelding he'd led and saddled him. Leaping into the saddle, he rode on. If this horse gave out before he could catch her, he'd follow Aurora on foot until he caught her. For he *would* catch her, and bring her back.

Late in the afternoon of the third day, he glimpsed Aurora and Pincus. He'd just crested a high ridge and saw them trotting across the grassy valley below. Beyond them was a long, rolling ridge, and beyond that he could see a long column of men and horses headed south toward them.

They were deep in Mexico, yet there was no mistaking the blue uniforms and yellow trim of the United States Cavalry. Although neither the soldiers nor Aurora and Pincus could see one another, the two parties would meet within the next couple of hours.

Unless he could get to her first.

Spurring the gelding, he sent the beast lunging straight down the slope. It was so steep and sandy

that the horse sat down on its haunches as they slid
to the bottom. There Wolf picked up Aurora's trail.
After nearly two hours of hard riding, he was
within a quarter-mile of her. She must have heard
his horse's pounding hooves, for she looked back.

"Aurora," he yelled, waving.

Aurora had stiffened as she heard hooves
pounding along behind her. "Please God, don't let
it be Wolf," she murmured. "Please."

Glancing over her right shoulder, she saw that
God hadn't heard her plea.

Seeing Wolf knocked the breath from her lungs.
He was magnificent. But she knew the truth about
him now, the voice inside her shouted, forced to
shout to be heard above her thundering heart.

"No!" He wouldn't have her, she vowed. Not
ever again. "Come on, Pincus." She leaned low
over her horse's neck and urged it on with the ends
of the rawhide reins.

"Aurora!" Wolf's shout floated across the grasslands and tugged at her heartstrings. "Wait."

Aurora sent her horse galloping up the long,
gradual slope to the ridgetop ahead. Her eyes
widened as she gazed at the horsemen in blue
uniforms flooding over the crest.

It looked like the cavalry was her first dazed
thought.

She was crazy was her second.

A bugle sounded. Soldiers galloped down the
slope toward her.

"Aurora!" This time the voice was ahead of her,
and it was her father's.

"Papa!"

The hooves were closing in behind her. She

glanced back and lashed her mare. Now she could pick out her father in the sea of blue as he sent his big gray horse leaping toward her.

But Wolf was so close.

"Papa," she screamed, holding out her arms as she galloped toward him.

Her father didn't even glance her way as he raced by, firing shot after shot from his revolver.

"Aur—"

Aurora turned as her name caught in Wolf's throat. She saw him jerk as her father fired again.

His eyes met hers across the distance, and she screamed at the agony in their dark depths.

The reins fell from Wolf's hand. Soldiers cut between them, blocking her view. When they had passed, Wolf's horse was hobbling away on three legs, his fourth broken and swinging uselessly. And he was riderless.

"No!" The word echoed in her heart long after the scream had left her lips.

"Aurora! Thank God, you're alive."

Someone was shaking her. Dimly she heard someone calling her, but she was still mindless with horror.

"Aurora, look at me."

She blinked several times, staring blankly at the brown-haired soldier who shook her. "Brit?"

"You're safe." He edged his horse closer to hers and clasped her ice-cold hands, giving them a gentle squeeze. "You're safe, Aurora. You've survived; your ordeal is over."

"No," she whispered hoarsely. "It's just starting." She glanced back over her shoulder, but troopers were milling about her father and she couldn't see anything. Another shot rang out, and she jerked as if the bullet had struck her.

"Don't look back," Brit said, pulling the reins from her stiff hands. He started up the slope, leading her horse.

She looked back once more at the clot of blue-uniformed troopers. Their horses shifted restlessly, and she glimpsed a horse's body on the ground—and not far from it, the body of a copper-skinned man.

She began to scream.

A part of her said this couldn't be happening, that she couldn't be screaming. But she was and she couldn't stop.

Leaping off his horse, Brit pulled her down off hers. He wrapped his arms around her and tried to nestle her against his broad chest.

Aurora fought him wildly, and all the time she screamed.

"Stop it, Aurora," he murmured. He held her loosely in his arms, stroking her, trying to soothe her, as he said over and over again, "You're safe. It's over. It's done."

But she kept screaming, deaf in her hysteria.

"I'm sorry to do this," Brit said, his eyes dark with sympathy. Then he slapped her.

The stinging blow snapped her jaw shut and she stared at him, stunned. Then, sinking to her knees, she doubled over, clutching her stomach. Now that she wasn't screaming, she hurt so much, so very, very much.

She covered her face, hiding from the curious eyes of the blue-coated soldiers who'd surrounded them.

Wolf was dead.

What had she done? Oh God, what had she done?

Chapter 23

〜⚬〇⚬〜

"**A**urora, I'm giving you my tent until we get back to Fort Bowie," Artemus Spencer said gruffly.

"What, Papa?" Aurora looked around, surprised to find that she was sitting on a boulder beside a stream. How had she gotten there?

"Over there." Artemus pointed at the cluster of white canvas tents dotting the grass near them. "After we eat, you can sleep on a real bed, child."

"I'm not a child." She tried to forget that he'd ridden right past her, more intent on killing Apaches than seeing how she was. "Papa, don't you want to know what happened to me?"

"I know it must have been terrible for you, being a captive of those awful savages, but you can put it behind you now. You're safe. You can forget those damn Apaches."

But she'd never forget one special Apache.

"Now, come and see how comfortable you'll be." He guided her across the grass with a dry, cool hand on her elbow. "I had Hester Porter pack some clothes for you. You remember her, don't you? She and her brother run the store at Fort Bowie. I've put your clothes on the cot. You can get out of those barbaric Indian rags and into some real clothes."

"These aren't rags! The women spent hours beading— Oh, what's the use of trying to make you understand?"

Pushing aside the flap—how different the coarse canvas felt from Stalking Wolf's wolfhide—she entered the tent and sat down on the cot. Everything had an unearthly quality, as if she wasn't really there. She pinched her arm and saw the red mark, but felt nothing.

Absently she opened the carpetbag. The sweet, cloying scent of English lavender assaulted her, making her rear back. It had been her favorite scent before, but now it was harsh and overpowering. She longed for the fresh, clean scent of sage instead.

She gazed numbly at the wrinkled lilac dress. It was the dress she'd been wearing the first time she saw Wolf, she thought dully, feeling as though everything was happening to someone else, not to her.

The white cotton petticoat and underdrawers seemed strange. Had she once worn such things? The stiff, whalebone corset made her shudder and grimace. She'd known the freedom of drawing a deep breath without having her ribs pinched. She'd never again wear a corset.

She piled the alien clothes outside so that they could air, then curled up on the cot and stared at the white canvas ceiling. There was no smoke hole to let in the twinkling stars, and she felt closed in and alone.

So alone.

*   *   *

Wolf opened his eyes and stared at the midnight heavens.

Slowly he gathered his senses. A cold wind blew over him, chilling his sweat-damp shirt. Other than the lonely moan of the wind, a great silence surrounded him.

The smell of blood was strong, and his shoulder felt as if it were on fire. But if he hurt, he reasoned, then he wasn't dead.

He tried to sit up and discovered new fires in his side and leg. Breaking out in a sweat at the sudden agony, he fell back, panting.

Slowly memory came back to him. Seeing Aurora. Almost catching her. The soldiers pouring over the ridge. The whinnies of the horses, the sulfur smell of gunpowder. The searing agony as Spencer's bullet tore into his shoulder. And the feeling that this couldn't be happening to him. But it was.

And it was the most amazing irony that the red-bearded man had shot him. Finally, so many years after he'd killed Wolf's mother, he'd shot her son, too.

Then had come the other bullets as the Bluecoats surrounded him. They thought they'd killed him.

Wolf gazed at the stars. "I will survive," he gritted through teeth locked in pain. "I swear it."

Something nudged his moccasin, then sharp teeth tore through the buckskin and brushed his big toe. "Hey!" he grunted, and whatever it was dropped his moccasin. With a monstrous effort, he rolled to his good side. His eyes met the steady yellow gaze of a coyote that sniffed at his feet.

"Go away, little wolf." He tried to shout, but his voice was a breathless croak. "I am a big wolf."

The coyote's ears swiveled around as it kept an eye on Wolf, but it bit at the moccasin again. Wolf shook his foot, driving it away, but he knew this retreat was only temporary. He felt around on the ground, found a fist-sized rock, and heaved it. The coyote snarled, then trotted away into the darkness.

But the coyote would be back. And maybe others, also, drawn by the scent of blood. Though coyotes were normally no threat to him, Wolf knew that in his present weakened condition he didn't have the extra energy it would take to keep driving the curious creatures away.

Slowly, painfully, using his good arm for leverage, he managed to sit up. Looking around, he spotted the looming bulk of his dead horse several hundred feet away. It was cold and getting colder, but maybe there would still be some warmth left in the beast's body.

Dragging himself on his good arm, he crawled toward the horse. Every movement sent agonizing pains shooting through his chest. Once he bumped his arm and waves of pain washed over him, leaving him dizzy and nauseated.

When he could sit up again, he glanced at the horse. Was he any closer? Or was he just fooling himself? The hunting cries of the coyotes goaded him. Were they coming nearer? They wouldn't have any trouble finding him. He could smell the trail of blood he was leaving.

Finally he leaned against the horse's haunch and took deep breaths. A glance at the stars told him it had taken him hours to cover the distance. Pulling himself up, he squirmed over the beast's long legs and fell into the space between its front and hind legs.

Wolf leaned against the belly and drew his heavy knife from its sheath on his belt. He should open the horse and crawl inside to stay warm during the night. One half-hearted slash with his knife told him he didn't have the strength. Holding onto the knife in case the coyotes grew bold, he huddled against the horse's still-warm belly and dozed, waiting for the winter sunrise.

When the sun rose, Wolf was surprised and pleased to see that his rifle was still in the saddle scabbard. He managed to stand up long enough to pull the rifle loose. When the tip of the barrel finally cleared the scabbard, he was breathless and sweat poured down him in rivers. He slumped against the horse, husbanding what little remained of his strength.

A distant line of bright-green mesquite trees told Wolf where there was water. Using his rifle as a crutch, he hobbled toward it.

He paused once, looking back at the empty valley and the trail that led north into the United States. "I will find you, Aurora," he muttered. "I will come for you. No matter where you go, I will come."

When morning came, Aurora dressed in the strange White-eyes clothes and went down to the stream to wash. When she returned, her father was waiting for her.

Glancing at the camp stool where she'd left her beautiful beaded Apache clothes, she frowned. "Where are my clothes?"

"Those Indian rags? I had the corporal burn them."

She glared at him, horrified. "You what?" Anger ripped through the pain. "You had no right! Those were mine."

"I had every right. You're my daughter and—"

"The women made them. They were all I had left."

"They're gone and you should be glad," he bellowed. "Have you lost your senses, girl?"

Aurora's shoulders straightened and her head came up. "No, Papa, I've found them. And for the first time, I'm seeing you as you really are. Those buckskins were beautiful, and anyone who wasn't so damned prejudiced against the Indians would have seen that. I treasured them."

"How dare you accuse me of being prejudiced? Have you forgotten that Indians murdered your mother?"

"The Indians didn't kill her! I was there. You weren't. And I saw her bleed to death from a small wound because the doctor was too drunk to do his job. The Army doctor killed her." She paced away three angry strides, then swung back. "But you couldn't accept that. Oh no, you had to have your revenge and kill Indians—all Indians. You should be very proud of yourself. First you killed Stalking Wolf's mother; now you've killed him."

"What the hell are you talking about?" Artemus raked his hand through his rusty-white hair, ruffling it wildly. "What have the Apaches done to you?"

"Opened my eyes. Think back—remember the first time you were stationed in Arizona, when you raided an Apache village? You were about to shoot a young boy when his mother pushed him out of the way and took the bullet you'd meant for him."

Her father stared at her, his washed-out blue eyes wide. "Damn!" He smacked his fist against his palm. "I knew I should have killed the little nit then."

Aurora stiffened with shock. "You remember?"

"Of course. He would have killed me that day. He would have made you an orphan. But I made sure he woke up in chains." He stomped away, then back, clasping and unclasping his fists. "I should have killed him then."

"He was a thirteen-year-old child. You were a grown man. He had a bow and arrow. You had a gun. You call that a fair fight?"

"Fair has nothing to do with it. The Army has a job to do. Either we tame these heathens or we exterminate them. They can't be allowed to stand in the way of progress."

A chill iced her bones. Aurora turned away, sickened. "I can't believe this," she murmured, shaking her head. "You're more of a savage than they are." She whirled back, her hands clamped to her waist. "Stalking Wolf hated you for murdering his mother. That's why he kidnapped me. He wanted to steal the thing you treasured most. But I don't mean anything to you, do I? Only the killing is important, isn't it? That's all you can think about—killing and more killing."

"What have the Apaches done to you? You used to be a sensible woman, but now you're—" He turned at the sound of nearby horses' hooves. "Here comes Lieutenant Chance with your mount. Maybe he can talk some sense into you."

"I am fully in control of my senses!"

"Take care of her, Lieutenant. I've got to see to the troop." Artemus Spencer hurried away.

Resting his arm on his saddle horn, Brit slouched on his horse for a moment as he contemplated Aurora. "You look a lot better than you did yesterday," he said, giving her an approving nod.

"It's called anger and horror," she snapped. Instantly she waved the words away. "I'm sorry. I didn't mean to take it out on you." Her lips thinned when she glanced at her retreating father. "I'm just so furious."

"Anger's better than numbness. Want to talk about it?"

She shook her head. "I don't think I can. Not yet, at least."

"Then come on." Dismounting, he came around his horse. "Let's get going, and then we'll talk about whatever you want to talk about."

His hand was warm around her elbow as he guided her between the horses. "What's this?" she asked, frowning at the sidesaddle as if she'd never seen one.

"Your father thought you'd want to ride in a civilized way, so he brought this saddle along. Privately, I think it's kind of silly."

"He's made a lot of assumptions, hasn't he?" she murmured tightly. She bent her left leg at the knee, but when Brit gripped her ankle, she stiffened. He glanced up and she knew he'd felt her tense. "Sorry," she said, gathering the reins in her left hand. "I guess I'm not used to a lot of things anymore." Brit boosted her up and she settled into the sidesaddle, even though it felt strange and awkward not to be riding astride.

"Aurora," Brit said as they rode along side by side. "If you want to talk about what happened, I'm here. And if you don't want to talk about it, I'm still here."

"Thanks, Brit." She flicked him a grateful glance. "I don't know what I want to do yet, but I appreciate your concern."

The long ride back to Fort Bowie was a blur. Aurora got up, ate whatever was put in her hand, and rode all day with Brit at her side. She didn't speak unless someone spoke to her, and then she answered yes or no.

Day after day, as they rode north, she felt an icy numbness growing in her. It was a deadness such as she'd never known, not even when her mother was killed, and it grew and grew. Day after day, she gazed at the rugged Chiricahua Mountains on their right. Wolf's home. But Wolf would never see them again.

Wolf was dead.

Her heart cried his name a thousand times a day and a thousand times a night.

But there was no answer.

After that first morning, Aurora and her father spoke only about unimportant things. The distance between them grew with each passing day. Every time she looked at him, she saw him raise his gun, saw him take aim; she heard the shot and smelled the acrid, biting sulfur scent of gunpowder.

Every time she looked at him, she relived Wolf's death.

On the last night, she huddled near the fire, sitting on a camp stool and sipping a mug of hot coffee. The steam curled up around her face, carrying the rich scent of fresh java. She wore the old, thick navy-blue wool cloak that she'd worn during her years at the Women's Medical College of Philadelphia. It was moth-holed in spots but still serviceable, and its warmth was welcome.

Brit walked over and poured himself some coffee from the heavy gallon pot that sat at the edge of the coals, then hunkered down on his heels beside her.

"Going to be another cold night."

"Yes." She couldn't help wondering how cold it would be for the Apaches on the hidden mesa.

He sipped his coffee. "Are you prepared for tomorrow?"

Her brow furrowed. "Prepared for what?"

"Facing everyone. So far the men have been relatively good, not making any suggestive remarks, but tomorrow you're going to have to face the women and civilians at the fort. They're going to—"

"Wonder how I survived? Wonder what I had to do? And what it was like?" She shrugged. "So what?"

He drew aimless patterns in the dust. "Some of them are going to be sure they know what you had to do to survive."

"I survived." She banged her hand down on her knee. "Isn't that enough, Brit? Am I supposed to feel ashamed because I survived?" Though not all of her had survived, not her heart.

"It's going to be damn rough. There's going to be a lot of curiosity, most of it ugly." He threw the last of his coffee into the fire, where it steamed and sizzled, then reached over and lifted her hand off her knee and squeezed it gently. "But I'll be there. Remember that, and don't be afraid to call on me."

"Thanks." She gave him a wan grimace that she hoped looked like a smile. "You and Pincus have shown me what true friends are."

Rising, Brit hooked his thumbs in his back pockets and glanced down at her. "At least you weren't a captive long enough to come back with a babe at your breast. Be thankful for that."

She glanced up at him wide-eyed, shocked by the idea. "God forbid." She set her cup in the tin washpan and walked into the darkness.

Aurora paused beneath a mesquite tree and

gazed at the newly risen moon. She felt newly risen, too. For the first time since Wolf's death, she felt alive. Why hadn't she realized? she wondered, rubbing her stomach gently. She was a doctor, for God's sake; how could she have missed the signs?

But she'd been too busy just surviving. Now that she thought back, she couldn't remember when she had flowed last. The knowledge flooded her with overwhelming joy. The icy darkness that had filled her receded, its place taken by something much greater, something growing in her. Wolf's legacy.

A shooting star flamed across the midnight sky. It was an omen, she decided. Wolf was dead, but his seed grew within her. Their child would grow up to be brave and strong like him.

For even though he hadn't trusted her, she'd loved him. She carried his gift. She would never love again as she'd loved him—she knew that with a frightening certainty. But in the long, lonely years that lay ahead, she would raise their son. And she would instill in him a great love for the Apache chief who was his father.

Chapter 24

❦

As she rode into Fort Bowie, Aurora held the reins in her left hand while her right rested protectively against her stomach. Except for a glance at the corral between the hospital and Headquarters, she looked neither right nor left at the men and women lining the wagon road. Not one person waved, and their silence resounded through the fort.

She rode straight to her father's quarters—there was no way she could call it home—and dismounted. Her head was high and she didn't look back as she marched up the steps. Then Rob Roy bounded around the corner of the veranda, and suddenly she was greeted with joy.

She knelt on the top step and hugged the wriggling dog. "Oh, Rob Roy, I'm happy to see you, too." No matter what she did, the collie would always love her. Burying her face in his fur, she fought the sobs welling up in her.

She was home, but she wasn't home. She felt more of a stranger at Fort Bowie than in the Apache camp.

The following weeks were an unending nightmare. Wolf was in her mind every moment of the day. His life—and his death.

Hester Porter, from the post store, was her only feminine oasis of warmth and support. The other women at the fort treated her with disdain and hostility, as if she had shamed them by surviving.

She was used goods, she overheard a woman say.

Aurora took refuge in helping Pincus catalog his pictures. She wrote tiny captions in India ink on the backs of the powerful images of the Apache lifeway.

"Aurora, I've been thinking more and more about your idea of doing a book," Pincus said one day, as they sat at the big, round mahogany table in his quarters. Late-afternoon sunshine spilled through the open front door. "You know, there's a deep curiosity about the Apaches back East. I telegraphed my editor at the *Sentinel*, and he loved the idea. He's already wired me funds and said to go ahead." He glanced at her. "Would you work on the book with me?"

"I'd love to, Pincus. It'll give me something to do while I decide where I'm going."

"Aren't you staying here?"

"No, I don't think so." She picked a piece of white lint off her hunter-green wool skirt. "Frankly, I don't feel very welcome here. I'm sure you know what I mean. Sometimes I think I felt more at home in the Apache village. Anyway, I'll be moving on soon." Before the baby began to show. "Oh, look, here's a picture of Many Tongues holding her son in his cradleboard." She sighed and grieved for the young mother whose life had been cut short. "I wish we could get him a copy, so that he'll be able to see what a beautiful woman his mother was."

"Maybe some day we will." He coughed into a white handkerchief. "You miss the Apaches, don't you?"

She gazed out the window. "You know what I miss."

"But he's gone. There's no one to go back to."

"Except his people." Turning back to the photos, she stroked one of the pictures as if she could feel the life in it. "His people were what he loved above all else."

"No, you're wrong. He loved you more, Aurora. That's why he came after you."

"And I killed him." She looked at Pincus and opened her mouth to say more, but suddenly the sobs she'd fought for so many days boiled over. She covered her face with her hands, unable to bear the searing knowledge any longer. "Oh God, Pincus," she whispered, "I killed him!"

"No! You did not."

Aurora whirled on hearing the deep masculine voice that came from the open doorway. "Brit!" Hastily she looked away and wiped her eyes on her skirt hem. "What are you doing here?"

"I came over to talk to you, but I guess I'd better clear something up first." His spurs jingled as he knelt in front of her, clasping her icy hands in his. "Stalking Wolf chose to come after you. He made the choice—not you. Your father chose to shoot him. He made the choice—not you." He gently squeezed her hands. "Do you understand? Both of them are adults, and you couldn't control their choices."

"Y-yes." She gazed through the front door at the parade ground. "But that doesn't make me feel better."

"Brit's right, you know." Pincus added his somber voice. "And Wolf would be the first to tell you that. You and I both know it, Aurora."

She swallowed, took a deep breath, and gave them a wobbly smile. "I am blessed with two wonderful friends. What would I ever do without you, Pincus?" She patted his hand. "Or you, Brit? How can I ever thank you?"

"For starters, you can come for a ride with me." Drawing his leather gauntlets out of his belt, Brit crushed them in his hand.

"I'd love to, Brit. I'd really enjoy getting out of the fort, but as you can see, I'm not dressed for riding." She'd have to stop soon anyway to protect the babe.

"I brought a buggy."

"A buggy? Getting fancy, aren't you?" She stood up with what she hoped looked like a genuine smile. "Then I would love to go with you, Lieutenant Chance."

"It will be my pleasure, Miss Spencer." Wrapping his hand around her elbow, he guided her outside.

They'd crossed the porch and were going down the wooden steps when a woman gasped loudly. Aurora glanced at the wagon road and met Mrs. Kreutz's angry glare. Young Sophie was barely visible behind her mother's barrel shape.

"Good afternoon, ladies," Aurora said, determined to be nice.

"Hrumph!" Mrs. Kreutz's mouth pursed until she looked as if she was sucking a very sour lemon.

"Lieutenant Chance, I'm surprised to see you with this . . . this person."

Brit's hand tightened on Aurora's elbow. "Miss Spencer has a name, Mrs. Kreutz. And she is my friend."

"Really?" The woman's icy eyes skimmed over Aurora as if she were beneath contempt. "I'm sure Captain Kreutz would like to know that."

Brit bowed slightly. "I'm sure he would, ma'am. Don't forget to tell him." He handed Aurora into a shiny black buggy.

"Well, I never!" Mrs. Kreutz's mouth hung open as he followed Aurora into the buggy and snapped the reins over the back of a chestnut horse. As they started to roll away, Mrs. Kreutz said, quite clearly, "Apache leavings."

"That does it," Aurora muttered. She would have turned and given the old biddy a piece of her mind, but Brit's hand closed over her knee.

"Don't give her the satisfaction of turning around."

"I don't want being seen with me to affect your career."

"You forget, the pompous Prussian was in charge when Stalking Wolf captured you. He wouldn't dare do anything."

"That's right, I'd forgotten." For the first time in days, she smiled a real smile. "I think I'll enjoy going for a ride with you."

As they reached the end of Officers' Row, a white-haired officer on a mule waved them over to the side.

"Aurora, have you met General Harris?" Brit said as he stopped the horse. "The General arrived at the fort just this morning."

Aurora nodded to the officer and extended her hand. "General."

"Miss Spencer, how nice to meet you." General Harris leaned forward in his saddle and shook her hand with his left one. That was when she realized that the right sleeve of his blue Army shirt was empty. "You are one of the people I most wanted to talk to. I understand you have lived with the Apaches and know them quite well."

Aurora threw Brit a wary glance. Was the General yet another officer who believed in exterminating the Apaches?

"It's all right, Aurora," Brit said, answering her unspoken question. "General Harris is well known for his respect for the Indians and their lifeways."

"Yes. All over the West, we've stolen Indian lands and driven them from their homes. That's wrong. We've got to start working with them, do something to help them survive and adapt to the white man's ways."

Aurora cocked her head and frowned at him. "Are you sure you're in the Army?"

"I'm known as Bible-Quoting Harris, Miss Spencer. I'd like to talk further with you about your experiences and how you think we should deal with the Apaches."

"I would be happy to talk to you anytime, General. Even though I was their captive, I came to respect them a great deal."

The General nodded and tipped his broad-brimmed black hat to her. "I'm glad we had this little chat, Miss Spencer. Thanks, Lieutenant," he added as he backed his mule away from the buggy. "I'll talk to you later."

As they drove on, Aurora studied Brit. "That meeting was no accident, was it?"

"No. You're the reason the General came over from New Mexico. He's hoping you have some new insights into how to deal with the Apaches."

"Give them back their land."

"We're working on it." Brit shot her a quick glance, then snapped the reins and clucked to the horse, sending it into a flashy, high-stepping trot as they left the fort.

After a while, Brit pulled over and stopped the buggy in a grove of oaks surrounding a tiny spring. "Aurora, I brought you out here to talk," he said, helping her down.

"Oh?" Pausing on the lower buggy step, she gave him a wary look. "Should I be worried?"

"No." But his rain-gray eyes didn't meet hers. He pulled a wicker picnic basket and a red, white, and green plaid blanket out from behind the seat, and led the way over to an large oak, where he spread the blanket. "Be seated, my lady."

She leaned back against the tree trunk and stretched out her legs, crossing her ankles and studying her new, black patent leather high-topped shoes. Hester had assured her they were the height of fashion back east. She didn't care. All she wanted was the comfort of Apache moccasins.

Brit knelt beside the basket and pulled out a bottle of wine and two beautiful crystal goblets. "Before you start wondering where I got these, I borrowed them from Hester." He inserted the corkscrew into the cork and began to turn it.

"Hester does a lot for a lot of people."

"She does, doesn't she." He popped the cork and poured wine into one of the goblets and handed it to Aurora.

"Did we come out here to talk about Hester?" Aurora sipped her wine.

"No. We came to talk about us." He poured wine into his goblet and raised it in a toasting gesture. "To us," he said, taking a sip.

"I don't want to be obtuse, Brit," Aurora said, tilting her head and eyeing him warily, "but what us?"

"Hmm." Brit walked back to the horse, slipped the bit out of its mouth, and attached a feedbag to its bridle. As he returned, Aurora noticed the jingle of his spurs.

"Why do your spurs sound different from the enlisted men's?"

"The men's are iron and ours are brass."

"You'd better be careful. The Apaches must have noticed that, and they'd use it to find officers in the dark."

He smiled. "You see, that's one of the ways you've changed. You're so much more observant."

"Really? What are some of the other ways?" She'd never thought of her captivity as changing her.

"You're stronger." He shook his head admiringly. "You are so strong now. In the old days, you would never have stood up to your father the way you did that first morning at your tent."

"I was that way before."

"No. You may think you were, but now you have a bone-deep strength."

"It comes from surviving," she said softly, watching a blue jay scolding them from another oak.

"You're also softer. I know that sounds like a contradiction, but you are. You're fighting for the Apaches even after all they did to you."

"No, I'm not. Well, maybe." She picked up a twig and began to pull the dried brown leaves off.

"It's just that I feel so sorry for them. They're fighting to save their land. We've moved in and taken it over and driven them off, and it's so unjust. If they were white, we could understand their love of the land, but because they're different from us, they just don't count."

"You see? You have changed. You always cared about people, but now you're not afraid to come right out and speak your mind. More wine?"

"A little. Thanks." She rubbed her hand over her abdomen absently.

"Aurora, are you ill?"

Did a broken heart count? "No, why?"

"Why do you rub your hand over your stomach so often?"

"What?" Aurora stared at him, wide-eyed. "I don't."

"Yes, you do. And you've been losing weight ever since we found you. What's wrong?"

She made a wry face. "Whew! I'm not the only observant person around here."

Brit drew up one knee and rested his forearm on it. "Did you love Stalking Wolf?"

"What a strange question. I got bitten by a rattlesnake, almost killed by Mexicans, fought smallpox, and lived like an Apache. And you ask if I loved the man who kidnapped me? Why would I?"

"Why, indeed?" He sipped his wine pensively. "You haven't answered my question."

She studied a ruby-throated hummingbird flitting back and forth around the horse's ears. "I respected him. He was a very honorable man." She glanced at Brit. "I know, how can an Apache be honorable? But he was. He led his people into exile rather than see them become farmers at San Carlos. Everything he did, he did for his people, and they were always foremost in his mind." And she loved him, by God. She'd love him to the end of her days.

"He couldn't learn to trust a white person." She ground a dried leaf into dust between her fingers. "He'd been betrayed by white men so often that he couldn't trust. Not even me."

"I see." He exhaled slowly. "You still haven't answered my question. No, I take that back. I think you have, in your very eloquent defense of him." He clasped his hands around his knee and studied her quietly for what felt like a very long time. "Are you with child?" he asked gently.

"No! Of course not," she almost shouted. "Whatever gave you that idea? Besides, how could I be?"

"You're a doctor. You know very well how."

"I think I'd like you to take me back now." Rising, Aurora brushed bits of grass off her skirt. She glanced at Brit. He hadn't moved. "I said I want to go back." She walked toward the buggy.

"Running away won't help, Aurora, and you know it. Sooner or later other people will notice. I want to help."

She froze with one foot on the lower step of the buggy. "I can leave." Her voice was a bare shred of sound. "No one has to know. I can move to Tucson or Phoenix or go back to Philadelphia."

"There's no need for you to. We can get married."

"What?" She whirled. He was walking toward her and she felt a moment's panic. "What do you mean?"

"We can get married," he repeated very calmly, as if she were slightly slow.

"Why would you do that? And don't say because we're friends. Marriage is much more of a commitment than friendship. Why would you suggest such a thing?"

"You're right. It is a large commitment. That's why I've thought about it a lot these past days. I wanted to be sure before I asked you." He hooked an elbow over the buggy frame and leaned against it. "I've wanted you ever since you stepped off the stagecoach; you know that. We like each other and enjoy talking to each other—I happen to think that's important. I realize you don't love me right now, but who knows what could happen." He shrugged. "I'm willing to take that chance."

"I don't think that's all there is to it, Brit, and if we're going to be honest with each other, I want the whole story. Why would you offer marriage to me when you know I'm carrying another man's child? It doesn't make sense."

Brit dragged his hand through his dark-brown hair. "It would if you'd grown up knowing the pain of being called a bastard every day of your life."

She put her hand on his arm and looked up at him for the longest time before she spoke. "I am so sorry," she said softly. "I know nothing I say can take away the hurt you must have endured."

"There's no reason for you to be sorry. You didn't have anything to do with it."

"Still, I can imagine your pain and—"

"Keep on imagining that pain, because your child is going to face it every day of his life. On top of that, he'll be a half-breed, too. Do you know what the kids will call him in school—if he ever gets to school?"

"He won't be a half-breed," she shot back fiercely. "Wolf was half white."

"So he was a bastard, too."

"No. His father joined— Oh, what does it matter now?"

"It will matter a great deal to the child you're carrying. Say yes, Aurora. Give yourself a second chance. Give the baby a legitimate name."

Tears misted her eyes as she looked up at him. Tears for what lay behind. And for what lay ahead.

"A second chance? As Mrs. Chance? Y-yes." She held up her hands as he reached for her. "Wait. Wait." Her eyes met his. "I want you to know that I'll be"—she swallowed hard, trying to accept all she couldn't change—"I'll be the best wife I can to you."

He swept her into his arms with a triumphant grin. "I know that."

An icicle touched her heart. Aurora pushed it away. Never again would Wolf hold her in his arms. Never again would he whisper her name and crush her to him. Now she had to go forward for the babe's sake. "Thank you, Brit," she whispered.

Wolf, please forgive me. I do this for our child. The child of our heart. I love you, Wolf. Only you.

Two weeks later Aurora stood in her bedroom, trying to recognize the woman who stared back at her from the mirror.

"Aurora, you look lovely." Hester fussed with the white lace mantilla she'd arranged over Aurora's fiery curls. "All brides should look as beautiful as you."

"Thanks, Hester, for all you've done." Aurora pulled at the nipped-in waist of her turquoise dress. "I'm glad it's a winter wedding so I could choose a color I liked." Turquoise reminded her of the Apaches and pieces-of-sky.

"That color is wonderful on you, especially with the white lace trim framing your face. I'm glad I had the material in the store."

"So am I." Aurora dabbed a few drops of orange blossom cologne on her pulse points. It was a very light, fresh scent, unlike the overpowering sweet fragrances she had come to hate after living with the Apaches.

"Your father is waiting in the parlor. He wants to escort you to the chapel and give you away."

Aurora sat down abruptly. "I can't, Hester," she whispered. "Every time I see him, I think of—"

"Aurora, you're all he has. He loves you. He'll never have another chance to give his daughter away in marriage. Please, Aurora." The women's eyes met and an understanding flowed between them.

"All right," Aurora said resignedly. Opening the door, she marched down the hall.

Her father sat stiffly on the edge of the burgundy horsehair sofa her mother had purchased so long ago. He held his hat in his lap. He jumped to his feet when Aurora entered.

"My little girl," he said in a tone of wonder. "You look beautiful. I can't believe how you've grown."

"Thank you, Father." He was her father, but she still couldn't forget what he'd done. "Shall we go?"

"Not so fast. There's something I want to say first. Need to say, actually." Artemus turned his hat nervously in his hands as he looked at her. "Why don't you sit down, child?"

Her first impulse was to say no, but he looked so nervous, shifting his weight from one foot to the other like a five-year-old, that she relented. She sat straight and tense on the edge of the sofa.

"I want to apologize. I thought a lot about what you said, and finally I talked to Dr. Wharton about your mother's wound. I want you to know I've come to the same conclusion as you did so many years ago. All these years he's told me how terrible her wounds were, that there was nothing he could do for her, but now I know it was Wharton's bungling that killed your mother. Not the Indians."

She turned to him, her eyes wide. "Wharton was the doctor?"

"Yes, didn't you know?"

"I was only seven. All I saw was a bloody white coat and a drunken, red-faced man. I never realized—" No wonder Wharton hadn't wanted her around.

"Aurora, that's not all I've been thinking about. I'd like to add that maybe if I was wrong about the Indians killing your mother, maybe I've been wrong about some other things, too."

Her blue eyes sharpened. "Meaning?"

"Meaning that I might be open to learning more about the Indians. Pincus says you two are working on a book about them, and I wondered if you'd show me the pictures."

"I'd like that, Father." Maybe she could show him some of the Apaches' good qualities. The chapel bell tolled and she jumped, still ill at ease with him. "It's time to go."

"Yes, it is." Standing up and clamping his hat on, he offered her his arm. "Your mother would be proud of you, Aurora Elizabeth. So am I."

He guided her down the steps, then they began the long walk across the parade ground. A light breeze carried the scent of sagebrush. The chapel bells began to peal joyously.

Everyone was gathered around the chapel steps, and the women looked like a bouquet of brilliant winter flowers in deep colors. Brit waited for her on the top stop, standing straight and tall in his dress uniform with his bright yellow cummerbund and his saber at his side.

Aurora pressed her bouquet of tiny white roses to her stomach. *We will survive, my son. You'll see. And someday I will tell you of the great Apache warrior who was your father.*

Her father cleared his throat. "I hope you'll be happy. As happy as your mother and I were."

"Brit's a good man," she said, staring straight ahead.

"Yes, he is. But he's—" He looked away from her at the corral between Headquarters and the hospital, where he'd imprisoned an Apache prisoner. "But he's not the man you love," he murmured.

Aurora shot him a startled glance, not sure she'd heard him correctly. "What did you say?"

He glanced at her and his eyes were suspiciously red. Then he shook his head sharply, as though pushing away unwanted memories. "Nothing," he said in a tight voice. "Nothing at all."

They were halfway across the parade ground when the ground began to shake with the thunder of pounding hooves.

Her father looked past her at an Indian galloping down the hill toward them. "What the hell—"

Aurora turned and stared. The sun was too bright, and she couldn't see the rider well. Yet there was something familiar about his shape. Shading her eyes with her hand, she studied the rider on the big black stallion intently.

In disbelief she took several steps toward him, as if that would help her see better. It couldn't be, she told herself, her heart beginning to pound. She took another couple of steps. Could it . . . could it really be?

Oh God, was it? A sunbeam touched her heart, then flickered and began to glow. It grew stronger and stronger with each beat of the horse's hooves.

"Stalking Wolf!"

She ran to meet him, arms outstretched. Her love was coming for her.

The rider bore down on her at a full gallop. He leaned low to the side of his horse and reached out to clasp her waist and lift her into the saddle in front of him.

It happened so quickly that no one even moved. As Aurora looked over Wolf's shoulder, she saw Brit run out to her father and rest a hand on his arm as he spoke to him.

Then the big horse rounded a curve in the road, and she couldn't see the fort anymore.

"Oh, Wolf," she cried, as sobs of joy bubbled up inside her. "I thought you were dead."

"I am alive, Aurora. And I have come for you."

Chapter 25

Wolf locked his arms around Aurora and crushed her to his broad chest as they galloped away.

Wrapping her arms around his sturdy neck, she hung on tightly. She could feel his sinews and tendons flexing beneath her fingers, tapping out their miraculous message. *Alive. Alive.*

"I thought Papa had killed you." She nestled her face into the hollow of his shoulder and dropped a trembling kiss against his throat. He was alive. He was alive.

"He failed." He squeezed her gently, just enough to let her know he'd felt her lips.

She sat across his hard thighs, hanging onto him. His heart thundered beneath her ear, and she reveled in that pounding beat she'd thought never to hear again. She drank in the unique mix of horse and leather and wild sage and male sweat that was his alone, drinking in the scent she'd thought never to smell again. Closing her eyes, she absorbed the feel of him, touching the man she'd thought she'd never touch again, being held in arms she'd thought would never hold her again.

"But I saw your body lying on the ground. I thought you were dead."

"Almost. I lost consciousness when the horses trampled me, and when I came to, I was alone and my horse was dead. I dragged myself to a stream, but couldn't go any further." There was no need for her to know how close he had come to dying. "Geronimo had sent riders after me, and they found me and loaded me on a horse and carted me back to the village."

"If only I'd known."

"Would it have made a difference?" He rubbed his chin against her hair. "You were running away from me, if you remember."

"I remember." She traced his rugged jawline, unable to get enough of touching him. "I also remember looking back and seeing you gaining on me and then the cavalry pouring over the ridge"— her voice faded to a shred—"and you jerking when the bullet struck . . . and looking at me one last time and your lips forming a word."

"I remember that also." He gave her a look so intense that her bones softened to taffy.

"You said Aurora." Her voice was tight with tension.

"Yes." And there was no need to say more.

Wolf reined his stallion off the wagon road and sent it hurtling along a narrow deer path, dodging bushes and low branches. Even as they twisted with the horse's movements, Wolf moved his hands over her, feeling the soft hills and valleys of her. Relearning her shape, remembering. Touching the woman who'd stolen his heart, the woman he'd sought for so long and almost lost.

Finally they emerged onto a small, brush-covered ledge high above Fort Bowie. "I first saw you from here," Wolf explained as he let her slide down the horse's side. Instead of dismounting in the usual way, he lifted his leg over the beast's withers and also slid down.

"Are you fully recovered? How bad were your wounds?" Aurora assessed him, looking for signs of pain. "I don't even know how you survived."

"I had to. I vowed I would find you." He opened his arms wide. "Come here, Aurora."

She ran into his arms. The low winter sun fired his obsidian eyes with golden lights as he nestled her against him. "I want to feel you close to me. I want your arms around me, holding me close, and I want your heart beating against mine, my *kun isdzán*."

Aurora felt as if she was falling into the sky. After so many weeks of worry, of feeling dead inside, she was alive as never before. She closed her eyes and absorbed his heat, surrounding her, sheltering her.

Slowly she tilted her head back against his arm. "How is it that you happened to show up today just as I was getting ready to marry Brit?"

"It was no accident." He brushed his thumb over her eyebrow as he smiled down at her.

"Somehow I didn't think it was."

"Brit sent for me. He sent Apache scouts to spread the word to the villages that Stalking Wolf's woman was taking another man today. I think he knew that if I was alive, I'd come. And he was right. But I got the message so late, I didn't know if I'd be in time."

"Just barely." Slowly, reluctantly, yet knowing she had to put some space between them, she pushed herself out of his arms and stepped back.

Squaring her shoulders, she stood tall, facing the man she loved. "Wolf, there's something I have to tell you. It's important to me that you know I believe what you said about Papa." She gazed down at her clasped hands. "I think I believed you for a long time, because I realized you were an honorable man and you wouldn't lie. But he's my father and I had to be loyal to him."

"Just as I had to be loyal to my mother." His voice didn't give her a clue to his thoughts.

"Oh God, I have so many questions." She walked to the rim, and afraid to look at him when she asked her questions, stared down at the blue figures running across the parade ground. "You told me once that you kidnapped me for ransom. Was that all it was?"

"Yes."

Her heart dropped all the way to her toes.

"That's what it was in the beginning. As soon as I saw you, I knew I wanted you. Then, to find out you were *his* daughter was like rain on the desert. My God, after searching for him for years, I would finally get revenge.

"But then as I got to know you, when you defied me time after time and never gave up trying to escape, when we fought tooth and nail, I became fascinated. You were strong and smart, a worthy adversary who kept me alert and on my toes. You were different from every other woman I'd ever met. I'd realized you were remarkable when you came to me in the corral, but I didn't know how unique until later."

"You're fascinated by me?" she said faintly as she dug the toe of her new shoe into the dust.

"No. That doesn't even begin to cover what I

feel. You know I want you." He paused, but she didn't move, didn't dare look at him. He went on, his voice hesitant, as if he found it hard to speak, "Once you told me you loved me, *kun isdzán*. I'm hoping you still do. Because . . . because . . . I love you."

Aurora gave an inarticulate cry and whirled to face him. "I'd like to believe that. But I don't understand how you can speak to me of love when you don't even trust me."

His brow furrowed into a deep frown. "What are you talking about? Of course I trust you."

"No. You may think you do, but you don't. On that last day, when we argued, I took the biggest chance of my life and told you I loved you. Surely you must have known I wasn't a threat to you, that I wouldn't do anything that would endanger you. But you didn't trust me enough to tell me Papa had left Fort Bowie. You just rode away." She wrapped her arms around her waist, holding in the agony that threatened to break her into little bits.

"Aurora, I trusted you by the time I went for the vaccine. And when I returned, I asked you to stand in front of me and hide my weakness from the others. I trust you enough to lean on you when I'm hurt or exhausted. That's a great deal of trust from an Apache warrior. Don't you know, my *kun isdzán*, I've trusted you more than I've ever trusted anyone?"

"Then why didn't you tell me Papa was coming?"

"I didn't know he'd left!"

"But Destarte told me—" She clenched her hands in front of her, afraid to hope.

"She spoke with a forked tongue. I didn't know

until I returned from the war raid. Only then did
Geronimo tell me that a runner had come with the
message that *Nantan* Spencer had left the fort with
guns and ammunition."

"Why would Geronimo wait to tell you? He
wanted the guns and ammunition as much as you
did."

"Because he didn't want me to be distracted by
thoughts of you. He was afraid I'd cut the raid
short, because he knew what you did not—that I
love you."

A smile as sweet as Christmas candy slowly lit
her face. "You *do* love me!" She threw herself into
his arms. "You do!"

"It isn't easy for me to say." He cupped the back
of her head in his large hand and dropped a deep
kiss on her lips. "After all, warriors are not known
for admitting such weakness."

She pulled back, intently studying his features.
"Is that how you feel about love? That it is a
weakness?"

"No. Loving you makes me stronger." He
paused and cleared his throat. "Only a man who
loved you could have heard your cry on the battlefield. That should have told us both. I think I knew
it long before, but I couldn't accept that I'd fallen in
love with the daughter of my enemy."

"When I told you I loved you, why didn't you
say anything before you left? Why couldn't you at
least tell me you cared?"

"My people believed I was obsessed with you—
a White-eyes woman. That's why I had to lead the
warriors—to prove to them and to myself that I
wasn't. That's also why I didn't dare turn around
when you told me you loved me. I was afraid I'd
take you in my arms and never let you go."

He raked his hand through his hair. "I don't know how to say the words that are in my heart, Aurora. But when I returned and found you gone . . ." He paced away from her. "Your fiery hair lit the darkness in my wickiup. Your fiery spirit lit the darkness in my heart. But I knew no matter what I felt for you, there could be no future for us. At least I thought I knew—only after you were gone did I understand how important you were to me. That's why I came after you."

Spinning around, he grasped her upper arms and spoke with an intensity that wrapped around her like a warm coat. "You are the fire that lights the darkness in me. I love you. I want to spend the rest of my years with you."

Aurora brushed her fingers over his warm lips. "I never thought you'd say these things to me, my love."

"I say them because they're true. I lay in a wickiup for many days, regaining my strength. With you gone"—his dark eyes were full of smoke and flame—"I had nothing to do but think. I have spent years seeking to avenge my mother's murder. It has always been the Apache way to avenge the dead."

Aurora eyed him intently. "Yes?"

"I decided I would have to choose another path. Otherwise, our past would hold our future hostage. To me, our life together is more important than any vengeance." His long fingers threaded through her upswept hair as he gazed down at her. "I can't offer you a soft life with servants or—"

"That doesn't matter, Wolf, because I love you." Their mouths met and melded in a potent kiss. "I love you."

"I can guarantee that this Apache warrior will never love anyone as he loves you, *isdzán*."

"*My* Apache warrior," she whispered. Slowly, as though ice was growing inside her, she went painfully still. The smile faded from her rosy lips, and the joy faded from her eyes.

"What is it?" Wolf asked. He shook her slightly, but she just stared at him. "What's the matter?" he shouted, frightened by the sudden change in her. She was so white, so stricken.

She struggled wildly, pushing at his chest with her small hands until he let go of her. She stumbled over to a mesquite and stopped with her back to him, holding onto the trunk with one hand while the other rested on her stomach.

"What is it?" Wolf cried, standing behind her.

She shook her head.

He rested his hand on her shoulder. "It's all right. Whatever it is, you can tell me."

She began to sob softly. "I'm sorry; I seem to be crying all the time lately."

"Maybe it's the child you carry."

She glanced back at him. "You knew I was *enceinte*?"

"As soon as I lifted you, I could feel that you were lighter, but there is a new fullness to your breasts, and your belly is more round."

"Heavens, am I showing already?" She tugged at her dress, embarrassed.

"Only to a man who knows your body as well as I do. Now what is it that troubles you?"

"If you know I carry a child, then you can understand why I can't come with you." She gulped, trying not to give in to the pain of a breaking heart. This was worse than when she'd fled the Apache village. Then she'd thought Wolf didn't love her. Now she knew he did. But she would still have to give him up, would have to live alone, would have to raise their child alone.

His hand stiffened on her shoulder. He turned her around. "I thought you loved me. I know I love you."

"Don't you understand? Love isn't enough," she whispered, choking on the lump in her throat. "Our child—"

"That's it? The baby? But why? Our children are loved. They are never struck. They are our future and we treasure them. Apache children grow up strong."

"If they survive, Wolf. Only if they survive. Our child deserves a future where he's not surrounded by enemies. But every time I think of what you told me, I shudder and vow that will not happen to him."

"What?" he cried. "What did I tell you?"

"That you were nine before you saw someone die other than by violence." She rubbed her hands over her arms, fighting the ice that was freezing in her veins.

Wolf's eyes widened, and he stared at her for a long heartbeat. Then his hands slowly slipped from her shoulders and he turned away.

"I had a lot of time to think when I lay wounded." He paced to the edge of the cliff and studied the Bluecoats below. "I knew that we could no longer survive surrounded by enemies. And you had shown my people that not all White-eyes are bad—that some are good. I decided that my distrust of White-eyes was blinding me to what The People needed to do." He walked over to her slowly, purposefully. "You were right; I hadn't considered the San Carlos Reservation, since I knew the warriors couldn't become farmers."

A flame was flickering in her heart. "And?"

"I have been in contact with General Harris in New Mexico, who believes in treating my people with respect. I've told him I won't take my people to the San Carlos Reservation to be farmers. But since we are horsemen and we are good at stealing cattle, perhaps it is time for us to raise them. This is something my warriors would do. General Harris is a far-seeing man. He has come to Arizona, and we are negotiating peace for my people." His eyes were dark pools of fire as he drew her into his arms.

She nestled against his broad chest and held him close. She'd come home. She'd come home forever.

"Working together, we could do so much for your people."

He tangled his long fingers in her curls and tilted her face up. "After all that's happened, you would help my people?"

"Shouldn't a wife help her husband?"

"First a woman must become a wife." His gaze fell to her turquoise dress and the white lace foaming up around her slender throat. "I like this," he murmured in a tone that rubbed across her skin like black velvet.

He drew a single finger from the pulse point in her throat down into the shadowed valley between her breasts. Her eyes drifted closed, and she gave herself up to the delicious tension that came with his touch.

"Oh, Wolf, I've missed you so," she murmured. His silky hair brushed her cheek as he lowered his head and nibbled the sensitive flesh in the hollow of her shoulder.

"I have something for you." Reaching down into a fold in his moccasin, he drew out the necklace of turquoise and heavy silver links that he'd given her so long ago.

"Pieces-of-sky," she said, touching it with a trembling finger.

"Pieces-of-sky," he echoed, as he fastened it around her throat. Stepping back, he regarded her with a smile. "Now that you have your wedding present, shall we go back?" He held out his hand. "The minister is waiting."

"Today? Now?"

His gaze slid over her like hot rum. "You're wearing your wedding dress, aren't you?"

They rode back into Fort Bowie at a slow walk, two riders on one horse. The troopers watched them, but no shots were fired. It was as if a truce had been declared. Aurora's father left the officers and women still clustered in front of the chapel and walked across the parade ground, alone to meet them.

Stalking Wolf and Aurora married that afternoon, but not in the darkness of the chapel. Aurora's father escorted her across the parade ground to the flagpole, where the minister stood, clasping his Bible.

Artemus' and Aurora's eyes met in a look of love and understanding. Then Artemus placed her hand in Stalking Wolf's.

And so they were married under the bright Arizona sun, with the thirty-seven-star flag snapping above them. The Apache warriors and women didn't come into the fort, but silently as ghosts they appeared on the ridges surrounding Fort Bowie and watched from their horses.

And when the minister asked, "Who marries this woman?" Wolf gazed deep into Aurora's eyes.

"I do. I, Ethan Allen Winthrop, take this woman to be my wife."

Later that night, Wolf and Aurora lay on the buffalo robes they'd brought into the special wedding wickiup the Apaches had constructed for them high in the pine forests of the Chiricahua Mountains. Slowly, savoring every splendid moment, they loved and loved again.

Aurora lay in Wolf's arms, secure in his love, and stared up through the smoke hole at the stars sparkling in the crisp December night. "Wolf, let's get married in the Apache way, too."

"We are, *isdzán*." He filled his hands with her wildly tousled hair. "We've been married in the Apache way for many moons—ever since I took you to my wickiup."

She rose up on her elbow and leaned over him. "Then why did you go through the White-eyes ceremony today?"

"Because it was important to you. And if I would live and succeed in the White-eyes world, it is best that I follow their customs." He pushed her over on her back and rained kisses of fire over her breasts.

"Besides, I wanted you and our son to carry my White-eyes name. He is blood of our blood. He carries the blood of two peoples, the Apache and the White-eyes. It's important that he has my White-eyes name, because he will be the bridge between our worlds. He will bring our peoples together. He will be destiny's warrior."

"No, Wolf, you're wrong." She laid a finger over

his lips to still his protest. "You are the one who has led your people from the old lifeway. You are the one who is helping them build a future in the White-eyes world," Aurora said. "You are destiny's warrior."

Avon Romances—
the best in exceptional authors and unforgettable novels!